WHERE HAVE ALL THE YOUNG GIRLS GONE

ALSO BY LEENA LEHTOLAINEN

The Maria Kallio Mysteries

WHERE HAVE ALL THE YOUNG GIRLS GONE

A MARIA KALLIO MYSTERY

LEENA LEHTOLAINEN

Translated by Owen F. Witesman

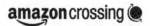

Text copyright © 2010 by Leena Lehtolainen
Translation copyright © 2019 by Owen F. Witesman
All rights reserved.

Previously published as *Minne tytöt kadonneet* by Tammi in Finland in 2010. Translated from Finnish by Owen F. Witesman. First published in English by AmazonCrossing in 2019.

Published by AmazonCrossing, Seattle

www.apub.com

Amazon, the Amazon logo, and AmazonCrossing are trademarks of Amazon.com, Inc., or its affiliates.

ISBN-13: 9781542040310
ISBN-10: 1542040310

Cover design by Ray Lundgren

Printed in the United States of America

For Anna and Hanna

CAST OF CHARACTERS

THE LAW

Akkila: ....Patrol officer

Haatainen, Assi: ....Forensic technician

Hakkarainen: ....Forensic investigator

Halli-Rasila, Irma: ....Detective, White Collar Crime, Tampere PD

Himanen: ....Patrol officer

Honkanen, Ursula: ....Detective, Violent Crime Unit

Kallio, Maria: ....Commander, Special Crimes Unit

Koivu, Pekka: ....Detective, Special Crimes Unit, Anu Wang-Koivu's husband

Lehtovuori: ....Detective, VCU

Mikkola: ....Patrol officer

Oinonen: ....Paramedic

Puupponen, Ville: ....Detective, VC

Puustjärvi, Petri: ....Detective, VCU

Rasilainen, Liisa: ....Patrol officer

Söderholm, Kaide: ....Ballistics expert, Helsinki PD

Ström, Pertti: ....Detective, VCU, deceased

Sutinen: ....Patrol officer

Taskinen, Jyrki: ....Director, Criminal Division

Timonen, Roni: ....Detective, VCU

Wang-Koivu, Anu: ....Juvenile Unit, Pekka Koivu's wife

THE GIRLS CLUB

Korhonen, Heini: ....Girls Club executive director

Jansson, Susanne "Susa": ....Girls Club member, Noor's friend

Sandelin, Sylvia: ....Girls Club founder

Saraneva, Miina "Adey": ....Girls Club member, Ayan's friend

Sarkela, Iida: ....Girls Club member, Maria Kallio's daughter

Vesterinen, Nelli: ....Girls Club activity coordinator

THE AFGHANS

Hasan, Ali Abdi and Mohammed Abdi: ....Aziza's brothers
Hasan, Aziza Abdi: ....Girls Club member
Jussuf, Omar: ....Afghan warlord
Mohammed, Abdi Hasan: ....Father of Aziza
Omar, Issa, AKA Issa Jussuf Hasan,
       AKA Mohammed Salim Hasan: ....Son of Omar Jussuf
Salim, Selene: ....Mother of Aziza

THE SUDANESE

Ali, Aisha Muhammed: ....Mother of Ayan
Hassan, Ali Jussuf: ....Father of Ayan
Jussuf, Ayan Ali: ....Girls Club member

THE BOSNIANS

Amir, Mikael: ....Sara's father
Amir, Mira: ....Sara's mother
Amir, Samir: ....Sara's brother
Amir, Sara: ....Girls Club member

THE IRANIANS

Ezfahani, Farid: ....Grandfather Reza's son
Ezfahani, Hamid: ....Noor's brother
Ezfahani, Jalil: ....Farid's son
Ezfahani, Noor (the elder): ....Noor's mother
Ezfahani, Noor: ....Girls Club member
Ezfahani, Rahim: ....Farid's son
Ezfahani, Reza (the elder): ....Noor's grandfather
Ezfahani, Reza (the younger): ....Noor's father, Iranian immigrant
Ezfahani, Vafa: ....Noor's younger brother, Iranian immigrant

SUPPORTING CAST

PROLOGUE

I had just nodded off when the machine-gun fire started. The sound of a Kalashnikov jolted me awake. When I opened my eyes, I saw muzzle flashes on the east side of the road less than a kilometer away from our armored vehicle.

"Should I try to turn around?" our driver, Corporal Jere Numminen, asked his superior officer. Behind us there was only darkness. The gunfire hadn't reached us yet, but the two four-wheel-drive patrol vehicles in front of us were taking hits. They were carrying EU police officials too. We had all been participating in the opening ceremonies for the new EUPOL-funded Afghani police academy near Jalalabad. Now we were on the road back to Kabul.

Major Lauri Vala didn't have time to reply before the lead vehicle exploded. It was carrying two German police instructors, Helmut Lindemann and Ulrike Müller. A young officer was acting as their driver, but all I could remember about him was that his first name was Sven.

The Germans' vehicle was the same as ours, a light armored RG-32 Scout. Rifle fire alone couldn't have destroyed it, and the shooters were too far away for their weapons to be very effective anyway. The road was supposed to be perfectly safe, but roadside bombs must have been the cause of the explosion. The French delegation driving in front of us stopped. The British team driving behind us was already backing up.

Vala pushed his helmet down more firmly on his head. I had taken off my own, because the combination of helmet and hijab had been too hot. Now I fumbled around for it, even though it wouldn't be able to give me much protection from what we were facing. In the light of the flames started by the explosion, I could see the French vehicle opening fire in the direction of the assault rifle muzzle flashes.

"They only have one weapon," Vala observed. I could feel the weight of my revolver in its shoulder holster. I felt like rushing over to the Germans to see if there was anything I could do, but that would have been suicide.

Antti and my mother had been right: only a lunatic with a death wish would go to Afghanistan. I'd been an irresponsible imbecile to agree to come on this trip, and now I would never see my children, Iida and Taneli, again. When Vala picked up a Heckler & Koch MP5 submachine gun from the back of the jeep and slipped its barrel through the vehicle's purpose-built firing port, I found myself praying. I realized I didn't know to what god I was addressing my entreaties, the Lutherans' or the Muslims', but the latter probably had a stronger foothold in these parts.

Vala's face held a blank expression as he opened fire. The attackers were far away, and he was mostly just shooting as an intimidation tactic, but he emptied the entire thirty-round banana magazine. The French continued to lay down fire, and gradually the distant muzzle flashes faded away. Beyond the flames of the Germans' blazing vehicle, the world was impenetrable darkness again. Vala pulled his submachine gun back into the vehicle and started looking for his satellite phone. Before he had time to punch in the code sequence, the telephone began to ring.

"Moose." That was Vala's codename. He continued in English; apparently the caller was the driver of the vehicle waiting behind us. New Scotland Yard assistant chief of police Albert Shaw was the highest ranking of the officials who had participated in the opening ceremonies of the police academy.

As Vala spoke, his subordinate, Numminen, reached back into the rear compartment. In addition to weaponry, backup rations, and water, the standard equipment in the vehicles included a metal detector. Vala cut the conversation short. I saw the door of the French vehicle open. Its driver also had a metal detector.

"According to the Americans, this road was supposed to be clean. The French confirmed it with them too. How the hell did anyone manage to plant anything here? Don't get out," Vala ordered Numminen. "If the Parisian boys want to risk their lives, they can be my guests. I'm calling Baxter."

Colonel Steve Baxter of the US International Security Assistance Force contingent was in charge of safety for the foreign visitors participating in the police academy opening. Vala didn't hold back any of the English expletives he knew as he spoke with Baxter and even dropped in a Finnish *perkele* too.

Until now everything had gone according to plan, and Vala had seemed cool as a cucumber, the type of guy to whom even a law enforcement professional could entrust her life. Now he was furious that the plan had fallen apart.

I watched the cautious movements of the young French officer with the bomb detector. He looked like a Halloween witch dancing in slow motion around a bonfire with a modernized broomstick. Even though the Finnish soldier's ethic was to never leave a fallen comrade, we had been given strict instructions not to risk our own lives to save our companions.

Ulrike and I had been responsible for training the female police officers, and we had become friends. I thought of Ulrike's strawberry-blond bun and the curls that were always trying to escape it, falling to her cheeks and neck. I smelled the stench of burning hair. I could only hope she had been killed instantly. It was just by chance that the Germans' vehicle had been at the head of the convoy.

The second French soldier had brought out a foam fire extinguisher, but its spray didn't seem to be having any effect on the flames leaping into the sky. The Brits left their vehicle as well, to bring a more effective fire extinguisher. When Numminen tried to leave the vehicle again, Vala grabbed him by his upper arm. Numminen sat back down behind the steering wheel.

Vala had finished his phone call. "Baxter doesn't know what went wrong. Fox Company from the 112th was supposed to be monitoring the road. No one can get ahold of them. Reinforcements are on their way. The choppers are already lifting off from the nearest NATO base, which is about ten clicks from here. The cavalry will arrive but very late. What did they say in those speeches today? 'The new police academy is an important step toward democracy and a spark of hope for a war-torn nation.' Quite a fire from one little spark."

I didn't feel like responding. It's normal for people experiencing mortal danger to run at the mouth. But I wished he would shut up. I couldn't stand any more chatter. I had never felt so impossibly small and helpless as I did at that moment, looking on as the lives of three people faded into ash in the middle of a dark and desolate wasteland.

1

The February evening was still luminous. The sun painted the waist-high snowdrifts in our yard a delicate blue. When I opened the front door, the scent of cocoa greeted my nose.

Taneli was seated at the kitchen table, slurping from a mug and reading a comic book. I could hear music coming from Iida's room; I recognized Nina Hagen's femme fatale voice. My daughter had partially inherited my taste in music. As usual, Iida had brought the mail in from the mailbox when she got home from school. On the kitchen table waited the normal Friday magazines, a cell phone bill for Antti, and a thick A4-size bubble wrap envelope for me, the original address of which had been clumsily blacked out. The letter had first been addressed to the Finnish Interior Ministry Police Division, from which it had found its way to my home. The envelope was tattered; it had obviously run a full gauntlet of metal detectors, bomb dogs, and X-ray machines.

The postmark said Munich, and the sender was Helga Müller of number 13 Kurfürstenstrasse. I took a pair scissors from the pencil cup and carefully opened the envelope. Inside I found a glossy, polished jewelry box that looked like birchwood and a letter with *Oberkommissarin Maria Kallio* on it. Because I knew who the letter must be from, I hesitated before reading it.

The letter was written on linden-green paper, the handwriting meticulous and clear, but there were a few grammatical errors in the simple English. Frau Müller had known that my German wasn't that great.

> Esteemed Detective Lieutenant Kallio,
> Only now has my strength returned enough that I am able to fulfill my daughter Ulrike's final wishes. She made out a will before leaving for the Afghanistan, and in it she asked that her jewelry be left to her friends. I have never met you, but I think this piece of jewelry fits the Finn. Ulrike valued you much and said she had her best discussions about the police profession and the place of women in the work with you.
> We held the quiet funeral within the family, even though all the world press and other curious people wished to come see the war casualty. This is why we did not invite you, and the journey would have been long as well.
> Respectfully,
> Helga Müller

"What's in it, Mom?" Apparently I had let out a choked sob, because Taneli had interrupted his reading and was staring at me in alarm.

"A gift from a friend. A piece of jewelry. Let's see what kind." I tried to look delighted; my work troubles weren't anything for a nine-year-old to worry about. I opened the box, which was lined with green satin. The necklace was a thin loop with three forged silver pendants, about two inches long, in the shape of spruce twigs. I'd seen it on Ulrike's neck at the graduation dinner for our Afghan colleagues, who'd attended the course we'd hosted at the Police University College in Tampere. After that, our students had gone back to Afghanistan to establish their own police academy, and Ulrike had returned to Munich. She had lived with her mother near the Englischer Garten and the Pinakotheks. I'd planned to visit her when spring came to southern Germany. But then Ulrike had died, and now all that awaited me in Munich was her grave.

I took the necklace into my room. The cats were lying side by side on the bed on top of a throw. Gray-striped Venjamin had gotten a new friend in the fall when we'd picked out Jahnukainen, a tortoiseshell, at the animal shelter. Iida had been feeling sorry for Venjamin for a couple of years because he was all alone, and she had promised to manage introducing the kitten to him. After a couple of weeks of hissing and batting at each other, the cats had grown used to the new situation. Sometimes they play fought, and sometimes they licked each other's necks like adoring siblings.

The music from Iida's room had gone quiet, and I could hear her coming downstairs.

"Hi, Mom. Guess what! I got a 10+ on my math test! What time are we going over to the Koivus'?"

I couldn't help but smile at my daughter. It seemed that today the storm clouds had lifted and it was the sun's turn to shine. Just yesterday she'd been grumbling because she had to go to the Koivus' and hang out with the little kids. Juuso was a good year younger than Taneli, Sennu was six, and Jaakko's fifth birthday was next week, which was the excuse for the party invitation.

"We'll take the 6:45 bus. So, a 10+? Where did the plus come from?"

"Teach gave me an extra problem cuz I did the others so fast."

Iida had inherited her math skills from her father. I stroked her dark hair. She was about an inch taller than me, already a young lady. Her hair was dyed black, which was also the only color of clothing she'd been willing to wear for the past year. I still remembered fighting with my mother about clothes, so I let Iida dress the way she wanted, even though the goth-style lace and purple eye shadow were sometimes

7

so over-the-top that I had to disguise my laughter as a fit of coughing. I'd still been wearing jeans and boyish shirts when I was thirteen, but then the safety pins and torn stockings had entered the picture. Ulrike had told me stories about how, as a girl, she'd used punk music to rebel against traditional Bavarian gender roles, and our similar adolescent experiences had strengthened our relationship, even though she'd been ten years younger than me.

My grief over her death, which had started to ease, returned with such force that I could have screamed with rage. Luckily Iida retrieved her test paper from her room, because she wanted more praise, and I obliged. With a thirteen-year-old, it was best to savor every moment that she wanted to connect.

I put on slightly nicer everyday clothes for the visit, and the necklace Ulrike's mother had sent. Anu and Pekka Koivu were close friends, so I could share the story of the necklace with them. Antti managed to get home just five minutes before we were supposed to leave for the bus and of course didn't notice the accessory. He'd recently returned to the university, somewhat against his better judgement, to take on a mathematics professorship. Apparently, the work itself was rewarding, but the red tape associated with new requirements to be "results oriented" had chipped away at academic freedom so thoroughly that Antti came home seething at least once a week. He seemed to be tense now too, so I didn't even ask how things were going.

Once we got out the door, Iida trudged to the bus stop a little ahead of us, and Taneli alternated between waltzing and split jumps. Iida had announced the previous summer that she was giving up synchronized skating, but Taneli was training for singles competition as enthusiastically as ever and was already executing the easier double jumps with confidence. The fact that he was no longer skating in his sister's shadow seemed to have increased his motivation. Skating was his own thing now, and something he was clearly more gifted at than his older sibling.

On the bus, Iida began to insist that she be allowed to ride to Tapiola instead of getting off in Leppävaara. She'd been increasingly involved in the Girls Club there, and they had improv theater on Friday nights.

"You can go next week," Antti snapped, crossly enough that Iida fell silent. Antti didn't usually raise his voice at the children, preferring to leave the bossing to me. Iida glared at her father and then, in protest, began adding gloss to her already glistening lips.

The Koivus' apartment smelled of chilis and lemongrass, so I guessed Anu had fixed Vietnamese food. Despite her grousing, Iida immediately began playing hairdresser with Sennu, while Juuso dragged Taneli off to play Star of Africa, and Jaakko followed them. It was a simple enough board game that even the smaller kids could understand. Pekka brought aperitifs, and after a few sips Antti visibly relaxed. He even noticed my necklace and asked if it was new.

"It came today in the mail from Ulrike Müller's mother."

"To Ulrike," Pekka said immediately, raising his glass. He and Anu had met Ulrike when we took the Afghan course participants on a tour of the Espoo Police Department. We clinked glasses in silence. Iida and Sennu's laughter came from the adults' bedroom, where they had gone to work on their hairdos in peace. Finally, Pekka broke the silence.

"Did they ever figure out how the IED got on the road? It was supposed to be safe, wasn't it?"

"The army company that was supposed to have been watching that part of the road had come under attack, so first surveillance failed and then intel. The next week there was a roadside bomb in the same place that killed some Red Crescent workers. There were women in their group too. Most likely the drug lords were responsible, because the strengthening of the police force is a threat to them. It's impossible to negotiate with those types."

During my visit I had toured the Afghan women's prisons. Most of the prisoners weren't criminals at all by Finnish standards; some were women who had been raped and young teenage girls who had fled arranged marriages to men decades their senior. The prison was almost a refuge, although it wasn't always possible to trust the guards any more than the people the prisoners were running from.

The Taliban opposed the police academy, even more so because women were allowed to train there. The protocols we established at the academy were not based on Sharia law, but rather on the idea that democratic police forces should be incorruptible and treat everyone equally. Though I'd only been in the country for ten days, I'd seen the futility of the enterprise. Most of the current police officers couldn't even read, and corruption was a matter of course. One of the worst setbacks so far had occurred in early February, when a man dressed in a police uniform shot two Swedish soldiers and an interpreter. There had also been Estonian casualties, and it was only a matter of time before a Finn died.

After the Afghanistan project, I'd continued teaching intensive courses at the police college in the Hervanta suburb of Tampere. In my next course for foreign female police officers, there had been students from several war-torn African countries: Sudan, Somalia, and Congo, just to name three. The end-of-term party had been in early February, and the EU-funded police training program was now being moved over to Swedish administration. I'd been offered the opportunity to work on that project as well, but I wasn't thrilled about flying back and forth between Gothenburg, in Sweden, and Espoo, in Finland. Just being separated from my family two hours away in Tampere had been hard.

"In a little more than a week, you'll be able to get back to safer work again," Anu said with a smile. "And you won't be wasting time commuting."

"It's good you can see the positive side of things. And, besides the short commute, I already know I'm going to like the people I'll be working with."

For the past five years, I'd been working in various short-term positions. Before the international training assignments, I'd earned my daily bread from a domestic violence research project under the auspices of the Ministry of the Interior, which they'd pulled me away from once on temporary orders to the Espoo Police Department. Now I was returning to that same department again, but its organizational structure had been turned inside out over the last year. Police departments all over the country had been merged, and the Espoo police station was now the headquarters of the Western Uusimaa Police District, which also included the towns of Raasepori, Lohja, and Vihti. The lead architect of the reforms at my old workplace had been my former boss, Jyrki Taskinen, who had stretched the limits set by the Interior Ministry Police Division as much as he possibly could. The Espoo police station still housed a Violent Crime Unit, which Anni Kuusimäki had been assigned to head up after me, but she'd had triplets a little over a year ago and was on parental leave. Her interim replacement was Markku Ruuskanen, a veteran police officer in his fifties. According to Koivu, Ruuskanen was a decent boss, if a bit distant.

A year and a half ago, Taskinen had tried to lure me back to fill in for Anni, but to no avail. I didn't want my old job or the stress that went along with it. Then he'd tried a new tactic. A couple of weeks after I returned from Afghanistan, he'd called and proposed a meeting at the Espoo police station.

"I'd like to hear about your trip," Taskinen said. "My heart almost stopped when I read about the police academy delegation driving over an IED. I was so relieved when we heard there weren't any Finnish victims."

I always had time for Taskinen, so I agreed to coffee in the reception room upstairs at the police station. Anyone else in the upper echelons of the police force would have served jelly donuts with the coffee, but

Taskinen was a health enthusiast and had ordered cheese and lettuce sandwiches. He was still able to run a marathon in three and a half hours, even though he was well past his fiftieth birthday. Nowadays, Taskinen spent more time chasing grandchildren than competing in races. His daughter, Silja, had moved her family from Canada to Finland and was coaching at the club where Taneli skated.

After I told him all about my travels, Taskinen looked at me in a way that told me there was a larger purpose for the meeting. I prepared to respond with an absolute no to anything he proposed.

"You're up to speed on the organizational restructuring that led to the merging of the police departments, right?"

"Well, I don't know the specifics."

"Here in Espoo, we're theoretically responsible for all violent crimes in the entire police district. Simple cases are still dealt with at the local level, but the more complicated ones come to us, along with all the atypical ones. Anyone can investigate drunken homicides and domestic violence incidents with witnesses, but we get the special ones: the cold cases, racially motivated crimes, school shooting threats—you know what I'm talking about. Investigating these cases requires a separate unit, a cell if you will, that comprises experienced detectives. A lieutenant and two sergeants. The lieutenant handles administrative duties but also does fieldwork and interrogations, assuming she's the right type. This is not going to be a paper-pushing job—it's going to be hard work. And I want you to take it on as commander of our new Special Crimes Unit. I've already spoken with Koivu and Puupponen. They've both had enough of wrangling alcoholics, and they're willing to accept the assignment if you agree to lead the cell."

"Cell? That sounds more like a terrorist operation than a police unit," I said. I was dumbfounded.

"It has a sort of modern, dynamic ring to it. The top brass embraced the term with enthusiasm. In this job, what everyone wants now is specialization and flexibility, and this is precisely that kind of police work. You'll specialize in a particular subset of violent crimes, and other staff from the Violent Crime Unit will be brought in to help your cell as necessary."

"And what if there isn't anything special going on?"

"Koivu and Puupponen will assist Violent Crime, and you will do research in the meantime."

"So, you are offering me paper pushing after all?"

Taskinen grinned. "This was how I got the brass to swallow it. You have experience both from that domestic violence project and your training work. During downtime, you could prepare some sort of report about what kinds of unusual violent crimes occur in the district. Welcome to the modern world. You can get anything past the policy-makers if you use the right terminology."

I stood up and walked to the window. Pine trees swayed in the November wind. Rain clouds approached from the north, darkening the midday sky. It was true that I didn't have any idea what I was going to do after the Police University College project ended in February. The coffee tasted bitter in my mouth. Its quality hadn't changed at all in the time I'd been away from the department.

"I don't have very many years left until retirement," Taskinen said. "I'm giving myself permission to be selfish: I want to spend the rest of my time here with the most competent group of people I can. And that includes you."

I let Taskinen sweet-talk me for another fifteen minutes before answering in the affirmative. The thought of letting Antti support our family alone horrified me. I already had enough of a moral hangover from when we'd bought our Nihtimäki apartment with money he'd inherited from his father. The package Taskinen was offering included all the perks. The independence of the job description intrigued me, and I missed Koivu, and Puupponen's corny jokes. I couldn't imagine two better partners.

"A week from Monday, and it's back to the mines. But let's not talk about work," I said quickly, because Antti's expression had grown dark again. Sometimes he complained about feeling like an outsider when Anu, Pekka, and I started talking cop shop. Anu was still in the Juvenile Unit and the liaison between Patrol, Violent Crime, and Juvenile, as well as social services. Taskinen had also tailored her gig specifically for her, when it had become clear the Koivu family couldn't survive two parents working unpredictable hours in the department. Taskinen had become the veritable éminence grise of Finnish police work, pulling strings however he saw fit.

Koivu told stories about the strangest crimes that had occurred over the winter, including a flasher who'd been skulking around the Haukilahti neighborhood wearing nothing but tennis socks.

"Now there's a 'special' streaker for you. You'd think he'd get some serious shrinkage, being out in the cold like that. Puupponen calls him the King of Swing."

"Hopefully not when anyone else can hear. We're not going to be expected to investigate cases like that, are we?"

Koivu answered with a shake of his head. With Sennu and Iida's help, Anu began carrying small dishes of various Vietnamese delicacies to the table. Iida thought no food could be too spicy, and Juuso seemed to agree. It was amusing to remember what Koivu had been like ages ago, when we first met in the early nineties, and any fresh herbs or spices had been exotic to the boy from nowheresville Nurmes.

"We made satay sauce in cooking class at the Girls Club. The week before last we cooked Vietnamese food. When it's the Finns' turn, I'm going to make Grandma's Karelian pies." Iida batted her eyelashes at Koivu, her godfather.

"You go there a lot, to the Girls Club?" Anu asked. "I'm planning on coming next month to talk about youth policing."

"What night? Don't tell anyone you know me!"

"I think it's totally stupid that boys can't go there," Taneli muttered. We'd had this conversation before. When the city of Espoo decided the previous spring that it didn't have the money to fund the Girls Club project, the retired former chair of the Central Chamber of Commerce of Finland, Sylvia Sandelin, had raised a stink and announced that she would pay for it herself. Sandelin had given notice to the accounting firm that was operating on the ground floor of an apartment building she owned in Tapiola, then turned the space into a girls-only youth center. She also paid the salaries for the two Girls Club permanent employees and the activity leaders, and she spent a lot of time with the girls herself. The seventy-year-old, in a skirt suit and without a single hair out of place, was a curious role model for the teenagers, but Iida thought Sandelin was "totally cool." The Girls Club had been modeled on the Helsinki Girls' House, and Antti and I had been overjoyed when Iida found a new hobby there after giving up skating.

"Are they still having trouble with those catcallers over at the club?" Anu asked once the children had run off to resume their games after the main course. "Has Iida mentioned anything?"

"There were boys hanging around sometimes, but Sylvia Sandelin drove them off single-handedly. They felt the same way as Taneli: irritated that there are places they can't go. It's hard to explain to some of them that there are immigrant girls who are only allowed to be with other girls."

Even though we'd given up on separate girls' and boys' schools in Finland a couple of generations earlier, sometimes gender segregation was imperative. Like in the case of the female-only prison in Afghanistan, which served as a refuge for abused Afghan women. Though, when all was said and done, that wasn't anything more than a temporary and problematic solution.

It had been four months since the police academy in Afghanistan had opened, and they'd been able to remain in operation so far, although some students and their families had received threats. In

January, NATO ISAF forces had narrowly averted a suicide bombing at the training facility. I stayed in e-mail contact with my students, but sometimes their Internet connection would be down for days at a time. They all used initials instead of names in their e-mail addresses to maintain anonymity.

My life had been threatened a few times in the line of duty, but those situations were transitory, caused by individuals—they weren't systematic attempts to kill me. In Afghanistan, respect for authority didn't always extend to the police: Malalai Kakar, who had headed up a unit working on crimes against women, had been killed in the fall of 2008 as a warning to other women.

Ulrike's necklace felt heavy around my neck. I had to watch my movements so the sharp, silver twigs wouldn't scratch my skin. Perhaps the necklace was meant to be worn over a high-necked blouse. Anu began to clear the dishes from the table, and Antti rose to help her. I drained my wineglass and was about to go into the kitchen when Pekka took me by the shoulder and pressed me back into my seat. At first, I thought he was just trying to stop me from helping to clear the table, but then I saw his expression and knew he had something to say.

"I didn't want to say this in front of Antti, since he's a civilian. I've been waiting all night to tell you that I'm already set to tackle our first case. We don't have to hem and haw about where to start. Three young immigrant girls have disappeared in the last five weeks. No one has been taking it seriously, though they should have."

"What disappearances? I don't remember seeing anything like that in the papers."

"Markku Ruuskanen didn't think they were that important. He's a decent guy, but he doesn't want any trouble, and especially not publicity. There's no definitive evidence of a crime having been committed, but what other explanation could there be? The families claim to be completely baffled. But I have a gut feeling that the cases are connected."

2

"What do you think, Maria? Do we have a case?" Koivu asked excitedly. It was the afternoon of my second day of work, and Koivu had finally had an opportunity to give us the rundown on the series of disappearances. I was sitting with him and Puupponen in my new office. The men had a spacious shared workspace next to mine, which we could use as a case room or a conference space as necessary. In addition to a desk, my office also fit a sofa, a coffee table, and an armchair. Koivu was standing in front of the whiteboard, writing. He'd pinned a picture of a young girl in a headscarf to the cork board right beside it. Dark eyes full of life looked out from a face framed by a multicolored scarf. On her lips I thought I could make out just a hint of light-red lipstick.

"First disappearance: January second. Aziza Abdi Hasan, native of Afghanistan, seventeen years old. Moved to Finland four years ago. Family has a temporary residence permit. Aziza was in the eighth grade at Leppävaara Middle School, so she had one more year of compulsory education left after this one. She was studying with younger students due to insufficient language skills and a total lack of primary education—she entered school for the first time only after moving to Finland. Before that she didn't even know how to read. But she'd been progressing well. According to the parents, she went to Stockholm with her uncle over Christmas vacation to visit relatives living there. When Aziza didn't show up at school after the break and the parents weren't able to say where she was, the school officials filed a missing person report. The Finnish embassy contacted the Stockholm police, who went to interview the relatives. Neither Aziza nor her uncle had ever arrived at their home. The uncle is a Swedish citizen who, according to the ferry company's travel information, arrived in Finland on December twenty-seventh. There was no record of a return ticket being purchased. The Swedish police have a search underway. The family also has relatives in Denmark. If Aziza disappeared with the family's consent, they're covering for one another.

"Second disappearance: January twenty-fifth. Sara Amir, Bosnian Muslim, age fourteen, also in the eighth grade, but at Espoo Central. Same story as Aziza's—parents had not filed a missing person report. The school contacted social services, who requested that the police investigate. The parents say she returned to Bosnia, but there's no evidence of that. The family has permanent residency, and all of them have applied for Finnish citizenship. I went with social services to interview them. The father, Mikael Amir, didn't allow the other members of the family to speak. Sara is the family's only daughter, the middle child of five. The mother looked like she'd been crying, but she didn't get a chance to say anything. The school picture is from last year. She missed pictures this year due to illness."

The girl in this picture still looked like a child. Her face was thin and unsmiling; you could see fear in her eyes. I'd been under the impression that the Bosnian Muslims were a secularized bunch, but Sara's scarf was pulled around her head so snugly that not a single lock of hair was visible, and it was tied tightly under her chin.

"I would've liked to interview the mother one-on-one, but no dice. Of course, the father promised to notify the police immediately if they received any information about Sara's whereabouts. We haven't heard anything." Koivu adjusted his glasses higher on his nose. He'd been forced to get bifocals just before Christmas.

18

"Third disappearance: February fourteenth. Ayan Ali Jussuf, from Sudan, a permanent resident in Finland just like the rest of her family. Eighteen years old, considered an adult by Finnish law and no longer required to attend school. The parents didn't report her missing, but her friends at the Girls Club got worried when they couldn't reach her. The parents claim not to know where she is. She hasn't registered a new address with the state. We have no information about her whereabouts."

"And what do they all have in common?" I interjected.

"None of these young women has exited the country, at least not under her own name, by sea or by air. It is possible that they've gone north by car and crossed the Swedish border at Tornio, but since we're in the Schengen Area, that would be impossible to track. They may also have used false identities."

"Didn't Ruuskanen think these cases were worth investigating? Three teenage Muslim girls living in Espoo disappear without a trace. It wouldn't take much of a reporter to start connecting the dots. How has the department managed to keep this under wraps?"

"The families haven't wanted any publicity, and Ayan's friends have been afraid that speaking out about it might put her in danger. But Ayan is already an adult, and she could have disappeared voluntarily. Aziza and Sara could have done the same—girls have been known to run away from home before."

"Are there any rumors online?" I asked. Koivu seemed to have been taking this seriously, and I suspected he'd been making his own inquiries despite Ruuskanen's reluctance.

"There was some discussion of Ayan on the MTV3 message boards, but the administrator deleted the thread because it contained information that violated privacy protections. Apparently, one of Ayan's friends from the Girls Club started the discussion. Some people suspected the family had sent her out of the country because she had a Finnish boyfriend. But the family denies knowing anything about a boyfriend. Their Ayan only had girlfriends. One of the posters on the discussion board claimed that Ayan's older brothers killed her, but the messages were deleted after that. I haven't been able to subpoena the deleted messages because the investigation hasn't been official."

More than ten years of living with Anu Wang-Koivu, who had arrived as a Vietnamese Chinese refugee, had shown Pekka what it was like to be a member of an ethnic minority in Finland. Anu was as Finnish as could be and spoke the language perfectly, without any hint of a foreign accent, but sometimes people still addressed her in English or treated her like she was mentally deficient. Because police officers with immigrant backgrounds still didn't grow on trees, Anu had been assigned to deal with new Finns, regardless of their race or religion, even though her background was completely different from, say, Somali asylum seekers or Polish cleaning ladies. Through all this, Koivu had developed an allergy to racial categorization.

Puupponen began to hum a familiar tune, Pete Seeger's "Where Have All the Flowers Gone." Where had all these young girls gone? Koivu pushed the plate of donuts closer to Puupponen, who grinned and stopped singing.

"Hey, guys, isn't it pretty normal to marry off fourteen-year-olds in Muslim countries? What if their parents just wanted to marry them off to some cousin so they shipped them somewhere our laws don't apply?" Puupponen turned the donut back and forth, inspecting it, but he didn't take a bite. The pink frosting was smearing on his fingers.

"An eighteen-year-old could have gotten married here," Koivu observed.

"But against her will? If they dragged her back to Sudan, they could have done anything they wanted. By now she probably has a new name, and her Finnish social security number is only a memory. Someone more paranoid than me might think we were on the trail of a serial killer with a taste for immigrant girls, but it's going to take more than this to get an old-fashioned realist from the backwoods of Savo to swallow a theory like that. I can understand why Ruuskanen hasn't taken the case any further. If they were kidnapped for marriages, it would just pour gas on the fire of all the neo-Nazis."

"But Finland is governed by the rule of law, and in a state governed by the rule of law, when people disappear, we investigate. Especially when it's minors who are disappearing. For God's sake, don't smear frosting on your shirt!" Koivu snapped at Puupponen, who had just wiped his fingers on his extraordinarily ugly hand-knitted sweater. Its design was evidently meant to depict bears, but it had stretched so much they looked more like pine martens. Maybe the sweater was an expression of Puupponen's mother's or sister-in-law's sense of humor.

Both of my subordinates stared at me as if I was a referee. The power to start an investigation or leave the case on ice was mine. But I knew Koivu well enough to know that he wouldn't get so worked up over nothing.

"We could go and have a talk with the families again. Maybe Sara's mother would be able to speak one-on-one with another woman. Who made the report about Ayan's disappearance?"

"Nelli Vesterinen, the activity coordinator at the Girls Club. Ayan's girlfriends had asked her what to do."

Iida had mentioned Nelli countless times. Nelli wasn't uptight like the other Girls Club leader; Nelli never got on their case for joking around and even tolerated some horseplay. Anu was going to give a talk at the Girls Club, but she wasn't my subordinate. I could still tell her to keep her eyes and ears open, though; maybe Ayan's friends who had made the missing person report would be there. But we needed to interview Nelli Vesterinen as soon as possible.

"Pekka, you've been collecting the personal information and addresses of the lost girls' relatives, right?"

"Correctamundo. In a file folder, just like in the old days. The computer system has been acting up recently, so it's best to keep a hard copy of anything important."

"Haven't you heard of backups?" Puupponen asked.

"Ville, since you're such a computer genius, why don't you get online and see what you can dig up? Start by searching the girls' names; maybe the discussion about the disappearances has started up again. We'll send requests for assistance to Europol and INTERPOL. Pekka, you met all of the families personally?"

"Yeah, Ruuskanen palmed the foreigners off on me because I have an immigrant wife and three slant-eyed kids."

"Aren't we bitter today? I thought you'd be happy now that Maria is back in the department," Puupponen said, finally biting into his donut in such a way that the topmost pine marten/bear on the sweater received a splat of jelly on the head.

"It just sticks in my craw how helpless we are with things like this. 'Just don't investigate. What does it matter if we lose an immigrant or two? Better they leave the country anyway.' Of course, Ruuskanen didn't say anything like that, but you can sense the attitude. It almost reminded me of the Pertti Ström days. But let's get down to business, even though we're late leaving the starting gate. How about we make our office the case room so the boss lady can have some peace and quiet?"

Now that Koivu had gotten his way, he was finally smiling.

"It would be good to get DNA samples for each girl. Hopefully they haven't thrown away their toothbrushes and hairbrushes. Although the ones who were traveling may have packed them . . . But let's try anyway. Koivu, you make appointments with the families. All three of us will go so we can talk to people separately. I'll get in touch with the Girls Club."

"Is this another one of these clubs where they don't allow men?" Puupponen asked.

"A policeman can go wherever he wants," Koivu said, grabbing the last donut off the plate and exiting the room. Puupponen remained sitting in the armchair.

"Have you had a chance to meet Ruuskanen yet?" he asked.

"We officially met yesterday. I've crossed paths with him before, years ago at an officers' event, but I doubt we've ever exchanged more than a few words. But Ruuskanen doesn't have anything to do with this. We operate as an independent unit, and besides, he's just a temp. I don't think we should expect too much trouble from that direction."

Puupponen shook his head. There were only a few freckles on his pale skin; the winter sun didn't exactly lure them out. While their donut habit had expanded Koivu's midsection, it didn't seem to have any effect on Puupponen, even though he'd be celebrating his fortieth birthday in the summer. His hair glowed a shade of red that would have been difficult to conjure out of a bottle.

"I found an interesting link when I was doing some research online. Ruuskanen's twentysomething son, Miro Ruuskanen, is an active member of an anti-immigrant group called Finnish Heartland. It's one of these small groups that are disappointed that the True Finns Party doesn't condemn immigration strongly enough. Of course, the opinions of father and son don't necessarily have anything to do with each other, but it'd be good for you to be aware. I didn't dare mention it to Koivu; he's already got enough conspiracy theories running around in his head."

"No point making Ruuskanen's disinterest out to be more than it is. It's more likely a question of the lack of resources, which our new unit is meant to address. But go dig around online; I'm going to try to line up our first interview. Shoo!" I waved Puupponen out of my office like a wasp, and it worked. He left, laughing, leaving behind the sugary smell of donuts.

I spent a moment collecting my thoughts. Unlike Koivu and Puupponen, I suspected that in leaving the disappearances uninvestigated, Ruuskanen had been trying to avoid a racist backlash. It might be that, because of his son, he knew the thought patterns of immigration critics well enough that he guessed they would raise a stink over the girls' disappearances. In doing so, Ruuskanen had failed to focus on the most likely explanation. The girls had probably just been sent out of the country. There wasn't any reason to suspect honor killings, because no bodies had been found.

The Turku Highway hummed its familiar drone outside my window; my new office faced south, and in the summer it would turn into a furnace. I looked up the numbers for the Girls Club and called Nelli Vesterinen's cell phone. I reached her voice mail and left my contact information. I took care of the rest of the startup routine for my new job, like sending people my work e-mail address and transferring my family phone numbers and other standard contacts onto my work phone. That took a surprisingly long time, and I was just about to go investigate whether the department's lunch offerings had changed in the last few years when I received an e-mail at my new address. The subject line said "Greetings from Kabul" and the sender was Lauri Vala.

> Hey Kallio,
>
> It looks like you've started a new gig, apparently with a police department instead of at the college. I'm glad. Active duty cops get more respect than academy instructors anyway.
>
> I'm coming to Finland next week, and we need to meet. I don't want to say anything more over e-mail. I'll let you know when I'm in the country.
>
> Lauri Vala

Major Vala had been the highest-ranking Finnish military official in the unit that ran security for the civilians participating in the opening ceremonies at the police academy in Afghanistan. His posting was Mazar-i-Sharif, like all the other Finnish units, but he'd been at our disposal during the whole trip. At first, Vala had been cool and businesslike, but on the evening after the IED attack, he'd tried to get better acquainted. After help had arrived and combed the area without finding any more mines, we continued our journey to Kabul. The Germans' exploded and badly charred jeep was left behind; the ambulance would come later to retrieve the bodies. We didn't say anything beyond what was absolutely necessary for the rest of the journey. Numminen drove us the rest of the way, and after we reached the city we ended up stuck in traffic, even though it was already late. While in Kabul, Vala was staying in the same carefully guarded hotel as I was, and when we arrived, he asked for my key as well as his at the reception desk and escorted me to my room.

"I don't want to leave you alone. I'll be back soon. I'm just going to get something that we both need. I'll knock three times, twice. Bap, bap, bap. Don't open up for anyone else."

Vala was used to being in command, and as a police officer, I was used to the chain of command being well defined. At that moment I didn't have a will of my own. My head was a mess of grief and gratitude. I was alive! I sat down on the bed. The stench of burning flesh clung to my hair, and I was afraid showering might not be enough to wash it out. I took off only my shoes before lying down. Outside someone was shouting the call to prayer in a shrill voice, and then it was lost in the din of traffic. There were dark splotches on the ceiling, like tears.

I don't know how much time passed before Vala knocked on the door. Apparently, he'd managed to change into a clean uniform and wash up, since his short, steel-gray hair was still wet. The hotel had a functioning plumbing system, which was still a luxury in Kabul. On the streets you saw women carrying water from the public wells. We'd been strictly warned against drinking anything but bottled water, and on top of that we were supposed to check the seal of the cap.

I let Vala in, even though I wasn't sure I wanted company. In his hand Vala had a wooden box that was about sixteen inches square, and about half as tall. He sat on the only chair in the room and set the box on the table. On its cover was a picture of a sailboat.

Vala opened the box, producing two glasses and a bottle of whiskey. It happened to be my favorite brand, but in that moment I was worried that the taste of peat and smoke would remind me too much of what had happened.

"I think we could both use a drink. How many fingers?"

"Can you drink on duty?"

"Right now, I don't give a rat's ass." Vala filled his glass halfway. "What? Are you in shock?"

I sat upright. Probably not, since I could still remember the signs of shock. I was just so tired that I felt like I was about to pass out. I asked Vala to pour me a couple of fingers. The Laphroaig was cask strength, 120 proof, and its burn flowed from my throat into my stomach. If I drank everything Vala had poured, nothing would hold back the tears.

"What on earth are you doing in a war zone? You have two kids. Your youngest isn't even ten. Why aren't you at home with them?"

Up to that point, Vala and I had stuck strictly to business in our conversations. He must have overheard me telling Ulrike about my children. I'd known Ulrike through the European Network of Policewomen before she joined the Afghanistan policewomen's project. She'd even met Iida and Taneli when they'd visited me in Tampere.

"I was closely involved with the Afghan academy project and trained the female police officers in Finland. I wanted to come here because I respect their courage."

"Do you respect their courage more than your children's right to a mother?"

Antti had asked essentially the same thing, as had my mother. Only my father had been silent, letting me do what I felt was right. He would probably be hearing about it from my mother for the rest of his life.

"My female students, Sayeda, Muna, and Uzuri, can't choose any other road than the one they're on, no matter how big a risk it is."

"But this is their homeland. You're a Finn."

"So are you. What's the difference?"

"My sons are already out on their own, and my wife left me years ago. Listen to me, Kallio. Throughout history men have done the fighting and women have looked after the home and the children. That's just how it's meant to be. Both are equally important. Would your children have thought you were a hero if that IED had hit us instead of the Germans? No, they would have thought you were a selfish bitch."

The person I'd been before that night probably would have thrown the malt whiskey in Vala's face. But that person had been left on the road between Kabul and Jalalabad, and the new me wanly drank the peaty, copper-gold liquid.

"Our safety was supposed to be guaranteed," I said lamely.

"This country is in a civil war. Nothing is guaranteed under these conditions. They don't play by Western rules here. We're facing off against a pack of men who think completely differently than we do. Their own lives aren't worth much, and their enemies' lives aren't worth anything. It's easy to be an optimist over in Finland. You saw the prisons here. How soon do you think those conditions are going to change? How long do you think your students are going to stay alive? They'll be lucky to live past Christmas. To the Taliban, having women work at the police academy is even worse than having it run by Westerners."

I could feel the whiskey starting to lift my thoughts. My head felt light. I'd met Lauri Vala before; it wasn't like a career soldier serving a peacekeeping mission would win any prizes for optimism.

"Don't misunderstand me. The folks at the police academy are a damn fine bunch. We wouldn't have anything to do in this country if everyone acted like them. My place is here, but yours isn't."

"Why the hell are you preaching to me? I'm leaving tomorrow, and I don't have any intention of coming back. You don't have to worry about me."

"So, you aren't going to accept the police academy director's invitation? He wanted you to stay on as a visiting lecturer."

Vala was drinking the whiskey like it was water, but nothing in his outward appearance indicated he was a drunk. The tan skin of his face didn't have any broken blood vessels, his nose wasn't red, and there was no sign of bloating in his muscular body from the booze. And someone with a drinking problem wouldn't have been able to do his job anyway. Booze was probably just Vala's way of dealing with setbacks.

"I might have considered it when we left the academy. But not anymore."

"So, you understand that you should be afraid?"

"Hey, soldier boy, don't you think we learn that in the police?"

That was exactly what we practiced: healthy fear and the ability to function regardless. I was drinking my whiskey too fast as well, even though the taste of it was like the stink of Ulrike as she burned. The strange words of a poem Uzuri had recited in Pashto during the opening ceremonies weighed on my mind. She'd written it herself. The poem said that home was like a poppy flower, the seeds of which the birds spread far and wide, and that *nanawati*, forgiveness, would fall upon all those who atoned for their evil deeds before the law. There was a direct translation of the poem in English in my bag. Uzuri had written it by hand with a ballpoint pen, and even her handwriting was like a little work of art. What did Vala think of nanawati?

"You must know, Kallio, the best way to drive away the presence of death?" Vala leaned toward me and touched my shoulder. "Sex makes a person feel alive better than booze or drugs."

It took a second for me to realize what Vala was talking about, and I could hardly believe my ears. I managed to sputter that I was married, though Vala already must have known.

"Faithfully married?"

I didn't like Vala's smile and drew back farther from the edge of the bed.

"Yes."

"Of course, that's an excellent thing, if not terribly common. Guess how many of my subordinates' wives have discovered they can't stand the waiting and the constant threat of death and so go off with a more stable guy who will actually be around? I made my own sons swear to never get into this job, but the younger one is in cadet school. The older one is going to be a commercial pilot."

I felt like saying that even if I was going to have an affair, I wouldn't do it with him, but I didn't have time before he got another call. The cell phone network was unreliable, so the soldiers had two-way radios. I realized that the roadside bomb attack would soon be in the headlines around the Western world and that I should notify my family that I was uninjured. The hotel had a fax machine, but no one in my family owned one anymore. There was one at Antti's work, but he wouldn't get the message until morning. Sometimes e-mails went without a hitch, but other times they simply vanished.

Vala's conversation in English was brief, his part of it mostly negative responses. While he was talking, I emptied my whiskey glass. I wanted to sleep, even if it meant taking a sleeping pill. But more than anything, I wanted Vala out of my room. When he ended the call, I thanked him for the drink and asked him to leave. He got up slowly and looked me in the eyes in a way that made me want to turn my head away.

"My room is number forty-six. It's on this same floor. Don't hesitate to knock if anything happens. Maybe we'll see each other at breakfast. Numminen will take you to the airport. The French are leaving on the same plane to Frankfurt." Vala shook my hand.

To my relief, we didn't run into each other at breakfast.

There was an empty seat next to me on the flight to Frankfurt, which had been reserved for Ulrike. I didn't dare drink any alcohol. I had to keep myself together, to forget . . . I didn't want to remember anything from the past twenty-four hours, including Lauri Vala.

We hadn't exchanged a single word since that night in Afghanistan, but now he wanted to meet, supposedly for some reason he couldn't reveal over e-mail. Just what I needed right now.

Vala left my mind when Nelli Vesterinen returned my call.

"Finally, someone is taking Ayan's disappearance seriously! We've been amazed that the police haven't done anything. Ayan's girlfriends have had enough bad experiences with the police in their own countries, and now the Finnish police are letting them down too. Ayan never would have left Finland voluntarily. She had a job and friends here."

I asked Nelli who Ayan's friends were.

"Some people from her work. She was working part-time at the Tapiola Stockmann, in the grocery department. She came to the Girls Club straight from there all the time. I never saw anyone with her but her older brother, who came to get her sometimes. But Miina, Ayan's best friend, is sure to know more. She was the one who got worried when Ayan stopped showing up. She went to Ayan's house, and they told her that no one knew where Ayan was. Maybe they really don't."

"What is this Miina's last name, and how can I reach her?"

"Miina Saraneva. She lives close, a few buildings away from the Girls Club, on Otsolahti Street. She's in her first year at the technical college—math, I think. She should be here tonight, same as every Tuesday. She sits and waits for Ayan to come back. You can find her here."

3

In the end, I went to the Girls Club alone, because I didn't want to draw needless attention by bringing in my male colleagues. I'd been to the entrance before, when dropping off and picking up Iida, but I'd never gone into the club itself.

Otsolahti Street was in the old part of Tapiola, an area built up in the 1950s, and in some places the snow-covered trees extended as high as the roofs. The property on the ground floor of the three-story building had originally been a grocery store. Sylvia Sandelin owned several units in the building and lived in a town house at the end of the street near the shore of a small bay. The local paper had done a full-page story when the Girls Club was founded, and I'd found more articles about Sandelin through Google. She was the rare woman who showed up in both women's magazines and the business pages.

I'd stopped off at home to eat before coming over to the club. Taneli was at an extra skating practice, so I'd pick him up on the way home. In a fit of belt-tightening, the Espoo Police Department had done away with personal official vehicles, except for the very highest levels of management, so I was using my own car, and I planned to stop by the supermarket while I was out. It was hard to find a parking spot at the Girls Club because of the piled-up snowbanks, but I finally got my vehicle squeezed in along the curb.

I recognized Nelli Vesterinen from Iida's description: she was a small, athletic-looking woman, with heavy red-and-green harlequin dreadlocks and several facial piercings. She smiled broadly at me and extended her right hand, the wrist of which was circled by Rasta-colored tribal tattoos. The handshake was firm enough that I struggled to match her grip.

"Nelli Vesterinen. Nice to meet you. Miina hasn't shown up yet. How about we go back into the employees' office? At least it has a door we can close."

The largest space at the Girls Club was a room of about six hundred square feet. It had beanbag chairs, a television and DVD player, and a hand loom with a half-finished rag rug on it. Next to the loom was a carpentry bench shielded by a screen. In a side room was the music space where Iida played with her friends. There was a drum set in there, along with a couple of amplifiers and a 1980s vintage keyboard. The kitchen smelled of cardamom, not from *pulla* sweet rolls but from someone cooking basmati rice. At the end of the hall, behind the kitchen, was a closet of a room, just big enough to fit a table and a couple of chairs. The room didn't have any windows, but the wall sported a picture of a wintry mountain vista that could have been Afghanistan.

"Would you like some green tea?"

"Why not."

Nelli opened a thermos and poured tea into two cups. The green liquid tasted a little bitter but still beat the police station's bags of Lipton.

"What can you tell me about Ayan Ali Jussuf? How long had she been coming to the Girls Club?"

"Since the beginning. A whole gaggle of Somali and Sudanese girls, who obviously had nothing to do, joined in, and Ayan was one of them. She wanted to be called Ayan Ali, without the Jussuf. Jussuf was her grandfather, and she didn't want his name, but that was the name she had in the population register. She wanted to change it."

"Why?"

"As I said, a Muslim's family name is her grandfather's name, and her middle name is her father's name. She wanted a name that wouldn't define her through any of her relatives. Ayan admired the Finnish system, where a child can be given her mother's surname, and a woman doesn't have to change her name when she gets married."

"So, was Ayan rebelling against Muslim culture?"

"Maybe in thought but not in deed. Though we don't know what's happened to her now. As far as I know, she didn't have a boyfriend, but Miina can tell you more. We don't go prying into the girls' private lives here; we just help the ones who need it. Ayan asked me about the possibility of changing her name, and I told her that, according to Finnish law, any adult can do that."

"Did she also want to leave her religion?"

"She never talked about that, at least not with me."

Someone knocked on the door, and Nelli invited whoever it was to come in. The newcomer was a slight, willowy girl with short-cropped hair that was so blond it was almost white. She was dressed all in white too, and her coveralls reminded me of the protective suits used in technical crime scene investigations or the jumpsuits worn by astronauts. But these overalls were made out of cotton and didn't have any patches on them, just small, bright-red embroidery on the collar and cuffs.

"This is Miina Saraneva. Detective Kallio from the Espoo police would like to chat with you about Ayan, Miina."

The girl's pale face flushed, and an angry heat flashed in her eyes.

"The police! Finally! Ayan has been missing for over two weeks. We were supposed to meet on Valentine's Day—there was a Valentine's Day party here—but she never showed up and didn't even send a text. I couldn't get ahold of her. The next Tuesday I went to her apartment, but her parents said they didn't know where she was. They didn't let me inside, so I don't know if they were lying. I asked Nelli to file a missing person report right after that."

"The police have already interviewed Ayan's family, but with the same results. Her family doesn't know anything. Did Ayan have a boyfriend?"

"No." Miina's answer was sure and quick. "She didn't want any man ordering her around."

There was another knock at the door, and the Indian-looking girl who had been working in the kitchen asked for Nelli. Nelli left the room, closing the door behind her. Miina looked at the landscape painting instead of me as she continued.

"Ayan didn't usually talk about these things; she was shy . . . she was from a world so different than mine. But once she said that she didn't want a husband or children, because it would be too painful. I guess she'd been circumcised in a refugee camp in Somalia when she was nine. She called it 'the operation.' Once she was with me when I was buying tampons. She was really embarrassed and barely had the courage to ask me why I used them. 'Doesn't it hurt?' she said. I explained how they work, and she was totally confused. I could see she wanted to ask more but didn't have the nerve, and I didn't want to force it. I doubt her mother even told her about periods. Ayan got all her information from the school nurse and magazines."

"Did Ayan fight with her family?"

"No. She didn't like everything that happened in her family, but she never said anything to them about it."

"There was a claim online that Ayan's brothers killed her. Who might have started a rumor like that?"

Miina's face went white as snow, and her voice began to shake.

"Really? Who said that?"

"It didn't say."

Miina closed her eyes. Her head rocked back and forth slowly. "Which brother?"

I explained that I hadn't seen the thread. She told me that Ayan had two older brothers, Gutaale and Abdullah. Both lived with their parents and worked at a cleaning company.

Miina had never visited Ayan's home when the men of the family were there, and the only family member she'd met was the mother. Ayan had not been willing to go over to Miina's house, even though she lived right next to the Girls Club. The girls had met at various coffee shops in Tapiola when one or the other happened to have some extra money.

"Ayan was proud of her job, even though it was just part-time. She would have liked to go to high school and then study nutrition. She talked about that sometimes, and she was really excited when she heard about the Finnish student financial aid and housing allowance systems. Earlier this year she went to the Adult Education Center to ask about taking night classes. Of course, I encouraged her to do it."

Tears had started to run down Miina's face, but the color of her cheeks didn't change. Her nose gradually started to redden. She took a paper napkin from the stack on the table and wiped her face with it. If I hadn't known Miina's real age, I would have let her travel on a child's ticket.

"Where do you think Ayan is?"

"Somewhere she'll never come back from! Maybe dead, maybe in Sudan with her grandparents, maybe sent off somewhere else where she can't get in touch with me. She would have told me if she was going to run away on her own. We were best friends. At least that's what she said. Sometimes she called me Adey—it means 'light skinned.' Sometimes we compared the skin on our faces and wrists. Such different colors, from such different worlds, but so alike . . ." Now Miina broke down completely. She buried her face in the napkin.

Music had started to come through the door, first the thumping of a bass guitar and then the sound of drums and cymbals. The rhythm was six-eight time, which the bass couldn't quite keep up with. Then the drums shifted to five-four, and a girl's voice yelled, "You can count to five, can't you, you effing blond?" The guitar stopped at that, but the drums stubbornly continued, now adding a bass drum, which played the first and fourth beats of the rhythm. My foot started to tap along.

35

The music took me back to my teenage years of band practice in a dingy basement, where I was usually the only girl. In Arpikylä, where I grew up, the only club for girls had been at the local church, and that wasn't my scene, even though they did do scouting.

I let Miina cry in peace. When she finally continued, her voice was hopeful.

"If Ayan is alive, she'll get in touch. There isn't any reason to think she's dead, is there? You haven't found anything to make you think that, have you?" Miina was like a dog whose owner had left her waiting at the door of a store. Her face had the same resigned look, mixed with just a hint of hope.

"We're going to do our best to figure this out, but not all cases get solved quickly." I offered Miina my business card, which had come from the printers just that morning. I asked her to contact me immediately if she heard from Ayan or discovered anything related to her disappearance.

"Will the police tell me things in return? I don't want to have to read online that my best friend has been found dead."

"In theory our duty is to inform just the family."

"They're only her family on paper! Ayan was forced to live with them. They didn't know anything about her thoughts and dreams. I'm the only one she really talked to. They weren't interested in what she had to say as long as she did what she was told! I told her that in Finland an adult doesn't have to explain herself to anyone, that women can live together and without men, that she could be a scientist or anything if she wanted to . . . Do you understand? Many of us are closer to our friends than our families. That's what Ayan loved about Finland. She didn't have to worry the whole time about her relatives and what they thought."

I promised Miina that she would hear immediately if we received more information about Ayan's whereabouts. When we left the office and went back into the recreation room, Miina flopped down in an armchair and stared at the wall. Nelli came in through the outside door and asked if I still wanted to interview her. She was followed by a tall woman who looked about thirty, whose hair was plaited in two thick, blond braids.

"Heini Korhonen, Girls Club executive director," she said by way of introduction. "You must be the detective. Finally. Three of our girls have disappeared without a trace, and no one has done anything about it. It's like the police are afraid to get involved in anything having to do with immigrants."

"Three? Were Sara Amir and Aziza Abdi Hasan coming to the Girls Club too?"

"Not as often as Ayan, but once or twice anyway. You didn't know they were all connected? We try to help girls integrate and become independent, but not all immigrant cultures see that as a good thing." Heini Korhonen had clearly said this before, and she seemed used to speaking in public.

I would need to leave soon to pick up Taneli. He didn't have a cell phone, so I couldn't warn him I'd be late. Antti didn't think kids under ten should have phones. Taneli was counting down the days to his birthday in April when he would finally get the coveted gadget.

"So, you know Sara and Aziza?" I asked Heini. "Who are their friends here?"

"Aziza only came to the club once, and Sara twice, first with girls from her class at school for a tour and then once for a cooking class. But I remember them, just like I remember all the girls. They're important to me. It's good the police have finally woken up. I've been thinking about tipping off a journalist I know. I imagine the public would be interested in something like this, though I'm sure the uproar would be greater if the missing girls were native Finns."

The volume of Heini's voice had attracted the attention of the girls in the room. I raised my own voice and asked if any of them had known Sara, Aziza, or Ayan. A girl named Niina said she'd been in the same school as Sara, but in a different grade. Apparently, there were rumors at school that she'd been sent back to Bosnia because she had a Finnish boyfriend, someone named Tommi.

"He wasn't from our school; he was from somewhere out in Siuntio or something. I never saw him. Someone just said on Facebook that Sara had been seen holding hands with a boy with long hair down at the Cello Mall a few days before she stopped coming to school. I'll look and see if I can still find the message."

I gave her my business card as well. It felt so old-fashioned, like I should be sending my contact information straight to her smartphone. The girl would probably throw the scrap of paper in the nearest trash can. If she just remembered my name, she could find me later using the Espoo Police Department address.

I was about to leave when Heini Korhonen's voice stopped me. "One more thing about Sara's family. I've met them a few times in other contexts. I speak Serbo-Croatian and work as a public service interpreter when I'm needed. They didn't like that Sara came here. That's probably why it was only a couple of times."

When I asked Heini about the possibility of Sara having a boyfriend, she said she didn't know. Then I had to leave to pick up Taneli. On the way back, I stopped by the grocery store, where I kept seeing Miina's pale face in my mind as I tried to come up with something quick for dinner. Antti was going to a concert, so I was in charge of getting everyone fed. Local perch fillets cost two and a half times the Vietnamese catfish, but I still chose the perch. My first day at work had also been my birthday, and Antti had pampered me with a mutton-chanterelle meat loaf, Iida had made brownies, and Taneli had fixed a salad. At work I'd served a raspberry jelly roll, which was the absolute upper limit of my kitchen skills. Koivu had politely taken three pieces. He had remembered my birthday even though I wasn't making a big deal about it because it wasn't a major milestone year.

There were potatoes left over from the weekend, so back at home I fried them up as a hash to go with the perch. I thought of the three families that now had an empty place at the dinner table. Maybe they knew the whereabouts of the person who had once held that seat, or maybe only some of them knew and the others were settling for a lie they'd been told. I didn't have any illusions about being able to tell if a person was lying just by looking at them. But in order to move this case forward, I would have to meet their families. I thought of them as Ayan's, Sara's, and Aziza's families, because none of the families, except the Amirs, shared a common surname. I had agreed to giving Iida Antti's last name, bowing to my husband's argument that everyone knows who a child's mother was, but you could never be completely sure of paternity. This cynical, Strindbergian view had seemed logical at the time, and later on we'd realized the wisdom of our children being Sarkelas, even though Kallio is a fairly common name. I could never perfectly insulate my family from the dangers of my job, but I could at least grant them this one protection.

Because our meal was delayed until a very Mediterranean nine o'clock in the evening, Taneli had to go to bed right afterward. Since Christmas he'd refused bedtime stories, which he now considered childish because he knew how to read to himself. Iida asked me to drill her on her Swedish vocabulary because there was a test the next day.

"I just got a text from Anni. She says you were at the Girls Club, but you didn't notice her. What were you doing there?"

"Work stuff."

I never talked about work with my children, and I tried to maintain confidentiality with Antti too, although occasionally I slipped. Sometimes I needed someone to bounce ideas off of. But I'd asked all the girls at the club to contact me if they had any information, and since Iida would hear about my visit from her friends anyway, I explained briefly what was going on. Maybe she could help.

Iida only remembered Ayan, and only because she was best friends with that "weird girl who always dresses in white." Iida mostly spent time with girls her own age, but she looked up to some of the older ones. When she started to press me about what I thought had happened to Ayan, I had to cut the conversation off.

"I'm sure we'll figure it out. Don't worry. There isn't any reason to think anything bad happened to her."

I hoped Iida believed me, even though I doubted anything good had led to Ayan's disappearance.

The next day was typical for March, cloudy with temperatures close to freezing. Enormous piles of dirty snow were heaped alongside every street and driveway. Ayan's family lived in a public housing project, the address of which was regrettably all too familiar to the police. The Amirs lived in the next building over, but we hadn't managed to contact them yet. Ayan's father, Ali Jussuf Hassan, would soon be on his way to his evening shift as a bus driver. We assumed the mother would be home as well, since she didn't work as far as Koivu knew.

"I tried to ask my neighbors, the Keiras, if they knew Ayan's family; they're from Sudan too. They knew who I was talking about, but the families see each other only sporadically at the mosque. The Keiras are going there less and less these days," Koivu had explained in the car. "Mehdi Keira went to a soccer match with us once and commented on how little spirit Finnish fans have in supporting their teams."

There was an elevator in Ayan's family's building, but it had a sign that said "Out of Order. Repairman Has Been Called" posted on it in Finnish, plus writing in two other languages whose characters I didn't know how to read. Maybe they were Somali and Persian.

We climbed the stairs to the third floor. Two-thirds of the names on the mail slots were written in something other than Finnish. On a couple of doors, there were pieces of paper with more handwritten names next to the white plastic letters. One mail slot even had four Finnish names. During my childhood in Arpikylä, divorce and kids without fathers were uncommon. The fatherless boy in my elementary school class had made a Father's Day card for his granddad, and I remember the teacher getting irritated because a girl named Minna didn't even have a grandfather to send a card to. The teacher just told her to draw whatever she wanted while the rest of us scribbled flowers and cars on our cards. Were Father's Day and Mother's Day culturally neutral enough for immigrants to feel comfortable adopting them, regardless of their religion? Did Muslims celebrate Women's Day? Iida would probably know better than me. The only immigrants in her class were a Russian and an Estonian, but more than a dozen cultures were represented by members of the Girls Club.

On Ayan's family's apartment door it said "Hassan." The man who greeted us looked familiar, and I realized that he often drove the regional bus that went from our house into Helsinki. He spoke Finnish with a strong accent but fluently. We'd left our overcoats in the car, and we wiped our shoes carefully on the mat in the entryway before Mr. Hassan led us to a room where IKEA met East Africa: the sofa with light-colored upholstery and wooden legs and the birch-veneer television stand could have been from any Finnish living room, but the colorful textiles and other decorations would have been more common in the family's land of origin. When Finns were in far-off countries, they claimed to miss *salmiakki* licorice and rye bread. What homeland flavors did the Sudanese miss? Were they content as long as they could get rice, and live in a country where peace prevailed?

Ali Jussuf Hassan motioned for us to sit. He did not look at me, and no one shook hands. Koivu began by asking if they had heard from Ayan and if her mother was home.

"Not a word. Two weeks she's been gone, and not a word. We don't know what to tell you. No one knows anything—not the neighbors, not the relatives. My wife is in the kitchen. She doesn't know anything either."

Ayan had left for the Girls Club Valentine's Day party, but she never arrived, and no one saw her get on the bus. Ali Jussuf Hassan had asked his coworkers who'd been driving that night, but the driver on shift didn't remember seeing his daughter.

"I didn't know this could happen in Finland. In Sudan, life is cheap, but here we were supposed to be safe," he said seriously. He had on straight-leg black pants, which he could wear while driving, and his white dress shirt was pressed and spotless. I heard a clatter in the kitchen, so I stood up and moved toward the sound. The door to the kitchen was closed, but I could hear water gurgling, like the sound of dishes being washed. When I opened the door, a woman turned toward me and cried out in surprise. I don't know what or who I looked like to her. I didn't have on a police uniform, but I had purposefully worn a black skirt that would cover my knees, violet boots, and a loose wool jacket, so that I would look more approachable in Aisha Muhammed Ali's eyes. According to our information, she was the same age as I was, but she was much thinner. The skin was stretched tight over the bones of her face, though the areas around her eyes and mouth were full of wrinkles. She had round eyeglasses and a long, multicolored dress, the sleeves of which were rolled up for dish washing. She quickly rolled them down when I stepped into the room and pulled the white scarf covering her hair farther forward on her head.

"Hello. I'm Detective Maria Kallio from the Espoo police. We're investigating the disappearance of your daughter, Ayan."

I'd told Koivu and Puupponen to press Ayan's father about the rumors that Ayan's brothers had killed her. Puupponen had been in contact with the Internet message board the rumors had appeared on, and the administrators had sent him documentation of the accusations. They were currently looking into who had posted them. When our cell was first being set up, we'd been given authority to subpoena the identity of anonymous Internet users when technically possible and when the crime in question was one that could bring at least two years in prison.

Ayan's mother didn't answer me. She dried her hands on a cloth that was as unwrinkled and gleaming white as her husband's shirt. There were teacups and a salad bowl in the sink. The kitchen didn't have a dishwasher.

"Do you speak Finnish?" I asked. Then I closed the door, which startled her.

"Not well. Ayan . . . found?" There was hope in the woman's eyes, which told me more than a verbal reply could. Aisha Muhammed Ali had no reason to believe that her daughter was dead.

"No. We're trying to find her. Do you know where she is?"

She shook her head. "She go Girl Club, never come back. Not know what happen. Husband and sons look for her all time—ask everyone." Though she spoke slowly and deliberately, there was a fierceness in her voice.

"Did Ayan have a boyfriend?"

"No. She was good girl. Went work, come home, give all money father. Sometimes Girl Club, but not too much. Someone take her, said, 'You beautiful girl, I take picture, you get money.' Ayan believe. Then . . ." She shrugged and spread her hands. "I hope come back. Someone find. Maybe Finland police good."

"What sort of relationship did Ayan have with her brothers?"

Aisha stared at the floor and then asked, "Relationship, what does mean?"

"Were they friends? What did Ayan's brothers think about her going to the Girls Club?"

She thought for a long time before answering. Perhaps she just had to search for the words. It would have been easier with an interpreter, but we hadn't been able to get one on such short notice.

"No fights. Ayan good. Boys not like she walk alone. Finnish boys not know respect girls. My boys get Ayan from club. Safe. Good boys, work much. Bring money home."

I knew not to place too much weight on Internet rumors. The people who had commented about Ayan's fate were probably professional xenophobes who didn't have any real information about Ayan. It felt cruel to ask a mother if one of her children could have killed another, but if we wanted to find out what had happened to Ayan, we couldn't shy away from even the most painful subjects.

"There are rumors that your sons killed their sister. Do you have any information about that?"

Aisha's breath caught, and then she said she didn't understand my question, but I could see from her eyes that she did. It was like she shrank, like she pulled back into herself, to protect herself from the harshness of the world. I could see that she didn't know what had happened to Ayan, but also that she didn't consider the theory I'd presented impossible. I felt chills.

4

After my question, Aisha closed up completely. All she would tell me was that Ayan had slept in the living room. The apartment had a common layout with three rooms, not including the kitchen. The bedroom that the parents shared was a reasonable size. Beside the bed was a wardrobe. The other room barely fit two beds and, between them under the window, a narrow table with a computer on it. The only thing on the walls was a Sudanese flag.

The men were sitting in the living room. It was clear from everyone's body language that my colleagues had presented the message board murder allegation to Ali Jussuf Hassan as well. He was staring at the floor, his fists clenched, and shaking his head in fury.

"We need some of Ayan's things, like a hairbrush or a toothbrush. Where did she keep her clothes?" I asked Aisha. "And did she sleep here on the sofa or somewhere else?"

Aisha pointed at a rug in the corner behind the couch. The sofa was arranged so the corner formed its own little nook, and on the other side a wooden chest served as a privacy screen.

"There. On mattress on rug. No bigger apartment. Sleep ground with sisters in Sudan. Not in bed."

"Sisters? Do you have other daughters besides Ayan?" Koivu had only mentioned the two older brothers.

"Two other girls. Left there. No food for everyone in camp." Aisha's voice was faint. "Many have all children die."

What could I say to that? Did the fact that the same thing had happened to others make losing children easier? Or that at least some had survived? Was it easier to stomach the agony if you had already experienced the loss once before? Would Ayan's parents have voluntarily sent her back to the hell where their other daughters had perished? Suddenly I wanted to be with Iida and Taneli, protecting them, making sure that nothing could threaten them.

"Ayan things there." Aisha pointed at the chest, on top of which was a colorful sitting cushion. It looked like it could have come with them all the way from Sudan.

I didn't ask permission to open the chest; I just got to work. Koivu got up from the couch and came behind me to see what was in it. I heard Ayan's father protest. It was inappropriate for a man, even a policeman, to see his daughter's undergarments. That was most of what was in the chest, along with a pair of loose, dark-red pants, three colorful tunics, and a black headscarf. Unfinished embroidery depicted roses and cornflowers. I wondered if those grew in Sudan too. Lipstick and a tube of mascara were hidden at the bottom of the chest. There was no lock on it, making it a poor hiding place. Ayan had slept night after night with only the chest and the sofa to give her privacy.

I stood and looked around the room, trying to focus all of my senses, sniffing like a bloodhound. But I wasn't a TV sleuth who only had to concentrate hard to know what had happened in a place. Of course I sensed the fear and stress; they'd taught us that in our first interrogation courses at the police academy. We'd had one lesson about the Roma, to help us understand the unique aspects of their culture, but basic training had focused overwhelmingly on interactions within mainstream Finnish culture. Antti occasionally listened to an avant-garde comedy album from M. A. Numminen, which included a passage of Wittgenstein delivered in German in a bizarre, crowing voice: "What we cannot speak about we must consign to silence." Finland wasn't the only place with a culture of silence. No matter how much lip service people gave to the idea of talking openly about problems, that alone wasn't going to change generations of habit, and it was just as easy to use words to conceal the truth as it was to illuminate it. White-collar criminals seemed to have a special gift for drowning our investigators in floods of meaningless words. Most suspects didn't use words, though—they just clammed up.

When I was teaching at the Police University College, I encouraged our interrogators to be gentle with immigrants who had spent time in refugee camps. Most native-born Finns trusted the police for good reason, but the situation in these newcomers' countries of origin was often quite different than ours, and threatening a person who had suffered extended periods of torture could trigger serious psychological problems. Now, however, I couldn't sit around wondering whether I'd made a mistake by suggesting to Aisha that the male members of her family might be behind Ayan's disappearance. I had to keep working to uncover the truth.

Aisha said Ayan's hairbrush was in the bag she always carried with her. Aisha had thrown out the toothbrush, and all of Ayan's clothing in the trunk was clean. Finding a DNA sample wouldn't be easy, but for the time being we didn't really need it anyway. We took the bag from the vacuum at any rate, which made Ali Jussuf Hassan look at us, perplexed.

It felt like we were leaving the apartment empty-handed. Koivu and Puupponen hadn't gotten anything out of Ali Jussuf Hassan, other than a fervent assurance that none of the family members knew where Ayan was. He looked for her every day, asking his bus driver coworkers if they'd seen her. He chalked up the rumors about his sons to Finnish racism.

"He said the boys had already lost their other sisters. Ayan is important to them, and they've been looking everywhere for her too, in the other neighborhoods around and along their route to work, at every bus stop and in the surrounding areas," Koivu said. "The police can't go around accusing people of crimes based on what anonymous Internet trolls say. But Ville and I will talk to the boys tomorrow anyway, OK?" Koivu's voice echoed in the stairwell like in a church. If there'd been violence in Ayan's family, the neighbors most likely would have heard, due to the poor soundproofing in the building. We could hear music and the crying of babies through some of the doors as we walked down toward the main entrance. We'd wait to start ringing doorbells.

Outside, a swarm of children played on a snow pile. There were about a dozen of them, all preschool age, with skin tones ranging from fair to very dark. Their mothers stood chatting near the wall. I approached, introduced myself, and asked if they knew anything about Ayan's disappearance.

"Is she missing?" one of the light-skinned mothers asked. "I thought it'd been a while since I'd seen her. She babysits for us sometimes when my sister can't. Has something happened to her?"

"We don't know. Have any of you heard fighting coming from Ayan's apartment?"

Silence fell over the group. Then one of the dark-skinned young women wearing a headscarf asked another dressed like her something in a language that I guessed was Somali. She answered in what sounded like the same language. The women's animated conversation ended in head shaking.

"Amina does not know Finnish very well and did not know what the word 'fighting' meant," one of the Somali women said. "She is Ayan's neighbor. No fights. Very peaceful family. Keep to selves, yes. Not many visitors. Feel a little sorry for them."

The other Somali woman nodded, confirming the first one's words. The woman who had used Ayan as a babysitter asked about her disappearance and wondered why nothing about her had appeared in the newspapers or on the Internet.

"It would be awful if she was found dead around here! Like, in a trash bin. Or if the children found her. She couldn't be under that snow pile, could she?" the woman asked, almost hysterically.

"Doubtful. But get in touch with the Espoo police if you hear or see anything out of the ordinary. The switchboard will know who to contact."

Puupponen had been watching the children's snow castle construction, while Koivu stood to the side, typing on his phone. Puupponen didn't have children of his own, and he had never expressed a desire to have a family, at least not to me. He got all sorts of ribbing about his single status around the department, including insinuations about his sexual orientation, but Puupponen took it like he did most things in life: with humor. Now he was smiling at a little girl with black curls spilling out from under her pink winter hat. The girl struggled to stay on her feet, plopping down in the snow every so often, but always stubbornly getting back up.

"Police material," Puupponen observed. "Falling on her ass over and over but not giving up."

"Maria!" Koivu called to me. "Let's go see if anyone's home at Sara's place, since it's over there, across the courtyard. I tried calling her father, but he isn't answering."

Sara Amir was the youngest of the missing girls, at just fourteen years old. Koivu told us that she had four brothers, two older and two younger. The smaller boys went to a nearby elementary school, while the younger of the bigger boys was in tenth grade trying to learn the language well enough to start vocational school.

"Sara's father is a taxi driver, and her mother is training to be a florist. They've been here since '96. The younger children were born in

Finland. The father was a teacher in Bosnia, but his education didn't transfer over here. The mother might be home."

"And the older son?" I asked, but Koivu didn't answer, instead tromping off briskly toward the next building. I followed him and soon heard Puupponen's steps behind me.

"Nice kid," he said as he opened the door for me. The lobby of this building was dirtier than the last. Someone had spray-painted "Niggers Get the Fuck Out" on the bulletin board, apparently very recently. Underneath somebody else had scratched an answer in pencil in another script I couldn't read.

The Amirs' apartment was on the second floor of the building. There were dents in the white paint of the hallway's concrete walls, as if someone had tried to move a piece of furniture that was too big to fit. On the Amirs' door was a wreath made of pink artificial roses and gold ribbon. The family was Bosnian Muslim, but many families in that particular population were religiously indifferent. Perhaps the Amirs had started celebrating Christmas in the Finnish style too, and the wreath was left over from that. Though it had been two months since the holidays, there seemed to be a Christmassy fragrance of cinnamon, cardamom, and ginger hanging in the hallway.

Koivu rang the doorbell. The sound was surprisingly loud, louder than a normal doorbell. When nothing happened, he pressed the button again. After the echo of the bell faded, we heard a strange howling coming from the apartment.

"Is there a dog in there?" Koivu said and then lifted the mail flap. The howling became clearer, but it wasn't coming from the entryway. It was coming from somewhere farther back in the apartment, and it didn't sound like something a human would make. But it wasn't like an animal noise either. Whoever or whatever was making the noise was clearly in distress.

"Open up! Police!" Koivu yelled through the mail slot, but his yell only made the howling intensify. At that moment the door to the next apartment opened, hitting Puupponen squarely in the back and crushing him between the door and the wall.

"Who's out here making all that racket?"

When Koivu saw the speaker, his face registered mild shock, and I think my own jaw probably dropped too. The woman was small and round, and her housecoat, her slippers, and the curlers under her babushka were like a costume from a black-and-white World War II movie. To top it all off, she had a rolling pin in her hand, which she brandished menacingly.

"Is someone behind the door? It's your own fault. You should be more careful," she said as Puupponen scrambled out, his nose red but, luckily, not bleeding.

"Espoo police. Good afternoon. We're trying to find the Amir family."

"Oh, so it's the police, is it? I'll need to see your badges."

We each presented our police credentials, which the woman turned this way and that to inspect. The nameplate on her door said Kämäräinen. She was standing with her feet firmly planted in the doorway, looking like she had no intention of allowing us into her apartment.

"They seem to be real, although you never can tell nowadays with all those fake doctors and all. You can never be too careful. My father was a policeman in Ruovesi, and he taught me that you shouldn't trust people too much. The ones who look the nicest are usually the biggest crooks. None of the Amirs are home except their crazy son, Samir. What do you want with them? Nothing bad has happened, has it?"

"Why is Samir making that sound?" If Kämäräinen didn't know about Sara's disappearance, I didn't intend to tell her about it. "Is he in trouble?"

"He was just born like that, or at least he's been strange since he was a child. Sometimes he's afraid of the doorbell. Do you want to speak with him? I have the Amirs' spare key. I sometimes go over to calm him down when he has these fits."

According to Finnish law, in missing person cases we were authorized to enter the missing individual's apartment without a search warrant. Weeks had passed since Sara's disappearance, so the family would have had plenty of time to hide anything that might indicate that Sara hadn't left of her own free will. And because we were being handed the keys on a silver platter, I said, "Yes, thank you." Kämäräinen closed her door while she went to retrieve the Amirs' keys.

"When did you last see Sara Amir, Ms. Kämäräinen?" I asked when she returned with the Abloy key. The keychain had an artificial rose attached, identical to the ones on the Amirs' door.

"I haven't seen her since she left on that trip more than a month ago. Strange she hasn't come back yet. You can't stay away from school like that, even with the winter break."

"What have Sara's parents said about her trip?"

"That she was seeing relatives in Bosnia and going to school there. That it's perfectly safe there nowadays. I do miss her, though. She's very helpful. She sometimes runs little errands for me and helps me take my rugs out. A nice girl, even though she does chase after the boys a lot. But then they all do at that age."

I inserted the key in the lock, but Koivu continued questioning Kämäräinen.

"How would you describe her interest in boys?"

"Giggling and flirting, wearing a lot of makeup. She curls her hair and doesn't wear a headscarf, which is probably not such a big sin in that family, unlike the other neighbors. Some of the men in those families don't dare look at me if I'm out without a scarf, and look at me: I'm just a wrinkled old woman!" Kämäräinen chuckled to herself.

When I turned the key in the lock, the howling began again. The smell of Christmas grew stronger, and when I peeked into the kitchen, I saw a spice cake on the table.

"Is anyone here?" I hollered. Puupponen followed after me. The howling had stopped. The entryway opened up into the living room, which had a door on the other side that led to the rest of the apartment. The decorations and furniture in the living room were the same as any Finnish home, where practicality and price were the most important considerations. The room was dominated by a dark-blue sofa set and a flat-screen TV. There weren't many books on the bookshelves, but there were plenty of knickknacks and artificial flower arrangements. The bouquet of roses on the coffee table looked real, but when I sniffed it, I discovered the flowers were silk.

I heard a scream behind me. I turned to see Puupponen standing in the door of the bedroom trying to fend off a young man. Puupponen was half a foot taller than his opponent, but the boy had armed himself with a bread knife and was waving it around blindly. Now and then he would let out a low roar or a screech that sounded like the cry of a bird.

Hearing the screams, Koivu charged into the apartment from the hallway, and we both rushed to Puupponen's aid. Puupponen backed into the living room, allowing Koivu to circle behind the attacker. I threw myself on the floor and grabbed the young man's legs. They were bare, and there weren't any toenails on the last two toes of his right foot. I was able to throw him off-balance by locking his ankles together, after which it was easy for Puupponen to grab his knife hand and disarm him. Koivu pulled the boy's arms behind him and pushed his head down, at which point Samir went limp, and Koivu had to work to keep him upright.

"Don't hurt him!" yelled Kämäräinen, who had come into the room behind Koivu. Puupponen was fishing for a pair of handcuffs in his briefcase, but I shook my head. The boy looked like he was calming down. He was very slender; his body looked more like a teenager's than a twentysomething's, but the black stubble on his jaw said otherwise.

When Koivu let him lift his head, I saw large brown eyes surrounded by eyelashes that would have been long enough for a mascara ad. The eyes were filled with terror.

"We don't want to hurt you," I said gently, as if speaking to a shy cat. "We're from the Espoo police, and we're looking for your sister, Sara."

Tears started to run from Samir's eyes. Koivu led him over to the sofa to sit. Kämäräinen sat down next to the boy and wrapped her arm around his shoulder.

"Don't worry, Samir. Auntie Aune won't let anything bad happen to you." Kämäräinen pulled a handkerchief out of the pocket of her housecoat and gave it to the boy, who clutched it in his fist but didn't use it. I guessed that a policewoman would probably be much less scary to Samir than two large men.

"Which room is Sara's? My colleagues could take a look at her things." I addressed my question to Aune Kämäräinen, because Samir was still sobbing.

"She slept in the little room with her mother. That door across from the kitchen. They called it the women's room."

Puupponen and Koivu didn't need any instructions; they knew what to do. After they left the room, Samir gradually began to calm down. Though Aune Kämäräinen was an outsider, she seemed to know the Amir family and Sara's business well enough, and so I let her stick around.

"You said that Sara is still in Bosnia. Have—"

I didn't have time to finish my sentence because at the word "Bosnia," Samir started shaking again and screamed, "Not back there! Not Samir!"

Kämäräinen had to press the boy down to keep him in place, and Koivu poked his head out of the women's room, ready to intervene.

"No one is taking you anywhere," Kämäräinen and I both said at the same time in an attempt to calm him down.

From what we could piece together, Samir had been born in the fall of 1989, so he had been a small child when the Bosnian War began. His father had been on the Serbs' hit list, but the family, only three people at the time, had managed to stay one step ahead by moving from one refugee camp to the next. The family's second-oldest child, Alen, was born in 1993 amid the chaos of the camps, and Sara had been less than a year old when the family escaped the Srebrenica bloodbath by the skin of their teeth. Samir had been six then and old enough to understand terror and to fear pain and death.

"Sara didn't want to go back there either," Samir suddenly said, clearly and sensibly. "But Father said she had to go, that Sara was learning the wrong ways here. She was with the wrong boys. Uncle Emir came to take Sara to her real home in Bosnia, even though Sara didn't want to go. Father will be angry that I told you. He said that I would follow Sara if I wasn't quiet."

"Why would it be better for Sara in Bosnia?"

"There the old ways are respected. No infidel boys. It's better for girls there; boys fine in Finland. My younger brothers were born in Finland. They don't remember anything about Bosnia. They want to play hockey like Finns."

Koivu had returned to the door of the women's room.

"Maria, we need your expertise in here. Will you come take a look?" Koivu walked into the living room with the deliberately gentle expression on his face that he often used with his own children. Even so, Samir retreated toward the back of the couch as Koivu approached. I stood up and went into the women's room, leaving Koivu to keep an eye on Samir. It was the same size as Ali Jussuf's family's smallest room, but the Amirs had solved the space problem with bunk beds. Next to the window was a writing desk with a hulking desktop computer that looked ten years old and a pile of books about flowers.

"There aren't any sheets on the upper bunk, so it must be Sara's. There are sheets on the bottom," Puupponen observed. "As a woman, can you tell which things are Sara's and which are her mother's? I don't understand anything about women, and Koivu's daughter is still too small to be using makeup and wearing trendy clothes, so he's no help either."

I opened the closet doors. One side was full of linens, and another section had mostly long skirts and demure, high-necked tunics that didn't look like something a normal fourteen-year-old would wear. The third section had only a few pieces of clothing, mostly the latest looks from the fast fashion chains, but also strappy tank tops, belly shirts, and miniskirts that had already gone out of style. The pink checkered leggings were a style that Iida had worn a couple of years ago before her black phase set in.

"This must be Sara's part of the closet, with the clothes she left behind in Finland."

"Yep. But if she doesn't intend to come back, why are the clothes still here? Why haven't they been thrown away?" Puupponen asked. "And what about these?" He opened the desk drawer, which was full of jewelry, and pulled out a package of contraceptive pills. "There's no name on them. Sara's mother is forty-seven, so she could still need the pill too."

"Give them here." I took the round pill dispenser. Four tablets had been taken from it. I tried to recall Sara's picture. She'd had some pimples, but not enough acne to warrant a prescription for birth control pills. I remembered the talk I had heard at the Girls Club about a boyfriend named Tommi.

"See a prescription anywhere?" I asked. When Puupponen answered in the negative, I told him to keep searching. "We'll have to ask Sara's mother about these when we get ahold of her. Sometimes the pill is prescribed for teens for reasons other than contraception, but fourteen years old is pretty young to be taking hormones."

"Better to take them than get pregnant, I guess," said Puupponen. "All of Sara's schoolbooks are here, since there probably wouldn't be any use for Finnish books in Bosnia."

"I'll look through Sara's side of the closet more carefully." All of the winter clothes and shoes were missing. On the upper shelf there was a worn-out pair of size five and a half figure skates, the cheapest brand from the department store sporting goods section. They had probably been bought used. A small cloth bag behind the skates was full of girls' underwear. There wasn't any more jewelry or makeup in her closet; that was all in the desk drawer.

On the wall above Sara's bed was a poster of a half-dressed Shakira. It spoke to the Amir family's lenient religious views. But the fact that they'd left the poster in place indicated that Sara would be coming home someday, contrary to what Samir claimed. How much could we trust the confused young man?

I thumbed through Sara's schoolbooks. There were a lot of drawings in them; apparently, Sara had been bored during lectures, because she had either touched up the pictures in the books or added her own in the margins. The drawing style was the same in all the books, so I felt safe assuming the pictures were Sara's work, even though textbooks rotated from one middle school student to another, and drawing in them was strictly forbidden. The history book had hearts in it. I noticed that at the center of almost all of them was written $S + T$. Hearts had begun to appear in her English workbook as well, just before Christmas, which I could tell because Sara had dated each homework assignment. Finally, in the math book, I found a large heart, pierced with an arrow and dripping blood, inside of which Sara had written T's name out in full next to her own: *Sara + Tommi*.

I was about to go back into the living room to ask what Samir and Aune Kämäräinen knew about Sara's friend Tommi when my phone rang. It played the theme music to *Pippi Longstocking*, Iida's ancient ringtone, which she was constantly demanding I change to something with more street cred. Because Iida never called during school unless it was important, I answered. Was she sick and needing to come home?

I could tell immediately that it was something serious.

"Hey, Mom, I just got a text from Anni. Noor, our friend from Girls Club, has been murdered. I'm not kidding. She was found in the snow somewhere in the woods in Olari. Anni texted that she'd been strangled with her own headscarf."

5

I tried in vain to calm Iida down by saying that her friend might be wrong. Puupponen had turned on his laptop, and as we spoke he logged in to the Espoo police intranet where information about new cases was posted. If a homicide had occurred in Espoo, the Violent Crime Unit led by Markku Ruuskanen would of course be the first to investigate.

"I'll be home at about four thirty. Yes, I'll find out. Don't get hysterical," I tried to say and then heard the school bell ring in the background. Iida's break had ended. Thankfully there was a strict cell phone ban at Iida's school during classes, so she wouldn't be able to stoke her fears by texting the whole time with her friend Anni. The emotional part of me wanted to rush to my daughter's side to protect and comfort her, but that wasn't possible right now. Iida had mentioned Noor a few times and said she was as beautiful as a Persian princess. She was several years older than Iida.

"There is a priority one here. The deceased is a young woman," Puupponen said from the computer. He was sitting with it on his lap on the desk chair in the women's room. "The body was found in Central Park behind the school in Olari at 10:15 a.m. The discovery was made by a retiree named Juhani Huttunen, seventy-six, who was out walking his dog." Puupponen's tone of voice grew more intense the further he got in the report. "The body was later identified as Noor Ezfahani, sixteen years old. She is the daughter of an Iranian family with Finnish asylum status. Cause of death one-three, strangulation."

"Has anyone been arrested?"

"No."

The body had been found about four hours earlier, and already there were text messages circulating about the incident. Presumably there were also rumors being spread online. Ruuskanen's team would be up to their necks in it by now.

"I'm sure this has something to do with our girls. There has to be a connection here. All of the girls are teenagers, immigrants, and Muslim, though the Amirs seem to be pretty liberal. Just think what kind of shitstorm this is going to set off!" Puupponen said, almost shouting.

"I agree that this is connected to our cell's existing cases and should fall to us. I'll get in touch with Ruuskanen and Taskinen as soon as we leave."

My desire to rush to Iida's school and take her home to comfort her was almost overwhelming. Today I wouldn't be the only parent who would have to answer questions about why things like this happened. To people who didn't know her, Noor's death would be just another story in the daily parade of horror on the news, but to the girls who went to the Girls Club, to her schoolmates, and to her neighbors it would be a gruesome part of their own lives. The mass killings in Finland over the past few years may have woken some people up to the fact that anything could happen to anyone, but who wanted to prepare for the worst? Who even knew how? All I could hope for was to never have to bury my own children, but there were no guarantees. Two of Aisha's daughters had died of hunger. People my grandmother's age had been forced to watch their children succumb to epidemics right here in our own country. You could get an insurance payout for a child, but that was only money; it couldn't make up for a lost life.

Puupponen and Koivu decided to go find Ayan's brothers, but they would drop me off at the station first, so I could ascertain the status of the inquiry into Noor's killing. I didn't have any desire to get into an argument with Ruuskanen about who would handle the investigation.

"Oh, hell no," Koivu swore when I told him about Noor Ezfahani's death. His face turned a shade paler. Koivu drove while Puupponen clicked at his computer. We'd left Aune Kämäräinen with Samir Amir to keep him company, and she had gotten the boy to calm down. I still didn't know the original reason for the howling. According to Kämäräinen, Samir didn't take antipsychotics and didn't go to therapy, but for the time being he was receiving a disability pension.

"Luckily he can live with his parents. He wouldn't make it on his own," Kämäräinen said as I was closing the door behind me. Thankfully, she hadn't started asking questions about Noor's murder, even though she'd probably overheard what Puupponen had read to me.

"A press release was issued at twelve o'clock about Noor's killing, so the family must have been notified and they must have identified the body. The armchair detectives online are already at their battle stations." Puupponen sighed. "They always know how things went down better than us. The cause of death is already out, but at least this site doesn't say that she was strangled with her own headscarf. That isn't in the press release. Where did Iida's friend hear that?"

"Anni is Iida's old skating partner and goes to the Olari Middle School. It's in the same building as the high school. All it would take to get rumors started is one of the students having seen the body."

Koivu turned into the police station parking lot, and I jumped out of the car. The building had just been completed when I first came to work for the Espoo police. It wasn't the slightest bit inviting, giving the impression that the only reason to be there was if something had gone wrong, though downstairs there was also a permit office for getting passports and driver's licenses. I walked past the people waiting in line, opened the door to the stairwell with my keycard, and climbed to the second floor. I dropped off my coat and bag in my office, then went to find Markku Ruuskanen. We had talked very briefly on the day I returned to work, and we'd agreed to cooperate with each other. Ruuskanen had said he was happy that there would be more resources for investigating violent crimes. In recent years the focus had been more on white-collar crime, and those investigations could drag on for years. Those perps were a far cry from the alcoholics Violent Crime usually dealt with, who tended to confess after the first night in the cooler, when the withdrawal symptoms hit.

The Violent Crime Unit hallway had its familiar stale-coffee smell, but there was also a new scent in the mix, a deep, musky perfume. Its source, Sergeant Ursula Honkanen, was just stepping out of the women's restroom into the hallway. I hadn't had a chance to greet her yet, and I didn't know how happy she would be about my return to the force. During the last string of cases we'd worked on together, she'd been overcome by a sudden surge of emotion and told me that she wasn't able to have children because of a hysterectomy. Later she clearly regretted the revelation, distancing herself from me yet again.

She didn't rush to give me a hug or even shake my hand. She just stared at me with a crooked smile.

"Look what we have here. Maria Kallio! Are you lost? Isn't your special unit or cell or whatever you're calling it over on the other side of the building?"

There was a time when Puupponen and I had made bets every morning on how high Ursula's heels would be that day. We hardly ever saw anything under three inches, but now Ursula had on nearly flat, trendy, knee-high boots made of a mottled black-and-purple suede. The perfume smell grew even stronger—perhaps she'd added some in the lavatory—and she had more makeup on than I used in a week. She looked familiar, unchanging, safe. I guess I'd missed her too.

"Hi, Honkanen. I hear you have a homicide in progress."

"Yep. And a teenage girl at that. Lehtovuori is putting the case wall together right now. Ruuskanen is in Turku giving a speech, but we'll do just fine getting the basic investigation together without a lead investigating officer. We have three detectives, including me and a trainee who starts next week. Apparently, her father worked here sometime in the Stone Age. The guy who shot himself."

I knew immediately who Honkanen was talking about. Halfway through my last teaching stint, a young, blond police cadet had come up to me in the police college cafeteria. There was something familiar about her, though I wasn't able to put my finger on what it was. She had brown eyes, and her straight hair, cut short in a trendy, asymmetrical style, was delicate as a baby's. She'd covered her skin with foundation, but the marks of adult acne were still visible if you looked closely enough. She was nearly eight inches taller than me and broad shouldered, and her police jumpsuit fit her perfectly.

"Hey, aren't you Maria Kallio?" she'd said.

"Yes. And you are?"

The young woman extended her hand in greeting. A showy amethyst ring glinted on the ring finger of her right hand.

"You probably don't recognize me. Jenna Ström. Pertti's daughter."

I had known that one day I would run into Pertti Ström's children. Nearly a dozen years had slipped by since his death, but I still thought of him often. Jenna had inherited her father's skin, his physique, and his facial features, but her eyes were from her mother, Marja, whom I had only met twice, once when I informed her of Pertti's death and once at the funeral.

I shook Jenna's hand, then pulled her into a hug. Jenna responded to the hug without hesitation, which felt good. When we released each other, I looked at her again. The patch on her breast said "Ström," and the familiar name brought back painful memories. Pertti and I had attended the old police academy together, lived in the same dormitory, and taken each other's measure on the firing range and the track. After school our paths diverged for about a decade, but then they met again in Espoo. Jenna had been eleven when Pertti died.

I'd then returned my lunch tray, but I wasn't in a hurry. My courses for the day were finished, and the ride a colleague had offered back to Espoo wouldn't leave until the evening. I asked Jenna if she had time for a cup of coffee, and we made our way to the most secluded table we could find.

"So, you're a police cadet," I said as we stirred our cappuccinos. Pertti Ström had steadfastly refused to drink this kind of "foreign sissy coffee."

"The latest batch. I went to military police school and then applied here. My brother, Jani, is doing his service right now and then he intends to enroll too. Mom isn't too thrilled about it, just like everything else connected to Dad."

"How is your mother doing?"

"Just fine. She lives with Kai, her current husband, and their kid Hannina, and runs a private rest home. Kai works there too, and Mom wanted me to take over the business from her someday. This job is more stimulating, though. I want to work in Violent Crime, just like Dad. Jani is more interested in highway patrol."

Jenna had also inherited her style of speech from her mother, because I didn't hear Pertti's tone in her voice. Hopefully Kai Hirvi had been a good stepfather. I could see in my mind the good-bye letters I'd found in Pertti's apartment. In the one addressed to his children, Ström had left all of his police equipment to Jani and his mother's amethyst ring to Jenna. Jenna noticed me looking at the ring.

"I imagine you recognize this?"

"I know what it is."

"Dad didn't leave much. We didn't see him very often, and Mom doesn't like to talk about him. She just says he was an unhappy person. But was he a bad policeman? You knew Dad, or at least that's the impression I get from Mom."

"We were in the same cadet class, and then we were colleagues. We competed for the same position once. I don't think I made life any easier for your father. One reason for his suicide might have been that he lost out on the position of unit commander to a woman younger than himself who, to add insult to injury, was about to go on maternity leave."

"Really? Who would promote someone starting maternity leave?"

"No one nowadays. That was during the economic boom, and times were different. And it was also a rap on the knuckles to your father. He wasn't a bad policeman by any means, but he didn't work well with others. Our idiot bosses made him my temporary replacement while I was on leave, supposedly as a consolation prize. Wasn't that considerate?" Jenna Ström seemed like a woman who didn't need the facts to be sugarcoated. She had also inherited that trait from her father.

"Mom said that Dad had a serious drinking problem and that sometimes he beat up people he was questioning. I think she hoped I wouldn't get into the police academy and have a chance to follow in his footsteps." Jenna smiled faintly and stirred her coffee, which she hadn't even tasted yet.

"I only saw your dad get violent once. The guy your father was interviewing intentionally provoked him." I remembered from the interrogation video Ari Väätäinen's triumphant expression when Pertti hit him. It was just what Väätäinen had wanted. "It is true that he drank too much. The rest of us should have intervened, especially me, since I was his immediate superior during that last period. Your father stopped me from jumping into an icy lake—I was going after a criminal who was trying to commit suicide. I was pregnant then, and my daughter, Iida, might not be here if your father hadn't acted so quickly. There wasn't only one side to Pertti, just like with all of us."

"Mom claims that Dad was in love with you."

I burst into laughter, which was so loud that everyone in the cafeteria turned to look at us. Jenna turned red and stared steadfastly at her cappuccino. I started hiccupping and had to hold my breath to make it stop. Of all the things I never thought I'd hear, that was the last.

"Sorry," I said once I'd gotten myself under control. "If that's true, your father had a very strange way of showing it. Your mother was probably just imagining things."

After we met, I kept in touch with Jenna Ström via e-mail. In her last message she had complained about not being able to find a trainee position. But apparently her luck had changed.

I'd mentioned our meeting to the Koivus only once, and over the years, even Puupponen's distaste for Pertti Ström had abated, so Jenna's arrival in the department wasn't likely to cause any feelings other than astonishment at how fast time flew.

To Ursula Honkanen, Ström was just a name. I noticed there was a ring on her left hand, but instead of congratulating her I decided to keep quiet. She had rings on so many fingers, and the one in question wasn't necessarily an engagement ring. I would hear about Ursula's romantic life before long anyway, at least if the guy on deck this time had any significant social standing.

"About the Noor Ezfahani case," I began, but I didn't get any further before Ursula interrupted.

"You aren't my boss anymore. There isn't any sort of chain of command between us, so I don't have to tell you anything."

"But you must know what our cell is investigating. Three teenage girls with immigrant backgrounds have disappeared. No bodies have been found, but there's no evidence that they aren't dead either. Don't you see that this could be part of the same case?" What on earth had gotten into me, missing Ursula Honkanen?

Ursula closed the door to the conference room behind her so I wouldn't get a glimpse of the case wall. Her smile was still crooked.

"Poor little Kallio, you have about as much authority to stick your nose in our case as a beat cop directing traffic. Meaning none. Sure, I know you're going to go cry to Taskinen about how nasty I am. He's on cloud nine now after getting you back in the building. That man has always had a perverse taste in women."

I laughed in response and set off for my office. Ruuskanen was in Turku, so there wasn't any point in negotiating about the division of labor right now. Back in my office, I started putting together a memo on what we'd discovered about Ayan's and Sara's disappearances. I wanted to ask Sara's mother about the birth control pills, but she didn't have a cell phone. We'd have to wait for her to come home. Maybe I could meet her tomorrow on her lunch break from the florist class.

I clicked open the police bulletin about Noor's death. The larger newspapers' websites had already been updated, but so far, their information about the slaying was limited. Could Ruuskanen's team know that Noor had been a regular visitor at the Girls Club? How would the club react? Heini and Nelli would probably be questioned by the police and also interviewed by the newspapers. Then, if it hadn't already, the disappearance of the other girls would make it into the press, and the media circus would begin in earnest.

I couldn't question Heini and Nelli about Noor's killing in my official capacity of police investigator, because I didn't belong to Ruuskanen's unit, but I could call them as Iida's concerned mother. I would be furious if one of my own colleagues went behind my back like that, but the temptation was too great. I looked up Heini Korhonen's number in my case file. She answered after the first ring.

"Finally the police call! Guess how fun it is to find out from a text message that one of our girls has been murdered!" Heini's voice was simultaneously furious and tearful. She was obviously outside on a street, the background noise of the cars making it difficult to hear.

"Yes, this is Detective Maria Kallio from the Espoo police. I'm not really—"

"Can I call you right back? I'm walking to the club. I'm just a couple of blocks away. It's really hard to hear next to this road."

"Sure."

Fate was giving me an opportunity not to go through with my scheme, but I didn't take it. When Heini called back, I let her jabber away unrestrained.

"I assume you know that Noor wanted to stop dressing according to the Islamic faith and start wearing Western clothes? You know what that means in some families? Noor's father couldn't stand that she came to the Girls Club, but Noor was a smart young woman and knew how to stand up for her rights. She was one of the best we've ever had here." Heini was crying as she talked. "I can't understand how something like this could happen in Finland!"

"Had Noor's father and brothers threatened her?"

"Not just her father and brothers, but all of the male members of the extended family. Her grandfather, her uncle, and her two male cousins live in Espoo. They're a very tight-knit bunch. Noor wouldn't even have gone to high school if Sylvia hadn't given those men a talking-to. They seemed to listen to Sylvia, but Noor still ended up dead. This is a nightmare! What am I going to say to the girls?"

"You can help by telling us as much as possible about Noor. The police have a professional obligation to maintain confidentiality, as you know. Nothing from our conversation will leak to the tabloids."

I promised myself I would pass on everything I learned to Ruuskanen's unit. And besides, Heini Korhonen really needed someone to talk to.

"Our purpose here at the Girls Club isn't to alienate anyone from their native culture. We encourage cultures to meet," Heini rattled off, as if by rote. "And we help the girls defend themselves. Noor asked for advice about clothing. What else could we say other than she should be able to wear whatever she wanted? Now this happened."

"Had Noor stopped wearing a headscarf?"

"Partially, at least at school and here. She still wore it when she was with her family."

"Do you know about anyone she might have been dating? Did she have a boyfriend?"

"You police are so quick to stereotype. Why couldn't she have had a girlfriend? But yes, Noor had a boyfriend, a Finnish boy. It was because of him that Noor wanted to dress like Western girls. Someone is coming now. Hey, Nelli! Have you heard? Sorry, I have to go!" Heini said, then suddenly hung up.

Every police officer knew to start looking for the perpetrator in the victim's close circle, and that honor killings were usually carried out by one of the victim's male family members, typically a brother or father. Ursula Honkanen and company would start their interviews with the close relatives. Even if they had nothing to do with her death, they would know Noor the best.

The newspapers hadn't reported Noor's time of death, so I logged in to the intranet again. It took an eternity for the page to load. There were probably a lot of other people looking at the same thing. I stared out the window as I waited.

Outside, the sun was dazzlingly bright, and the temperature was climbing above freezing for the first time in months. I realized that the roads must be slick when I saw some of the cars slowing down on the Turku Highway. A red Corolla narrowly avoided rear-ending a Škoda as it braked. It looked like spring, but I shivered from the draft coming in around the window frame.

Noor's precise time of death wasn't known, but she'd probably been lying in the forest, in the cold, for several hours, perhaps overnight. Surely the family would have been concerned if Noor hadn't come home for the night? The pattern of events seemed depressingly obvious, which put a damper on my enthusiasm about getting the investigation turned over to our cell. Noor had rebelled and consorted with an infidel, so she had been killed. That wrecked the serial killer theory, at least in Noor's case.

I called Iida around three o'clock.

"Hey, it's Mom. I'm sorry to have to tell you that the text message you got was right. Noor Ezfahani is dead."

"I know. We had computer class, and the boys looked it up online," Iida replied, her voice shaking. She was planning to meet Anni and a couple of other girls from the club right after school. They were going to take flowers and candles to the scene of Noor's murder.

"That may not be possible right now. The area is probably still roped off, and outsiders crowding around might hamper the criminal investigation."

"Mom! Don't start talking like a cop! We're not strangers. We were Noor's friends."

"An even better reason for you to not interfere with the investigation. What if you go home after school instead, and we'll go there later tonight? I can take you, and the others too if they want to come."

"I want to go with my friends."

"Then I'll come pick you up there. What time?" I didn't want to leave my thirteen-year-old to face the scene of a violent death alone. Though solving these kinds of crimes had been a part of my work for years, even I wasn't numb to it.

"Are you investigating it?"

"In a way. Do you know if Noor had a boyfriend?"

Iida sighed. The situation was strange to both of us. Iida hadn't ever really said much about my profession, other than opining that the name of our police band, the Flatfeet, was "mortifying." We agreed that I would come get her. It was only half a mile's walk from the police station to our house. I'd have plenty of time to get the car and drive to meet her by four thirty.

I knew that I was partially deceiving myself: I wanted to see where Noor's body had been found, and picking up my daughter at the site would be a halfway legal way to do so.

I was soaked by the time I got home, since the melting snow had formed huge puddles along the road, and the passing cars splashed slush on the pedestrians. It was impossible to get across the crosswalk without stepping in a pond. Taneli had gone to a friend's house, so only the cats were home. I grabbed the car keys from the entryway and started driving toward Olari. The windows of the car fogged up, and I had to turn the heat on full blast in order to see at all.

I left the car in the school parking lot. There was a path trodden in the snow to where Noor's body had been found. The area was still roped off, so the forensic investigation was still underway. The pair of patrol officers standing guard were new to me. There were a couple dozen teens standing around, most of them Noor's schoolmates judging by their ages, including some boys. Was one of them Noor's boyfriend? Candles and flowers had been placed in a little pile at the base of a pine tree as an unofficial altar. Nelli Vesterinen stood next to Iida and Anni. Besides the flowers, her dreadlocks and multicolored coat were the only splashes of color in the starkly bright early March afternoon.

I walked over and hugged both Iida and Anni. Nelli Vesterinen didn't pay me any mind, and I suddenly felt like it would be tactless to start questioning her. No one in the group was sobbing audibly, but sorrow pushed the young people together, and many huddled with their arms around each other.

When Iida finally turned to leave, she took my hand like a little girl. After we were out of earshot, she asked in a small, scared voice, "Mom, are you going to solve this? Will the police catch Noor's killer?"

"Yes, absolutely." I had never made any promise with so much of my heart.

6

"Of course, we'll take any extra help we can get. With so many people to question, you are welcome to come join the party!" The expression around Detective Markku Ruuskanen's mouth was genial, but there was irritation in his eyes. I was sitting with him and Captain Jyrki Taskinen in the command officers' conference room on the top floor of the Espoo police station. On Wednesday night I'd called Taskinen and reported my suspicion that Noor Ezfahani's murder was connected to the disappearances of the other three immigrant girls. Ruuskanen's unit was working on a few battery cases, and they were also finishing up an investigation into the death of a married couple. For weeks the police had been trying to decide who had started the game of knife tag and who had died first. So, there was plenty of work to go around, and for the time being, Noor's killing was a dead-end case without a prime suspect. The combined investigatory resources of Violent Crime and Patrol had been sorting out the girl's movements during her final night, with little success. The family said Noor had come home from school a little before three p.m., as usual, and eaten with the family around six p.m. Then, according to her father, she'd gone out for a walk and hadn't been seen since, until her body was discovered.

"We know from experience that we can't trust Muslim families, because they don't trust the police. They decide together what to say and then stick to the story because they think they have Allah's permission to lie to infidels," Ruuskanen ranted. He'd come to Espoo from the Itäkeskus precinct in Helsinki, where, according to rumors Koivu had heard, they'd wanted to get rid of him. I didn't completely believe the gossip, because I knew what kind of wild stories were floating around about my own job changes. Supposedly, the reason for my departure from the Espoo police was either a nervous breakdown or an affair with Taskinen, and my return to Espoo had apparently given new life to the latter theory. I didn't bother with them as long as Jyrki's wife and my Antti knew they weren't true.

Ruuskanen had purportedly neglected to investigate a couple crimes in which there were clearly interracial tensions between different ethnic populations, but he'd always immediately taken up cases involving native Finns assaulting immigrants. Some colleagues complained that Ruuskanen was too lax when it came to immigrant criminals. Because of this he was accused of being a "raghead ass-licker" and a communist. What he was now saying about Muslims seemed to discredit these accusations.

"So, you think the Ezfahani family members are all fundamentally unreliable witnesses?" Taskinen asked, wrinkling his brow.

"Of course not, but their family culture is so different than ours— they stick together. There are cases of Finnish-born children protecting their parents too, of course."

"The perp could just as easily be an outsider." I poured more water into my teacup. Before, I'd knocked back at least ten cups of coffee a day, but while I'd been away from the police department I had slowly transitioned to tea.

"Kallio's cell seems to have latched onto the idea of a serial killer. Get Honkanen started on profiling, since she went through that FBI training program in Washington. It doesn't take an all-expenses paid vacation to America, though, to notice that the three other girls disappeared without a trace while Noor Ezfahani's body was left in the snow near a walking path, out in the open for anyone to find. And don't say the perp was interrupted. You can get these cases to match up if you force it, but that may not be the best thing for the investigation," Ruuskanen said with a snort. He'd obviously been good-looking when he was young, with an athletic body and a head full of curls, but now his hairline had receded, forming a shiny surface that extended almost to the top of his head, and flesh hung loosely beneath both his eyes and his jaw. His sideburns were cropped close, and he obviously had to work to keep them trimmed so neatly. He wore muted-brown cotton slacks and a sport coat. The top buttons of his light-blue dress shirt were open, revealing thick, curly chest hair.

"The immediate family, Noor's parents and two brothers, have been called in here for questioning at noon. According to Honkanen, you're excited about investigating the homes of suspects. The Ezfahanis' home was a regular Arabian rug store, in case you were wondering. I'd planned to have Honkanen interview Mrs. Ezfahani, but you can too if you want. Apparently, she can't speak to strange men without her husband or some other woman present, but that's how it usually is with these people."

I didn't ask what Ruuskanen meant by "these people." As if the word "Muslim" were so politically incorrect that he didn't dare use it. The phrase "these people" tied all immigrants together in a single, vague bundle that could just as easily include a refugee from Afghanistan and a top lawyer from Moscow who had gone through a protracted selection process before coming to work in Finland. Ruuskanen's reputation as an immigrant coddler must have been someone's idea of a joke.

Taskinen cleared his throat dryly. He'd complained to me about an odd cough that didn't seem to want to go away, though he didn't have any other flu symptoms. "Do you mean, Markku, that you want Maria's cell to take over the Noor Ezfahani case?"

"No, just to collaborate. Kallio and her gang can help us figure out if there's a link between the Ezfahani affair and these three others—I can't keep their Goddamn names straight in my head!"

"Just say ASA." In our morning meeting, Puupponen had become tired of listing the girls' names in a row and had abbreviated Ayan, Sara, and Aziza to ASA.

Ruuskanen was trying to find a compromise that would give us both what we wanted. I didn't have any reason to complain. During our little tête-à-tête I'd remembered again how intensely I despised meetings, especially the kind that turned into power struggles. Swedish colleagues said that I wouldn't last two days with them because even their junior field officers spent more time in meetings than chasing bad guys or making traffic stops.

"The other men in the Ezfahani family, the grandfather and the uncle and his children, Noor's two male cousins, are coming at two. Noor and her mother are the only women in the family. Men are more likely to survive." Ruuskanen rolled his eyes to show what he thought about the issue. The whites around his pupils were bloodshot, and there seemed to be a hematoma in the right one.

"The reports from Forensics are on the intranet. The password is 'Persia.' You can tell your team. I decided to put passwords on all incomplete investigations because of the leaks you've had here before. This place bleeds information like a stuck pig. And don't start griping, Taskinen. It's perfectly legal."

In the past I'd suspected that Ursula Honkanen financed her wardrobe by selling confidential information to the tabloids. I'd never found any evidence of it, but apparently the rumors had reached Ruuskanen too. Honkanen would certainly get the password just like the others, but the number of people who knew it was limited, so there wouldn't be any room for malfeasance. Of course, "Persia" was simple enough for someone to guess it after a few failed attempts to access information about a murdered Iranian girl.

"With this case we're going to have the vultures, jackals, and hyenas at our necks in record time. I've promised to issue a statement at four. Until then I'm not taking any calls from the media." Ruuskanen's face brightened. "But hey, you could take responsibility for PR. Your serial killer theory is much more interesting than my assumption that Noor's killer is a member of the family—or the boyfriend. In any case I've reserved two interrogation rooms downstairs, and Maria, you can take the wife to your offices. She'll be less afraid up there with you. Yesterday she was as skittish as a baby rabbit. She just sat there, perched on the corner of the sofa and not saying a word."

"Does she speak Finnish, or will we need an interpreter?"

"She's had two years of language training. I imagine she's learned something in that time, unless she's a complete ignoramus."

The screen of my phone, which was set on silent, lit up. My father was trying to reach me. He was coming to stay with us for a few nights, for his fiftieth college class reunion that weekend. Dad had said he would take a bus from the train station to our house, but maybe he'd run into trouble. There was no way he'd "waste" money on a taxi. I sent him a text suggesting he call Antti as I replied to Ruuskanen.

"It's difficult to give updates about a case we don't know much about. But let's put together whatever we know by four. Agreed? Is there anything of note in the forensics report? When is the autopsy?"

"They're going to open her up tomorrow. Read the rest yourself. You and the other interrogators will meet the Ezfahanis at noon downstairs, and the three of us will meet back here at 3:45." Ruuskanen stood up, clearly in a hurry to get somewhere. He left the door open behind him, and I saw him disappear into the nearest men's room. There were still more of those than women's restrooms; at the time of the building's completion in 1996, the force had been significantly more male than it was now, a decade and a half later.

Taskinen poured more milk into his coffee. I needed to go back to work, but it seemed like he had something he wanted to talk about. I let him stir his coffee in peace. Outside it was sleeting again, and the pine trees swayed in the wind, their branches wet. The sleet melted as soon as it touched any surface. They didn't, of course, put pictures of this kind of thing in Finnish travel brochures. At least the days were growing longer, and spring would shake winter off its feet as we moved further into March. It was a spring Noor Ezfahani would never see.

"Let's do our best to solve this case," Taskinen said finally. "It's good that Ruuskanen is so cooperative. His unit has too many cases and can't seem to finish a preliminary investigation of a simple stabbing, even when the suspect has confessed. Hopefully Ms. Ezfahani's murder is a straightforward affair. Was she one of Iida's friends?"

"Just an acquaintance, from the Girls Club. They're holding a memorial for Noor there today. I promised to take Iida."

"Without any ulterior motives, right?" Taskinen smiled.

"You know me. I never have ulterior motives."

Taskinen finished his coffee in one gulp, and we stood up at the same time. I walked down the stairs to our case room. Puupponen had pinned two pictures of Noor up next to the missing girls. In one she was a smiling, dark-eyed beauty. In the other she was a lifeless corpse. Her face was dark blue and swollen. Her distended tongue hung out of her mouth, and there were frozen lumps of snow in her hair. The same violet, gold-trimmed scarf that had veiled the girl's hair in the previous picture was wrapped tightly around her neck.

Rage flooded through me. This kind of thing wasn't supposed to happen. To cut short a young life, to take another person's existence in your hands and wrench it away! The logical, experienced police officer in me knew that my job wasn't to hate, but to solve the crime. I would have to turn my anger into a whip that would drive me to find the culprit. A few months earlier I'd been forced to look on as my friend died, a victim of a roadside bomb, and I hadn't been able to do anything to bring her killers to justice. The same thing would not happen with Noor's murder.

My computer was already on. First, I logged in to the intranet, then in to the Western Uusimaa Police District page, and finally in to the folder Ruuskanen had created. The password, "Persia," worked once I thought to type all the letters in uppercase. The report on the location of the body was still in process. Some of the things found at the scene, such as a single dark-gray wool mitten and an empty beer bottle, were still being processed. The report was also not able to say definitively whether the location of the body was also the scene of the crime. It was clear that Noor had been lying there since at least early morning because snow had fallen on her, and according to weather bureau records, it had snowed in the Olari area between 5:00 a.m. and 6:30 a.m. When she was found, the temperature was 31 degrees Fahrenheit, so the snow hadn't had a chance to thaw. The temperature of Noor's body had been 86.4 degrees, but even that wasn't enough to deduce a precise time of death. The contents of her stomach, which would be revealed during the autopsy, would help answer this question.

We also needed to find out where Noor had been going when she left home. Ruuskanen had asked Patrol for help interviewing the neighbors and anyone out and about around the school, and a request for information about Noor's movements had been delivered to the print media and the radio stations and put up on the police public website. Dozens of tips had already come in, but I hadn't had time to do anything more than glance at them. It would take quite a bit of work for the department secretary to record them.

A pouch of instant tomato-basil soup would have to serve as lunch. When I was teaching for the Police University College, I'd developed the habit of always carrying an energy bar and a packet of soup with me. My foreign students were often eager to chat after class, so my breaks were frequently cut short. I continued to slurp the soup from its paper cup while taking the elevator downstairs to meet Mrs. Ezfahani. Her first name was also Noor. Did her husband just call her "Mom" too, to avoid confusion? I'd told Antti that I would divorce him immediately if he ever addressed me as "Mom," unless he was talking about me to our children.

The waiting room was full, but even so the Ezfahanis stood out from the crowd. They weren't the only immigrants by any means, but they exuded a deep sorrow; it was like they were curled up around each other, even though only the oldest man and one of the younger men were standing with their arms around each other's shoulders. Mrs. Ezfahani stood at the edge of the group, her head bowed. She wore a floor-length, dark-blue woolen coat and a white scarf covering her head. Puustjärvi and Lehtovuori were there, and Koivu scampered into the lobby just behind me. This was so there would be a separate interviewer for each member of the family, a tactic chosen by Ruuskanen. I didn't know if it would save time. The information would have to be combined afterward anyway, so we could compare notes and look for holes and contradictions. Even Noor's mother couldn't be crossed off the list of suspects. In the Afghan prison I'd met young women who'd had to flee their mothers after attempts on their lives for entertaining overly Western ideas. One of the young women had been badly burned by her mother, who had thrown hot oil over her when she declared she didn't want to marry the man—thirty years her senior—the family had chosen for her.

Still, I couldn't help but remember that the woman standing before me had lost her only daughter. Her teenage daughter.

"Mrs. Ezfahani? Detective Maria Kallio. We'll be going upstairs. Please follow me."

The woman said something to her family in a language I didn't understand a single word of. The men muttered something disapproving in reply, but no one tried to stop us from leaving. I took Mrs. Ezfahani to the elevator. She did not have a purse, but she was clutching an embroidered handkerchief in her gloved hand. Her gloves were made of caramel-colored leather, and they were worn at the knuckles. I took her into my office, because I didn't want her seeing the pictures of her dead daughter that had been hung on the case wall. I kicked the door to the conference room closed as we walked by. Ruuskanen's passwords were useless when the door to our room was open and anyone could peek in. I asked Mrs. Ezfahani if she would like coffee or tea, but she shook her head.

The beginning of the interview felt formal as I asked for her personal details. She'd been born in Iran, in Ilam Province, in April thirty-eight years before. The exact date was unknown, so she'd chosen the eighth of April as her birthday, because it sounded beautiful, and having an exact date was necessary to get a Finnish social security number. The family had ended up in Finland six years earlier, as UN quota refugees from a camp in Afghanistan. They'd been forced to flee Iran because the grandfather, Reza Ezfahani, had run into trouble with the authorities because he'd refused to pay protection money for his butcher shop. I'd read all this from the background report, and Mrs. Ezfahani confirmed what I'd heard with nods, shakes of the head, and monosyllabic responses. She had spent four years in Finland without even the most rudimentary knowledge of the language, and even after two years of study, her language skills were still very basic. In my early years at the Espoo Police Department, I'd been called on to speak Swedish to elderly Finnish Swedes and Swedish nationals who ran into trouble in our country, since our official bilingualism was highly theoretical in the police force. Now a Finnish police officer was supposed to be proficient in languages I'd never even heard of back in school in Arpikylä.

Mrs. Ezfahani had not taken off her gloves or unbuttoned her coat. It was so loose that only hints of her body's contours were visible. The uniforms of female teachers at the Afghan Police Academy had included long, dark-green skirts and scarves of the same color. Only Muna had chosen the long pants worn by the men, even though she knew how risky that choice was.

"It's hard to climb in a skirt. I'd rather be able to function, even if that means someone will disapprove of my outfit. Hopefully the next generation of policewomen won't need to think about things like this."

Loose trousers peeked out from underneath the hem of the elder Noor Ezfahani's coat. Her shoes were low topped and looked awfully thin for the slushy weather. The toes were streaked from having been soaked repeatedly.

"When did you last see your daughter, Noor?" My instincts told me to be more formal, but I knew that informal speech might be easier for her to understand, because no one used formal forms of address in the Finnish media or on shows on television.

"Tuesday. Six."

"By Tuesday do you mean Tuesday the second of March, at six in the evening?"

"Yes."

"Where was Noor then?"

"At home. Went out."

"Where? Who was she going to see?"

"Don't know."

"Doesn't your family have a practice of asking where your underage daughter is going?"

Mrs. Ezfahani didn't answer. Her nose started to redden, and she blew it noisily, afterward wrapping the cloth handkerchief into a careful bundle.

"Weren't you interested in where Noor went?"

Still no answer.

"Did Noor have a boyfriend?"

"No!"

"The police have been told otherwise."

Mrs. Ezfahani was quiet. Drops of sweat trickled from beneath her headscarf, but she still didn't open her thick coat. Was it part of Islamic culture to not speak ill of the dead? Was keeping the wrong company something that had to be kept secret?

I asked about the boyfriend again.

"The police know that Noor had a Finnish boyfriend. Didn't you know? Didn't Noor tell you?"

Now Mrs. Ezfahani was completely red. "He was not a boyfriend! He was one stupid boy who wanted to be with Noor, but Noor didn't like him! That bad boy killed my Noor, believe me, policeman!" Mrs. Ezfahani sighed deeply and clenched her handkerchief. Then she dried her brow with her other gloved hand.

"Do you or your family have any evidence that this boy is the killer? What is the boy's name?"

"Not remember." After losing her temper, Mrs. Ezfahani went back to speaking simple Finnish. I wondered if she was pretending to have poorer language skills than she really did. "Finnish names hard. Not remember."

"Did the boy come to your apartment?"

"No! Was in Noor school."

"Noor's school friend?"

Again, violent head shaking. "Bad, bad boy." Water was flowing down Mrs. Ezfahani's cheeks, partly sweat from her forehead, partly tears from the corners of her eyes. Her facial features were delicate, but she was not stunningly beautiful in the way her daughter had been. The Ezfahanis' eldest son was twenty-one, so he had been born when she was seventeen years old.

"When we bury Noor? Two days already gone."

"How do you know that Noor died on Tuesday? She was only found yesterday."

Mrs. Ezfahani flinched and fell silent, shaking her head and muttering something in her own language. I thought about whether her slip could be considered a breakthrough. We still hadn't been able to determine Noor's time of death with any precision.

I asked what they had eaten for dinner that night.

"I make rice, egg . . . what is it?"

"Eggplant?"

"Eggplant, yes, and chicken. We eat at five. Then said she going and did go."

That was useful information in terms of the autopsy that would be carried out the next day, since it could help narrow down the time of death by a few hours. Noor's last meal had been perfectly ordinary. Could a mother have fed her daughter eggplant with chicken and rice and then sent her off to die at the hands of her father, brothers, or grandfather? Not that her being a mother ruled her out—mothers could still enact violence toward a child. I remembered the sixteen-year-old Afghan girl who had killed her three-month-old infant as a sacrifice to Allah. That wasn't why she was in prison, but rather because she was psychotic and had also threatened to kill the god who had demanded such a thing. Prison was her refuge from the rage of society, though she should have been in a mental hospital.

"Noor's body is in the care of the police for the time being. It will be turned over to you when the forensic analysis has been completed."

"When? Allah wait to receive her. Not good if wait."

"Our law trumps religion at the moment. That's the way here."

"Inna lillahi wa inna ilayhi raji 'un," Mrs. Ezfahani said tearfully. That phrase I understood, since I'd heard it several times in Afghanistan. *Surely we belong to Allah, and to Him shall we return.* Did murdered Muslims get into their heaven? What if they'd been killed because they'd transgressed against their religion?

I tried to ask more about Noor's life, but Mrs. Ezfahani was growing increasingly uncommunicative. It was as if she'd said what she'd come to say, and that was all we were going to get out of her. So I took her downstairs. None of the male family members were back yet. She sat on one of the uncomfortable chairs in the waiting room and stared at her gloves.

When I opened the door to the stairwell, I almost ran into Ursula Honkanen. She sneered at me, revealing a smudge of lipstick on her front teeth.

"Ruuskanen sure is showing his sensitive side, sending you to interview the mother of a murdered teenage girl. Did you get anything out of her? It's a miracle they even let her be interviewed. Aren't the women not supposed to know or say anything?"

"It isn't exactly like that."

"Come on, Kallio, take off the blinders! Guess how many times I've been in some restaurant where these holy Muslims throw back beers just like the Finns, and no matter how big the litter of pups they have at home with the missus, they still want to get in my bed."

"Not all of them practice their religion actively, just like Christians."

"Oh, you poor liberal patsies! Miina Sillanpää and Helvi Sipilä must be rolling over in their graves. Can you imagine one of those feminists hearing about Finnish women wanting to convert to Islam and return to the oppressed state they all did their best to free us from? Why do so many women need men to boss them around? I don't understand. Do you, Kallio?"

"No. But I don't suppose religion is meant to be understood logically."

Our cell phones beeped at the same time. It was a message from Ruuskanen: *Have ordered arrest of boy harassing Noor Ezfahani. Tuomas Juhani Soivio, 19. Ezfahani men all claim Soivio killed her.*

"So, this Tuomas Soivio was infatuated with Noor and wanted to date her, but Noor wasn't interested in him." In questioning, all of the Ezfahani men had told the same story.

We were sitting in the Violent Crime Unit's big conference room. The table was packed: in addition to the violent crime detectives, we also had the forensics crew and a group of patrol officers. Liisa Rasilainen, who was in her final year of police service, was also there. Her hair was completely steel gray these days, and she'd painted her nails the same color.

"We're tracking down Soivio. We didn't find him at home, but he could still be on the way back from school. He's in his third year at Olari High School, but he's going to have to stay for a fourth. So he's a real genius." Ruuskanen was trying to be witty, but no one laughed, and Puupponen looked as if this attempt at humor had been so wretched that it was a personal insult.

"I had a conversation with Heini Korhonen, the director of the Girls Club, on the phone yesterday, and she had a different understanding of the boyfriend situation. Korhonen claims that Noor was dating a Finnish boy, and that her male relatives had threatened her over it," I interjected. This caused murmuring among those gathered, which Ruuskanen was forced to silence by knocking on the table.

"Are you claiming that all of the Ezfahanis are lying? Seven men told the exact same story," said Ruuskanen.

"I'm just reporting what Heini Korhonen said. Mrs. Noor Ezfahani also talked about a 'bad, bad boy' who had threatened her daughter. I think it would be important now to talk to Noor's friends and figure out what they know about Noor and Tuomas Soivio's relationship."

"Don't tell me how to do my work! I intend to tell the press that we have a suspect and have issued an arrest warrant."

"If Soivio really is guilty, that will only make him go on the run!" Ursula snapped. "Let's issue the warrant, but not tell the media yet."

Ruuskanen's expression was that of a man mentally counting to ten. "I'm in charge of communications, and I'll take responsibility for the consequences of my actions. If I hear even a whisper of what has been said in this meeting from a single newspaper or Internet chat room, I will personally find the leaker and hold him or her accountable. That is all. This meeting is now adjourned. Whoever wants to can come to the press conference, but keep your mouths shut!"

Part of me understood Ruuskanen. Eight witnesses who agreed was eight witnesses who agreed, and every police officer wanted homicides to be solved as quickly as possible, especially when the crime attracted a lot of media attention.

Ruuskanen had distributed Tuomas Soivio's photograph to the meeting attendees, taking it from the same Olari High School roll as Noor Ezfahani's picture. Soivio was a handsome boy with perfect skin and short, curly blond hair. His blue eyes were open and sincere, and his smile was happy. He would have been a perfect fit for one of those travel brochures about how idyllic Finland is. Tuomas lived with his parents in Tapiola, close to the Girls Club, and was on the math and science track at Olari High School. He was just a regular high school kid, with no criminal background. He wouldn't be able to evade the police for long.

I exchanged a few words with Liisa Rasilainen. Liisa had been on the patrol that had informed Noor Ezfahani's family of her death.

They hadn't found any identity papers on Noor's body, and her bag was missing, but she'd been wearing a locket around her neck that said "Noor," and there weren't many girls with that name in the metro area. Identifying her had taken only a couple of hours. Unrestrained weeping and wailing had begun in the Ezfahani household, and everyone had been so hysterical that there had been no point in trying to conduct interviews.

"It isn't often you see grown men crying like that. It could do Finns some good."

"Whatever! Who the hell wants to watch men blubbering?" Ursula had snuck up behind me and Liisa. "And you have to remember that it's a lot easier to fake extreme emotions than restrained sorrow. You just splash some onion juice in your eyes and start bawling." Ursula contorted her face like some C-list soap opera actor.

"I've been ordered to interview Noor's girlfriends," Ursula continued. "Koivu managed to squeeze a few names out of Noor's older brother. Do you gals have any tips on how to approach them? I'm sure they're tracking the case online, so it would be silly to think we can get unbiased information from them."

"Tell them that we only want to talk to the boy because he was close to Noor, not because he's guilty. Her girlfriends will know whether she really wanted Soivio's attention or not."

"Maybe she didn't know what she wanted. At sixteen you don't necessarily know who you want to be with, and any attention can be flattering," Liisa said. "Although that can go for sixty-year-olds too," she added with a grin. "I'm going to go do the rounds in the Ezfahanis' neighborhood. You going home, Maria?"

"In theory." I told my colleagues about the memorial at the Girls Club. "Maybe we could better connect with Noor's friends there than in an interview situation."

"Oh, so you're saving the cherries for yourself, and I get the shit jobs. Just like old times," Ursula snapped. "At least tell me who you talk to, so we don't do the same work twice. That would be a complete waste of resources, don't you think?" Ursula rummaged around in her bag, pulled out a bottle of perfume, and started spraying it on her neck without a second thought. Liisa and I took a step back.

But the musky scent clung to me as I left to walk home. The sleet had stopped. There were a few blue patches in the gray blanket of the sky, and they were expanding promisingly. A brook babbled down the street as energetically as if it were late spring. My cats, Jahnukainen and Venjamin, were lounging on the porch. They rushed over to butt against my legs but didn't follow me inside. I assumed that my father had arrived, because his presence made the cats shy, though Venjamin was likely to be purring in his lap before the night was out.

My dad and Taneli were slapping down cards at the kitchen table. Iida was doing her homework at one end, trying to look like the game of Egyptian Ratscrew couldn't interest her less. After we said hello, my dad told me that Antti had gone for a run but would make supper when he got back.

My dad was looking a little shorter and whiter haired than he had the last time we'd seen each other, when I'd been startled to realize that in two-inch heels I was taller than he was now. He'd been the only person in my close circle who had considered my decision to visit Afghanistan with some sense.

"Of course you have to go, if that's how you feel. Your mother will just have to take sleeping pills until you come back," he'd said to me on the phone. I'd intentionally called his cell phone before my departure, even though I usually talked more with my mother. But she'd had a sobbing, raving fit when she heard about my plans, and I wanted to avoid having to deal with that again. I'd inquired after her health from my father.

When I was young I'd been a daddy's girl, unruly and stubborn. My mother and I had fought frequently, especially about how I dressed. Mom had despised my punk getups and how I hung around with boys so much. It wasn't until I was an adult that I realized she might have been taking my attitude as a critique of her own feminine style; she wore high heels and jewelry even around the house.

Taneli shouted with satisfaction when he won the card game, and it was only then that Iida raised her eyes from the history book. She'd obviously been crying; streaks of eyeliner had run down her cheeks.

"Have you caught the . . . have you caught him?" she asked.

"Not yet, but we're working on it."

"So you're working a serious case?" my father asked, trying to be subtle. He wanted to keep Taneli in the dark, but it was no use.

"At school they said someone was murdered at the high school! I said my mom was investigating it since she's a murder police."

"Homicide detective, you idiot!" Iida said angrily.

"Taneli, let's go look at your new Lego ship," my dad interrupted, standing up. He started to half drag Taneli toward his room. Just then Antti appeared, all sweaty, and said he was going to make chicken couscous once he got out of the shower. Family routine seemed to calm Iida down, but after dinner, once we were in the car on our way to the Girls Club, I saw her wiping away tears again.

"At school people were saying that Noor's brothers didn't like Noor's boyfriend because he was from the wrong religion. Can they really kill someone because they don't believe the right way? Isn't that from the Middle Ages?"

"You've heard rumors that it was someone from Noor's family?" I felt strange questioning my own child, even informally.

"Everyone knew. Susa will probably be at the club; that's Noor's BFF. Noor told her that if she went outside without a scarf one more time, she was going to get a beating. It's just like if Dad or Taneli told me I couldn't wear jeans. It's sick!"

I turned off the Ring II Beltway toward Tapiola. I didn't say anything, because I didn't feel like getting into a conversation about cultural diversity just now. Traffic was moving slowly because of road construction. Espoo was a city that was never complete. Every time you felt like you were getting used to the landscape or had figured out the best way to get somewhere, a road disappeared or was cut off. Even the names of places changed, according to the sponsors: recently the ice rink had changed from the WestCar Arena to the Barona Arena.

We arrived to find the Girls Club full of young women. Most were dressed in black, and the Islamic girls had on white or black headscarves. They'd formed a circle, and I stayed back as Iida went to join the group. Nelli Vesterinen stood at the center of the circle. She had exchanged her colorful clothing for black harem pants and a long, black tunic with gold embroidery.

"Noor liked poetry, both ancient Persian and modern Finnish. I'm going to read you a few poems that she and I discussed. Then we can sing something, if someone has a suggestion."

I saw a few scarf-covered heads bowing, and I heard murmuring. Islamic extremists forbade music. I remembered again a couple of my Laestadian classmates from elementary school who weren't even allowed to do folk dancing, let alone go to PE class. Were that denomination's attitudes still the same, or had the Conservative Laestadians had to modernize too? When I was young I'd thought that religious fundamentalists were wackos. As I got older I'd tried to understand their worldview, but I hadn't been able to accept any belief system that subordinated one sex to the other, no matter what the religion.

I felt like an intruder at the girls' memorial service. Because Heini Korhonen wasn't anywhere to be seen, I knocked on the employee lounge door.

"Who's there?" The voice wasn't Heini's.

"Detective Maria Kallio, Espoo police."

The door opened so fast that it almost hit me in the face. Inside, Heini Korhonen sat next to the small table. The woman who had opened the door was only familiar to me from pictures. Sylvia Sandelin had on a black pantsuit with a white blouse. Her blond, shoulder-length hairstyle was that of someone who had the leisure to spend hours preening. Even Ursula would have envied Sandelin's jewelry, which adorned her neck, wrists, and ears; the overall effect was just short of ridiculous. Sandelin's makeup was straight out of whatever textbook advised women over sixty on how to present themselves without looking clownish.

"Is it normal for the police to show up unannounced in the middle of a memorial service? Is that your tactic?" Sandelin didn't shake my hand but indicated that I should enter, then closed the door behind me. There were only two chairs, and Sandelin sat down in the free one next to Heini.

"Hello, Heini," I said to the young woman, who looked like a ghost next to the polished, manicured Sandelin.

"Oh, you know each other?"

"My daughter is a regular here at the Girls Club. Iida Sarkela."

Sandelin's eyes flashed, and she looked me over again, this time more closely.

"So, you're Marjatta Sarkela's policewoman daughter-in-law? Marjatta has talked about you." Now Sandelin extended her hand, but she didn't go so far as to stand up. "Sylvia Sandelin. Just call me Sylvia, like all the girls here do—if they dare." She gave a crooked smile. "Noor Ezfahani never had the nerve. She respected her elders, as is the custom in her home culture. Native Finnish girls now, few of them even know how to politely address people. Marjatta's grand-daughter does, I've noticed. Heini, maybe you should go look and see if they need you at the service. Then Detective Kallio will be able to sit down too."

Heini Korhonen stood up obediently, and I slipped into her seat. I smiled to myself. I should have guessed that all the wealthy old women in Tapiola would know each other. My mother-in-law wasn't much older than Sylvia Sandelin, and I could imagine them sitting together at a play at the cultural center or at a Tapiola Sinfonietta concert. I found it amusing that I was able to get into Sandelin's good graces because Iida knew her yes ma'ams. My Finnish teacher at the police academy had pounded into my head that you had to speak to people with respect, and maybe that had rubbed off on Iida too.

"You obviously came here because of Noor Ezfahani. Would you like some tea? Heini just put water in the kettle. The white tea will take a little while to brew. I can't stand teabags."

"Then I don't recommend visiting the Espoo Police Department. Although the coffee is tolerable. A cup of tea would be lovely."

Sandelin stood up, took a teapot made of thick blue porcelain out of the cupboard, and carefully measured a few tea flowers into the bottom of it before pouring water from the electric pot. On the table she placed teacups that matched the pot and a glass jar of honey, as well as a pair of silver spoons. The last time I was here, I'd been offered a tea bag. Apparently, Heini Korhonen wasn't as much of a tea enthusiast as her boss.

"You're right. I came because of Noor Ezfahani. The police have been given conflicting information about her social life. What's your understanding here at the Girls Club?"

Sandelin stroked the handle of her silver spoon. "I'm not terribly up-to-date on all of the girls' business. I know your daughter by name, and I've talked with her because she's my friend's granddaughter. Some of the girls are only faces to me, even though of course I want to help and support all of them. But Noor Ezfahani was an exceptionally intelligent young woman. She knew how to question everything, not only the religion of her home but also the Western culture of mammon. She wanted to be a doctor, just like her Finnish boyfriend. I also know Tuomas Soivio's parents and grandparents. The family was a little disappointed when Tuomas didn't go to Tapiola High School, where both of his parents went, but at Olari he could specialize in natural science, and that's a good foundation for getting into medical school. The family was a little concerned about Tuomas last spring because he was starting to run with the wrong crowd, but thankfully he met Noor then and changed his mind."

"Changed his mind about what?"

"Immigrants. Just think, an intelligent boy like that getting mixed up with those anti-immigrant ruffians. The racists, I mean." Sandelin wrinkled her nose at the word. She poured our tea. The flowers had opened and fell decoratively into our cups. Sandelin added a large spoonful of honey to her cup before continuing.

"I sometimes wonder whether there's any sense even trying to educate some of these boys. They barely know how to read and only seem to express themselves through verbal vomit on the Internet. Do you visit these forums often, Detective?"

"No. But some do say they advance free speech."

"Free speech is a wonderful thing. Everyone defends it. But I don't support stupid, hateful people's right to spew their mental excrement in a public forum. There isn't any benefit in that. Intelligent conversation is utterly impossible on sites that are open to everyone. I'm not ashamed to say out loud that I am more intelligent than ninety-five percent of people. It doesn't have anything to do with my race or my sex—it's just because I am who I am. I've earned my wealth with my wits, and now I have an obligation to help others. Unfortunately, the politicians decide what my taxes are used for. I'm more intelligent than ninety-five percent of them too."

Sylvia Sandelin stopped to sip her tea. I couldn't resist a comment on her logic.

"So, you think there are twenty intelligent members of Parliament? And two wise ministers in the government?"

Sandelin smiled like a teacher at a clever student.

"You seem like a police officer who knows how to read, write, and even count. No, not all politicians are stupid and self-serving, although it's easy to think of many of them that way. Some of them are utterly hopeless, but luckily the least clever of them don't usually get enough power to do real damage. There are more than two wise people in the government, I have to admit. Poking fun at politicians is a base pastime, and maybe it's best that our stupidest citizens don't bother to vote. The results would be ghastly if they did, as we have seen."

I could hear singing through the door. There wasn't much chance Noor Ezfahani had gone to Lutheran confirmation class, but the song being sung in her memory came from the Christian youth hymnal I too had used long ago. It was Kari Rydman's "So Beautiful the Earth." I understood the choice, because even though Christians had claimed the song as their own, its message wasn't specific to any one religion. I thought I could pick Iida's voice out of the chorus. She had a surprisingly clear soprano, also inherited from her father's mother. Sylvia Sandelin stopped to listen, and we were silent until the end of the song. The girls' voices broke in the last stanza at the words "departed now friend most beloved," and I saw how Sandelin's necklace shook as she tried to hold back her tears. After the song ended, Sandelin said that she had to go talk to the girls. I hung back, standing in the doorway. Iida's world and my work were now crashing together, and this time the mother won out over the police officer. Several times I'd felt like a sort of cleaning woman who'd come to the scene of an accident after the fact, scrubbing away the bloodstains, collecting all the broken pieces of pottery, and trying to leave the area looking like nothing had ever happened. I also made sure that the person who had made such a mess wouldn't be able to do it again. But I didn't believe that my work could stop scars from forming or remove the burden of the memories they would carry with them for the rest of their lives. Would Iida ever forget Noor's murder?

I heard Sandelin's low, peaceful voice, but I couldn't make out the words. I turned back into the room, took a seat, and sipped my tea. Just then Heini Korhonen returned, flopped down in the other chair, and put her hands in front of her face. After a moment she uncovered her face, and I could see anger boiling in her eyes. She raised her cup of already-cooled tea to her lips and gulped it down as if she hadn't had anything to drink in hours.

"Ayan's disappearance was already horrible enough, but at least there's still hope that she's alive. We can't do anything for Noor. Many of our girls have experienced terrible losses, but they thought they were safe here in Finland. But they aren't, not as long as there are people in Rome who haven't learned to do as the Romans."

"What do you mean?"

"Noor's male relatives. The cousin, Rahim, is the worst. He runs with one of the extremist gangs. They are always starting fights. He's been in jail a few times after fighting with skinheads and Russians, but the police must know that already."

I hadn't heard about this, though the Ezfahanis' criminal records must have been examined. Perhaps the person who had gone through them hadn't thought it worth mentioning or that gang fights were relevant to the murder of a young woman.

"According to the Ezfahani family, Tuomas Soivio wasn't Noor's boyfriend at all; he was just obsessed with her, and Noor didn't want his attention. The family suspects that Soivio killed Noor out of jealousy, because he couldn't have her."

Heini was struck with a sudden coughing fit so powerful that I worried she would choke. Tears came to her eyes, and in the end, she stood up and rushed out the door, presumably to the restroom. I heard the sound of retching, then Heini blew her nose, and finally she flushed the toilet before returning. She sat down and then seemed to be searching for words. The rage in her eyes had intensified.

"Are the police complete idiots? Tuomas didn't kill Noor. They were dating, and they were happy. Are you afraid of being accused of racism, so you aren't looking at her family? That's where you'll find the murderer," Heini said, fuming.

"Everyone knew," was what Iida had said about Noor's boyfriend.

"I understand that Noor's best friend's name is Susa. Is she here now?"

"I don't know if she was Noor's best friend, but they were close. Susanne Jansson. We haven't seen her. Should I call her?"

"Could you give me her contact information? An officer can go and interview her. First, tell me everything you know about Noor and Tuomas Soivio's relationship."

Males were only allowed to come inside the Girls Club to give lectures or provide professional services, but Heini had seen Tuomas dropping Noor off and picking her up several times.

"Noor didn't want to lie to her family. I'd guess that sometimes she said she was going to Tapiola, which was true, but that instead of coming to the Girls Club she went to see Tuomas or stopped at the club for a few minutes and then left with him. This isn't some sort of nunnery meant to turn girls away from boys; it's meant to simply give the girls a place to take a break from boys and the constraints of home. Noor didn't hide the fact that she was going out with Tuomas. I run a discussion group in which we talk about dating and sex, and Noor, who wanted to be a doctor, was very curious about anatomy. She had never seen any of her adult female family members naked, much less the men. Once she brought in a cross-sectional picture of a penis from a Finnish biology book, and she wanted to know what it would really look and feel like."

Noor obviously hadn't visited any Internet porn sites or watched late-night movies. It would be a shame if young girls' knowledge of male anatomy only came from those sources, but they at least provided the opportunity to get information, however inaccurate or unsavory. Iida had yet to bring up our going into the sauna together as a family, but Antti was already careful not to say anything about her body or look at her too closely.

Heini looked up Susanne Jansson's phone number for me. Maybe Ursula had already gotten it. Sylvia Sandelin's voice had been replaced by the buzz of conversation. I didn't know how long Iida wanted to stay at the Girls Club, and I was just thinking I should go and find out when I heard a cry of shock, then others. I stood up and ran into the main room.

I recognized him immediately, because I'd seen his picture that morning. The boy in the picture had been smiling broadly, but this young man looked haggard. His pants and jacket were covered in mud, as if he'd been riding a bicycle through puddles without any concern for getting wet.

"Where is Heini? Is she here?"

"Tuomas, you know the rules," Sylvia Sandelin said, talking over the boy.

"Fuck the rules! Noor is dead, and I have to talk to Heini!"

Heini shoved me aside and ran to Tuomas. She embraced him. She was four inches shorter, but she still pulled his head against her shoulder like a big sister trying to protect a little brother. She whispered something in Tuomas's ear and led him toward the door so we wouldn't hear what she was saying.

Heini knew the police were after Tuomas. I had to act. I took out my phone and called Dispatch.

"Detective Kallio here; ten-twenty Otsolahti Street, one-six Charlie. On the ground-floor door it says 'Girls Club.' I'm on scene, but I need backup."

I waited for the operator to figure out the location of the nearest patrol car, keeping a close eye on Tuomas and Heini. They had stopped, and now Tuomas was whispering something to Heini. I tried to work my way between them and the door.

"Six-three-seven was getting coffee at the Teboil station a couple of blocks away. They'll be there momentarily."

"Good. Out."

Because the phone had prevented me from hearing with one ear, and the noise of the girls had interfered with the other, I hadn't been able to hear Heini and Tuomas's conversation. I stepped closer to them and touched Tuomas on the shoulder.

"Tuomas Soivio? Detective Maria Kallio, Espoo police. We've been trying to reach you. We need to talk."

Tuomas broke away from Heini. The shoulder of her shirt was wet with his tears.

"A patrol car will be here soon. We're going to take you to the police station to be interviewed."

"Are you seriously going to arrest Tuomas, you moron? He hasn't done anything!" For a second, I thought Heini was going to attack me.

"He's not being arrested, but I would recommend that he cooperate with the police." I heard the van pull up outside, and the Black Maria's front doors rattled familiarly as they were pushed open. The doorbell rang, and when I opened the door, a familiar officer marched into the room. Five years before I'd been with Officer Himanen for one of the most harrying arrests of my life. The other policeman's shirt said "Sutinen," and he looked like he was fresh out of the academy.

"This is Tuomas Soivio, the one Violent Crime has been looking for. They want to question him about Noor Ezfahani's murder." I tried to keep my voice down, though I knew the girls could still hear every word I said. "Take him to the station and put him in a waiting room. I'll see if someone from the investigation team is still there and can interview him, or I'll come down myself. Don't worry, Tuomas. We're just asking for your help."

The boy looked at me like he didn't understand a word I said. Then he shrugged. Neither Himanen nor Sutinen had to use any force; Tuomas followed them out like a trained dog.

My next task was even more difficult than handing Tuomas Soivio over to the police patrol. I looked around for a familiar face. Iida didn't need me to say anything. She knew that it was time to leave. And I knew that it would be a long time before she forgave me for what had happened.

8

"Where are you going now?" my father asked as I dropped Iida off at the door. He was just stepping out to empty the trash. I was letting him play housemaid. Maybe, as a retiree, he felt that it was his responsibility, given how long my workday was dragging on.

Since Iida had already seen how Noor's murder investigation was going, I'd called Ruuskanen as we were driving away from the Girls Club and asked where the officers in his unit were. Koivu and Puupponen had both checked in around seven p.m., saying they were leaving the station after having finished interviewing the Ezfahani cousins, the uncle, and the grandfather. Their reports would already be online. Ursula had gotten in touch with Susanne Jansson's parents and, after questioning them, had also contacted the doctor who had given the order to keep people from disturbing Susanne for the time being.

"The family is protecting their little princess now that she's seen what life is really like. It sounds like they've poured about half a drugstore into her. She wouldn't be any use, even if we could talk to her," Ursula said over the phone. "I did get out of them that Tuomas and Noor had been at their house with Susanne sometimes, and that they were clearly a couple. Or however it was the old lady said it, *så gulliga,* so cute. They're *bättre folk,* the Janssons, Swede Finns. The husband is some sort of bigwig at Aktia Bank and looks good enough to eat."

Luckily Iida was listening to music, not Ursula. Because the rest of Ruuskanen's unit was busy, I called Puupponen and asked him to meet me at the station. He was at the gym and promised to be there in half an hour. Koivu's children could have a night with their dad. Puupponen could have managed Soivio just as well without me, but I wanted to be there. I was the one who found him—even if it was just by luck and at poor Iida's expense.

The only person in the lobby at the station was the duty officer, but he knew what was going on and told me that Soivio had been taken to an interrogation room downstairs. Koskinen, the guard on duty in Holding, was keeping an eye on him. The boy had been calm when he was brought in, and a text message to Koskinen confirmed that he still was. There was no rush.

Outside it was already dark. Silence enveloped the station. The ticking of the clock was the only sound. The department's mascot, a giant yellow stuffed octopus wearing a police cap, looked tired. I felt like tying its arms together. Liisa Rasilainen appeared, coming from the coffee machine with a fresh cup in hand.

"Maria, you're still here?"

"We found Tuomas Soivio. What are you up to?"

"I came in to write up a report on what the Ezfahanis' neighbors told us. I only have a desktop computer. Anyway, it's better for my back than a laptop. Old dogs and all that."

"What did you learn from the neighbors?"

Liisa took out her notepad. "They confirmed what we already knew: the Ezfahani family was very tight-knit. The grandfather, his second son, and his two grandsons lived a couple of buildings away from Noor's family, but all nine of them ate together every day and night, meaning Mrs. Noor Ezfahani is the extended family's full-time cook. Some of the neighbors were irritated by the family constantly running up and down the stairs. The Ezfahani men are supposedly an upstanding lot, not coming home drunk like the Kurds in the next stairwell over, who 'drink like Christians,' as a Somali neighbor put it. Loud voices come from the apartment now and then, and sometimes the mother looks like she's been crying. Noor leaves home with a headscarf on but takes it off on the bus if none of the family is around. Sorry, I have to go get more sugar. The coffee is even worse than usual today!" Liisa made a face and went back to the coffee machine.

In my office I logged in to the department's intranet, typed in "PERSIA," and looked up the reports on the Ezfahani family interviews. The seven Ezfahani men's version of Tuesday evening's events was identical to the one Noor's mother had given me. They'd all said that the nine family members had gathered at five to eat chicken, eggplant, and rice. Grandfather Reza Ezfahani and his second son, Farid, and grandsons, Jalil and Rahim, usually ate with Noor's family because they lived nearby and because they thought it was good for a family to have their meals together. They also covered part of the cost of the food. The grandfather was already retired, one of Noor's brothers was in trade school studying to be an electrician, and the other was currently unemployed. The cousins didn't have work either, but the men in the middle generation were driving freight trucks, mostly transporting groceries and produce from the harbors to distribution centers.

All of the Ezfahani men had the same impression of Tuomas Soivio—although no one could remember the boy's name, because "Finnish names are so hard." Mrs. Noor Ezfahani had used the exact same words. Every member of the family had been interviewed separately, but there seemed to be no cracks in their story. Either they believed they were telling the whole truth, and Noor had been spinning her family a yarn about Tuomas, or they had figured out in advance what they would say. The family had come from an environment in which even the slightest slip of the tongue could mean death. That taught you to choose your words wisely. I intended to recommend to

Ruuskanen that we reinterview the whole family together, with almost the same number of police officers there, five at the least. If the family had agreed on a common lie, they would probably start needlessly embellishing it, and one of them would eventually talk them all into a corner.

Could Tuomas Soivio have gotten so angry about Noor denying their relationship to her family that he killed her? Or had Noor been forced to end the relationship because she had to choose between her family and this Finnish boy?

"Howdy." Puupponen bounced into my office. "It's good you called. You saved me from ending up in the gutter. I had promised to go with Liskomäki for a beer after my workout, and knowing him, it would have gotten out of hand. Although I did my last set of leg presses a little faster than normal to make it here sooner, and now my legs feel like spaghetti." Puupponen put his recovery drink bottle to his lips and drank in big gulps that made his Adam's apple bounce up and down like a fishing bobber in the water.

"We have contradictory reports on Tuomas Soivio's relationship with Noor Ezfahani. Numerous witnesses, including my daughter, Iida, believe that Noor and Tuomas were dating. Supposedly everyone knew. Everyone except those in the Ezfahani family."

"I interviewed both the grandfather and Noor's oldest brother, Hamid. We needed a Persian interpreter with the grandfather, since he knows only a few words of Finnish. With Hamid we spoke pidgin. He mixed in English because his Finnish is so bad. But it still felt like the two men were saying the same things, almost word for word. The only difference was that, according to Hamid, they also had roasted nuts with the eggplant, which his grandfather didn't mention. Is learning Persian very difficult? It's starting to look like it would be useful to know a bit. For this interview with the boy, are we going to play some roles, or are we just going to be us?"

"Scare Soivio with a bad joke at the beginning."

"Scare? Telling jokes is more of a trust-building tactic. But I'm guessing Tuomas won't be in a joking mood. Does he understand that even the word of eight people won't have much weight if we don't have any concrete evidence?"

"Let's go see what he understands."

There were two windowless, bleak interrogation rooms in the basement holding cell area. I had asked them to take Tuomas to one of these rooms, because the Holding guard would be able to keep an eye on him. As usual, the patrolmen had taken his cell phone, belt, and anything else that could be used as a weapon, though Soivio didn't seem like he was a danger to himself any more than he was to someone else. He wasn't locked up. According to Koskinen, he'd asked for something to drink and been given orange juice. He'd also gone to the restroom under Koskinen's watch and only spent a moment in there.

"He seems to have his wits about him. Patrol gave him a breathalyzer, and it came up negative. He doesn't seem to be on anything. However, he is as dirty as a dog that's been rolling in the mud."

Puupponen and I entered the interrogation room. The overhead light was switched off, and only the glimmer of the table lamp revealed the room to us. Tuomas Soivio had tried to make himself comfortable: he was sitting in the only armchair in the room and had reclined it as far as possible. His feet were up on the table and his eyes were shut. He'd taken off his muddy shoes and wrapped his coat around himself like a blanket. He looked like he was asleep. A few drops of drool had dribbled from the corner of his mouth.

"Tuomas? Tuomas Soivio?"

The boy awoke with a start, and when he opened his eyes, it was obvious he didn't know where he was for a moment. I turned on the overhead light, and the brightness made Soivio's eyelids flutter.

"I'm Detective Kallio. We met earlier in the evening at the Girls Club. This is Detective Puupponen. We wouldn't have had to bring you in to the police station if you had answered our calls."

"So, am I under arrest?"

"No. Why didn't you respond to any of our messages?"

Tuomas lowered his feet to the floor and pressed the chair's reclining button, making the back bounce upright. Puupponen sat down on the other side of the table. I rolled the third chair over to the end of the table between the two men. Soivio rubbed his face and shook himself.

"I didn't get any messages."

"Not the voice mails, the messages we left with your parents, the texts, the e-mails?"

"I haven't been home since yesterday, and my cell phone died. Sorry. I didn't know anyone was trying to reach me." I could almost believe him.

"How close is your friendship with Heini Korhonen?"

This question surprised Tuomas. He swallowed a couple of times before he answered.

"We aren't close at all. I barely know her. But she was Noor's friend, and I wanted to be with someone who . . . I thought Heini would understand."

"So, you know that Noor Ezfahani is dead?" Puupponen asked to make sure.

"That's what it says online. It must be true, since Noor isn't answering her phone."

"How have you been able to try to contact her, when your own phone doesn't work?" Puupponen latched onto the boy's words instantly, but Tuomas wasn't thrown off-balance.

"There are other cell phones in the world, and I know Noor's number by heart. Where is she now? Can I see her? It doesn't say anywhere how she was killed. Did she suffer?"

Again, Soivio almost sounded believable, and his expression would have convinced anyone. But there had been rumors about the scarf online, so his question didn't hold water. Or maybe he was the rare teenager who didn't believe everything people said online.

"When did you last see Noor?"

"Tuesday . . . at school, during lunch. I didn't have any classes after that, so I went home. We agreed to meet at eight at my house. She was supposed to come straight from the Girls Club. She was going to drop by there so she wouldn't be lying to her family. Noor hated not telling the truth. But she never came and didn't answer any of my texts. I thought maybe those lunatics weren't letting her out again. I felt like going to find out, but I didn't. I should have. Maybe I could have saved her . . ."

"What lunatics?"

"Those dicks in her family! They're always lurking somewhere. The cousin, Rahim, is the worst. He thinks Noor should quit school and forget all her dreams of becoming a doctor and instead marry him and start pushing out babies for Finland to support."

I remembered what Sylvia Sandelin had said, that Tuomas used to run with an anti-immigrant gang but had changed his mind after falling in love with Noor. Maybe his change of heart only applied to female immigrants.

"Tell us again what you thought when Noor didn't show up as you'd arranged," Puupponen said.

"That they hadn't let her leave home again."

"Did that happen often?"

"Now and then. Sometimes Noor got away. They didn't dare beat her anymore, because Heini and Nelli had said that Noor could notify the police and that the Girls Club would arrange for a lawyer. Noor knew her rights, but she didn't feel like constantly fighting with those dicks, especially because it hurt her mom so much."

Now Tuomas was more alert and animated, and as he moved, dried mud flaked off his clothes onto the chair and floor.

"Were you home all night Tuesday?"

"Yes. Which was a mistake. I should have gone to get Noor, to keep her safe, by force if necessary."

"Can anyone confirm that you didn't leave your parents' home on that evening?"

Soivio sneered at Puupponen's question. "Oh, so you want my alibi! Don't parents count? I was chatting online with a couple of friends, because I was pissed. I'm sure you can still find the discussion threads. Dad's brother came by at nine thirty and brought me tickets to the Blues' next hockey game—he stuck his head in my room too. Or won't you believe him either, since he's a relative?"

"Name and contact information?" Puupponen asked, and Tuomas said the name, but that his uncle's number was in his phone, which was still dead.

"How would you describe your relationship with Noor Ezfahani?"

Tuomas must have assumed that the police knew about their relationship, but I wanted to hear him define it in his own words.

"We were dating. You wouldn't have dragged me here unless you knew I was Noor's boyfriend. We'd been going out since last September. There was a dance at school, and that's where it started."

"What did you do together?"

Tuomas blushed a little, even though I hadn't asked whether they'd had a sexual relationship. That would have bearing on the case, because Noor obviously came from a family where it was a given that a bride would be a virgin. Tuomas described a typical high school romance: they hung out in coffee shops, at friends' houses, or at his house; they watched movies and played video games.

"Noor went to the Girls Club a lot. Were you jealous that she enjoyed spending time somewhere you weren't allowed?" Puupponen asked.

Tuomas shook his head. "I have my own stuff. I play floor hockey and lift weights. The Girls Club is a really good thing for immigrant chicks. They learn that they don't have to follow the Stone Age rules their imams and stuff try to force on them. And a lot of the time Noor just stopped by there and then came to my place. Her dad and grandpa freaked out when Sylvia Sandelin lectured them about not wanting Noor to go to high school. No one really knows what Sylvia said to them, but after that they didn't dare stop Noor from going her own way. They tried, of course, when we started dating."

"Noor's family members all claim that you weren't dating, and that you were harassing Noor, that she didn't want your attention."

The main thing I saw in Tuomas's expression was astonishment, but after a moment I thought I could see something else, perhaps a mixture of satisfaction and grief.

"That's bullshit! Ask anyone in our school: the teachers, our friends, my parents . . . At least a hundred people can tell you we were dating. Maybe they don't count me as a real boyfriend because I'm an infidel, but who cares? One of them killed Noor because she was with me, but we weren't doing anything wrong! All I did was love her."

Up to this point Tuomas had been oddly calm, but now his voice started to shake, and he tried without success to slurp more liquid out of the empty orange juice box. Puupponen asked if he wanted more to drink and went to get something when Tuomas said yes. I stayed behind. Tuomas was doing everything he could to hold back his tears. When Puupponen returned, this time with a can of Jaffa orange soda, Tuomas opened it in such a way that liquid sprayed across the table and onto his pants, rewetting the dried mud, more of which dribbled onto the floor. Puupponen had to go back out to get some toilet paper, which he and Tuomas used to clean up the mess.

"S . . . sorry . . . ," Tuomas stuttered. "I didn't realize how tired I was. I haven't been able to sleep."

"Where did you spend last night?"

"Does it matter?"

"Yes."

"I was there."

"Do you mean where Noor's body was found?" A patrol had been on duty in the area all night because the forensic investigation was ongoing. It would be strange if they hadn't noticed a teenager sneaking around.

"No, that was in Olari near the school! I was in Kuitinmäki, near all the ragheads' . . . I mean immigrants' apartments. I sat in a swing and waited for a light to turn on in Noor's window. But the curtains were in the way and it was dark anyway."

"You talk about ragheads, but you were dating a Muslim girl. So are you anti-immigrant or not?" Puupponen had leaned closer to Tuomas, and the light shining on his hair painted it carrot-red.

"That's just talk, you know, ragheads, towel-heads, sand niggers and all that. They talk about us the same way. Rahim called me an infidel dog. I don't have anything against dogs or immigrants. Let whoever wants to come to Finland in, so long as they support themselves and don't try to make us believe like them. And not all the Ezfahanis are total bums—some of them work. Or so I thought before they killed Noor. Do you know which one of them did it?"

"We haven't caught Noor's murderer yet. Did members of her family directly threaten her life?"

Tuomas didn't answer immediately, first drinking more soda and looking over Puupponen's head at the wall, which was blank. Over the years I'd seen people I was questioning project all sorts of internal films on empty white walls. One of the interrogation rooms used to have calming seascape pictures, but in the confusion of some remodel they'd been discarded. The police station was a stark sort of place, not meant to be hospitable. Finally, Tuomas sighed, his eyes tearing up.

"Noor knew she could tell the police about the threats. Her family didn't like that she was with me. But she was a minor, and they tried to forbid her. Rahim and the grandfather were infuriated that Noor knew her rights. And she said she would rather die than let herself be ordered around when she wasn't doing anything wrong. She . . ." Tuomas paused. He closed his eyes as if that would make the tears stop flowing.

"Why haven't you made them confess?" he muttered, trying to catch the tears with his tongue and then wiping them away with his sleeve, leaving a smear of mud on his face.

"What do you mean by 'them'?" Puupponen asked.

"Come on! Noor's family and her relatives, of course. Haven't I been telling you the whole time that one of them did it!"

My phone pinged with a text message alert, followed by another. I looked at the screen. It was Liisa Rasilainen, saying she had just been called by one of Noor's neighbors, who hadn't been home when Liisa canvassed the neighborhood but had heard from her husband that the police wanted information about the girl. The neighbor had come home on Tuesday evening at 6:15 and passed Noor in the stairwell. She'd been crying and was barely able to say hello.

I went out into the hallway for a moment and called Liisa, even though she was only a few floors away. The neighbor, Irina Domnina, had called after getting home from Jorvi Hospital, where she worked as a physician's assistant. She hadn't seen her husband, who also worked a night shift, since Noor's death. When Igor Domnin told her that the police were interviewing Noor's neighbors, Irina Domnina called us immediately. According to her, Noor had always been friendly and usually stopped to chat when Domnina was out walking the family's smooth-haired Dachshund, who Noor liked a lot. This time she not only had been in a rush but was also crying. Irina Domnina had been worried but ascribed it to teenage disappointment that would quickly pass.

"Now Domnina is blaming herself. If only she'd taken the time to talk to Noor, things might have gone differently. Noor would have stopped to chat and maybe been prevented from meeting her murderer. I'm going to see Domnina tomorrow, because I'll be better able to judge her reliability face-to-face. But she doesn't seem like the kind of person to go looking for attention by claiming to have been the last one to see a victim before her death."

"At least that confirms what the Ezfahanis said about the time Noor left home."

"Yeah. I would think there would have been more eyewitnesses at that time of day, though. Given how many people live in and travel through that area, we haven't had very many sightings. We could always issue a request for assistance through the media."

"That's Ruuskanen's wheelhouse," I responded. I didn't bother to ask if she'd told the lead investigator what she'd just told me. I wasn't Rasilainen's boss.

When I'd started working for the police, we hadn't needed to consider the possibility that a witness might come forward out of greed or because they were seeking publicity. Career criminals built their reputations behind bars by recounting their deeds on the pages of *Alibi* magazine and other venerable publications, but a homicide had to be really extraordinary for the general media to interview witnesses and their mother's brother's dog's former owners. Miles of column space hadn't solved Kyllikki Saari's murder, the Tulilahti double slaying, or the Lake Bodom tragedy, and maybe that had put a damper on crime reporting. There'd been some cases of spotlight seeking in the eighties, but they were few and far between. Back then some witnesses were downright afraid of having their names mentioned in the media. Now we constantly had to be on the lookout for the attention starved. The worst part was that some of them didn't even care about living the rest of their lives with reputations as liars and frauds, and they had no compassion for the lives touched by a homicide. Once I'd tried to count how many people one death could touch, but I gave up in horror once I reached triple digits. In a way it was comforting, though: everyone left a mark on the world. Maybe the kids I'd seen lighting candles for Noor in the forest and singing together at the Girls Club would channel their sorrow into something that could help them heal their wounds.

Tuomas had calmed down while I'd been away. Puupponen had turned the conversation to the hockey game between the Espoo Blues and the Oulu Ermines, which the boy planned to attend the next day. Puupponen's team was actually KalPa from Kuopio, but apparently he also knew the Blues lineup better than the average fan. Soivio seemed to be responding mostly out of politeness—the game wasn't the most important thing on his mind at the moment.

"Let's go back to Tuesday night," I said, interrupting Puupponen as he speculated about whether the Blues would win their home match by a one- or two-goal margin. "Noor was coming to meet you in Tapiola. What mode of transportation would she have been most likely to use?"

"Airplane. Give me a break. The only way out of there is the bus. Nineteen, thirteen, or one ninety-five. Whichever one happens to come by the stop first."

"Did she always use the stop closest to her apartment?"

"How am I supposed to know? Probably."

Central Park wasn't even close to the route between her home and the Girls Club. Because there was so little information about her movements after leaving home, it seemed likely that she'd caught a bus soon after leaving her family's apartment. None of the Ezfahanis had their own car, but Noor's father and uncle did have access to trucks. We would have to verify with the trucking company about the garage where the vehicles were stored when they weren't being driven . . . I stopped that line of thinking; I wasn't going to start doing Ruuskanen's job. Of course, I would mention it to him when we met the next morning.

I opened my briefcase and took out three pictures. First, I showed Tuomas the pictures of Ayan Ali Jussuf.

"Do you know her?"

"Why should I?" Tuomas had barely glanced at the picture.

"Do you know her?"

"No. Who is she?"

"Ayan Ali Jussuf. She went to the Girls Club too." Then it was Sara Amir's turn. "What about her?" Tuomas looked at this one more carefully but denied ever having seen her.

When I took out Aziza Abdi Hasan's picture, Tuomas reacted in a completely different way than when I'd showed him the other photographs. His expression looked confused, but then he said that he had never seen Aziza. He demanded to know why he was being shown the girls' pictures, but I didn't tell him. I thought it was strange that Tuomas hadn't known Ayan. According to Heini, Noor had been aware of Ayan's disappearance, though the girls hadn't been connected by anything beyond religion and the Girls Club.

We didn't have any reason to keep Tuomas at the station, so we allowed him to call his father to come pick him up. Puupponen promised to wait for Tuomas's father so he could verify the boy's movements on Tuesday evening.

I felt like leaving the car at the station and walking home, but I didn't know if Antti would need it the next day. The evening had turned cold, and some puddles had already formed a thin layer of ice. After parking the car, I stood for a moment in our front yard and listened to the hum of the city. A few pale stars shone in the sky, but they couldn't compete with the lights of the city. Their brightness was just a question of where you viewed them from. I hoped I'd be able to find a new perspective on Noor Ezfahani's killing, an angle from which I could see the truth.

9

"Do you think I'm stupid, Kallio?" Markku Ruuskanen, in his nasal voice, practically shouted. "Of course I've checked whether Farid and Reza Ezfahani could have used a truck outside of business hours. The answer is no. They're big semitrucks, which don't fit in normal apartment building parking lots. The trucks are stored at transport centers. They're used to haul food, so they have strict hygiene regulations. So, you can drop the truck theory. We've checked with the taxi services to see if any of their drivers saw the girl on Tuesday. Zero results there too."

"There have been cases where the taxi driver himself was the killer," Ursula Honkanen reminded us.

"So far nothing points in that direction. Today we'll continue questioning the Ezfahani family, but we must consider the possibility that Ms. Ezfahani was the victim of a random attack by a stranger. Puupponen, how did Tuomas Soivio's alibi hold up?"

"The parents and uncle confirmed it, but you know relatives. Soivio was chatting online all night, but he could have done that from anywhere. We can't put a whole lot of weight on that. No one saw Soivio in Noor's neighborhood Tuesday night, but people did on Wednesday, so at least that part of his story checks out."

I was still inclined to believe Tuomas hadn't killed his girlfriend, but I also suspected that he knew more than he'd told us. Other than Tuomas and Noor's cousin, had there been other would-be suitors? It would have been in Tuomas's best interest to tell us about someone like that.

In addition to his own unit, Ruuskanen had called in our cell and representatives from Forensics for the morning meeting. Only Puustjärvi was missing: Ruuskanen had ordered him to observe the autopsy and report back if anything earth shattering turned up in the results. The pathologists knew how to do their jobs without us hovering over their shoulders, but it was up to the lead investigator to decide whether he wanted a member of his team present. I wasn't at all surprised that Ruuskanen was trying to make his mark on department procedures. Anni Kuusimäki wasn't likely to return to the role of head of the Violent Crime Unit, and Ruuskanen was already positioning himself to apply for the job.

"What has your team found out so far, Hakkarainen?" Ruuskanen asked the representative from Forensics, who cleared his throat and clicked open a file on his laptop.

"We've examined the site where the body was found, clearing the layers of snow and doing various cross-checks. Just based on that, it looks like the girl was not killed where her body was found, because there weren't any signs of a struggle. There was evidence that someone had driven a car on the walking path after the second-to-last snowfall, so before the body was found, and according to the revised snow radar report, the last flurry was in the morning at about five thirty, and the previous one was at three. So, we can assume the body was moved to the scene at some point between those times."

"Have you identified the tire tracks?"

"The tires were a basic Gislaved model that Biltema sold thousands of during a sale not too long ago. We're not going to collar anyone based on that alone. We're trying to analyze the wear pattern, but it's clear the tires were more or less new. I doubt we're going to get any solid lead from that direction."

"I have those same Biltema Gislaveds," Puupponen saw fit to announce. He received an irritated glare from Ruuskanen. Then Ruuskanen's phone rang. He answered and set the phone on the table with the speaker on. It was the most expensive smartphone on the market; there was no way the department budget could have covered it. The speaker distorted Puustjärvi's calm voice, but it was still recognizable.

"They've completed the external investigation here. They just started removing and weighing the internal organs. I came out into the hall to talk so I wouldn't bother them," Puustjärvi reported. Ursula winked at Puupponen, and Koivu smiled too. The autopsy had to be done, but watching it wasn't something that even an experienced officer would enjoy.

"The girl was five foot four and weighed 120 pounds. She had good muscle definition and clearly exercised. There were some old scars on the body, the longest of which was on the left rear thigh. It looked like a knife wound. Hard to say what caused the others. In addition, there were postmortem abrasions."

"So, she was moved after she died?" Ruuskanen shouted. After nearly falling off my chair in surprise, I realized that Ruuskanen must know that the speaker on his expensive gadget was junk.

"Yeah, it looks that way. We'll get the stomach-content analysis later, but given the degree of rigor mortis, the body was in the cold for three to six hours. That was as exact as they could get." Puustjärvi made a dramatic pause and then continued. "She wasn't a virgin, if that means anything."

"Was she circumcised?" Ursula's voice was cool, but I could see from her eyes that this information was important to her.

"No. There were no signs of sexual violence or semen found on her either. An obvious case of strangulation, the murder weapon being her own scarf."

Why had the strangler left the headscarf around her neck? Hadn't he realized we might be able to find his DNA on it? Of course, her clothes had been checked for fibers, particles, and cells, but they wouldn't be of any use until we found corresponding samples.

"Was her hair dyed? Did she shave her legs or armpits, or her genital area?" Ursula asked. Ruuskanen looked appalled, though Ursula's questions were completely relevant.

"I didn't notice. Should I go ask?"

"I think details like that can wait for the final autopsy report, but make sure it gets included. So, no breakthrough so far?" Ruuskanen sounded disappointed.

"No. Should I stay here?"

"Finish the job." Ruuskanen pressed the off button. He hadn't divvied up the day's assignments yet. It was a relief to not be responsible for organizing the entire investigation. If it were up to me, since Noor's home had already been searched for signs of a fight, next I would have moved on to the building nearby where Noor's grandfather Reza, her uncle, and her cousins lived. I was just opening my mouth when Koivu asked if we intended to question the entire Ezfahani clan together at the same time.

"Puupponen said that Tuomas Soivio's alibi can't be considered airtight because it was confirmed only by family members. It's the same with the Ezfahanis. Let's put them in a room together and see if they get their wires crossed."

"*If* they do," Ruuskanen said with a snort. "All we need now is an honor killing. What were you getting at with your questions about her hair, Honkanen?"

"It tells us how westernized Noor was. Puupponen, Kallio, did you even ask the boyfriend if they were sleeping together? You better believe that matters for the investigation! If Soivio went to bed with the girl, he made her unmarriageable in these Muslims' view. That's obvious, isn't it?"

I studied Ursula thoughtfully. Bright red glinted on her lips, and her skin was completely free of blemishes. Her tight black sweater was conservative compared to her usual wardrobe, because it was both a turtleneck and long sleeved. Her violet suede trousers clung to her body, which was a shape most of us could only dream of. Ursula's colleagues had grown numb to her beauty and heavy makeup, but sometimes it made people underestimate her, believing she was some bimbo who was too stupid to catch them in their lies. Had Ursula tried to hit on Ruuskanen? Had he been warned about the department vamp? I knew Taskinen had warned Ursula about sexual advances in the workplace. I'd never heard about her trying to hit on a member of the public while on duty. She knew that would get her benched.

"The imam from the Ezfahanis' mosque has gotten himself mixed up in the case too," Ruuskanen said. "He called me last night demanding the body be turned over immediately. There was a dispute about the autopsy as well, but I told him that religion doesn't trump the law in this country. The girl will be buried as soon as we're done with the body."

My cell phone, which was on silent, started to blink and vibrate. I didn't recognize the number. I thumbed in a message right away, replying that I couldn't answer right now but asking the caller to leave me his or her name. Rasilainen was reporting on the neighbors' stories, and the information about Noor crying as she left home probably prompted Ruuskanen to follow Koivu's suggestion about questioning the Ezfahanis together.

"Kallio will probably want to be there, along with Koivu, Puupponen, Lehtovuori, and Puustjärvi, who've already interviewed the individuals in question. I'll lead the interrogation, so that will make six of us. That seems like it should be enough. Honkanen, you'll go with Forensics to take a closer look at Noor Ezfahani's belongings, since you seem to be an expert on the feminine mystique. From there you can go with Rasilainen to continue interviewing the Ezfahanis' neighbors. I wouldn't be surprised if the murder occurred in one of those buildings."

"Have we been to the Ezfahani men's apartment yet? Do we have a search warrant?" Ursula asked.

"Not yet. Let's see what comes up in the interrogation. We'll have to catch Reza junior and Farid at work, and the other—Vafa was it?—will have to be fetched from school."

"Aren't they on sick leave? Surely people get time off when a family member dies," Lehtovuori said, perplexed.

"I don't imagine they're quite that familiar with the Finnish system yet," Ruuskanen said with another derisive snort. "And what good would sick leave do? It isn't going to bring anyone back. It's best to get back in the saddle as soon as possible, to get on with life."

Ruuskanen clearly wasn't someone who handed out contact information for victim support groups to the people he interviewed. Might he be speaking from experience? I couldn't ask with the others present. Perhaps someone would know—in a police station, everyone seemed to know everyone else's business. Our experiences molded us as professionals, but not all in the same way. As a young police officer, I'd had a tendency to handle suspects with kid gloves. Now I knew that the authorities weren't always the best people to offer comfort, though sometimes a police officer didn't have any alternative but to take a broken person in her arms until the cries subsided.

"We haven't discussed as a group yet that Noor's cousin Rahim Ezfahani has two assault and battery convictions. He's only twenty-three. One was in 2003, right after he arrived in Finland, and the other was last year. He wasn't deported the first time because he was a minor and the whole family was still waiting for approval of their asylum application. The incident last year was a gang scuffle that got out of hand, and Rahim wasn't the only person convicted. No one was seriously injured, and the Immigration Service didn't revoke Rahim's residence permit. In the latter case, one of the prosecution witnesses was one Miro Ruuskanen. Any relation?" Koivu sounded irritated.

"I'm sure you already know that Miro Ruuskanen is my son. But he was only a witness to the assault, not a party to it. There's no need for me to recuse myself," Ruuskanen said testily.

"But the fight was between Muslims, mostly Iraqis and Kurds, and some Finnish nationalists. The group calls itself Finnish Heartland, and your son is a member. He even has the gang tattoos to prove it."

"I see you've done your homework, Koivu. But my son and his opinions don't have anything to do with Noor Ezfahani's murder. My son is an adult who lives on his own, and I have nothing to do with his politics. We can continue this discussion in private, if you like, but there's no reason to waste the group's time on this."

"In my opinion, it's important for everyone involved in the criminal investigation to know that Rahim Ezfahani has two battery convictions. Not everyone had been informed," Koivu insisted. The red hue of Ruuskanen's face deepened to the color of brick, but he didn't reply. Instead, he rustled his papers, like it was time to move on to more important matters.

I'd heard about the battery convictions yesterday from Tuomas Soivio, so I should have brought them up, but I hadn't wanted to step on the lead investigator's toes. Apparently, they were going to get smashed anyway. The recent campaign finance scandal had made the media and the public more inclined to take conspiracy theories seriously, and if we didn't keep our house in order, people would start thinking the Espoo police were up to shady business too.

"The group of six I mentioned will remain on standby until all of the Ezfahanis have been rounded up. I'll arrange for an interpreter, since some of the family members don't speak very good Finnish. I'll send out a text when we're ready to go. Lehtovuori, will you make sure this conference room has enough chairs for everyone? Set up sound and video too. And give some thought to the seating arrangements. If we're in a circle, we can have one officer between each Ezfahani, but then situating the cameras will be difficult."

"In a circle?" Koivu asked, a note of skepticism in his voice.

"A little like we're sitting around a campfire. Won't that create a homey, trusting sort of feeling? I want them to relax and let down their guard, so they'll start talking. Then we'll get some results. I don't have to remind such an experienced group where murderers are usually found. Kallio, are there any urgent jobs for Puupponen with the other cases your cell is investigating, or can he keep going through the online discussions about Noor's killing?"

I didn't have to think. "A homicide takes precedence over any other investigations. By the way, should we get wiretap authorizations for the Ezfahanis' and Tuomas Soivio's phones?"

"First let's see what comes out of this interview," Ruuskanen answered sourly.

A text message had come in from the same number that had just tried to call me: *Vala here. I'm waiting in the Espoo PD lobby next to a gigantic stuffed octopus. The desk says you're in a meeting. Call me ASAP. Lauri.*

I almost burst out laughing. Vala had the gall to think I would just jump on demand, that all he had to do was give the word! Perhaps he'd gotten used to things working that way in the military chain of command, but I wasn't his subordinate. I listened to Ruuskanen assigning tasks with one ear. Noor's schoolmates and teachers would be questioned, and Puupponen and I would get another crack at Tuomas, if deemed necessary after the Ezfahanis' interview. On the night of Noor's killing, Tuomas had been chatting online about hockey and his favorite rock bands. It would have taken some pretty cool nerves to kill his girlfriend and then go right back to chatting, but Tuomas wouldn't have been the first teenager to hide a killer's heart from his family and the police.

"Apparently, Sylvia Sandelin managed to persuade Noor's family to let her go to high school. I've already talked to her once, and we had a good rapport, so I'd be happy to continue with her," I suggested when

Ruuskanen came to me in the rotation. He nodded and tried to smile. Maybe he hoped we would form a connection and then team up against our underlings. I didn't have any desire to get into something like that, but I didn't intend to start making waves either. I just wanted to make good on my promise to Iida.

After the meeting I returned to my office and left a message for Sylvia Sandelin to call me. I'd just logged on to the intranet when the switchboard called.

"I just saw Ruuskanen slip out for a smoke, so your meeting must be over. You have an eager visitor waiting for you down here in the lobby, a Major Lauri Vala. It's been all I can do to keep him from barging up the stairs and into your office. Do you have time to see him now, or should I tell him to keep waiting or come back tomorrow? You don't have an appointment with him, right?"

I mulled over my options. Vala was stubborn. I certainly didn't want him coming to find me at home. The workplace was a more neutral environment, and in the best-case scenario, Ruuskanen would interrupt his visit.

I promised to come down and get Vala. I stopped by the restroom on the way. The face that looked back at me from the mirror was in serious need of some concealer under the eyes. I returned to my office, dug the concealer pen out of my bag, and grabbed a lipstick while I was at it. Using a compact mirror, I touched up my makeup. I realized that I was doing so because of Vala—not because I wanted to look attractive, but because I wanted to give the impression of being at the top of my game. That annoyed me. I remembered what Vala had said about a woman's place, which had irritated me even in the midst of all that grief, and I didn't want him to think this murder investigation was too much for me.

I threw the lipstick and concealer back in my bag, then put Antti's and the children's pictures in a drawer. My family wasn't any of Vala's business. Maybe it would be a good idea to take the photos home.

Many Finnish peacekeepers had withdrawn from Afghanistan at the end of last October, before the second round of the presidential elections, but Vala had decided to stay in the country. The troops had been rotated again in February, but Vala had told me in an e-mail that he was on leave and after that he'd go back to Afghanistan. I hadn't received another invitation to the country after the events of early October; few messages came from the police academy, though they'd promised to report to the Finnish Ministry of the Interior, the school's partner organization. The academy was still functioning, but under difficult circumstances, because both the drug lords and the Taliban were doing everything they could to disrupt its operations.

I walked down the stairs and saw Vala through the glass doors, standing with his arms akimbo and his brow furrowed in front of the giant yellow octopus. He was wearing fatigues, and I realized I'd never seen him in civilian clothing. Surely, he was allowed to dress casually while on leave. Was he trying to stand out from the crowd? His hair was even shorter than before, just stubble really, which had become sprinkled with more gray during the intervening months.

I opened the door, and he turned suddenly, as if waiting for an armed threat.

"Hello, Major Vala." I extended my hand in greeting and received the familiar bone-crushing handshake.

"Detective Kallio. It's been a long time. Is there somewhere we could talk in private?"

"My office." I'd only been using it for a few days, but already it felt like my own. "Have you gotten your visitor badge? Good. Let's go." I opened the door and started jogging up the stairs. Vala's combat boots knocked along behind me, and the visitor card hanging from his collar clicked against the metal buttons of his uniform. Koivu passed us in the hallway.

"I'm getting coffee and donuts. Should I get some for you and your visitor?" he asked politely, unable to conceal his curiosity. I'd told Koivu what I could about Lauri Vala without risking a breach of confidentiality. His last name was sewn on his jacket, which was one difference from the uniform he'd worn in Afghanistan. There it was best for soldiers to remain anonymous.

"Do you want something?" I asked Vala.

"No, thank you. Police coffee is even worse than army coffee, and I haven't eaten a jelly donut since bible camp." Vala was the kind of guy who watched his waistline.

"No? OK. Maria, one small thing when you get a moment. Preferably before Ruuskanen's big meeting."

"OK." I opened the door for Vala. I'd been at work for less than a week, so the desk hadn't had time to collect piles of files and papers, and the bookshelves were waiting to be filled too. The computer screen saver was a picture of a three-month-old Jahnukainen stalking Venjamin's tail. But they could be any two cats from the Internet, not necessarily from our family.

Vala closed the door behind him and sat down in one of the armchairs. "So, you're riding the Espoo police gravy train again."

"For the time being. We have a murder investigation going on, and I'm on the clock. How can I help you? I can't waste my day catching up."

"Hey, slow down. Are there any surveillance cameras in here?"

"No. Just in the hallway."

Vala nodded. He pulled his cell phone out of his breast pocket and pressed a button that made the phone vibrate, and then the screen went black.

"Please turn off your cell phone. You never can be sure how these devices work."

Vala seemed serious. He stared at me expectantly.

"Lauri, dear, my phone isn't bugged. This is Espoo, not Afghanistan."

"Fine. We won't talk. I'm leaving."

That would have been a relief. I knew the military monitored the mental health of peacekeepers, so maybe Vala wasn't on leave—maybe he had been sent packing and failed to mention it to me. But he didn't get out of his chair; he just looked around the room as if searching for microphones or video equipment. I sat down behind my desk and opened the Espoo police homepage, logged in to the intranet, and started to read a report about car break-ins and traffic stops. Vala just sat there. "You were going to leave," I pointed out after several minutes. "Please do. I have work."

Vala sat quietly for a moment and then got up and walked around the desk, then stood behind me so he could see what was on my computer. A vehicle burglary in the parking lot of the old Matinkylä sports bubble. Anyone who knew anything about the incident was asked to contact the Espoo police. He was so close to me that I could feel his breath on my hair, and it took some effort for me not to turn to look at him. Then the computer screen dimmed, and the screen saver appeared, reflecting Vala's face in the dark background of the photograph. The strange expression in his eyes felt oppressive.

"At least turn off the computer. How many cell phones are there in this room?"

"Stop clowning around." I turned my chair toward Vala, almost kicking him in the shin. "State your business and then get out. I don't have the time or desire to play spy games."

"This isn't a game!" Vala roared. He paused, clearly alarmed by the volume of his voice, then continued in a near whisper. "Please turn off your computer and all of your cell phones. I'm begging you. I trust you but not the other police."

"My work phone has to stay on during work. I can turn off the other." I logged out of the intranet and exited all the other programs I had open, then turned off my personal phone. Hopefully the children wouldn't have any emergencies in the middle of the school day. That didn't happen very often, and besides, both my father and Antti were available. Why was I even worried about that?

Vala sat back in his chair. His posture was erect, his hands resting crossed in his lap, but he was twiddling his thumbs nervously. "I understand. At work you always have to be available. Do you have it in a safety-deposit box?"

"What?"

"The necklace. Ulrike Müller's necklace."

"How do you know I have that?"

"She asked for your address. Helga Müller, Ulrike's mother. Of course, I didn't give it to her. I reported her daughter's death to the next of kin. It was my duty. That was how she knew to contact me."

"Did Ulrike's mother tell you what she intended to send me?"

"Yes. She asked if I thought it would be appropriate. Where is it?"

"At home, in my jewelry box."

"It's locked, right?"

I started to get nervous. I kept my jewelry box in one of our bedroom dressers, because none of the jewelry in it had any particularly great monetary value. My great-grandmother's emerald earrings and brooch were dear to me of course, but the golden cross pendant my godmother had left me was entirely too big, and it represented a faith I was too unsure of to display front and center. I hadn't ever worn Antti's grandmother's hair comb, which was silver, with two aquamarine gemstones. The rest of my jewelry collection was made up of cheap earrings and punk-era kitsch. Even though Ulrike's choker was unique and clearly made by a designer jeweler, I hadn't thought it needed to be put under lock and key.

"So, it isn't locked up. How could you be so stupid? You're a police officer! Take it to a safety-deposit box before it's too late."

"What on earth are you talking about?"

Vala shook his head. "It wasn't a coincidence that we were attacked that night. And that roadside bomb wasn't intended for any random

ISAF or NATO personnel. They knew that Ulrike Müller was in the first vehicle."

That night on the road between Jalalabad and Kabul was still too clear in my mind. Vala's presence brought back the smell of smoke and the muzzle flashes in the blackness along the road. I hadn't even touched Ulrike's necklace, not since that night we spent with the Koivus. I'd felt its weight too heavily around my neck.

"Ulrike was killed because she knew too much. I'm sure that necklace was sent to you because it contains a hidden message about what she knew."

10

The war must have really messed with Lauri Vala's head. Customs, the Interior Ministry, and our own mailroom had checked the package that contained the necklace. It had been scanned repeatedly using X-ray machines and metal detectors. The package had most likely been opened, the contents checked, and the whole thing retaped. Helga Müller wouldn't have sent something with valuable or dangerous information through the normal postal service.

"Ulrike Müller was a German police officer. How much did she tell you about her mother?" Vala demanded. I tried to think. I'd pushed Ulrike into the back of my mind with everything else I didn't have the energy to think about right now, what with the new job demanding my full attention.

"Nothing, really. Her mother was a retired widow."

"Retired from what?"

"Not a clue."

"Helga Müller was also a policewoman. Strange that Ulrike didn't mention it. Why would she conceal that? It's not common for both a woman in her seventies and her forty-year-old daughter to be police-women. Isn't the German police force still predominately male?"

There was fire in Vala's eyes. He'd crossed his hands over his knees, but I could see that they were shaking. I was glad when my phone rang, though the caller wasn't Ruuskanen ordering me to come down for the interview.

It was Sylvia Sandelin. I didn't want to talk to her in front of Vala, so I went into the hallway, though I was certain that Vala would go through my desk drawers while I was away. They were almost empty anyway, but he would find my family photos.

"Detective Kallio, you left a message for me to call you."

"As you can guess, it's about Noor Ezfahani, or, more precisely, about her schooling. I've been told you were instrumental in persuading the family to let her continue high school. Is this true?"

"Yes. Noor asked Heini and Nelli for help, but they didn't think the Ezfahanis would listen to them. So, I got in touch with Noor's mother, who informed me that, in their family, the men made those kinds of decisions. I was forced to defend my position to both Noor's father and her grandfather, and I believe there were some brothers involved as well."

"Was it hard to convince them?"

"Yes. It took several meetings and consultations with Noor's guidance counselor and math teacher. At least we didn't have to call in Child Protective Services. The family calmed down once they understood that university studies don't cost much of anything in Finland and that there is financial aid available for high school textbooks. The Ezfahanis were most afraid of being sent back to Iran, because that would almost certainly mean death. They're religiously devout, but they oppose the politics of the current government. So, it pays for them to stay in the good graces of Finnish authorities."

"I'd like to talk more about all of this, say, early next week. Will you be in Espoo then?"

"I may go to Helsinki on Monday, but no farther than that. Have you made any headway in the investigation? The newspapers make it sound like the police are lost."

"We can't tell everything to the media. I'll be in touch early in the week. Have a good weekend!"

During the winter there had been political unrest in Iran. Several groups were gunning for power, and secular forces were trying to instigate a revolt against the Islamist government. We could expect to see more refugees soon. My sister Eeva had been enamored with the beautiful empress consort Farah and confused when Finns protested against her during her visit to Finland. That conflict was one of Eeva's earliest childhood memories. I didn't remember the whole event, even though I was two years older. Apparently, as a child I hadn't identified with queens and empresses.

Puupponen came out of the case room looking like he had something important on his mind and jogged off toward the stairway. I glanced at my phone, but there wasn't a text about the interview, so Puupponen must have been in a rush for some other reason.

When I returned to my office, Vala was sitting in the same position I'd left him in. My instinct was to take him by the scruff of the neck and tell him to get lost.

"I want to see the necklace," Vala announced. "It has to be checked and taken somewhere safe. When do you get off work?"

"I have no idea. And the necklace is none of your business. Do you understand? We were both forced to witness Ulrike's death, but the necklace isn't connected to that. It's just a memento."

Vala interrupted me. "Why would Ulrike's mother send it to you so long after her daughter's death? Why wouldn't she have given it to you as a Christmas present instead?"

"Maybe she couldn't bear to send it earlier! Maybe she didn't have the address yet! I'm in the middle of a murder investigation, if you hadn't heard. I have more important things to do than speculate about Ulrike's necklace. Please leave."

Vala rose so quickly that I instinctively drew back, expecting him to lunge at me. But he didn't. He just looked me in the eyes and bellowed,

"What the hell kind of bubble are you living in? First you come waltzing into Afghanistan, needlessly risking your life for some police academy opening ceremonies. You almost ended up being the next obituary in *Police and Justice*! Anyone could see that the country would be more restless than usual before the first round of presidential elections. Now you're missing something just as obvious. That necklace isn't just a necklace—it's a message!"

The tanned skin of Vala's face wrinkled around his eyes. Beads of sweat had appeared along his hairline, the smell of cologne growing stronger as he became agitated. I wasn't in any danger—the building was full of colleagues who would rush to my aid if necessary, but I couldn't bear the idea of Vala trying to force his way into my home to look at the necklace.

"Sure, you've trained Afghan police officers, but I don't think you really get how hopeless that country is. The drug lords and the Taliban live in an unholy alliance, which suits both just fine, and the international drug dealers hope the Western powers never manage to spread peace and democracy. The Finnish military command denies we're even at war, even though allied troops and civilians are constantly dying. And now you're turning a blind eye too."

"Are you really just on leave, or have you been discharged?"

"What do you mean? I'm on leave, of course! I'm going back midmonth. I'm not leaving there until all the Finnish troops are demobilized, or until they send me home in a casket. Fuck!" Vala looked at me again, the expression in his eyes like a punch. "It's useless talking to you. I'll go now."

I couldn't let Vala go wandering around the halls of the police station, so I set off after him and escorted him down to the lobby. He didn't say another word, but I had a nasty feeling that he wasn't going to let this go. My father was still at our house; his party wouldn't be starting until early evening. I thought about calling and asking him to hide the necklace in the lockable drawer in Antti's desk, but I didn't want to get my dad mixed up in Vala's meltdown. Besides, he would have wanted to know what was going on. He was the one from which I'd inherited my natural curiosity, after all. He was just as likely to meddle in other people's business as I was.

Still, my father had never tried to curtail my choice of profession or any of my other decisions, at least not actively. Since the time I was small, he'd encouraged me to pursue paths that were uncommon for women. My mother had worried I was making my life difficult by being different from the other girls, and she had opposed my desire to go to the police academy. Dad had probably just thought I wouldn't get in.

I was thirsty, so on my way back to my office I stopped in the restroom to get some water. When I opened the door with a full mug in hand, I almost ran into Puupponen, who was dashing along the hallway toward the case room with an enormous pizza box in his hands.

"Hot pepperoni pizza straight from the delivery man! I ordered me and Koivu a family size; there's enough for you too, if you want some."

"Which one of you has the hangover?"

"The only hangover I have is from reading racist websites. It's not like I started with a very rosy picture of humanity, but some people just seem to keep sinking lower. They're seriously depraved. But come have some pizza. It'll take the edge off. All Antti ever feeds you at home is health food. Take a break from the mushrooms and herring!" Puupponen balanced the pizza box with one hand and wrapped his other arm around me tightly enough to make water splash out of my cup onto both of our shoes. I let him lead me into the case room. Koivu was already sitting at the table, swigging Coke straight from the can.

"I brought the boss too," Puupponen announced, setting the box down on the table and opening it. The room filled with the scent of pepperoni, slightly singed cheese, and garlic.

"This is a secret Espoo police torture technique: they'll confess to anything just to get away from our garlic breath!" Puupponen said with a mischievous glint in his eyes. He grabbed a slice with a paper napkin and had it at his lips before he even sat down. I couldn't deny I was hungry too, so I joined them.

"Have you found anything in the anti-immigration websites, other than existential nausea?" I asked Puupponen after eating a few pieces of pizza.

"A few of the discussion boards mentioned that Tuomas Soivio was in police custody yesterday, and they were calling us idiots and raghead lovers. Sara Amir's name also came up. Someone claimed that she had been killed just like Noor. No one has jumped at that bait yet."

"I can't decide whether it was worse back when we used to get anonymous tips over the phone or now when it's always some weird online pseudonym." It was hard to understand Koivu because his mouth was full of pizza. A line of grease ran down the side of his mouth. "I think we should systematically work through all of Ayan's, Sara's, and Aziza's schoolmates, coworkers, and friends, and try to figure out who's spreading this stuff online. If they're doing it there, you can be sure they're doing it in real life too."

"One of the girls who goes to the club said something about a picture on Facebook with Sara and a boy named Tommi from Siuntio holding hands. Can you find it?" I asked.

"That isn't much to go on, but I'll try." Puupponen opened an energy drink. He grimaced as he gulped it down.

My phone rang. The screen said "Dad." Vala hadn't gone straight to my house, had he? I only lived half a mile from the police station, so he easily could have made it there already by taxi. I swallowed the pizza in my mouth and answered.

"Hey there."

"Hi, it's Dad. Hope I'm not interrupting, but where on earth do you keep the iron? I've looked in every closet, but all I've found is the ironing board. I can't go to my reunion in a wrinkled shirt. It got all crumpled up in my suitcase, even though I packed carefully."

"Did you look in Iida's room? Sometimes she forgets to put it away. Maybe she was ironing patches on her hoodie again."

"Wait a second." I heard my father's muffled steps. "Here it is, on a pot holder on Iida's desk."

"What time are you supposed to leave?"

"The party starts at six, so probably just after five. Yesterday Antti and I looked up the bus schedule."

"Did you talk about whether he would get home before you left?"

"No, but the children will be fine . . . And I can find my way to the bus. I did study in Helsinki. I'm not a complete country bumpkin!"

I laughed. My father had a legendary sense of direction. He never got lost, and you could drop him in the middle of a forest in the dark and he'd still know more or less where he was and which way was north. He'd taught me how to use a compass and read a map, skills that had actually been a lot of help during my police academy entrance examinations.

"Listen, Dad, if a man about fifty years old, muscular, with short, graying hair, shows up at the door, don't open it for him. I'll tell you more later. Have a fun time at the party!"

"I'll take a taxi back and try not to wake you all up. Do you have to work tomorrow too?"

"Possibly."

"OK, well, see you in the morning."

I ended the call and put the phone in my pocket. Of course, Koivu and Puupponen had been listening. What else could I have expected from them? "What fifty-year-old?" Koivu asked immediately. "Is it that same character who claimed that the last time he ate a jelly donut was at bible camp?"

"Yep. Major Lauri Vala. He's a peacekeeper I met in Afghanistan. He was up in arms about the necklace I was wearing last Sunday when we were at your house. He's just a head case. Koivu, do you want to split that last slice?"

As I was reaching for the piece of pizza, our cell phones beeped, indicating incoming text messages. Ruuskanen was calling us together at 1:50, in just over an hour. I scarfed down the rest of the pizza and grabbed more water to wash it down before going to my office to call Susanne Jansson and her parents. I got the mother, Ulla Jansson. When I asked whether she'd rather speak Swedish instead of Finnish, she said it was all the same to her.

"What is there to talk about?" she said when I asked her about Noor Ezfahani and Tuomas Soivio's relationship. "They were dating. Susanne was a little melancholy sometimes because she didn't have a boyfriend, but she still liked to invite Noor and Tuomas over to our house."

"What evidence do you have that they were dating?"

"Good Lord, they acted like young people who were dating: they held each other's hands, they sat next to each other, and they did everything else couples do. Do I have to draw you a picture?"

"No. It was important to hear you say it, though. Thank you. How is Susanne coping?"

"Poorly. She's probably going to have to be away from school for quite some time and finish her classes later. Your solving this quickly would help her a lot. Knowing who killed her dear friend will give her some closure."

"Has Susanne ever told you about Noor lying to her family about Tuomas? Specifically, did Noor tell them he was bothering her?"

"Susanne did say that it was better if Noor's family didn't find out about her relationship. My husband and I talked once about getting to know Noor's family, but we wouldn't have had very much in common. And I guess their kind generally keeps to themselves. But Noor was very Finnish, very integrated. She was a good example of an immigrant who would have been a benefit to society, not a burden."

After the phone conversation, I wrote up a summary of all the people who'd said that Tuomas Soivio was dating Noor. It was a long enough list to indicate that Noor might have been lying to her family. But how did I know she didn't enjoy lying? Did she see herself and Tuomas as a modern-day Romeo and Juliet, despite the lack of animosity on the part of Romeo's family? It was probably easier for a family to accept an immigrant daughter-in-law than to accept a son-in-law from another culture. I knew I wouldn't react terribly well if Iida decided to convert to Islam and start wearing a headscarf because of a boyfriend, but I probably couldn't stop it either. Back in the day, my mother would have looked down her nose at a boyfriend just for going to trade school instead of being on the college track. Nothing had ever been said directly, but I'd sensed it. Maybe it had been a relief for her when I spent almost all of junior high mooning over Johnny Miettinen, who was already in high school. Now thinking about Johnny just made me snort in amusement.

At 1:50 p.m. we gathered in the large conference room. Lehtovuori and the investigative secretary set up the video cameras while Ruuskanen gave the interpreter, a thirtysomething Iranian-born woman, a brief rundown of what was going on. She was a sworn translator who had come to fill in while the regular Espoo police Persian interpreter was out sick. She already knew Rahim Ezfahani and, through him, the whole family, because she had acted as their official interpreter a few times at the employment office and the tax bureau, as well as with Rahim and his legal counsel.

"We'll use you only when the family members are not able to express themselves in Finnish," Ruuskanen said. "The primary language for the interview will be Finnish."

Ruuskanen would lead the interrogation, but each of us could also present questions if we wished. However, the most important thing was to observe the Ezfahanis' reactions and responses to any contradictions that might arise. We six police officers would be a sort of human lie detector.

The Ezfahani family was prompt. All were dressed in black, with the men's white shirts gleaming under their suit jackets. The mother looked considerably more deflated than before, her dark eyes sunk deeply into her skull. Grandfather Reza immediately got into an animated discussion with the interpreter, who shook her head. The others were clearly disconcerted by the abundance of police officers. They stayed huddled together in a tight group, in the middle of which Noor the elder, frail and a head shorter than the others, looked like she might disappear altogether.

"They asked when they can bury Noor," the interpreter translated. "Is there any information about that?"

"Not yet," Ruuskanen replied. Puustjärvi hadn't shown up yet—maybe Noor's autopsy wasn't complete. When this was interpreted for the Ezfahanis, a general snorting and shaking of heads began, which the interpreter attempted to calm. In the discussions I'd had with Afghan police officers, I'd learned how seriously autopsies interfered with Islamic funeral arrangements. Their tradition of quick burial was related to climate: in ancient times there hadn't been morgues with sterile cold storage units for preserving a body. Islamic law did allow for an autopsy in the case of a crime. But Noor's mother wanted to wash the body as soon as possible. That was part of the custom too. Muna had told me heartbreaking stories of Afghani families searching through the rubble of their bombed-out homes, looking for pieces of their loved ones so they could wash them. The Ezfahanis came from a place where you couldn't escape the daily occurrence of death or only think about it as someone else's problem when watching the evening news. I didn't know whether that experience with loss would help them bear Noor's death any better.

Ruuskanen began to arrange everyone in a semblance of a circle, but where to place the interpreter presented a problem. Finally, she decided to sit in the circle with everyone else, between Reza senior and Rahim. I sat between Rahim and Noor. I tried to focus my senses, to attune to what was going on in the mind of the people sitting next to me.

Ruuskanen started by asking the family to again describe the events of Tuesday afternoon and evening. Grandfather Reza began, first asking the interpreter to translate what he said. He spoke slowly and clearly, as if that would help us understand his incomprehensible Persian.

"Rahim, Jalil, and I waited for Farid to come home from work and wash up. Then we went to my eldest son Reza's family's home. Reza's wife had prepared supper, as she always does. We took along rice and tomatoes. In Finland the tomatoes are hard and expensive. We hardly ever get good ones and never in the winter. My daughter-in-law Noor makes a delicious tomato sauce, which was on the menu for the next day, along with chicken with eggplant and rice. My granddaughter Noor set the table. She was bragging about getting the highest grade on her Finnish test, and that she would be able to become a doctor because she knew Finnish so well."

Sitting next to me, Noor's mother sighed, her muscles clenching under her loose black coat. Ruuskanen waited for Reza to continue his monologue, but the older man looked to his eldest son as if asking him to chime in. Reza junior remained silent.

"Did your daughter do housework willingly?" Ruuskanen directed his question in Finnish to Noor the elder, who was sitting to his left.

"Willingly? What that mean?"

The interpreter began to explain to her, and Noor answered bravely in Finnish.

"It her duty. She get go to school, she help at home. Everyone help—boys too. Father and Hamid go work. We no ask why do, we do. I say and Noor do."

Reza senior became agitated because he didn't understand what his daughter-in-law was saying, and the interpreter had to repeat what she'd said in Persian. Puupponen was sitting directly across from me in the circle, fidgeting. If I could have, I would have reminded him of the 90 percent rule in police work. Most of what we did was always a waste of time. Roni Timonen, a young investigator hired by the Violent Crime Unit while I'd been away, looked eager. He probably hadn't participated in a mass interrogation like this since he'd been at the academy.

"You all gathered at the dinner table. What did you discuss?"

The interpreter translated Ruuskanen's question.

"Soccer. We talked about soccer," Rahim said next to me. I was hearing his voice for the first time. It was hoarse, as though there were something wrong with his vocal cords.

"We talked about when the field would melt again so we could play," Hamid added, and the others nodded. The interpreter translated for the grandfather, who smiled and said something so quickly that I wasn't able to discern individual words.

"The boys are like little children when there is talk of soccer. They follow the Iranian league with the help of the satellite dish."

"Did Noor participate in the discussion?" Koivu asked. The men went silent, and then Noor's father, Reza, shook his head.

"No, probably not. Noor quiet girl. Listen much, not speak much."

"Did you have an argument about soccer?" Koivu asked. The answer was a firm no in two different languages. Both Rezas assured us that there was no disagreement at the dinner table. They started to talk over each other, and Noor's mother sank even deeper into her chair, as if she wanted to disappear. She exuded fear, but I wasn't able to tell of whom or of what. The men seemed calmer, if alert. They each repeated the same story almost word for word about how they'd eaten chicken and eggplant and how there had been too little sugar in the tea and they'd had to add more.

"Where did Noor go after dinner?" Ruuskanen was clearly beginning to be irritated that there weren't any holes in their story.

"To her club, to get to know the Finnish girls," Noor's father answered.

"Was there any difference of opinion about her leaving?"

Again, the answer came as vigorous head shaking and a profusion of words. I was already picking up on the word *nakheir*, Persian for "no."

"Noor always went there," her younger brother, Vafa, said. "It's a good club, since there are only girls. The girls get left alone."

"Did Noor's boyfriend, Tuomas Soivio, ever visit you?" Puupponen threw this out like a forward in a soccer match who has realized that the coaches' tactics aren't working and takes off alone on a mad dash that even he doesn't believe will work. Puupponen's question and the interpreter's version were followed by a silence that was almost more overwhelming than the exultation following the home team scoring a goal. They obviously hadn't agreed on a common answer.

"Noor did not have boyfriend," her father finally said.

"We have several witnesses who have stated that Noor was dating her schoolmate, Tuomas Soivio. Did Noor neglect to tell you?" As I asked this, I looked straight at Noor's mother, who avoided my gaze by staring at the floor and then by closing her eyes. The Rezas, father and grandfather, traded a few heated sentences in their own language.

"What are they saying? You have to translate everything!" Ruuskanen bellowed at the interpreter.

"Wait. That Noor wasn't a liar, that the boy is trying to ruin her reputation. That the boy was following Noor around even though Noor didn't want him and so he killed her."

It was the same thing they had claimed in previous interviews. Ruuskanen tried to steer the conversation back to Noor's departure for the Girls Club. According to her family, she'd been completely normal, not crying or angry. It was starting to get hot in the room. I reeked of garlic, and I could still smell its stink on Koivu's and Puupponen's breath. Maybe that was why Timonen was breathing through his mouth.

Noor had helped her mother clear the dishes from the table before going out. Vafa admitted, a little abashed, that he'd helped his mother wash the dishes while the rest of the men had been trying to fix the rear mudguard on Hamid's bicycle—the interpreter's help was needed for "mudguard." Grandfather, Farid, Jalil, and Rahim had gone home around nine p.m. Around ten p.m. Mrs. Ezfahani started to wonder why her daughter hadn't come home.

"Did you try to call her?" Ruuskanen asked.

"She not answer. Hamid go to Grandfather's house, see if girl there. She not. Everyone sleep. Then not sleep when hear Noor not at home. No one sleep that night. Not sleep anymore ever, not ever. No sleep with sorrow," Noor's father said quietly.

"You arrest the boy," Jalil said. "Or we take revenge ourselves."

His father, Farid, spoke angrily to his son, and the men of the family began another rapid conversation in Persian, which made the interpreter's head turn from person to person and her pen fly across her notebook. Then the grandfather gave everyone an order, evidently to be quiet.

"Mr. Farid Ezfahani says no revenge. Mr. Reza senior says that in Finland the police take care of revenge, and that we will trust the Finnish police. Mr. Jalil asks forgiveness but says that his cousin has been violated and that this cannot be done. A cousin is like a sister, his brother's future spouse."

Those final words made Rahim flinch next to me. He was sitting so close that I could see the blood drain from his face, and his skin turned a pale yellowish color, like grass after a night of freezing temperatures. Tuomas Soivio had mentioned that Noor was promised to her cousin, but it was good to hear the same from the cousin's younger brother's mouth.

"It not true," Noor's mother said in a louder voice than I had heard her use before. "Noor not promised anyone, not married. Wanted be doctor. Not promised anyone." She rose, stretched over me, and slapped Rahim across the face. Then she fell straight into my lap.

11

Mrs. Noor Ezfahani was incoherent after she regained consciousness. Her skin felt dry and hot, and she didn't react to the interpreter's Persian. I asked Noor's husband, Reza, to help, and together we carried her to the nearest room that had a couch for her to rest on. Koivu called the paramedics. They would get to decide whether Mrs. Ezfahani would need to be taken to the emergency room at Jorvi Hospital.

"Why did your wife hit Rahim?" I asked Reza when we were left alone with his wife.

"I cannot see into her soul," he answered, and I had to content myself with that. The paramedics arrived, and I left them to do their work in peace. Luckily one of them was a woman, which appeased Reza. Mrs. Ezfahani had an arrhythmia and was also seriously dehydrated, so further tests would be necessary. The men demanded to be allowed to follow her to Jorvi, and Reza attempted to climb into the ambulance as it was leaving. It took a good amount of police muscle to keep him out of the vehicle.

"Shall we proceed without the mother?" I asked Ruuskanen, though part of me wanted to dismiss the interpreter so she could go help Noor. The older woman's Finnish was passable, but medical terminology wasn't usually the first thing covered in language classes. But Jorvi was a big place—maybe they would be able to find another Persian speaker there.

There was a scratch on Rahim Ezfahani's cheek, left by his aunt's blow. Ruuskanen drove the men back into the conference room like a sheepdog with a flock. I walked back next to Vafa, and I could hear his stomach rumbling. He was eighteen years old, ideal cannon fodder for any army in any country, and he looked like he was on the verge of tears. Apparently, the combination of his sister's death and his mother's fit was too much for the boy.

We sat down in the circle again, and Ruuskanen began to press Jalil about what he'd meant when he'd said Noor was promised to her cousin Rahim. Jalil claimed that he hadn't said it at all, that the interpreter had misunderstood him, and the other men backed him up. The interpreter's face turned bright red.

"He said it, I swear! I understand my native language just fine."

The men of the second generation, whose Finnish was the best in the group, became agitated at this and began to berate the interpreter in Persian. Her expression turned even more wretched. Her feet were clad in elaborately decorated boots, which she swung under her chair like a little girl.

"What are they saying?" Ruuskanen asked amid the tumult.

"That I'm twisting their words, that I'm on the police's side," the interpreter almost shouted.

"We want another interpreter," Farid Ezfahani said.

"This interpreter will have to do." Ruuskanen had to work to control his temper. Puupponen's eyes glinted impishly—chaotic situations appealed to his sense of humor, so long as no one was in physical danger. He'd never been very good at tolerating authority figures, and Ruuskanen wasn't exactly his favorite boss. Koivu, on the other hand, looked concerned; he understood, as I did, that the interrogation had gone off the rails and hadn't moved the investigation forward at all. Rahim Ezfahani, who sat next to me, shifted restlessly. He'd smoked a quick cigarette as we escorted Mrs. Ezfahani to the ambulance, and now he probably wanted another one. He'd tried to sit as far away from me as possible for the whole interview; even though I was old enough to be his mother, I was still a woman and dressed wrong. Years ago, when I'd taken my children on bus trips in their baby buggies, the immigrant men, particularly Somalis, were often the ones who were most willing to lend a hand. The first time I'd gratefully looked the man in the eyes and smiled, but later I realized that that was a violation of their customs. Since then, at least some of the newcomers must have adapted to Finnish women behaving differently than they were used to. I'd worn a headscarf in Afghanistan, but in Finland I could wear my hair down and smile at anyone I wanted to.

Ruuskanen pressed the Ezfahanis about why they hadn't contacted the police when Noor didn't come home. Noor's father said that they hadn't wanted to bother the police, that they'd hoped she'd just fallen asleep at a friend's house. He said this in Finnish, pausing now and then to search for the right word.

"Did Noor often stay out overnight?" Koivu asked.

"No. Noor good girl."

"Did she say that she might not come home on Tuesday?"

"No. Everything the same as always. No fight, no nothing. Everything OK."

"Did you call her friends, like Susanne Jansson, or other girls from the Girls Club?"

"We not have their number."

"You could have gotten it from Information."

"We not bother strangers at night. When Noor not at grandfather's house, we try sleep. Not able very much."

The other men repeated the story: they'd gone home, and a little later Hamid came over to see if Noor had stopped by for a visit. No one had heard from her, and they hadn't been able to reach her cell phone. Noor's telephone records would tell us if she'd used her phone on Tuesday night. All the family members claimed they hadn't been able to get in touch with Noor after six p.m., just as Tuomas Soivio had said. Where had she disappeared to?

The Ezfahanis stuck to their story, and we didn't have any evidence that a family member had been party to Noor's killing, so eventually we had to cut them loose. Before they left, Ruuskanen forbade any of them from leaving the country and received a cutting reply from Grandfather Ezfahani in return.

"We're not going anywhere until Noor has been buried the right way!"

Once they were gone, we discussed the interview, and everyone seemed just as frustrated as I was. In Puupponen's opinion, the men had seemed agitated, but that didn't mean much; few people would be calm right after a close relative's murder. Koivu said he had watched Noor's mother, who'd struggled to keep her expression in check throughout the entire interview.

"That woman is the weakest link. It would be a good idea to question her alone. Maybe I could go with Maria," Koivu suggested, "once she's able to talk."

"You have to admire them. They played together like a pro hockey team," Timonen said.

"More like a soccer team," Puupponen corrected. "The strategy they agreed on held. Only the mother sent a stray ball."

"Maria, since you're a woman—," Ruuskanen said.

"Very astute observation, Detective," Puupponen interrupted.

"Could you be quiet for once?" Ruuskanen roared like a teacher to a misbehaving student. "Now, since you're a woman, and a mother, how likely do you think it is that a mother would protect her daughter's murderer?"

"I think anything is possible. Mothers even kill their own daughters. We've seen that before. And it could be that Noor senior doesn't know the truth, that only the men of the family have been initiated.

But their stories are too similar. And why didn't they go out to look for Noor? There are six able-bodied men in the family, plus the grandfather, who could have stayed behind to support the mother while the others went out to search for the girl. Their behavior doesn't seem logical, and I don't believe that it's just a matter of cultural differences."

During the interrogation the need to go to the restroom had hit me, so I was happy when Ruuskanen announced he was leaving to go review the results of the forensic investigation. I rushed to the nearest ladies' room. In it there was a sink and two stalls, one of which was occupied. I went into the free stall and did my business. I could hear a strange whimpering coming from the other stall.

The doors of the stalls didn't go all the way to the floor, but the wall between them did, so I couldn't see the shoes of the woman using the other stall. When I went to wash my hands, I bent over and looked underneath the door, where I saw the same low-heeled black suede boots with gold fringe that had been swinging in front of me for the last couple hours.

I stood up, dug my makeup bag out of my purse, and began to apply some mascara, though I already had plenty on. I added a layer, separated my lashes with a comb, and then added another layer; I was starting to look ridiculous.

The whimpering had stopped. Whoever was in the stall had not come out, so I decided to make a feint and opened the restroom door. I stepped out, waited a moment, and then slipped back in. The interpreter, whose name I couldn't recall, was rinsing her face. Her eyes were teary, and she blushed violently when she saw me.

"Are you OK?" I asked. "What's wrong?"

"I . . . I didn't make a mistake! They were lying." The interpreter's face contorted as she tried to hold back her tears.

"That happens. People change their stories. Sometimes they aren't even lying intentionally."

"But the oldest man said to me that I was putting them in danger with my poor translations, that I'm a stupid woman who shouldn't be allowed to work as an interpreter. That I lie to the police."

"The oldest man? You mean Reza Ezfahani, the victim's grandfather? Did he threaten you?"

"I've helped them a few times, explaining taxes and things like that, and I was with Rahim and a couple other boys in court when they were in that gang fight last year. Rahim didn't like that the interpreter was a woman. They think I've become too Finnish, that I'm on the side of the Finnish police, not my own people."

I was sure that they'd discussed the role of the interpreter during her training—interpreters aren't supposed to interpret, but rather translate as directly as possible. What was said wasn't the interpreter's responsibility, and of course the interpreter was supposed to be impartial. A person who couldn't stand conflict wouldn't last very long in that profession.

I looked for a highlighter in my makeup bag so I would have an excuse for extending the conversation.

"Does that help with redness?" the interpreter asked as I dabbed it on.

"Yeah, it covers it up a little. Do you want some?" She held up her hand, and I smeared a little makeup on the back of it. The shade was too light for her, but so be it. If sharing makeup helped create a sense of sisterhood, it was worth it.

"Did you leave anything out, other than the insults directed at you? There was a lot going on—the Ezfahanis and the police were talking over one another so fast at times."

The interpreter dabbed the highlighter under her eyes and then assessed her face in the mirror. She was about thirty, graceful and thin skinned; there were already small lines at the corners of her eyes. Her eyebrows were dark and thick, and her lashes didn't need any extra mascara. Interpreters were invaluable to the police, and I didn't want to intimidate this woman, whose name I still couldn't remember. Had Ruuskanen even mentioned it?

"The whole time I had the feeling that it wasn't about what was being said but what was being left unsaid. As if every word was precious and had to be conserved. Previously, Farid, Rahim, and Jalil were talkative, even at the tax office and in the courtroom. Today they didn't talk much at all. Maybe it's because they're sad. I don't know."

"Do you remember the reason for the skirmish between Rahim and his friends and those Finns? Who started the fight?"

It was the usual story. The gangs had been eyeing each other at the Big Apple Mall, and when the guards came to shoo them away, the teenagers moved to the courtyard of a nearby apartment building. The Iranian gang asked the Finns to let them be, and when they didn't, Rahim was the first to blow up. He tried to chase off the leader of the Finnish contingent, who then pulled a knife, at which point Rahim grabbed the nearest bicycle as a weapon. The others joined in the fray, and residents in the surrounding buildings called the police.

"People are afraid of what they don't know. Rahim only wants to be with Iranians. He thinks Finnish customs are dangerous, that they eat away at our own wonderful thousands-of-years-old culture, which was flourishing when the Finns were still living in igloos and gnawing on pine bark."

I laughed. It appeared that everything Rahim Ezfahani had heard during his social integration course had gone in one ear and out the other, possibly because he didn't want to learn what was being taught. It's easier to hate when you don't know much about what you're hating.

"His father, Farid, tried to calm him down when we were at the tax office. He said that the system was good, that it takes care of people, that Rahim should be thankful to the Finns, who had accepted the family. Rahim talks a lot about returning to Iran, but there aren't any relatives there anymore. His mother didn't make it through the refugee camp, his sister died in childbirth, and his brother-in-law was killed. The family experienced a lot of grief even before Noor's death."

"Did you know Noor?"

"I'd seen her a few times, but I'd never spoken with her. People said she was extremely smart, that she had a mind as sharp as a diamond."

Suddenly the door to the restroom swung open; my nose told me it was Ursula before I saw her.

"Hey, Kallio! It looks like we might have our breakthrough!" Ursula looked triumphant, but then she noticed the interpreter and went quiet. She slipped into a stall, from which then came the sound of buttons and a belt hurriedly being undone.

"I managed to miss your name during the introductions," I said to the interpreter. "What is it?"

"Gullala. It means 'tulip.' Did you still have something you wanted to talk about . . . Your name is Maria, right?"

"Yes. Let's talk later, when things settle down. I have to escort you to the lobby; you can't get out otherwise." It was a wonder she'd been allowed to stay in the building without anyone noticing her. Maybe the male police officers hadn't presumed to follow her into the restroom.

I walked Gullala down to the lobby. Business hours were over, so it was empty, and I had to let her out of the inner door. A patrolman named Akkila was drowsing at the crime reporting station between the doors. He'd been in the department since the new police station had been dedicated in 1996 and was known for his incredibly poor human relations skills. The police academy psychological tests had really failed with him, and I couldn't understand why he of all people would be stuck out here to meet the frantic citizens who came to report break-ins and assaults.

I went back upstairs, because I wanted to hear what Ursula had meant by a breakthrough. I finally caught up with her in the Violent Crime conference room, which was also functioning as the nexus for

Noor's murder investigation. Ruuskanen was there too; no one else was around.

"I found two neighbors who confirmed that Rahim Ezfahani sometimes drives a gray Toyota Corolla; it's a model from the midnineties," Ursula was saying. "According to the database, he doesn't have a Finnish driver's license."

"Was anyone able to tell you the license plate number of this gray Corolla?"

"Not exactly. One remembered that the first letter was a *C,* and the other recalled that the numbers at the end were 235, her daughter's birthday. According to the two witnesses, the owner is 'some Arab.' Their words, not mine. One was a Finn and the other a Russian. I'm going to start looking for the car in the motor vehicle registry."

"So, you discovered that Noor's older cousin might have a car at his disposal. Was that your breakthrough?" I asked Ursula.

"Isn't that enough? Was I supposed to find the murderer all by myself while the six of you sat here on your asses?"

"I didn't say anything about it being enough or not being enough. Of course this will affect things, especially since Rahim is one of the main suspects. It would be great if we could find that car and get Forensics working on it."

"If you didn't stick your nose into things that aren't any of your business, I'd already be looking for it," Ursula hissed and then walked out.

Ruuskanen stared at me with a self-satisfied look on his face.

"You two really do love each other," he said with a laugh. .

"Ursula is a good police officer."

"I still wouldn't assign her to interview a Muslim man, or if I did, she'd have to dress down for it. I've felt like calling her out on her clothes more than once. She looks more like a client of the old Vice Squad than a police officer. But I'd probably get a fake nail in the eye if I tried." Ruuskanen perched on the corner of the table. "Keep in touch with Koivu over the weekend. He's going to find out when we can visit Mrs. Ezfahani at the hospital. Rasilainen found out some interesting things while she was walking around the Ezfahanis' neighborhood too, and Puustjärvi is supposedly coming back from the autopsy any moment."

"That took long enough."

"Apparently the bone saw broke. Murphy's Law. I'm going to send another statement to the media as soon as I've talked with Puustjärvi. If your cell doesn't have something else going on, as far as I'm concerned you can go enjoy your weekend."

In a way it was a relief not to have to direct this murder investigation. At most I might need to hold the rudder sometimes and watch to make sure others kept the sails trimmed. I promised Ruuskanen that I'd be available by phone the whole weekend, and then I went back to our case room, where Puupponen and Koivu were sitting at their computers.

"I got an e-mail from the Bosnian police," Koivu announced.

"About Sara Amir?"

"Yeah. A girl named Sara Amir, born 1995, was registered for school last week in the city of Bihać. She doesn't have a passport or any other identification papers with her. The woman who registered her for school claims to be her aunt. According to her, the girl is from the countryside, and her identification papers were lost in the same fire in which the girl's family died. There isn't any record of a fire fitting that description, though. The police are going tomorrow to determine if this Sara Amir is the same girl who disappeared from Espoo."

"Tomorrow? Why not immediately? If she's our Sara, she might just disappear again. Have you notified her parents?"

"It probably isn't a good idea to raise false hopes. I'm going to wait to see what our colleagues in Bosnia find out. I'm leaving now, but I'll check my e-mail once I get home and let you know immediately if anything comes up. We should go to the hospital the moment

Mrs. Ezfahani is ready to talk." Koivu sighed deeply, logged out of the e-mail system, and turned off his computer. He removed his glasses and rubbed his face. When had such a deep furrow appeared on his forehead?

"Say hi to Anu and the kids. I'll be off to see my own soon too. Let's be in touch."

Puupponen's fingers were flying on the keyboard, his left hand quickly moving the mouse back and forth. "I'm looking for comments about Rahim's gang's throwdown with those Finns last fall. I mostly want to see if any of the commenters on the fight have usernames that match those of the people who've commented on Noor's murder. That will help me judge the reliability of the rumors I'm seeing."

"Is there anything new or interesting?"

"Nothing earth shattering. The online rumor mill thinks the family is guilty. I'd be willing to bet that the username 'In Memory of Noor' is either Tuomas Soivio or one of his good friends, since he knows so many details about how he ended up at the police station. At least he has the sense not to post the names of the officers who questioned him. I'm going to go through these one more time. What do you think? Would it be a good idea to throw some bait into the net, add a little bad information?"

"Like what?"

"Well, say for example that Noor was seen getting into a gray Corolla—I heard about Ursula's find. Maybe that would spawn something."

"Don't say anything about the Corolla if you want us to find it. Ursula is looking for it right now. And besides, you'd need the lead investigator's permission to plant any false rumors, like you would for an undercover drug buy. Are you going to be hanging around here long?"

"As long as I need to. I'm not in a hurry to get home."

"OK. Well, have a good weekend."

I stopped by my office, put my family pictures back on the desk, and then left. A familiar figure stood at the bus stop closest to my house: my father. Ever frugal, he had wanted to ride the bus to Helsinki instead of taking a cab. He was staring fixedly in the direction the bus would arrive from, which was opposite the direction I was coming from, so he didn't notice me. He looked strangely frail in his knee-length, dark-gray winter coat and blue brimmed hat.

My dad had always been a very strong man. He wasn't especially tall, but he was well muscled and, at my uncle Pena's farm, had been able to lift shockingly heavy sacks and logs like they were nothing. My mother, on the other hand, had barely been able to carry two full water pails from the summer kitchen to the barn.

As a little girl I'd admired my father's strength and wanted to be just like him. I'd worked hard to follow in his footsteps. Now I looked back on my bravado with amusement. I'd spent so much time trying to prove that I was just as good as the boys. But my desperate desire to keep up had been a sign of how little I valued my own gender. Had my father demanded that of me? There probably wasn't an easy answer to that question.

"Hi." Dad jumped at my voice. He obviously hadn't heard me approach. "When is the bus supposed to come?"

"Antti said it should be here in a few minutes. I like to be early, since you never know about these things."

"So, Antti is at home?"

"He came home early, at three thirty. He's cooking some sort of bread. Starts with an *f*."

"Focaccia. Yum."

"How was your day at work? Any progress?"

"A little."

"The news at noon said there had been an attack on that police academy of yours in Afghanistan. At least three students were killed. Hopefully no one you knew. Here comes the bus!"

I watched as Dad climbed aboard and then let the weight of that news wash over me. I felt like running to the nearest computer to look it up. If the first report said three people died, it was likely the actual total was much larger. The strike wasn't a surprise—there had been danger in the air since the school opened. Of course the drug lords didn't like that we were trying to create a force in the country that would threaten their operations. Some of them funded the Taliban and Al-Qaeda, and when you captured one bad guy, two always popped up in his place.

At home it smelled like rosemary and garlic. Taneli was helping his father make a salad, and I couldn't see Iida. I went into the bedroom to turn on my computer, and while I was waiting for it to come to life, I took out my jewelry box, which still had Ulrike's necklace in it. I got it out and carefully inspected every detail, searching for seams or cracks that would reveal something hidden inside. I didn't find anything. After thinking for a moment, I took out my smallest jewelry box, which had once had a pair of earrings in it. The necklace just barely fit. I fetched some cotton balls from the bathroom and lined the box with them. Then I wrapped it in newspaper and a plastic bag and put the whole assemblage in an empty ice cream container. I stuck a label on the top and wrote *Mushrooms* and a date in September on it. I showed the container to Antti in the kitchen.

"I'm putting this in the freezer. Don't ask why."

"Why?" Antti said anyway, but I had already gone back into the bedroom, where the computer had finally booted. I clicked my way to the Finnish Broadcasting news site: "Bomb Attack at Finland-Supported Police Academy in Afghanistan. At Least Three Students Killed." The picture that showed the familiar building looked, based on the season, like it had been taken just after the school opened. The article was brief, and I didn't find anything more on the NBC, BBC, or *New York Times* sites.

I dashed off a quick e-mail to Muna, Uzuri, and Sayeda, though the attack could have destroyed the school's Internet connection. I wanted to do more, but I was thousands of miles away and utterly powerless. I dug out the ten-afghani bill I'd been carrying around as a memento. The banknote was decorated with a greenish-brown picture of a palace and an edifice that looked for all the world like a European triumphal arch. I looked at the money for a moment and then put it in my drawer. I'd been saving it in case I went back to Afghanistan someday. I didn't know if I would ever be up to that again.

Then it was time for dinner. Antti had made Italian fish stew, pistou, and the focaccia my dad had mentioned. On a normal Friday night, I would have joined him for a glass of white wine, but because of the news about the explosion I felt like I was on standby. Iida asked about the investigation into Noor's killing, but I couldn't tell her anything more than that the work was coming along.

When my phone rang at seven thirty, I knew immediately that it couldn't mean anything good. I couldn't put my phone on silent, because someone from work might call. Lauri Vala's name flashed on the display. *Shit.*

"Why aren't you answering?" Taneli asked, and Jahnukainen stared disapprovingly at the device, which was playing a riff from Juice Leskinen's "Police Academy" as its ringtone. Puupponen had put it on my phone during a boozy night the previous summer, when he and I and the Koivus had been on a pub crawl around Helsinki.

"Not interested." Finally, the noise stopped, but then the voice mail notification chime sounded. Jahnukainen started rubbing against my legs. I looked under the sofa to find one of his toy mice on a string and started playing with him. Venjamin got up from his lounging spot by the fireplace, which for once was spick-and-span because my father had not only vacuumed but scrubbed it. The cats soon lost interest in the mouse and instead started fighting with each other. Whenever they noticed a person was watching, they would stop, looking sheepish, but after a moment go right back to their play.

When my cell phone rang again, my first thought was that Vala was a persistent bastard, but the call wasn't coming from his number. The number looked familiar, though it wasn't a police number, so I answered.

"Hi, it's Tuomas Soivio. I have Rahim Ezfahani here, and he just admitted that he strangled Noor. Come pick him up before I kill him."

12

"Tuomas, where are you calling from?"

"From the forest near Noor's building."

"And Rahim is there too, right?"

"He's right over there, handcuffed to a tree and whining. He's probably afraid of this knife. I could cut off his balls."

"Tell me the address."

"I don't know! The patch of forest behind the bus stop west of Noor's building. He admitted that he killed Noor. Take him to jail."

"OK, I'll be right there. Don't do anything stupid."

I called for backup and got moving. I found Noor's building on the GPS. I remembered more or less what woods Tuomas meant. The patrol car got there before I did; Himanen and Sutinen happened to be on duty again, and they told me where to find them. When I arrived on scene, I found Rahim shackled to a pine tree with his limbs around the trunk. Tuomas was holding a knife to his neck, and Himanen and Sutinen were trying to convince him to back away from Rahim. To top it off, inquisitive bystanders had started to gather—the tree was next to a popular walking path. We weren't very far from the place where a murderer had once threatened to kill me if I wouldn't agree to cooperate with him. I tried to push those memories to the back of my mind. Now the most important thing was to get Rahim and Tuomas out of this situation. Both seemed like they were out of their minds. Rahim was muttering something in Persian—I couldn't tell if it was a prayer or a curse. Tuomas was crying and ranting and raving.

"I'm going to say this one more time, Tuomas: give me the knife. There's already plenty for us to charge you with: assault with a deadly weapon, unlawful detention, and brandishing an edged weapon in a public place. Don't add resisting arrest and assaulting an officer to that list," Himanen said. Sutinen and Himanen had weapons, but using them in this situation would have been too risky.

"I want him to repeat what he just admitted to me. That he killed Noor because his future wife was dating an infidel. But you wouldn't have gotten to have Noor first anyway, you fucking pig! She lost her virginity to me in December. Suck on that!"

Rahim's next words sounded like a curse. I looked at these two young men who were doing their best to ruin their lives, all for the sake of anger and revenge. The world was full of armies of frustrated teenagers, blinded by hate, who were easy to goad into fighting senseless wars. All you had to do was promise them honor, eternal life, or endless sex.

"Sutinen, call for backup to help get the bystanders under control. Tuomas, I'm going to come closer now. I want you to throw the knife at my feet. You aren't stupid. I'm sure you understand that any confession you get out of him using violence won't carry any weight in court. It's the police's job to get guilty people to confess, not amateurs like you."

I tried to keep my voice calm, even though I was on edge too. Vigilante justice was the last thing our investigation needed. The media had stayed more or less objective up to this point, but we wouldn't be able to count on that going forward. This little duel was guaranteed to lead to more gang fights, and each act of vengeance would be more brutal than the last.

I started to inch closer to Tuomas. I didn't think he had it in him to stab a police officer. And, in any case, it was unlikely a young man like Tuomas would consider a middle-aged woman like me to be a physical threat. I was nearly a foot shorter than he was. Sutinen and Himanen, both in their thirties, were the ones who represented a danger to him. I hoped my colleagues would pick up on what I was doing and move around to either side of the tree.

More civilians had joined the crowd on the forest path, having heard the racket from the bus stop and wanting to see what real-life drama was playing out on their doorsteps this evening.

"Don't you flatfoots have your peashooters with you?" an old man yelled, making some of the other onlookers burst into laughter.

"Yes! Which is exactly why I need to ask you to move farther back. Now!"

"Bossy broad, eh? So, it's the women calling the shots these days, is it?" I didn't even turn to look at him because the Black Maria's lights were already flashing through the woods. Luckily the arriving patrol hadn't turned on their sirens. They could worry about getting the bystanders away from the scene.

I stepped carefully toward Tuomas and Rahim. I was only thirty feet away now. Tuomas had stopped crying. Rahim's brow and neck glistened with sweat. Rahim looked like he believed Tuomas was capable of killing him. I didn't know whether he thought he would be crowned as a martyr in the paradise of his religion if that happened, but if he did, it didn't seem to be making him any less afraid of dying.

An extremely tall figure appeared out of the darkness, followed by another nearly a foot shorter. They both looked familiar, but I didn't remember their names immediately and couldn't make out the name tags on their uniforms.

"Break it up," the taller one said, starting to shoo the crowd like they were a flock of chickens. "This isn't a public performance."

"Don't we get to be witnesses?" the old man grumbled.

"I wouldn't recommend it. The pay is terrible, and the trials aren't televised," the shorter officer said, and I recognized Mikkola's face. He began roping off the area by stretching blue-and-white plastic tape around trees. Tuomas Soivio looked on as if a snare was slowly closing around him, and instead of being the hunter, now he was the rabbit.

As I'd hoped, Himanen and Sutinen had also started to approach Tuomas. I took another few steps. I could already make out the color of the young men's eyes, Rahim's dark brown and Tuomas's Finnish-flag blue.

"What did Rahim admit to you?"

"Just like I said on the phone! That he strangled Noor."

"Did you strangle her, Rahim?"

Noor's cousin remained silent, which made Tuomas push the blade of the knife closer to the other young man's bare neck. Rahim felt its touch and flinched.

"Say it!" Tuomas shouted.

"Shut up, Tuomas!" I barked. Rahim flinched, nodded once and then again.

The motion wouldn't have any evidentiary value, because even the worst defense attorney would be able to demonstrate that the confession had occurred under duress. I doubted anyone but Tuomas and I had seen him nod. Maybe Rahim was making a calculation too, knowing this small movement of his head might both free him from Tuomas's clutches and keep him from having to answer a murder charge.

"There you go, Tuomas. You got your confession. We both saw it, as did my colleagues here. Now you can stop. Give me the knife and unlock Rahim's handcuffs."

Tuomas turned his face from Rahim to me. I tried to look as reassuring and satisfied as I could, like a policewoman whose case had been solved with the help of an upstanding citizen, though in reality the upstanding citizen would now have to be arrested and hauled off for questioning. His defense attorney would be able to appeal to the trauma his client had experienced and the public's sense of justice. I would rather have bet on a horse I'd never heard of than on what sort of sentence Tuomas would get in the end.

I took one more step toward Tuomas. The knife he was holding looked like it had grown heavy—it was starting to pull his hand down, and when his arm was at a twenty-degree angle, the knife fell to the ground. Because I was closest, I walked the rest of the way and bent over to pick it up.

"Hands up, Soivio," Himanen shouted. He hadn't drawn his weapon. "Stay where you are. We're going to have to search you. And give me the key to those handcuffs."

Tuomas looked like he'd been betrayed in some horrible way, but he stayed put and slowly raised his hands. Himanen and Sutinen could handle frisking him. I turned my head away.

"You'll have to figure out how to open the handcuffs. I think I dropped the key when that pig tried to get away. You might be able to find it if you get a metal detector." There was ridicule in Tuomas's voice. Himanen went through the boy's pockets; all he found was a wallet, a bus pass, and two paper clips.

The tall policeman had walked to the other side of the tree Rahim was attached to and was looking appraisingly at the tightly stretched chain of the handcuffs.

"These bracelets are kiddy toys. They probably wouldn't even hold up in serious bondage play," he snorted derisively. "Hey, Mikkola, do we have those bolt cutters in the van? They'd slice through this chain like a hot knife through butter, and then we could jimmy the lock with a paper clip once we get back to the station."

"Did you have a bad experience with toy handcuffs like that?" Mikkola asked his partner with a grin. The situation had de-escalated, and now we all needed a little humor.

"You don't want to know," the tall policeman answered. I still didn't get a look at his name tag, because he left to get the tools from the vehicle.

It was already growing late, and I really didn't feel like spending my Friday night doing more interviews, but my mental law book said that even though we had multiple grounds for detaining Tuomas Soivio, the same was not true of Rahim Ezfahani. Despite that nod of his head, he was the victim here, not the suspect. On the other hand, the best time to question Rahim would be right now, while he was still frightened. Tuomas could spend the night in a cell thinking about how idiotically he'd behaved. We would also take Rahim down to the station so he could tell us what Tuomas had done to him before the police showed up. If he wanted to talk about the cause of the ambush, he would of course be given that opportunity.

I sent Antti a text message saying I had to go to the station. Rahim went in the van, Tuomas in the patrol car. We wouldn't talk to him until tomorrow. Rahim was not technically under arrest, but he didn't question why he had to go with the police. I asked Himanen to wait with him in the lobby. I followed the patrol vehicles in my car, and while driving I heard a text message alert on my phone. I thought that it would be Antti responding to my text, likely commenting on how quickly the workdays had become ridiculously long after my return to active policing, but when I looked at my phone in the station parking lot, I discovered the sender was Ursula.

I'm pretty sure I've found the gray Corolla, model year 1992, license COI-235. The owner's name is Omar Hassan. Should we pick up the car for forensic analysis?

I wondered if the message had been sent only to me or if Ruuskanen had received it too. Obviously, Ursula hadn't heard about the incident with Tuomas and Rahim, so I called her.

"Hi, it's Maria. I'm in the parking lot outside the station. I'll be in shortly. We have Rahim Ezfahani with us. I'll meet you in my cell's case room."

Then I started to think about what tactic to use with Rahim. Ursula and I could play bad cop/bad cop, but would intimidation get us results? Or would sympathy and kindness work better? And would he even be able to understand us? This late at night we might not be able to get an interpreter. I left the car in the parking lot but went in through the back door, which was used by employees only. I got a double helping of coffee from the vending machine and a sparkling water—it was time for the big guns. Then I went hunting for Ursula.

"Good work with the car. Does Ruuskanen know?"

"Oh, I think I forgot to send him the message. My fingers must've slipped."

"You need permission from the lead investigator for a forensic analysis."

"Oh, OK." Ursula shrugged dramatically. "But I want to get my hands on that Toyota ASAP."

"Remember that civilians usually don't know how little it takes to put together good forensic evidence. No matter how thoroughly the car has been cleaned and vacuumed, we may still be able to find fibers and fingerprints. Call Ruuskanen so we can pick it up today. I think the suspicion that Rahim might have had access to the car will be enough at this point."

I told Ursula about what had happened in the forest. Any police officer could sense the opportunity the confession gave us to solve the case, but Ursula was more enthusiastic about the forensic evidence than Rahim himself. We agreed that I would get in touch with Ruuskanen about both issues: questioning Rahim and what we were going to do with the car. I had to leave two messages on Ruuskanen's voice mail before he called me back.

"Well, so arrest him already!" Ruuskanen said over the phone, exasperated. "I mean the Ezfahani boy. I would have thrown him in a cell days ago, but I was afraid that all the PC bleeding-heart liberals would accuse me of racism. And make sure the Soivio brat doesn't talk to the tabloids. Damn it! His little stunt is going to be all over the web."

Ruuskanen didn't sound entirely sober, but I didn't know him well enough to judge his degree of intoxication. He wasn't on duty, but in theory leadership of the investigation was his responsibility 24-7.

Obviously, I wouldn't be getting him down to the station tonight, so we arranged to talk on the phone the next day. Someone would have to question Tuomas Soivio, and I was sorely afraid that someone would be me.

I went to the bathroom to splash cold water on my face. It washed off the last of my makeup, not that how I looked mattered. Another text came in, this time from Lauri Vala. I remembered that I hadn't listened to his voice mail yet. There was no point putting it off, since the rest of the night was going to be one disagreeable thing after another anyway. I punched in my passcode and discovered a voice mail and a text.

"Vala here. You probably already heard. Your work has been bombed to shit. Omar Jussuf, the drug lord, made good on his threats. You should have listened to me. Call me, Kallio. I think I can help you."

The text message was more of the same: *Is something wrong with your phone? Call me ASAP.*

Just having Lauri Vala's name in my telephone irritated me. I felt like erasing it, but then I might accidentally answer one of his calls. At some point I would have to talk to him, but now was not the time. I used my phone to check if I'd received any new e-mails. My inbox was empty. I imagined my former students had other things to do right then than reply to my message. At that very moment they might be digging through the ruins of the police academy, trying to save those who were still trapped. Perhaps they were waiting to be rescued themselves. My powerlessness ate at me.

I sent an appeal for protection upward, even though I didn't know whose god I was addressing. Every now and then I had a confused theological discussion with Pastor Terhi Pihlaja while we were out Nordic walking together. I would have liked to believe in a higher power, but I didn't know how to articulate what that was, and I got annoyed with myself for being so indecisive. Saying I had faith, just not in the way the churches teach, sounded so hackneyed. Antti was a committed atheist, but sometimes I wanted to believe that everything had a purpose. Pastor

Pihlaja claimed I didn't need to analyze so much. Faith and doubt didn't rule each other out. Doubting was something I could do.

Himanen and the tall policeman were with Rahim in the Violent Crime Unit's conference room. One of them had started the coffee machine, and the smell of cheap grounds and the rarely cleaned pot wafted through the air. The tall policeman was picking the lock on the handcuffs, which were still around Rahim's wrists.

"Welcome to metal shop class," he said, laughing. "This wasn't as simple as I thought. I can coax this one open, but that other one is going to need cutters. It's messing up the blood flow to his wrist, so we have to get it taken care of now. Mikkola went to find tools."

Rahim was still pale, and he sat with his eyes closed, mumbling to himself. The tall policeman got Rahim's right wrist free. The handcuff had pressed into the skin, leaving behind a deep red indentation, which oozed blood in places. It would have to be cleaned and bandaged. I turned toward the first aid cabinet, which used to be in the corner of the conference room, but it wasn't there anymore.

"Where can I find Band-Aids, gauze, and disinfectant?" I asked Himanen.

"In the locker room. Should I go get some?"

"Yes, please. Then you and Sutinen can go about your business. I can manage here. Rahim, do you want coffee or something else to drink? Should I let someone know that you're at the police station?"

No reaction. My head was starting to hurt—I should have asked Himanen for some ibuprofen for myself. Mikkola came back with some heavy-duty bolt cutters, and the tall policeman took them from him. The beanpole clearly enjoyed this. He ordered Mikkola to hold Rahim's left hand in place and then started breaking the hinge of the handcuff. It wasn't easy, because there wasn't any space between the metal and the skin. Rahim opened his eyes, and the last of the color drained from his face when he saw the compound cutters.

"Don't cut it off!" he screamed, startling us. The bolt cutters slipped from the tall man's hands.

"I have to. Otherwise we can't get it off."

"Not my hand. I'm not a thief!"

"Rahim, we don't cut thieves' hands off in Finland," I said quickly. I could have added that at least the police didn't; some criminal gangs had taken up the barbaric practice. Even worse was done to murderers.

Though my Afghan students had been an enlightened group, with some of them I'd been forced to have long philosophical discussions about the justness and equity of sentences, because some of them strongly supported capital punishment. I remembered a discussion in which Ulrike Müller had reported crying when Saddam Hussein was executed. Not for Saddam Hussein's sake, since he was pure evil. Ulrike's tears had flowed in shame because, by allowing Saddam's execution, we had lowered ourselves to his level. We weren't supposed to demand an eye for an eye anymore. It was the twenty-first century, after all. But there would always be people who thought our punishments were too lenient.

The tall policeman couldn't get the handcuff open, so he started in with a hacksaw. Himanen returned with the first aid supplies, and I began to clean and bandage Rahim's other wrist. The young man sat, completely passive, seeming to have lapsed into his own world in which none of the rest of us were allowed. Sometimes his lips moved, but there was no sound.

By the time the tall officer got Rahim's left wrist free, the boy's fingers were completely numb. The policeman rubbed them for a while, and then I bandaged them.

"Do you need anything else?" Mikkola asked, nursing his cup of coffee. "They're shorthanded out in the field, and it's Friday night."

"Go on. And hey, let's be careful out there!"

Mikkola was probably too young to understand the *Hill Street Blues* reference, but the tall policeman laughed and replied that he was always careful. Then they were gone. Now it was just Rahim and me, and he was still in another reality. I'd have to find a way to get in there with him.

"Rahim?" I said, testing the waters. "Does your wrist hurt? Do you need some painkillers?"

He opened his eyes, glanced at me quickly and then at the rest of the room, and closed his eyes again. I wasn't sure what I was seeing. Was he unable to see me, or did he just not want to? Was being alone with a woman without a headscarf so dangerous that he couldn't even look at me? If that was the problem, then my situation was hopeless. I tried again.

"Rahim, Tuomas Soivio shouldn't have handcuffed you. He's going to be facing criminal charges for doing that to you. Do you understand?"

A slow nod.

"You should tell me how Soivio captured you. If you need an interpreter, we can arrange one, but not until tomorrow. You would have to spend the night at the police station. If you tell me what happened, you might be able to go home by tomorrow."

Now Rahim's color was more normal, but he still didn't open his eyes. Because I was addressing him as a victim instead of as a suspect, I didn't need to worry about getting him a lawyer. I gave him time to search for words as the clock ticked on the wall, reminding me that Taneli had gone to bed ages ago. Finally, he opened his eyes but kept them glued to the floor. Then he spoke in a quiet voice.

"Don't know anything. Tuomas came to bus stop and threaten to hit me with knife. Put on handcuff. Me told send away from Finland if fight again, so I not fight. Tuomas take to forest, put on tree."

"Did he ask you if you murdered Noor?"

Rahim nodded.

"What did you say?"

"Not say anything. Tuomas not police."

"He claimed that you admitted you murdered your cousin."

His brown eyes closed again.

"He said kill if no say what he want."

"You admitted to doing it because you didn't want to die?"

Rahim nodded.

My head was hurting even more. I was sure even Rahim would be able to hear the pounding in my temples. The smell wafting from the coffee machine became increasingly difficult to bear, and the siren that suddenly screamed to life outside sliced right through my head. I stood up and turned off the coffee machine, picked up the filter, and emptied it into the trash can, which had finally been upgraded to a system for separating recyclables. Thin snowflakes were falling outside again. It might not be too long before snow was a distant memory here in southern Finland and all that would fall would be rain. It felt crazy to think there might come a time when we would long for sleet.

I walked back to Rahim and sat down in the chair across from him.

"You confessed to Tuomas because you didn't want to die. But were you telling the truth? Did you strangle Noor?"

Rahim didn't answer, but tears started running down his cheeks.

13

Rahim ended up spending the night in the cell next to Tuomas Soivio. I didn't get anything more out of him; he just continued to cry. I decided to try again the next day with an interpreter, unless Ruuskanen wanted to handle the interrogation himself. I was also preparing myself to take responsibility for Rahim's arrest if anyone raised a ruckus about it. My police sense told me that keeping him locked up while his friend's car was with Forensics would be justifiable. Maybe he wasn't just a young man who'd been scarred by the refugee camps and was mourning the death of his last female cousin. He might also be his cousin's murderer. I wasn't a psychologist or a clairvoyant, so I didn't know how a night in jail would affect him.

I walked home because I needed some fresh air and exercise. The cold had brought frost with it, creating a sheet of ice over the puddles. It was a quiet Friday night in our neighborhood, though there were lights visible in almost all of the houses. There wasn't any music playing, and no one was out and about except for a lone smoker on a terrace. It wasn't until just before our yard that I passed a dog walker, but I didn't recognize her. As I entered the yard, a taxi pulled into the driveway. It was my dad coming back from his party. I stayed outside, waiting for him while he paid the driver. The walkway was slippery, and I didn't know how boozy class reunions for math teachers got. At least the way he was walking didn't indicate excessive imbibing.

"Hi," he said in surprise. "Where have you been at this hour?"

"I had to stop by work again. Was the party good?"

"Well, if realizing that we're all old and that some of us are already in the grave is good, then yes. Are the children asleep?"

Taneli's window was dark, but there was still a light on in Iida's room. She was always up half the night on weekends, and Monday mornings were always full of foot-dragging. It was probably some sort of karma: my parents had had to nag me to go to sleep too.

"I was just thinking in the taxi that it's good you aren't in Afghanistan anymore. The people who died there are someone else's daughters and sons too, but at this age I don't have the energy to carry the whole world's cares. My own are enough to bear," Dad admitted as we stepped inside. "Do you have any juice? I'm thirsty."

While I hunted down some black currant juice for him, Antti came downstairs to greet us. I sent one more text message to Ursula to let her know that Rahim had not confessed, and that he would be in a cell overnight. Then I went to turn on my computer. The police academy explosion in Afghanistan was all over the Finnish media now. No one had claimed responsibility for the strike, but information about what had happened was lacking in general. The number of victims had climbed to nine, but there were still people missing. I hadn't received any messages from my students. I checked my e-mail at five-minute intervals, but no turquoise envelope icon appeared in my inbox. I tried to convince myself that that didn't necessarily mean anything ominous.

Just when I was going to bed, I saw that my phone, which was on silent, was ringing. From the beginning of the number, I could tell that the call was coming from Radio Finland. They probably wanted me to comment on the terror attack or Tuomas's rampage. I didn't feel like talking about either. Antti was still sitting up watching a French movie on Canal+. I knew I would wake up when he came to bed, but I let him watch TV in peace. The cats, on the other hand, immediately showed up at the foot of the bed, and I was just falling asleep when they started fighting.

"Rascals," I mumbled, half-awake. But then I couldn't fall asleep again. I just tossed and turned, thinking about whether I should go back to the computer. Instead I grabbed my phone and checked my e-mail. Nothing. But Lauri Vala had decided to grace me with another text. I begrudgingly opened the messaging app, hoping Vala would know something about my students.

"If I were you, I'd take out more life insurance, Kallio. If those drug lords decide to take revenge for founding a police academy on their turf, no one will be safe anywhere."

The smell of explosives and burned flesh returned to my nose. That same smell now hung over the ruins of the police academy. The powers that be in Finland had been squabbling all fall and winter about how seriously Finland should participate in the ISAF forces' operations in Afghanistan and whether Finland was at war or not. I'd lived my own childhood and teenage years in the shadow of the Cold War and fear of the bomb. Finland had the Agreement of Friendship, Cooperation, and Mutual Assistance with the Soviet Union, which in theory meant that in the event of an attack on our eastern neighbor through Finland, Finland was supposed to defend its WWII-era enemy. We'd been cowed by visions of American bombs falling from the sky, even though there was hardly anything in Finland that would have interested the United States. We were just a convenient buffer zone between East and West.

In the twenty-first century, it felt like religions had built much higher fences than political ideologies ever had. All around these new walls hung the gnawing awareness that, the way things were going, there wasn't going to be enough food or water for everyone. It wasn't possible to ensure a Finnish-style standard of living for everyone. It was easy to think the flood would come during our lifetimes, but it was harder to see any further than that. During my own parents' lifetimes, the world had changed so completely that *their* parents would never have believed it. People composed broadside ballads about the war in Japan and the sinking of the *Titanic*, but it took weeks for the message the songs contained to circle the globe. My father recalled the ballad about the *Titanic* as being one of the great horror stories of his childhood. Finland, as a grand duchy of Russia, had citizens fighting in Japan, and Finns died in the *Titanic* disaster, so even though these events occurred far away, they became a part of my father's life. Now there was no refuge from war, not even in neighboring Sweden, which had lived in peace for almost two hundred years.

I fell back asleep, and my dreams carried me to Afghanistan, to the police academy, shiny and new, the cold stone and ruddy wood floors gradually being covered with rugs, bookshelves, and decorations. Before my trip I'd seen pictures of the building in various stages of completion. Their own new building was a magnificent symbol of the country's efforts to create a democratic, corruption-free police force, but more important than the building were the people who worked in it. In my dream I was listening to Uzuri's Pashto recitation again, but it was interrupted by a young girl in a headscarf who rushed into the room yelling in Finnish: "Everybody out, the building is rigged with explosives!" In the dream I recognized the girl's face: she was the Afghani girl who had disappeared in January, Aziza Abdi Hasan, whom I had never seen except in pictures. I awoke to a terrible crash and at first didn't know where I was. Afghanistan? But soon I could make out the outlines of our bedroom, traced by the light from the streetlamps shining through the shades, and Antti, who swore as he lay next to me.

"Effing cats. We shouldn't let them in the bedroom! They were fighting with each other again and knocked my book off the nightstand. It's only six. Let's try to get some more sleep."

I tossed and turned for a while but couldn't get back to sleep. Antti started to snuffle, and from downstairs came my father's chain saw snoring. He'd forgotten to attach the ball to his pajama top to stop him from rolling onto his back. For once he was getting to sleep in the position he preferred.

I got up to go to the bathroom and brought along my phone. No text messages, one e-mail from Ursula. It had been sent to me and Ruuskanen.

"I got ahold of the Corolla's owner. He freely admitted to having loaned his car to Rahim Ezfahani and claims that he thought Rahim had a legal driver's license. He was afraid of the police, or at least of me. Or he thought that I was tempting him to sin because I wasn't wearing a headscarf. The car is in our possession and on the way to Forensics."

The message had been sent at 3:32 a.m. Anyone would have been afraid if the police came ringing the doorbell in the middle of the night and started asking questions about whether the family's Corolla had been loaned to anyone recently. Ruuskanen hadn't answered the message yet. I finally admitted to myself that I was fully awake and tiptoed down to the kitchen to turn on the coffee maker and pull on clean running clothes from the drying line. I drank a cup of coffee with cream and went outside into the cold.

I ran at a relatively leisurely pace for a half an hour, more to clear my head than to actually exercise. Since the Afghanistan trip I'd been having nightmares on and off, and the best medicine had been getting outside. The skyline glowed promisingly—today I might even need sunglasses. The winter had entailed record-breaking snowfall, but soon the coltsfoot would emerge and the blackbirds would start warbling. Completely irrationally, I felt happy. Hell, at least I was alive and able to run on my own two feet, though it had been a good while since my fortieth birthday, and without the dye bottle my hair would have streaks of gray.

My cheerfulness fell flat once I went inside. Dad had woken up, made more coffee, and turned on the TV. He'd muted it and put on the subtitles so as not to disturb the others.

"Twenty dead," was the first thing he said as I started stretching and reading the news ticker. Vala had been right for once: the drug lords were the prime suspects in the bombing. One of the main goals of Afghanistan's reconstituted police force had been to get the flourishing drug trade under control. Afghanistan produced 90 percent of the world's heroin. If even half of that could be taken off the market, the distributors' financial losses would be enormous.

After a shower I read the morning paper, which also reported on the bombing. The paper had a grainy picture of the smoking building, apparently taken by a cell phone. An American agency was credited for the image. Even though I couldn't help but imagine the stench of burning in my nostrils, I forced myself to eat a good breakfast.

There hadn't been any word from Ruuskanen, and I didn't feel like doing his work for him. Another call came in to my cell phone from the Radio Finland number. I went to the sauna to answer—it was the only place in the house where I could talk in private.

"Good morning, this is Aija Heikkinen from Radio Finland News. Am I speaking to the Detective Maria Kallio who was training instructors for the new police academy in Afghanistan and who participated in the opening ceremonies?"

"Yes, that's me."

"I'm sure you've heard by now about the terror attack at the police academy, in which at least twenty people lost their lives. Would you like to comment?"

"Are you taping this conversation?"

"Not yet. I'll ask your permission before taping."

"I don't know enough about it yet to really say anything. I'm completely dependent on the media for information right now."

"Were you threatened during the training or the opening ceremonies?"

"Not until right after the opening ceremonies. As you most likely know, our convoy was hit by a roadside bomb. But we never had concrete evidence about who carried out the attack."

"What do you think about Finland being involved in international projects of this sort? Is it sensible to invest tax revenues paid by our citizens on risky undertakings with the potential for such catastrophic losses?"

I swallowed the first answer that came to mind, that the tax revenues paid by our citizens always seemed to be going astray, no matter what they were intended for. Of course, we had to take care of the elderly and the children, and the few WWII vets still around, but investing in almost anything else always seemed to be grand larceny in someone's mind.

"It's a question of global responsibility. Founding the police academy was in the interest of Finland and other Western countries, because an active, well-organized police force will hinder the drug trade in Afghanistan." I repeated my oft-quoted rationale, which was sure to sound just as rote as it was.

"Can I have that last comment again, this time on tape?"

I repeated the sentence, and the reporter asked again if I knew whether any of the instructors trained in Finland were among the victims. I just said again that I didn't know anything about the identities of the victims.

I'd barely gotten rid of the reporter when Ursula called. She'd started canvassing the Ezfahanis' neighborhood early that morning with Puupponen, trying to find any witnesses who might have seen the gray Corolla or Rahim on the night Noor was killed.

"The initial tire-tread analysis hasn't ruled anything out. Mark my words—it was Rahim who did it. Should we put up warnings in the mosques? When this comes out, the anti-immigration types are going to be all over them."

"No provocations, Ursula," I managed to say, and then my phone beeped again. This time it was Ruuskanen. He was announcing that my cell and the Violent Crime Unit would be holding a joint meeting at the station at ten thirty. There would be no way to know how long the workday would be after that.

Taneli had skating practice, but he already knew how to use the bus, and besides, my dad could go with him. Grandpa's visit had happened to come at the perfect time.

There wasn't any more specific information in the newspaper about the terror strike than I'd seen on TV, so after finishing my breakfast I went to check online for more details. American sources were saying that communication links to the police academy were down; it was silly to draw any hasty conclusions about the fate of my students just because they hadn't answered their e-mail. I found a video clip on the CNN website and tried in vain to look for people I might recognize, but everyone was just the same faceless blob rushing back and forth. And besides, the women's heads were covered with headscarves, and after being gone for several months I couldn't remember how each of my students moved.

I discussed practical arrangements for the day with my dad and Antti, and promised to let them know once I knew when I would be coming home. My father was sewing on a button that had come off the collar of Iida's winter coat, grumbling all the while. It made me smile to remember that once he had played Tailor Halme, a sort of Finnish Don Quixote and his favorite character from Finnish literature, at the community theater in a production based on Väinö Linna's Under the Northern Star trilogy.

I didn't have the energy to put on makeup or style my hair, so I pulled my stocking cap down low over my head as I left to walk to work.

Despite the sunshine, the wind was blowing so hard that the end of my nose felt like it was freezing solid, and my eyes started to water. On my way, Söderholm, the guitarist and lead singer of the Flatfeet, texted me the date and time of our next rehearsal. It was impossible for me to commit to anything, and all of my bandmates had the same problem. Sometimes months went by before all the band members had time to practice together. We only played occasional gigs. There was always demand during the Christmas office party season, and if we were up to it, we would perform in late summer at the police department open houses in Espoo, Vantaa, and Lohja.

Söderholm was the Espoo Police Department weapons expert and a ballistics analyst with an international reputation; he was also the most un-policeman-looking man I'd ever seen. Even when he went abroad to give lectures, he wore his battered leather jacket and boots, and had been stopped by airport security more often than all of my other Finnish colleagues combined. I texted him back, suggesting that we get together for lunch when we both had time. The other members of the band were working for the Helsinki police and the National Bureau of Investigation these days.

In our ten thirty meeting, Ruuskanen wasn't exactly what you'd call perky, and Ursula also gave off a vibe suggesting she'd slept only a couple of hours, apparently on the lumpy bed in the on-call room at the station. Her makeup was minimal, and some mascara had flaked onto her cheek.

From the very beginning of the meeting, it was apparent that Ursula thought Rahim was guilty. Forensics had already found his fingerprints in the car, and under the front driver-side seat they'd found a broken bracelet with pink glass flowers and the name "Noor" in Persian script.

"Noor was in the car. I checked with her mother, and the bracelet belonged to the girl. The owner of the car denies ever having met a female cousin of Rahim Ezfahani. He isn't an Iranian; he's Somali."

"The Somali could be lying," Puustjärvi pointed out. "Who knows? Maybe he strangled the girl himself."

"Don't confuse things. I'm just saying what we know so far."

"One at a time!" Ruuskanen snapped. He didn't have a tie on, and the top couple of buttons of his shirt had been left open. A thick gold chain and graying, curly chest hair were visible through the collar opening. I hadn't noticed Ruuskanen wearing any jewelry before except a wedding ring, which was a simple, narrow band.

"The interpreter will be here at 11:15. Kallio tried to question the Ezfahani boy alone yesterday. It was a good attempt, but they won't talk to women. That's just the name of the game," Ruuskanen said.

"Oh, come on!" Ursula snapped before I had time to say anything. "Omar Hassan talked my ear off, in perfectly good English. Apparently, he lived in London before he fell in love with a Finnish au pair and followed her to Espoo. At first, he was a little shy, but then he sang like a bird. Maybe their desire to speak depends on which woman is asking the questions."

"At two in the morning I would talk too, just to be able to get back to sleep," Puupponen put in. "I looked up this Omar Hassan guy online. There's more than one person by that name in Finland, but our Omar was married to a Finnish girl and got a residency permit six years ago. The couple live at different addresses now, but they haven't divorced. And Omar is unemployed at the moment."

"But he still has enough money for a car," Ruuskanen pointed out.

"It would be nice to know if Omar lends his Corolla to people out of the goodness of his heart or if he charges for it," Ursula continued. "In any case, he's loaned the car to Rahim several times, including on the day Noor was killed. Rahim returned the car the next morning. Clean, as it always is when he borrows it. We'll see what Forensics finds. Does Rahim know how to use a car vac, or is that women's work?"

"If you talked like that about a Finnish man, I would be offended," Koivu cut in. "I have three half-Vietnamese children, two of whom look more like their mother than me. We run into this labeling constantly. How do we know Tuomas Soivio didn't kill his girlfriend himself, and now he's trying to frame Rahim? OK, Soivio has an alibi that his family and uncle are backing up. But so does Rahim. Which one are we more likely to believe? Soivio."

"Omar Hassan's story blows Rahim's alibi out of the water. Let's see what he has to say. If you want to get Tuomas Soivio to admit to doing something he didn't do, Koivu, then you can do the interrogation yourself. And take Puustjärvi with you while you're at it. The rest of us are going to stay here and question Rahim Ezfahani." Ruuskanen fingered his gold chain as he talked, freeing some chest hair that had gotten caught in the necklace.

Koivu looked at me, shaking his head. There wasn't any point in grousing about little things. Koivu was technically my subordinate, and ordering him around was my job, even though our cell was assisting Ruuskanen's unit in this homicide investigation. The sooner it was over, the faster we would be able to get back to looking for Sara, Ayan, and Aziza.

A knock came at the door, and we looked up to see Akkila from the crime reporting desk.

"Um, since there isn't anyone on the switchboard right now . . . I had to leave my station because there's a man downstairs demanding to see"—Akkila had to cheat and look at the name on a piece of paper—"the lead investigator for the Noor Ezfahani murder case. He claims his son is being held here at the station without cause."

"Mr. Soivio, presumably," Koivu whispered to me.

"Tell him we don't have time to meet anyone right now! Tuomas Soivio has been arrested legally and will be released when we're done questioning him and charges have been filed." Ruuskanen wiped the sweat off his upper lip; apparently his mustache felt hot. "Take down his phone number. I'll call him when I have time. I repeat: when I have time."

Akkila shrugged and disappeared. We went through a few more details from the forensic investigation and the autopsy report, and then Koivu and Puustjärvi left. The rest of us, seven all together, stayed to wait for Rahim Ezfahani and Gullala, the interpreter, whom Timonen, as the youngest in the group, was ordered to fetch.

Gullala arrived first, seeming keyed up. She didn't look anyone but me in the eyes. Then Rahim was brought into the room. When he saw how many police officers there were, he tried to make a break for it, but Puupponen grabbed him by the sleeve, and Timonen blocked access to the door. Thankfully, no one had put handcuffs on Rahim's maimed wrists. The bandages I'd put on the night before were still in place; they made Rahim look like a suicidal man who hadn't been able to decide which wrist he was going to slash.

Puupponen started the audio recorder and the video camera. Rahim stared at his hands as Ruuskanen, with Gullala interpreting, asked him to state his name, age, and address for the record. Rahim did so without any trouble, but when Ruuskanen started to ask questions about the events of Tuesday night, the young Iranian wouldn't say a word. Apparently, he'd had enough time in the cell to think about what the wisest course of action would be and had decided it was silence.

"Once more: Did you meet your cousin Noor Ezfahani after she left her apartment building and went to the bus stop?" Ruuskanen was starting to lose his cool, and Gullala's voice had risen a couple of octaves since the beginning of the interrogation, as she translated the same words for the tenth time. Ursula tapped the table with her fingernails. The shiny silver polish on her thumbnail had chipped a little, and her perfume smelled a day old. I could tell she was really irritated.

"There's no point trying to deny it," she said suddenly, standing up and walking straight over to the boy, who was sitting a few steps away from the rest of us. He didn't raise his eyes. "We know you did it. Translate!" she almost yelled at Gullala.

"Hey, Honkanen . . . ," Ruuskanen began.

"You be quiet! I'm not afraid of anyone accusing *me* of racism. You don't have to translate that. Instead, tell young Mr. Ezfahani that Finnish prison won't be fun for an immigrant child murderer. They might even feed you pork if you aren't careful. So, it would be best to confess now so you get off with a shorter sentence."

"Don't translate that, Gullala. Come on, Ursula, we're not at Guantanamo Bay, we're in Espoo," Koivu said, interrupting.

There was another knock at the door. This time it was Liisa Rasilainen.

"Someone is asking for you, Maria."

"We're in the middle of something!" Ruuskanen snapped.

I stood up and slipped out the door.

"Who's asking for me?"

"She says she's the mother of the murdered girl. She just stopped me in the parking lot on my way in. She said she didn't dare talk to the man who was sitting in the lobby, but that she could talk to me."

"Where is Mrs. Ezfahani?"

"She's waiting in the lobby. I had to leave her with Akkila."

Ruuskanen and company could get by just fine without me, as long as Ursula and Ruuskanen didn't come to blows. I followed Liisa down the stairs into the nearly empty lobby. Mrs. Ezfahani was standing next to the octopus mascot, stroking its yellow tentacles. Her face was completely expressionless. It was like a deep well that had permanently dried up.

"Detective Kallio. Rahim here?"

"He is currently in police custody."

"You know? He tell?"

182

"What should Rahim tell?"

Mrs. Ezfahani said something in Persian; her voice was quiet and tired. Then she flinched and continued in Finnish.

"Family is everything, and tribe, I always think. And man better . . . bigger. But man cannot kill my girl." Then she muttered something again in Persian. It sounded like she was pleading for strength.

"Rahim did it. Kill Noor. Maybe Reza kill me now, but they order it. All the men. They order, and Rahim kill my Noor."

14

As I made the trek to work on Monday morning, I felt like there was sand in my eyes. I'd slept just fine the night before, but a weekend full of work had taken its toll, and I didn't know when I would be able to take my comp time. My situation would be getting better, though, because it looked like Noor Ezfahani's murder had been solved. Rahim had not confessed—he'd stuck with the silent approach—but the evidence against him was piling up. The most damning, of course, was Noor's mother's statement. I'd gotten her a place in the Espoo women's shelter, because apparently her life wasn't worth much now that she had betrayed Rahim. I thought about how the judicial system would treat her. According to Finnish law, no one had to testify in a case that would incriminate next of kin. In Iranian culture all of the Ezfahanis were the same family, i.e., next of kin. In Finland, only the nuclear family counted. Rahim was Mrs. Noor Ezfahani's husband's nephew, so he was not a blood relative. At its most draconian, the court could charge Mrs. Ezfahani and the rest of the members of Noor's birth family with obstruction of justice. Oddly enough, Rahim's brother, father, and grandfather might be able to avoid that charge, but the prosecutors would certainly consider slapping them with aiding and abetting or even accessory to murder. Noor's mother's story felt true, but a skilled lawyer would be able to make it look like a sieve and lump her in with the rest of the family.

On Tuesday night Noor had left for the Girls Club and to meet Tuomas Soivio. The family had tried to stop her from going, because Noor's rebellion had gone too far—she wasn't wearing her headscarf at school anymore and was dating an infidel. Dinner had ended in a fight, because Grandfather Reza had forbidden Noor from leaving.

"Noor not afraid. She say Finland law on she side. No can forbid, no hit. Tuomas know, and friends at Girls Club. We have to let she go or she tell police."

But Noor had left crying, because the men of the family had called her names that her mother wasn't willing to repeat. The jealous Rahim had followed Noor. He had come to dinner in the car he had borrowed from Omar Hassan and offered Noor a ride. Though Rahim hadn't given us any details, we speculated that the young people had quarreled in the car, and at the end of the fight Rahim had strangled Noor.

When Mrs. Ezfahani came to that point, she lost her ability to speak Finnish entirely. I took her to our case room, offered her tea, and went back to the Violent Crime conference room, where they were still in a deadlock. I pulled Ruuskanen aside and repeated what Mrs. Ezfahani had told me so far.

"This could be our breakthrough. Maybe it would be a good idea to put Rahim's interrogation on hold and take Gullala over to translate for Mrs. Ezfahani."

"Why did she come tell you this all of a sudden?" Ruuskanen said, dumbfounded.

"You just said yourself that some Muslim men don't speak at all to women. The same goes the other way too. Gullala is also a woman. What if the two of us tried to get a statement out of Mrs. Ezfahani right now, which would have some actual evidentiary value? Then we'll have something concrete on the men of the family, including our main suspect."

Ruuskanen understood that the most important thing was solving the crime, not how it was solved or who actually did the solving. He shut down Rahim's questioning for the time being, sent him back to his cell, and instructed the others to pick up the rest of the family members for a new interview.

"Come with me. There's another job I need your help with," I said to Gullala. She followed me down the hall toward my case room. She didn't ask why the interrogation had been interrupted, and I didn't want to tell her where we were going. She was an interpreter after all, not a fellow officer. When she saw Mrs. Ezfahani, she nodded in deference to the older woman and straightened her headscarf.

"I'm going to be taping this conversation. Could Mrs. Ezfahani repeat in Persian what she just told me in Finnish?"

Gullala's eyes grew wide as Noor's mother's narrative progressed. Now she spoke in a perfectly calm, even voice, and I wondered if she was in shock. There were more details in the Persian version of the story. Rahim had strangled Noor as she sat in the front seat, covered her face with the scarf, and then driven to the parking lot of the Puolarmetsä community garden, where he put the body in the back seat and covered it with the floor mat from the trunk. Then he drove home and called the men of the family together for a meeting.

"Wait," I said, interrupting. "The neighbor who said she saw Noor leaving home crying Tuesday night at six claimed she didn't have a headscarf."

"She left with the scarf on her head but took it off immediately in the hallway. Or so I suppose. Of course, Rahim demanded that she put it back on. It was inappropriate to sit in the car with him with her head uncovered. And that was what started the fight. Noor didn't want to wear the headscarf anymore, didn't want Islam anymore. Is that what they were teaching her at the Girls Club?"

It felt like Gullala was joining in Noor's mother's question. I would answer her later if she still wanted to know.

"Nothing was said to me. The men just left, to smoke the water pipe and drink tea, to talk about men's business. No one came home for a long time. There was no sign of Noor. Then the men came back and ordered me to go to sleep—they were going to be up late. I said that I could not go to bed before Noor came home. Reza, my husband, said that Noor was with them. I knew at that point that all was not well. I thought that maybe they would beat her, or get an imam to marry her to Rahim, even though a marriage like that would not be legal in Finland. Noor had said that we could not force her because she had to be eighteen before she could get married according to the law. And then we wouldn't be able to tell her what to do anymore. She'd laughed when she said that, laughed in her father's face."

Mrs. Ezfahani hadn't been able to sleep, however, and instead she'd waited up and prayed that things would take a turn for the better. Allah was wise and all powerful. She had waited in her darkened room for the men to return, and when she saw them in the yard she quickly got in her bed and pretended to be asleep. But she could hear her husband and sons speaking quietly and, from the snatches of conversation, realized they hadn't beaten Noor or forcibly married her to Rahim but rather that she had been killed.

"I'd known that things would go badly when I heard about that boy. Rahim and Vafa saw Noor with him, and when they asked her who he was, Noor answered that it was none of her brother's business, and even less of her cousin's business, even though she had been promised to Rahim years ago. Noor would always do what she wanted, because in this country the law protected her. She would become a doctor who would treat both men and women. Noor was defiant and paid for it."

Gullala was barely able to keep her voice steady as she interpreted Mrs. Ezfahani's words for me, and now and then her eyes appeared to grow moist. I didn't know whether she was married, and if she was, if she had entered the matrimonial state of her own free will or if someone else had chosen her spouse. Mrs. Ezfahani continued her story as if the words were a river that had broken through a dam and were now impossible to stop.

"In the morning we got up to pray. No one said anything to me about Noor. When we prayed, I asked where she was. Reza ordered me to make tea. I said that I wasn't going to make any tea until someone told me where my daughter was. He ordered me to be silent. I made the tea. I was silent. Then the others came, without Noor, and they told me that I had to do exactly as they instructed, to say the words they told me to say, and then all would be well. But I heard during the night that it was Rahim. And Reza told me later in secret, away from the boys. He didn't want to have it weighing on his conscience. He wanted to be able to bury Noor according to Islamic tradition. He was sad. He hadn't wanted Noor to die, but he could not expose his brother's son, who had just been trying to defend his family's honor. And Reza said something even worse, but I couldn't believe it. Noor had told Rahim mockingly that he wouldn't want her anymore anyway, because she had given her virginity to that infidel boy. She must have just been teasing. That can't be true, can it? It is against everything I taught her. Did she really die having done something so terrible?"

I could imagine what had happened in the car. In anger Noor had belittled her jealous, sexually frustrated cousin. But Noor wasn't to blame for her fate. The guilty party was the one who had wrapped the headscarf around her neck and strangled her to death. I could see how Rahim had been able to convince himself that he had done the right thing. Over the course of my career I'd met enough Finnish wife beaters that I wasn't about to blame Rahim's act on his religious convictions alone. It was the unadulterated desire to possess that had been raging inside of him, though he used the old ways to justify it, the order of the world dictated by Allah.

"By Allah I had to tell, even though we may be sent back to Iran, and nothing good will come of it."

"I hardly think your residency permits will be revoked so easily. Rahim is the only one with a criminal history. I wouldn't vouch for his residency status, though."

"But what if my husband says that he will divorce me? Where will I move then? What will I live on? I probably won't be welcome at the mosques anymore. I've betrayed my family. Maybe they will kill me next." Now there was a teary sing-song quality to Noor's voice, the same sort of wailing as the professional mourners I'd seen documentaries about. Was that how things were even today—the men declared war and stirred up the masses, and the women wept over the consequences? Was that still how the world was now, at the beginning of the third millennium? I wanted to believe that humanity would be better off if there were more women in leadership roles, but it often felt like those who sought power didn't hesitate to use it for evil as well as good, regardless of gender.

After their arrest on Saturday, Ruuskanen changed interrogation tactics with the other Ezfahanis. Now they were isolated from one another and presented with a new line of questioning. Ruuskanen made it clear that next of kin meant, according to Finnish law, a direct descendant or ascendant, plus siblings. A cousin or an uncle wasn't close enough to count, so Noor's immediate family didn't have the legal right to refuse to testify against Rahim. After hearing this, Noor's younger brother, Vafa, started to cry, and then began contradicting the agreed-upon story. Koivu questioned him, and after a couple of hours, Vafa admitted that he had seen his sister dead in "some car." He was unwilling to name the perpetrator.

The Ezfahanis' interrogations would continue for days. All of the men were under arrest for the time being. Because they'd been arrested over the weekend, the cell block was busy anyway. Tuomas Soivio's father had returned to the station on Saturday afternoon and continued to demand for his son's release. Apparently, in his excitement Ruuskanen had forgotten all about Tuomas. Mr. Soivio brought a lawyer with him on his second visit, so Ruuskanen had thought it best to release the boy, but instructed him to stay reachable for upcoming questioning. I happened to be leaving just as Tuomas, his father, and their lawyer, who was none other than my school friend and short-term boyfriend Kristian Ljungberg, were making their way through the lobby, also on their way out. Kristian had been in a relationship with Ursula Honkanen a couple of years ago too, and I hoped desperately that the two of them wouldn't run into each other. I didn't feel like playing umpire.

"Maria, it's nice to see you're alive." Kristian took me by the shoulders and kissed me on both cheeks in the orthodox manner, his lips touching air, not skin. "Wasn't there some skirmish in Afghanistan in the fall? How did you end up in a place like that anyway?"

"Business, Kristian, business."

"It would appear that we have common business now. My client has been doing his best to help solve his girlfriend's murder, and as thanks the police threw him in jail for a night. A very unfortunate situation."

"You know the law as well as I do, and you know that assault and battery, assault with a deadly weapon, and unlawful detention aren't small potatoes. Charges will be brought."

"Has he confessed yet?" Tuomas interrupted.

"You mean Rahim Ezfahani? No."

"But it was him. Noor detested him."

"Let us do our work. We've been making progress." If I had been alone with Tuomas, I might have hinted that there was evidence of Rahim's guilt, but I didn't want to do it in front of Kristian. It wasn't really Tuomas's business anyway, even though Noor had been his girlfriend. My mind filled with a mixture of pity and rage when I thought about Tuomas. Did he have to go acting like some video game hero? And I had been dragged into his soap opera.

"We'll see you in court, Maria," Kristian continued. "My client called you to the scene, so for some reason he trusted you. You rewarded his trust with a trip to jail. I'm looking forward to questioning you on the witness stand."

I laughed. A lone avenger out of a video game and a sardonic defense attorney from an American courtroom drama—now there was a great pair. "Come on, Kristian. We've known each other for more than twenty years. You must know by now that intimidation doesn't work on me. I hope you all have a lovely rest of the day!" I headed for the door and turned to wave to Kristian as it closed behind me. The young policeman sitting at the crime reporting desk looked after me in confusion.

I walked home by a slightly different route than usual, cutting along a small forest path. A yellow house with wooden siding that I didn't usually walk by had gotten a new paint job since the fall, and someone had built fanciful snow creatures in the front yard. They'd already started to melt in the sun. A strange feeling of exuberance washed over me. Ulrike would never see this spring, so I had to enjoy it for her too. I'd already lived past the average life expectancy for Afghans, after all.

The lady who lived next door walked by with her children. Her daughter, Norppa, was pushing a children's-size kick sled as her little brother screamed in the stroller.

"We were just playing in the yard with your Jahnukainen," the neighbor said, "and now apparently we have to get a cat too."

"You can come over to our place to see the cats any time," I replied. I had been worried about how the neighbors would react to us letting our cats roam—we were breaking local regulations about loose animals—but so far no one had complained. Antti had a cover for the playground sandbox and did his best to make sure it was in place when no one was playing there.

When I got home, Iida ran up to me before I could take off my coat.

"Mom, did you leave so early this morning because Noor's murder has been solved? It says online that Tuomas forced Noor's cousin to confess."

"It does? On what site?"

"It's all over the place."

"Have you been surfing the web all day?" Antti and I had tried to establish ground rules for our children's Internet usage and to monitor which websites they were visiting. So far, there'd been no big problems, but now that the tabloid headlines had intruded into Iida's everyday life, it would be no wonder if the online world started to interest her more.

Iida told me the names of the sites, blushing. "The things on that racist forum were revolting, stuff like Rahim should be killed and why isn't there the death penalty in Finland. I'm glad there isn't."

"Don't go on forums like that."

I thought about who would have had time to leak the attack on Rahim. Tuomas had been under strict police custody and cut off from the Internet, so it couldn't be him. Puupponen would still be following the online conversations about the case. Maybe I didn't need to bother with it—I would get the important details from him anyway.

Now that Noor's murder was closer to being solved, I could turn my attention to what had happened at the new Afghani police academy. But Iida was the only one home and wanted some company. I boiled water for tea and chatted with her until Antti came home from the store. He recruited Iida to chop onions with him for paella, so I was finally able to get to the computer.

The Police University College spokesperson and the ISAF representative had both sent me statements about the explosion. The police college still didn't know the victims' identities, but they promised to inform me as soon as the names could be announced. The ISAF press release focused on who was responsible for the strike:

> Drug lords in the area made threats before the police academy
> was even completed, saying that they would hinder construc-
> tion activities or destroy the school later. Although no one has
> claimed responsibility for the attacks, one of the main suspects
> is the heroin producer Omar Jussuf, who is heavily involved

with the northern European drug trade and evidently has sev-
eral falsified European passports. Jussuf controls the Jalalabad
and northern Pakistani border-area drug trade. A search is
currently underway to locate him.

Lauri Vala had also mentioned Omar Jussuf's name, so apparently he wasn't as out of touch as I'd thought. Still I hoped I would never see him again. My Internet surfing was interrupted when Dad and Taneli got home from skating practice. My son announced that he'd landed his double flip several times and demanded to show his favorite figure-skating programs to his grandpa, who assented readily. During the 2002 Olympics I'd been on parental leave and had taken Iida and Taneli to spend a week at my parents' home in Arpikylä. My dad had completely surprised me by being moved to tears when the men's figure-skating champion, Alexei Yagudin, wept with joy. Personally, the male half of the winning ice-dancing pair, with his luxurious lion's mane, had had an even bigger effect on me than Yagudin. I'd used his picture as my computer screen saver for a while after that.

Iida also wanted her grandpa's attention and brought out the advanced math extra-credit work she'd been doing in school to show him. I sank into the corner of the sofa intending to read, but instead I fell asleep. When I woke up with Venjamin purring on my stomach, it was already nine and Antti was waiting for me in the sauna.

I took Sunday off, but Ruuskanen did inform me that Noor's fingerprints had been identified in Omar Hassan's Corolla, and that some of her hair had been found in the trunk of the car. A clever defense lawyer could probably shoot down this evidence too, but things were looking promising. I would hardly have to touch the Noor Ezfahani murder investigation at all until the trial.

More information came from ISAF too. Two of the people who'd lost their lives in the explosion had been women; they had been part of the kitchen staff. One female police instructor and two female cadets were in the hospital with minor injuries. After reading that message I went out for a run in the crisp evening air. The sky was a clear blue, and the ground was slowly freezing. Soon the stars would come out.

Back at home the news was on, and the hosts were discussing whether Finland should donate more funds to rebuild the academy, since we'd been involved in the project before. Three out of four people interviewed on the street had been against it. "How about we take care of our own people here?" was a common sentiment. Indeed.

On Monday I received a text message from Puupponen before I'd even managed to drink my morning coffee: *Have you seen the tabloids? One has an interview with Tuomas S on the cover and the other is already quoting him on their website. Dude's turning into hero. Internet full of TS.*

My first thought was to check the stories on my home computer, but I decided to wait until I got to work. The gas station on the corner by the police station was the closest place to buy the tabloids. The morning paper also had coverage of Noor's murder. Ruuskanen had issued a statement about the progress being made in the case and condemning the disturbance in Kuitinmäki. Most of the news media remained relatively objective in their reporting on immigrant crime, at times being so restrained that some accused them of holding back information. But online everything was different—there the anger and recrimination roiled freely, and I was afraid the tabloids and gossip magazines would soon have to follow suit if they wanted to please their readers. Reporters loved their scoops, but few of them really wanted to fan the flames of a race war, no matter how much attention the resulting headlines would garner. We wanted to hold on to our fairytale of tranquility.

How would I have reacted if I'd been forced to stay in Afghanistan? How closely would I have followed the customs of the land? I wouldn't have changed my religion, even though I didn't know exactly what I believed in. At least not for a religion that demanded I hate those who believed differently.

Ruuskanen hadn't invited my cell to his morning meeting, so after I got to my office my first task was to log in to the intranet. There wasn't any more information there about the investigation. There was an e-mail waiting for me, from the Bosnian police. They had talked to Sara Amir, who did not in fact have any kind of passport, and who, when questioned, admitted that she had last lived in Finland. Attached were a few pictures of a scared-looking girl in a headscarf, who looked very much like several pictures I'd seen of the Sara Amir from Espoo. We would have to go talk to her family members here. If they had sent Sara to Bosnia against her will, the case was more appropriate for Child Protective Services than for the police. At least she was alive.

I heard a commotion in the case room as Puupponen loudly fumbled around for something. There was a printer in there, so I could print the pictures I'd received of Sara for the wall. I went to see what the fuss was about.

"Hi, Maria. Did you already see these? Aren't we all just so glad that cell phones have such good cameras?" Puupponen tossed one of the two main tabloids to me. Even though the picture was blurry, I could make out Rahim bound to the tree. A black bar had been photoshopped over his eyes. The profiles of Himanen, Sutinen, and myself were even more unclear.

"Apparently, there's a video on YouTube too. It makes me long for the good old days of steaming letters open and tracking down anonymous tips pasted together with letters cut from magazines. So, I'm guessing that no one told Soivio not to talk to the papers? Although, in the interviews it was actually his lawyer doing the talking."

"None of this is our mess to clean up; Ruuskanen is leading the investigation. Now let's just concentrate on what we found out from Bosnia. Let's go meet Sara Amir's family. Koivu, will you find out if they're home? Then . . ."

My work phone rang. The number seemed familiar, so I answered.

"Good morning, Detective Kallio. This is Sylvia Sandelin. I have something I need to talk to you about. Would you be able to meet with me today? Perhaps I could offer you a light lunch at my home."

"What is it about?"

"I'm sure you can guess, Detective. Noor Ezfahani. I would very much like to talk with you about how we should present the truth about Noor to the girls at the club, what the police recommend. Something like this can't happen again. My girls have to be able to be themselves, to be free from this sort of thing." Sandelin's voice was agitated, oddly raspy, as if she'd been weeping violently just before calling.

"I have my hands full here." Then I realized that I was my own boss. I could send Koivu and Puupponen to meet Sara Amir's family. I owed the Girls Club this visit, and Iida, who would see the headlines and likely yell at me for not having told her what had happened. "But around one o'clock would work. You don't have to serve me anything, though."

"It's more pleasant to eat in company. The address is Otsolahti Street 5 C, down near the shore. I look forward to seeing you."

Koivu had already started making phone calls, and Puupponen was still grappling with the Internet, huffing and snorting as he read. The printer spit out the pictures of Sara. I thought about the birth control pill disk in her drawer. Was that why she'd been sent away? In early Finnish films, girls from the country were always falling into dens of iniquity in the cities, being corrupted, or having to serve as maids in manor houses where a bold university boy would be waiting to seduce them. Then the innocence disappeared, and sex became recreation, something that wasn't supposed to have much emotional impact. How would people who were used to Muslim standards of modesty react to this kind of world?

Our case room door opened, and there stood Puustjärvi. "Good morning! May I introduce the new Violent Crime trainee, Junior

Officer"—Puustjärvi nudged the young woman into the room—"Jenna Ström!"

Puustjärvi stepped in and closed the door behind him, and the four of us formed a ring around Jenna. She looked between us, at first bewildered by the wicked expression on Puustjärvi's round face, Koivu's confusion, and the sudden understanding that flashed in Puupponen's eyes.

"The four of us were your father's coworkers. That redhead is Ville Puupponen, and the pretty blond is Pekka Koivu," I told Jenna. "Welcome to the department."

We stood in silence for a long time, with only Jenna's eyes moving from person to person. In the end Puupponen took Jenna by the shoulders and hugged her. Koivu followed, then me, and finally Puustjärvi, who had known Pertti Ström for the shortest amount of time of any of us. We had all made mistakes with Ström, and he hadn't played favorites in being a bastard to all of us. With Jenna things would be different. We owed that much to Pertti Ström's memory.

15

I agreed to Sylvia Sandelin's lunch invitation because I wanted to know more about a few of the girls from the club. One of them had been killed, two were still missing, and a fourth had been sent back to her former homeland. Did some immigrants see a threat in multicultural activities that encouraged girls to think independently? Heini and Nelli probably knew the girls who went to the club better than Sandelin, but the idea for the Girls Club had been hers, and she funded the organization.

I took the bus to Tapiola and got off at the stop next to the Stockmann department store. I walked past the Tapio Square parking lot, a recently expanded hotel, and the church, toward the older part of Tapiola and Otsolahti Bay. The Girls Club was located just a few blocks from Sandelin's home. The trees along Otsolahti Street were enormous, many of them having grown undisturbed for half a century. The old WWII bunkers up the hill had been among Antti's favorite places to play as a child; his family had lived just a short distance away, on the east side of the bay. He and his friends had whittled rifles from tree branches to fight in and around the bunkers, but despite that early interest Antti had opted for civil service instead of the usual obligatory stint in the military. Like their parents had before them, children Taneli's age played with toy guns of the airsoft variety in the nearby woods. Boys and girls just a little older satisfied their need to shoot and blow things up in online games. War toys had been forbidden during my childhood, but even a piece of crispbread could be chewed into the shape of a pistol by the truly driven adventurer. It seemed that the impulse to attack and defend was written deep in our DNA. Maybe someday the scientists would be able to identify the anger gene and disarm it.

Sandelin's house was one of the most attractive buildings on the shore of Otsolahti Bay. The two-thousand-plus-square-foot home seemed too big for one person. I remembered someone saying back when the Girls Club was founded that of course the old bat wouldn't want to let teenage girls and who-knew-what thieves into her home, even though there would be plenty of space.

The doorbell played the opening strains of Johann Strauss I's *Radetzky March*. One of the New Year's Day traditions of my childhood had been watching the Vienna Philharmonic concert, and because of those concerts my sister Helena had started taking ballet lessons, which, like so many of her fleeting fancies, hadn't progressed beyond a single spring of experimentation.

Sandelin came to the door wearing a dark-gray skirt suit, reminiscent of a uniform, and patent leather shoes of the same color with four-inch heels. Her hair was perfectly styled. Maybe she went to the salon up the street every morning to have it done. The March wind had whipped my own hair into a tangle of frizz. I should have had the sense to put it in a ponytail. I took my shoes off in the entryway because I was afraid the gravel stuck in the soles would leave marks on the polished parquet and luxurious white rugs. There was still too much snow and ice for the city to start bringing an end to its yearly ritual of graveling and sweeping.

"Detective Kallio, welcome. Now we can talk without any interruptions. You don't have any food allergies, do you?"

"No."

"How singular. These days if I hold a luncheon for twelve people, I have to compose the menu based on what each person *can't* eat. It's very limiting. On the other hand, some of my girls have lived nearly their entire lives on only cornmeal or cassava, since in their fathers' minds girls are least in need of food. And still the undernourished twelve-year-olds get pregnant. But my eating carrot soup and oatmeal porridge for the rest of my life wouldn't save them, so let us enjoy some food. Mojca has prepared the drawing room. There is more light there than in the dining room, and God knows we need that after the long winter."

I followed Sandelin from the entryway into a space about seven hundred square feet in size, one wall of which was entirely glass, just a window opening onto the bay. The sea ice on Otsolahti Bay was dark and thin looking, but a couple of ice fishermen were still tempting fate a few dozen yards offshore. Though the house was between the West Highway and the Ring I Beltway, the sounds of traffic couldn't be heard inside.

"The windows are so well insulated that they don't allow any heat to escape. Sometimes I do wonder if it's dangerous to have such good soundproofing. If those daft men were to fall through the ice right now, I wouldn't hear their cries for help. Even at retirement age some men still imagine they are invincible. Sit facing the sea, Detective. I get to look at the view every day."

A round table, adorned with decorative carvings, was covered with a white linen tablecloth without even a hint of a wrinkle. Soup bowls had been laid out at the center of the table, with service plates underneath and bread plates beside. I didn't really know dishes, but I wondered how much my homeowner's insurance deductible was and whether the policy would cover it if I happened to break Sandelin's fine china. The water glasses were decorative as well, bringing to mind the glass shops in the Czech Republic or Poland that I never dared go inside because I was sure I would smash something.

"Mojca, you may bring the soup!"

A dark-haired woman of about thirty entered. She was wearing normal clothing, a light-blue blouse and jeans, but her hair was held back by a white headband and her clothing was protected by an apron even less wrinkled than the tablecloth. The soup tureen belonged to the same set as the plates, and the ladle was silver. At least they had taught us how to recognize that at the police academy.

"Burbot soup, a seasonal delicacy. I hope you like it."

Mojca disappeared into the kitchen and then returned carrying a bread plate and a butter dish. There were three different types of bread, and they all smelled freshly baked. My mouth began to water as I ladled soup into my bowl. I hadn't eaten burbot in years. Perhaps I wouldn't tell Sandelin that her offering had been my father's most despised food: the Kallio family's resources had been scant during the winters as they tried to keep their youngest son in high school, and so the family had lived on the burbot Grandfather and Uncle Pena caught. Dad had sworn that burbot would never be seen on his own family's table, and it hadn't been.

We ate a few spoonfuls in silence. The portlier of the two ice fishermen pulled a fish from his hole. The cars moved along the bridge from Helsinki like something out of a silent film. Sandelin offered me the bread, and I chose a slice of black Åland *svartbröd*. The butter was real.

"Last night I lay awake thinking about whether I could have prevented this," Sandelin finally said. "We knew at the Girls Club that Noor's family hadn't really adjusted to Finland. But one always hopes for the best, and the family's two older generations apparently understood, at least to some degree, that they must live according to the laws and customs of the place they are in. I understand that police officers are obligated to maintain confidentiality, and I am not expecting to be told anything more than a reporter for the gossip rags would be, but had they really all agreed that Noor should be killed?"

"It was Rahim Ezfahani who took the initiative. The others just didn't turn him in."

"Rahim, Rahim . . . Last spring, around the time the middle school graduates were choosing where to continue their studies, Noor came

201

to the Girls Club in tears. I was not at the club at the time, but Heini told me that Noor's family had forbidden her from going on to high school. If she wished to, she could work, if she could find a job, but mainly she was supposed to be preparing to marry her cousin Rahim. If the security situation allowed, they would have traveled to Iran to be married that summer—last summer, that is. According to the laws of that country, the marriage of a fifteen-year-old would be religiously and legally binding."

"So, the marriage had to be prevented."

"Exactly. I talked to Noor the next time she came to the Girls Club. Her answer was unequivocal. Under no circumstances would she marry Rahim or anyone else. She wanted to go to high school and after that study to be a doctor, preferably a gynecologist, and then return to her homeland to teach women about birth control and to try to prevent death from childbirth."

Sandelin had then taken up Noor's cause as her own and, by getting the social welfare authorities involved, managed to convince the Ezfahanis that Noor would be removed from their home if they did not allow her to continue her schooling. Sandelin blushed when she told me how she had offered the family a "small monetary gift" for doing so.

"I said to the younger men of the family that they would do well to take a cue from Noor, to get an education and a profession and learn Finnish thoroughly, which clearly offended them. After that I informed them that I would negotiate matters having to do with Noor with only her parents. That was what Finnish law mandated."

Tuomas Soivio and Noor had started dating soon after Noor entered high school, sometime in early October. Sandelin had first heard about the relationship from Tuomas's grandmother, who had met the dazzlingly beautiful Iranian girl with her grandson in the café on the third floor of the Stockmann department store in Tapiola.

"Aila was slightly taken aback at first, but then made peace with the fact that this is how the world is now, though the girl's headscarf did bother her a little. You see, she had been forced to wear a babushka herself as a young woman and vowed never to put a scarf on her head again after she moved out of her parents' house in the early 1950s. I discovered quickly that the girl she was talking about was Noor. I think associating with people from different cultures should be encouraged, because that's how we learn to understand each other, but in Noor's case I sensed that no good would come of it. And now we see what happened. She's gone."

Sandelin raised a napkin to her eyes, and although the gesture looked like she could have learned it in modeling school, it didn't seem faked. Sandelin's eye makeup was not waterproof, so some blue eyeliner smeared beneath her eye and caught in the fine wrinkles of her upper cheek.

"It isn't polite to cry at the dining table, but I imagine a detective has seen people crying in every sort of situation imaginable. It is just such a tremendous waste of a life! I should have followed my instincts and asked Noor to come live here. But I selfishly wanted to preserve my privacy. Mojca has a separate studio apartment at number sixteen on this same street. I own a few small apartments in the building. I've never imagined living under the same roof with someone else, but in Noor's case it felt like I might have to."

One of the fishermen out on the ice had begun moving toward the bridge, and the other was waving at him, apparently trying to stop him. The currents under the bridge made the ice thinner—it was insane to go there.

"But even if Noor had lived here, would you have been able to guard her all the time? Sometimes nothing stops a man looking for vengeance—not a restraining order, not even prison. When you invited me to lunch, you said you hoped we could discuss how to tell the girls at the club about Noor's murder having been solved. We could use the opportunity to our advantage by asking them to report any threats they receive. Not long ago, I was working for a domestic violence prevention project. We discovered that simply not leaving a victim alone with her fear helped her to build emotional coping skills and made her feel stronger. Unfortunately, there are always hardcore nutjobs, and as long as they're walking free, their victims will never be safe."

"Is Rahim like that? Will he kill again?"

"Who knows? His time in prison isn't going to be a cakewalk, and anger breeds more anger."

The fisherman had set out after his companion. I'd left my shoes in the entryway, and I couldn't see any garden shoes next to the back door that I could put on if the men fell through the ice and I had to rush to the rescue. I felt like opening the door and ordering them in the name of the law to stop risking their lives.

"Many of my friends are highly educated people with comfortable incomes, and they tend to think of themselves as sophisticates. They trend center right, voting National Coalition or Swedish People's Party, although one might go with the Greens on a lark. They wouldn't even consider supporting nationalists like the True Finns. They are precisely the people who think we have plenty of space for new immigrants, particularly those coming here to work, but also for refugees. And they are precisely the people who can give jobs to the newcomers. It doesn't matter what the nationality is of the man remodeling your home or the woman cleaning your floors, as long as they are honest. But they do not want to be friends with them. The worlds they come from are too different, they say. Our world can come into contact with their world, can influence it, but theirs is not supposed to shake our own. What do you think, Detective? Should we still sing the hymn '*Den blomstertid nu kommer*' at school graduations? Should everyone have to participate in our Christian public rituals?"

My phone rang before I could answer Sandelin's question. It was my father, who should have been at the station getting on the train for Joensuu. Maybe he just wanted to thank me for putting him up for three nights. I apologized to Sandelin, rose from the table, and answered.

"Hi, it's Dad. I'm in a bit of a fix."

"Did you make your train?"

"No! I was trying to move your bookcase so I could get behind it to vacuum, and my blasted back—I think it's lumbago. I'm now lying here on your floor cursing. At least I was able to get some painkillers out of my jacket."

"Christ almighty, Dad! Taneli gets out today at two, so he'll be home first. I'll try to get there as fast as I can. Do we need to take you to a doctor?"

"A doctor isn't going to be able to help. But if you could bring home an ice wrap . . ."

"There's a cooling gel pack in the freezer and a heat wrap in my room. I'll have to tell Taneli where to find them." The old men cavorting out on the ice were about my father's age. Thankfully they'd decided to move closer to shore. I promised my father I'd come home as soon as I could, hopefully by three. In the meantime, and without asking me, Sandelin had served me more soup.

"Bad news?" she asked. I told her briefly, and Sandelin laughed. "Yes, we don't always remember that we aren't young anymore. Sometimes I am nothing but aches and pains if I happen to do a few too many repetitions at the gym. Apparently, one never learns. Try the bread with the seeds. It's one of Mojca's Croatian specialties."

"Did she come to Finland for work or as a refugee?"

"Her family moved here during the breakup of Yugoslavia. The others have already returned, but Mojca wanted to stay. She's a home economics teacher by training, but I pay her a better salary than the state can, partially because I can claim the home services deduction on my tax return. We'll see how long it takes before our voters have another bout of jealousy over other people's success and snatch that away too, leaving hundreds unemployed."

The burbot soup was undeniably delicious. I ate another bowl and listened with amusement to Sylvia Sandelin's social views. She seemed to assume that I shared them. Perhaps she saw the police as a force that upheld the order of society, that propped up the position of whoever happened to be in power without question or complaint. According to Sandelin, Finland was only a quasi democracy in which the prevailing assumption of equality was merely an illusion.

"But the people who were only dealt a hand of twos and threes at birth certainly know how to blame society for everything that happens to them. Would you prefer coffee or tea to follow?"

I should have left, but I said, "Coffee. Thank you." The espresso was as strong as in an Italian restaurant, and with it Mojca served dark, obviously handmade, chocolates. Sandelin and I agreed that she would tell the girls at the club why Noor had died, even though everyone would already know.

"And Tuomas needs to be cautioned about his stupidity. Although I imagine it's better he received his fifteen minutes of fame this way than by actually hurting someone. Heini was utterly stunned by his stunt. She'd thought he had more sense than that. I told her she should never overestimate men. Luckily, I've never had to be dependent upon them. But they do have their good sides, as long as one does not see them too often. Friedrich lives in Hamburg; I'm flying there tomorrow for four days. That much is always fun, but any longer and it becomes routine." It was good I was sitting down, because Sandelin winked at me. I only barely managed to wink back.

I sat with Sandelin for another five minutes after I finished my coffee and then thanked her for the meal and left. She tried to convince me to come and speak at the Girls Club, but I declined, appealing to Iida's certain opposition.

"She doesn't want me getting too involved in her world."

"But she's your daughter. You're the one in charge. My mother was the chairperson of the parents' committee at my school and handed out the scholarships at every single Christmas and spring fête. I was proud of her because she wasn't just anyone."

I declined again. Sandelin then attempted to prolong my visit by asking after my mother-in-law, so I practically ran into the entryway, where I put on my coat and shoes. Sandelin shook my hand politely in farewell.

"About singing '*Den blomstertid nu kommer*,'" I said at the door. "For how many Finns is it a hymn about religious conviction, and for how many is it a tradition we repeat because we always have? I don't think it's dangerous to anyone. Secular oddities like myself would be perfectly willing to sing other religions' songs too, if the circumstances demanded."

Down on the street, I had to dodge a bicyclist who came screaming around the corner straight at me, his hair flying in the wind. I jumped into the middle of the road and swore, but the boy didn't even turn to look back. Of course, he didn't have a helmet on. So many young men believed they were immortal.

On the bus I switched my phone to silent and opened three frantic text messages from my mother. Then I looked at my e-mail inbox. Antti had sent a silly cat video with an overeager tabby jumping into cardboard boxes. I was much more interested in a message that had come from Uzuri in Afghanistan, written in English.

Hi Maria,

You've probably heard the bad news. I am sad to report that there was a traitor among us, one of the police cadets. He didn't have a religious fanatic background, so we didn't have any reason to suspect he was one of Omar Jussuf's men—apparently his own son Issa. It wasn't a suicide attack, and he got away. I'm attaching a list of the dead. We still don't know when the school will be repaired. Omar Jussuf has said that he will destroy it again, that his forces are everywhere. We are trying to stay brave.

Yours,
Uzuri

P.S. The cadet was very interested in Finland and said that his bride-to-be lives there. I wrote the girl's name down once in my journal, and it survived the explosion. I still haven't told this to anyone, but it just occurred to me that the cadet, Issa Omar, whom we knew by the name Mohammed Salim Hasan, might try to come to Finland to hide out with his fiancée if his father isn't able to guarantee his safety. The girl's name is Aziza Abdi Hasan, and the man whom we knew as Mohammed claimed that she was his cousin. But maybe the story about a Finnish bride was just as big a lie as everything else he said.

I read the message three times during the bus ride. Its contents didn't change. There might be thousands of Aziza Abdi Hasans in the world, but only one had disappeared from Finland. And Lauri Vala had talked about the drug lord Omar Jussuf. Had Omar Jussuf's son arranged for the roadside bomb that hit our convoy? It would have been easy for him to find out what our route was and when we would be traveling. Did Vala know more than he was telling me? Might he know that our cell was looking for a missing Aziza? There was nothing to be done about it: even though the humiliation was searing, I had to contact Vala.

Back at the station, Koivu barreled down the hallway toward me with a printout in his hand.

"Hi, Maria. We found Tommi."

"What Tommi?"

"Tommi Mäki from Siuntio. Sara Amir's supposed boyfriend. One of Sara's girlfriends called, and they transferred her to me. Apparently, Tommi was just a one-night fling, and Sara had been mad at this friend for putting the picture of Sara and Tommi on Facebook. Tommi didn't want to date her. Fourteen-year-olds shouldn't even be allowed on there! Maybe that picture led to Sara being sent to Bosnia. I could take a little business trip down to Bihać to check it out. I'm sure Anu could manage with the kids for a few days."

"I'd recommend taking a business trip across town to see Sara's parents instead. I'm sure they'll be thrilled when they hear we've found their daughter."

"I've been trying to reach them, but I haven't gotten through. We'll probably just have to go over there. Can you come, or should I take Ville?"

"Option B. I have something else I need to do. If Sara's mother won't talk to you, I'll go there tomorrow."

I stepped into my office and thought for a moment about how best to approach Vala. I came to the conclusion that I should use his own tactics, i.e., intimidation and shouting. Vala answered after the first ring, as if he'd been holding the phone in his hand, waiting for me to call.

"Vala here. What's up, Kallio? Did you miss me?"

"Yes. What are you doing tonight?" I would have to go home to see my dad and evaluate his situation, but I could come back to the office later in the evening.

"What do you propose?"

"Come to the Espoo police station at eight. I'll be waiting for you at the door downstairs."

"Sounds good," Vala said in a tone meant to make me understand that I had just promised him some wild sex. Maybe tonight I should dress the same way I had in Afghanistan, headscarf and all. The weather report promised sleet, and that would be a good excuse.

I googled Aziza Abdi Hasan, but I didn't get any relevant hits other than the newspaper stories about the missing girls and Noor's murder. There was plenty of information about Omar Jussuf. I logged in to the police department's internal system we shared with Europol and INTERPOL. A picture started to coalesce of one of the world's most unscrupulous drug runners, whose business had tentacles extending from northern Afghanistan deep into Europe. He was fifty-six. He hadn't forced his way into the booming drug markets of Russia, instead selling his heroin in the former Soviet Republics and Scandinavia. There wasn't any information about how many wives he had, but he had at least six sons. Daughters weren't mentioned in the report.

I should have gotten in touch with the Security Intelligence Service and asked whether they knew if Omar Jussuf had any connections to Finland, but I decided to be selfish and interview Vala first. There were enough coincidences that I doubted I was the only Finnish police officer aware of them, but I was the only one who had narrowly survived a roadside bomb. Our vehicle was supposed to have been at the front of the line, but fate had dictated otherwise. I would never forget that.

When I got home, my father was lying on the living room rug on his back, and Taneli was reading him a section of *Harry Potter and the Sorcerer's Stone*. I didn't know how effective that treatment would be. Iida was making tomato soup in the kitchen, because in her opinion sick people were supposed to eat warm, light food. My mother had already sent me six worried text messages. The living room's heavy bookcase had been dragged away from the wall, and behind it there was a shameful collection of dust bunnies. But still, my father had gone overboard with tidying up.

"Are you able to move at all?"

"I can crawl to pi . . . to the bathroom. Walking hurts."

"You said you took some painkillers."

"A couple of two-hundred-milligram ibuprofens. They were in my coat pocket, which, luckily, was on the back of that chair. I got water from the cat's bowl. I hope I don't catch anything."

"Let's put some pain gel on your back. What about going to see a doctor?"

"Nothing is going to help but time. Of course, something like this just had to happen!"

I massaged the medicated cream into my father's back. He took it calmly, but he started to have trouble when Iida asked to serve him his soup. She didn't understand how much pain her grandfather was in and that many motions were impossible for him. A shot of whiskey would have made it easier to bear, but booze and pain medication were a dangerous combination for an old man.

I made chanterelle risotto for the family and also cooked some hot dogs for Taneli, who thought that a real meal had to include meat. While I was cooking, a text message came from Puupponen.

I wasted three hours and then got to talk to Sara Amir's dad. He finally admitted that she had been sent to Bosnia because she was safer there than here. When I asked safe from what, he said from men. He didn't feel like her whereabouts were any business of the Finnish authorities, but I'm going to figure out when and how she left the country once I can get a Serbo-Croatian interpreter.

At five to eight I was waiting for Vala at the police station, inside the outer doors. The parking lot was almost empty, so I recognized him in his car when he pulled into the lot, parking as close as possible to the door. It was raining gently, and I had on rubber boots and a hooded raincoat. I'd pulled my hair up in a bun, put on my ugliest and loosest wool sweater, and carefully washed off all my makeup.

When Vala started walking from the car, I saw that he had a long, thin object in his hand. It was a rose wrapped in cellophane, and as he came closer, I saw that it was bloodred. I opened the door, and he extended the rose.

"Happy Women's Day, Detective Kallio. Are we finally going to start speaking the same language?"

"That depends on what language that is." I accepted the rose but didn't open the packaging. I'd always hated International Women's Day, which to me seemed like an import that epitomized Soviet-style subordination: on one day women get roses, but the next day they have a double workload waiting at home and the collective farm.

I took Vala to our case room, leaving the rose next to the coffee machine and deciding to forget it. I looked at Aziza, staring at me from the wall. She'd been illiterate until she was fourteen. I pointed to her.

"Do you recognize her?"

Vala had sat down in a chair from which he could see the case wall. He glanced at the picture first quickly, but then perked up, inspecting it carefully before answering.

"At first you think that everyone in a headscarf looks the same. They aren't even women, just forbidden fruit. Then you start to notice the differences. I doubt I've ever seen her in the flesh, and why would I have? Why would Issa Omar's fiancée be in my circle of acquaintances? Obviously, you're only finding out her true identity now."

Other officers had interviewed Aziza's family, so I'd never met them. The family claimed that Aziza had left with her young uncle over the Christmas holiday for Sweden, but she'd never arrived. Had Aziza's "uncle" been Issa Omar?

"Who knows that Omar Jussuf has connections to Finland?"

"I don't know that Jussuf does. Issa does, though. Strange that the Security Intelligence Service wouldn't inform the local police. The spy boys probably had a good laugh when they read in the paper that the fate of the missing immigrant girls in Espoo wasn't connected to Noor whatever-her-name-was's murder. Aziza doesn't have anything to do with those other girls. She's a shield whose job is to make it easier for Issa Omar to move from one country to another."

I didn't know if Vala was just talking out of his ass, but the e-mail I'd gotten from Uzuri seemed to support his claim. Vala sat in his chair, perfectly calm. Gone was the restless motion of our previous meeting. I looked him in the eyes; his pupils were normal. Maybe I should have checked with the Ministry of Defense about whether Vala really was on leave and not discharged for psychological reasons, though they probably wouldn't have told me anyway unless I had an official reason for knowing. Some Swedish soldiers had died in Afghanistan when an attacker dressed in a police uniform opened fire on them. Maybe he'd been on Omar Jussuf's payroll too.

An emergency vehicle's siren blared, and Vala flinched. He was about to stand up but quickly realized that the alarm didn't have anything to do with him. Over the years I'd learned not to react to sirens, unless an alert had come to my cell phone or pager right before.

"How well did you know Ulrike Müller?" Vala asked.

"I guess she was sort of a . . . friend. I liked her."

"But you didn't know the real reason she was participating in the Afghanistan police academy project?" Vala's voice was amused. "Apparently, she trusted you much less than she did me. Or maybe she didn't trust me. Maybe she was just spouting off in the heat of the moment."

"In the heat of what moment?"

"What, am I making you jealous? I told you that danger turns people on. At least the last night of Ulrike's life wasn't boring. The threat of a terror attack at the police academy on its opening day was very real, which you were obviously too naïve to realize. Ulrike did, though."

I listened to Vala's self-assured voice as he related that, after the opening ceremonies, he and Ulrike had ended up in the same bed, in her room. She had fallen asleep after they made love, and Vala had gone through her things.

"Ulrike was a police officer and a German intelligence agent. Of course, our German friends wanted to monitor what kind of new police officers were being trained for Afghanistan. Less than half of the current police force there can be trusted. No one knew whether the new recruits were clean or whether the drug lords could buy them. Ulrike admitted all of this when I pressed her after she woke up. She was amazed that the Finns didn't understand what a big risk we were taking by participating in setting up the police academy. Or did some of us realize after all? How do I know what the real reason is for your interest in Aziza Abdi Hasan? Maybe you want to find her so you can turn her over to Issa Omar. Ulrike said that the German police believed Omar's tentacles extended into Finland. Considering what the police get paid here, it would be no wonder if someone had been bought. Are you the mole, Kallio?"

16

Vala's question was so ridiculous that I couldn't respond with anything but a laugh.

"For Christ's sake, Lauri, get a grip. I'm not a mole, and Ulrike's necklace is just a piece of jewelry. Get that through your head already."

"What are you more offended by, that Ulrike wasn't honest with you, or that I doubt you?"

I answered that I wasn't offended about anything. Ulrike was dead, so Vala could claim anything he wanted about her.

"You've been there, in Afghanistan. You know what it's like. Finland is at war, no matter what the government says. Each momentary success in negotiating with one faction is followed immediately by a strike from another. The Taliban are fluffy little lambs compared to the drug lords. Drug runners aren't even bound by religious law. In Finland we imagine that if we play along nicely, we won't be touched. That's not how it works!"

Vala leaned toward me and grabbed my wrist. I felt like breaking away, but that would have seemed weak. Still, I could feel my pulse rate rising. My brain sensed danger and was trying to warn my heart.

"You must know what it's like. I know you joined the police while you were still in diapers. I applied to be a peacekeeper the moment I was old enough too. It seemed so noble. Peacekeepers protect peace, they don't fight wars. A little like freedom fighters taking up arms for some good cause. How naïve can a person be? But no one stays that way for long. When everyone around you is backsliding, you can't always keep your hands clean. You look the other way when the men in the next unit use excessive force on teenage boys. Then you go whoring, even though you have no clue who the money ends up going to or whether the girls are even of age. You get so damn apathetic—and lonely." Vala tightened his grip on my wrist. I grabbed his arm with my free hand and disengaged it.

"I know exactly as much about Aziza as I've told you. I also believe she may be in danger. I still have a few shreds of idealism left, but I'm not naïve. I'm . . ."

For a moment I was going to tell Vala about my own experiences, about my own close calls, about Ström's suicide, about why I'd left the Espoo police, but thankfully I had the sense to keep my mouth shut. I didn't want to be Lauri Vala's ally, and I wasn't the woman who could offer him comfort.

I was only able to get him to leave after promising to tell him what we found out after meeting with Aziza's family. Of course, Vala knew I might promise anything to get rid of him. He didn't have an official position in the police organization or any right to demand that I cooperate with him. However, he probably did think that our shared experience near Jalalabad bound us together and obligated me to keep my word somehow.

"I would have brought you poppies, but there aren't any around here this time of year. The first time I saw slopes covered with red I thought, *My God, how beautiful.* But it's because of those flowers that so many people are killed with so little thought. Fuck, we're risking our lives to guard the drug lords' property. What sense is there in that?"

When I had been in Afghanistan, in the fall, the poppies hadn't been blooming anymore, but crocuses had been planted near the police academy. The international community was trying to convince opium producers to switch over to saffron. Ulrike had picked one and pressed

216

it between the pages of her notebook, staining the pages with the yellow spice.

I didn't want Vala to infect me with his dark outlook, so I asked him again to leave. I left for home at the same time, and in the hallway, he suddenly reminded me that I had forgotten my rose.

"Go get it. Forgetting a gift given in goodwill brings bad luck."

I didn't know where Vala had gotten that from and even less whether he really had goodwill toward me, but I promised to go back to get the flower after I escorted him to the door. There he suddenly snatched me up in his arms. It lasted longer than a normal good-bye embrace, and I was starting to think about giving him a knee to the groin, but he finally let me go.

"Every good-bye could be forever. Take care of yourself, Kallio."

I didn't have any desire to ever see Lauri Vala again. I went back for the flower, though. It may have been a cut flower, but it was still a living thing, and I didn't want to kill it. The flower hadn't chosen who bought it or who received it, I reasoned as I trudged toward my house with the cellophane-wrapped bundle in my hand. At home I said that the department had passed them out to all the women for Women's Day.

The next day I went with Koivu to meet Aziza Abdi Hasan's family. They lived on the same block as the Wang-Koivus, and they even had common acquaintances. No one in the family was answering phone calls or text messages, so we went to ring their doorbell. No one answered.

Suspicion of terrorism would have been enough to get a search warrant, but I wanted to have more information before I set the big wheels turning. While we were waiting at the door, I found Corporal Jere Numminen's contact information in my phone's e-mail archive and sent him an otherwise vague message in which I first marveled about our good luck with the roadside bomb, then told of my receiving Ulrike's necklace from her mother, and finally asked how Major Lauri Vala was doing. The message was a shot in the dark, of course. And even if he did know something, Numminen might decide that discretion was the better part of valor.

After waiting for a bit, we decided that no one was home. I dropped a written contact request through the mail slot.

We had cleared up Sara Amir's fate the previous day without any serious drama. After seeing the picture the Bosnian police had sent, Sara's mother had admitted that she had been sent to live with relatives in Bosnia.

"It is better for her there," she'd said but hadn't been willing to say anything more. Koivu had gotten in touch with Child Protective Services, who would take over the case.

We didn't hear anything from Aziza's family all week. Koivu rang their doorbell every night, and a uniformed patrol stopped by a few times each day. On Thursday we decided to start going through the Border Patrol exit records. Aziza would have been caught at passport control in the airport or at the ferry terminal, but no alert had been issued for the rest of the family. So, I wasn't surprised when I finally found that Abdi Hasan Mohammed, his wife, Selene Salim, and their underage sons, Ali Abdi Hasan and Mohammed Abdi Hasan, had traveled by boat from Turku to Stockholm on the second of March. Both boys were still required to be in their classes—they were only halfway through elementary school.

We called the school, and the receptionist told us that the family had let them know in February that the boys would be traveling the week before winter break. They'd received permission from the principal to be away for the week, but there hadn't been any sign of the boys after the vacation, and their homeroom teachers hadn't had any luck contacting the family.

"I spoke with the principal. Our son, Juuso, is in the same school, and Sennu will be going next year. The Hasan brothers are already teenagers, but they're still attending grade school in the immigrant class.

Each has different developmental problems that slow down their learning. They haven't even learned to read properly. Apparently, the father
and Aziza are the only ones in the family who know how to read and
write Dari, and only Aziza understands Finnish well. According to the
principal, Child Protective Services was intending to contact the family
next week. But the rest of the family seems to have vanished into thin
air along with Aziza. However, their residency permit is valid until the
end of this year."

"Maybe we should take a look at their apartment. I take it there
aren't any suspicious smells coming from inside?"

"No smell of bodies," Koivu confirmed.

"When you first made the connection between the missing girls,
did you do thorough background checks? Did Aziza's family members
all come into the country at the same time, and were their papers in
order?"

Koivu promised to check. I filed the request for the search warrant
and sent another e-mail to Uzuri. I contacted the Security Intelligence
Service, but I received a curt reply that no minor by the name of Aziza
Abdi Hasan was on their watchlist. The officer who answered the call
refused to even discuss Issa Omar. Regardless, I was sure my call would
stir things up. That was fine with me. I wasn't looking for kudos for
finding Aziza. Lately Security Intelligence had expanded its jurisdiction
to include outright spying and had established units all around the
world. If Omar Jussuf's empire were to expand too close to Finland,
they would be sure to know, but of course they wouldn't be sharing
information with us regular police officers.

On Thursday there was a logjam of stabbings and domestic violence
incidents in Espoo, and Ruuskanen pressured Puupponen and Koivu
into helping his unit with the investigations. I kept in touch with Child
Protective Services and met briefly with Sara Amir's parents. They didn't
understand why they weren't allowed to decide where their daughter

would live. According to the Bosnian police, Sara wanted to stay in her former homeland. So what was the problem?

On Thursday morning I also received the search warrant for Aziza's home. Because the other members of the cell were busy with their investigations, I went over with Assi Haatainen from Forensics. In the hallway, we put on paper coveralls, shoe guards, shower-cap-like hair protectors, and disposable gloves. Haatainen had joined the department during my most recent absence. She was about thirty years old, very energetic and decisive seeming, and spoke so much on the drive over that it actually made me dizzy.

The building superintendent from the housing cooperative showed up just as we'd finished donning our gear. I'd heard from the co-op that Aziza's family's March rent had been paid, but that the family had been behind on their rent before. They hadn't given notice. The maintenance man watched us curiously.

"Do you have to put on those getups because you think you're going to find bodies?"

"Please exit the area. The possibility of contaminating the scene applies to you too," Haatainen said firmly. She let me through the door first and then closed it in the building superintendent's face.

It was a two-bedroom apartment, decorated much the same as many private spaces I'd seen in Afghanistan: lots of rugs, wall hangings, and low couches and tables. There were no cloths on the tables and no beds, but there was a pile of carefully rolled sleeping rugs. There were dishes in the kitchen, but there were no hygiene products of any kind in the bathroom. The hall closet gaped open, empty. Assi began to vacuum the rugs to find hairs and fibers. I peeked into the cleaning closet, which held only a lonely looking rug beater and an almost empty package of laundry detergent. The refrigerator had been turned off. The door was open, and from inside wafted a sour, astringent lemon scent. In the cupboards, there were a few bags of black tea, an unopened package of rice, and a can of crushed tomatoes, plus a few dishes, a battered pot, a dull-looking serrated bread knife, and a few colorful plastic mugs that looked like they'd been bought at IKEA.

In the closet in the bedroom, there were two pairs of tattered men's-size athletic shoes and a lone black sock. In the other closet was a soccer ball. Nothing else. Either Aziza's family lived a very austere life, or they weren't intending to return to Finland.

Assi was taking pictures and studying the rugs carefully, searching for possible bloodstains and DNA with a spectrometer. I looked out the window in the larger of the bedrooms and saw the building the Koivu family lived in. Where was Aziza? Where was her family? Was another small band of people wandering Europe now, a group that would never put down roots? Maybe they would get caught in Provence or Sicily for using false papers, or they would be forced into virtual slavery on the streets of Hamburg. Perhaps they would try to get back to their homeland, even though a human life was cheaper there than Lordi's second album on an online auction site. I would probably never know their fate.

Investigating murders had its downsides, but over 95 percent of homicides were solved eventually, which offered some semblance of closure. Of course, a violent death cast a permanent shadow over the lives of everyone closely connected to it. The lost, the missing, and the runaways who were never found would never really have their police files closed. A person was presumed dead after they'd been missing for ten years, but when Aziza's family got to that point, almost everyone would have already forgotten them, including me. Still, I felt a strange responsibility for them, even though the only things that tied us together were that they had come from a country whose democracy I had been doing my part to build, and that they happened to end up in my city.

On Friday, while Koivu was handling other matters, I got in contact with the Child Protective Services authorities and the police in Bosnia.

I asked my colleagues there about the possibility of getting Sara Amir to come in for a video interview. I was in no way questioning the competence of the Bosnians, but I wanted to know whether Sara was telling the truth when she said she was happy in Bosnia, or if she had been ordered to say so. I thought about the birth control pills we'd found in her drawer and about Tommi from Siuntio, who had only been a one-night stand. Had Sara's parents taken it too seriously? Then I forced myself to let it go. Child Protective Services would ask the police for help if they needed it.

One of the domestic violence incidents the previous day had been a fight between a man in his thirties, who was living with his parents, and his sister, who was about ten years his junior and had moved away from home. The sister had attacked her brother while he was sleeping and tried to smother him with a pillow. Ruuskanen and I decided that this should be classified as a "special" case and that my cell would take over the investigation. The attacker was currently in Jorvi Hospital under strong sedation. The alarm bells in my head said that it might be a case of incest, because neither family member had a criminal background. The brother drifted from one temporary job to the next, and the sister had cut herself frequently as a teenager. Now she was studying to be a licensed nurse practitioner, and in school they had been doing their section on psychology. Their sixty-year-old parents were completely baffled by the incident. However, the investigation could wait until after the weekend.

Friday evening, I started making dinner early. Antti was out swimming with his friends, so it was my turn to cook. My dad's back was already in better shape than before, but he still wouldn't be able to travel for quite some time. My mother called at least three times every day and had decided to come to Espoo the following week. Maybe my father could travel with her by air, since they weren't running sleeper trains to

Joensuu anymore. Progress was marching on in that regard too. While I was in school, taking the sleeper trains had been a sensible use of time, even though, after a scroungy night on the train from Tampere to Viinijärvi, I was always useless the next day.

Antti had managed to buy some local organic ground meat through a colleague, so I'd decided to keep it simple and make a ground lamb sauce. I was grabbing some shallots from the cupboard, hoping that they wouldn't make me cry as much as normal onions, when my work phone rang. I had saved Heini Korhonen's number in my contacts, and I didn't think she would call for no reason, so I answered.

"Kallio here."

For a few moments all I could hear was a strange, distant murmuring. Then a sob, and a voice said, faltering, "This is Heini . . . Heini Korhonen from the Girls Club. Is this Detective Maria Kallio, Iida Sarkela's mother?"

"Yes."

"I'm at home . . . in Hakalehto." She gave me the address. Then she said, "I've been raped."

"When and where? Who did it?"

"Just now, here at my home. The person who did it is sitting over in the corner. It's Samir Amir, Sara Amir's brother. Could the police come and take him away?"

Before, Heini's voice had contained a cool determination, but now she was talking in a shrill, little girl's voice. Of course, she knew what to do after being raped; she had lectured the girls at the club about it over and over. She was still probably in shock, though. Maybe that was why she'd called me instead of the emergency number.

"Don't hang up. I'm going to use my personal phone to send a police patrol over." I punched in the speed-dial code for the emergency call center with my other hand. My father looked at me from the mattress we'd set up for him on the floor with a quizzical expression, but there was nothing he could do to help. Thankfully the children were in their rooms, hopefully with headphones on or so engrossed in their books that they wouldn't realize what was going on. I put my work phone on speaker, so I would hear if Samir attacked Heini again. It took way too long for the call center to answer, even though in reality only about ten seconds had gone by.

"This is Detective Maria Kallio of the Espoo police. I just received a report of a rape incident. Send a patrol car to Hakarinne Street 6 M 765. The perpetrator is still on-scene, as is the victim. Exactly, the report came straight to me, because the victim is an acquaintance of mine. I'm on my way too. It would probably be a good idea to send an ambulance. The perpetrator is Samir Amir, a Bosnian immigrant with severe psychiatric problems."

I looked at the clock. Antti had promised to come home for dinner at six, and it was still half an hour until then. My family wouldn't die of hunger; there was bread and fruit in the cupboard if they needed a snack. I told Heini that both a police patrol and I were coming and ordered her to stay on the phone. I reminded her not to shower or change her clothes until she'd been examined by a doctor. I'd been in a similar situation myself, and afterward I'd frantically scrubbed my body and my teeth for weeks on end in order to get every last cell of my attacker out of me. But evidence was evidence. Sperm, ripped clothing, and bruised skin held more weight in a court of law than the word of an honest person.

I explained to my father that something unexpected had come up, but that it shouldn't keep me away too long. Luckily, Antti had taken the bus, so I took our car. Jahnukainen ran out from underneath when I started it. The cold engine coughed a few times, and the steering wheel was so ice cold that I had to put on my gloves. The line was still open to Heini's phone. No sounds came from her apartment other than an animallike whimpering, apparently from Samir.

"Heini, are you still there?"

"Yes. I need to go to the bathroom."

"Try to hold it. I'm sorry. Did penetration occur? Did he ejaculate inside you?"

"Yes . . ."

"An ambulance is coming. If you have to urinate, do it in a cup of some sort." It felt cruel to be giving clinical instructions like this to a person who had just experienced something so horrendous, but that was my job. "I'll be there in ten minutes."

Old Mankkaa Road was full of speed bumps, but they'd gotten rid of most of the traffic lights in favor of roundabouts, which I swerved through as recklessly as the best rally driver. The car bounced over the speed bumps. Thankfully there wasn't much traffic, and no pedestrians got in my way except for a Shetland sheepdog that had escaped its master. Fortunately it had on a high-visibility vest so I managed to avoid it in time.

Just as I was turning into Heini's neighborhood, I heard the doorbell ring through the phone speaker. The patrol had made it before me.

"Police. Open up," a familiar female voice said. Rasilainen. Thank God. "This is Officer Rasilainen and Officer Timonen from the Espoo police. We received a report of a rape."

I hung up the phone and turned onto Hakarinne Street. There weren't many parking spots, and some of them were still covered in snow, so I left my car parked illegally next to a pile, where it wouldn't be in anyone's way. The police van was parked next to the steps. I'd been in this building once ages ago, when I'd worked for a short time in a somewhat shady law office in North Tapiola.

Heini Korhonen's apartment was located on the third floor. There was an elevator, but instead of using it I jogged up the stairs. The door next to Heini's was open, and an elderly woman stood in the hallway, holding the door open by its key.

"Why did the police go into Heini's apartment?" she asked loudly, almost shouting. "She's always such a well-mannered young lady. There aren't thieves about, are there?"

"No, nothing like that."

"What?" the woman yelled. "I don't have my hearing aids in. I just saw the police come to the entrance, and I was looking to see where they went."

Due to her hearing difficulties, it would be pointless to ask her about what had happened in the apartment next door. I rang Heini's doorbell, and when it opened, there stood Timonen decked out in a protective suit, which made me jump. He couldn't be the detective from Ruuskanen's unit, because he was wearing a patrol uniform, so this had to be a twin brother.

"Hi. Yeah, I'm not my bro," he said, amused, but I wasn't laughing. The twin jokes would have to wait for another time. I took my own protective coveralls out of my investigation kit and put them on. The whining I'd heard over the phone was still going on, and when I stepped inside the apartment, I saw Samir Amir curled up in a fetal position in the corner. He was rocking back and forth and whimpering. I could see Heini's legs protruding from an alcove. She had on bobby socks, but her lower legs and thighs were bare. When I stepped closer I saw that her blouse had been torn open and she'd wrapped her lower body in a bath towel.

"I couldn't hold it," were the first mumbled words out of her mouth. "I had to . . ."

"Don't worry. We'll still be able to get a sperm sample from you." There was a contusion on her temple, and her nose was bleeding. Blood had dried on her jaw and her neck. "I know that being examined by a doctor after this will feel horrible, but the medical evidence we get from doing so may be essential for the trial. I assume that there weren't any outside witnesses to the rape."

"What?"

"There was no one in the apartment except you and Samir. Can you tell me briefly what happened?" I wasn't able to evaluate what shape Heini was in. That would be a job for the doctor. However, I took a recorder from my investigation kit and dictated the usual introductory details. Then I sat down next to Heini. The bed was made, the bedspread stretched tight. Had Heini put the covers back in order after the rape out of habit, or had the act been perpetrated somewhere else? In addition to the sleeping alcove, the studio apartment had an open kitchen and a small balcony with a drying rack full of clothes. Heini apparently wore lavender underwear.

"I know all about this. You're supposed to tell the police. You can't stay quiet, even though you'll want to." Heini's mouth formed the words slowly, as if she were struggling to move the muscles of her face.

"You don't have to talk if you don't feel up to it."

"I have to. I just have to. I just made the mistake I've warned the girls about. Don't let strangers into your home. But he wasn't a stranger. He was Samir, Sara's brother. The one the war broke. He was on the same bus as me. I invited him up for coffee. He was so happy because he got to speak his language with someone other than his family. I thought he might know something about Sara. I didn't even have time to put the grounds in the coffee maker before he attacked. And he's strong."

Heini was relatively tall, maybe an inch taller than Samir, and looked like she was in good shape, but she had apparently been so stunned that she hadn't been able to put up much of a fight. Timonen tried fruitlessly to question Samir, but it was like he was on another planet. The ambulance would be needed more for him than for Heini; I could take her to the Jorvi Hospital emergency room in my car.

"Please understand that I have to ask this: You're saying that you in no way did anything to make Samir Amir think that you wanted to have sex with him?"

"No!" Heini's whisper was emphatic.

"Where did the rape occur?"

"He knocked me down on the floor, choked me with one arm, and pulled my clothes off . . . I don't really remember the rest."

Rasilainen motioned me back toward the door.

"Hold on a second, Heini. I'll be right back." I stood up and walked over.

"Forensics won't be able to come over until tomorrow," Rasilainen said. "We'll have to seal the apartment. Ms. Korhonen will need to go to a friend's house or to her parents'. Otherwise the police can arrange a hotel room for her. And the suspect is totally messed up. I wouldn't dare put him in a cell."

"What happened when you arrived?"

"Korhonen came to the door. She'd wrapped a towel around herself and had a bread knife in her hand. I took it away from her and bagged it."

"Was Samir Amir already curled up in the corner like that?"

"Yes. The suspect hasn't said anything in any language the whole time. What does he speak?"

"A Serbo-Croatian dialect from Bosnia. He does know some Finnish, but we would need an interpreter to question him—if it ever gets that far."

The doorbell rang. It was the paramedics. They didn't seem particularly thrown by the fact that they were told to treat the suspect rather than the victim. A man whose uniform said "Oinonen" asked how Samir had collapsed.

"I don't know," Heini said, still speaking slowly. "He . . . he got off me and moved away. I had my eyes closed. I heard him open the balcony door. I still didn't dare move. He went out onto the balcony, and I crawled toward the kitchen to get a knife. When he saw it, he started to cry and sat down on the floor. I closed the balcony door so it wouldn't get cold and called the police."

Samir didn't react when the paramedics approached. It wasn't until Oinonen touched him that the volume of his whimpering went up. He didn't resist when they lifted him onto his feet. His pants were unbuttoned, he didn't have any socks on, and the nailless last two toes of his right foot looked raw. The men from the ambulance crew led him away, supporting him by his arms, and Officer Timonen followed after.

"I'll make sure they get him loaded up," he shouted back to Officer Rasilainen as he left.

I tried to find any signs of a struggle in the apartment. The main room contained the usual furnishings: a sofa, an armchair, a TV stand, and next to the kitchen nook a table with two chairs. None of the furniture had fallen down. If Heini had been standing next to the coffee maker in the kitchen, Samir might have been able to drag her to the rug between the sofa and television stand without banging into any of the furniture, if Heini weren't struggling too much. Her jeans were in a heap next to the sofa. A pastel purple-and-pink scrap of fabric had probably been a pair of panties.

Nausea rose in throat. I tried to fight it. I didn't want the same nightmare for Heini that I'd experienced myself five years earlier: retelling the violent act again and again—with the doctor, in the police interview, in court. The same questions were presented by different people, the worst being the defense attorney's claims that I had somehow been responsible for the crime. Even though I knew how irrational his questions were, they still felt like stabs at my soul. I could still feel that from time to time even now. If only I hadn't gone out running alone . . . I'd been attacked outside, but Heini had let the rapist into her home voluntarily. There were judges who would think that was a mitigating circumstance.

Timonen returned, putting new covers on his shoes.

"There were a few gawkers out in the parking lot. I told them to put their cell phone cameras away. If I were you, I'd put something on Ms. Korhonen so she can hide her face. Are we going to take her in to get checked out?"

I answered that I would handle it. Now I had to think about Heini, not my own past. This wasn't about me.

"Maria, are you OK?" Rasilainen asked. She knew me too well.

"Yeah, I'm fine. I'm going to take Heini to the hospital and make sure she finds a safe place to spend the night. You keep in touch with Forensics. Theoretically Ruuskanen will be heading this one up. I'll figure out with him how to divvy up the work. Heini just happened to call me because we know each other from before."

I wondered why Heini wasn't at the Girls Club tonight; on Fridays, they held their popular improv night. I searched the closet for some loose sweatpants, some underwear, and a shirt to go over the ripped one, which could stay on until she got to the doctor. Then I would take possession of it and deliver it to Forensics.

"Heini, do you have any maxi pads?"

"Why? I'm not on my period."

I didn't bother to explain. I just looked in the closets again and then went into the bathroom. There were only tampons in the medicine cabinet, but I was able to find a compress in my investigation kit. I asked Heini to use it as a pad. She dressed as slowly and clumsily as a five-year-old child trying to delay putting on her raincoat because she doesn't want to go to nursery school.

"Does it hurt much? Do you want some painkillers?"

Heini stared at me oddly. I felt like wrapping my arms around her, but instead I just grabbed a hooded jacket from the coatrack and offered it to her, asking her to pull the hood over her head as we went out.

"Should I get you anything for staying overnight, like a nightshirt or a toothbrush? What else might you need? Who could you stay with?"

"Why?" Heini asked again.

"Forensics has to inspect your apartment. It will be sealed until tomorrow. We need to go to Jorvi now, and then I'll take you wherever you want to go. Don't worry, Heini. I'm here for you. The doctor and I will have to ask you some questions, but only so Samir will get the sentence he deserves."

When Heini didn't answer, I grabbed a nightshirt from the closet, a purple-and-pink-striped affair from Marimekko, panties, and a pair of socks. I put them in one of the plastic bags from my kit. I also took along a toothbrush and container of moisturizer from the bathroom. Maybe the doctor would think it best for Heini to stay in the hospital overnight for observation—if there was space. We could end up having to wait hours for her to be seen.

Heini walked behind me to my car. There were a couple of oldish men standing around next to the police vehicle. They looked disappointed when, instead of uniformed officers, two women came out of the building, one of whom was a stranger and the other of whom was concealed under her hood. There was nothing about my car that would indicate it was being used in an official capacity. Heini got in next to me and fastened her seat belt. The Friday evening traffic was flowing at its usual pace along the streets of Espoo, with people returning from their jobs, going to the store or the movies, or hurrying to meet their loved ones. None of them had a clue that the life of one person in this town would never go back to the way it had been, that time would be divided in two, before rape and after rape. Heini probably didn't know it yet either. But I knew it all too well.

17

The wait at the emergency room was grueling. My worry that, by going to the bathroom at home, Heini would wash away the semen seemed ridiculous now. She had to go twice more before we got to see a doctor. I was sure she knew the drill and would be preparing herself.

Heini told me that her brother lived nearby, so I called him from her phone. He was taken aback when, instead of his sister, a complete stranger started talking. I said that Heini had been assaulted and was at the Jorvi Hospital emergency room waiting to be seen by a doctor. The brother promised to come as soon as he could; currently he was stuck in a business meeting.

"What happened to her? Is she going to have to stay in the hospital?"

"She'll have to tell you herself, and the doctor will decide whether to admit her. I can say this much: her life is not in danger and there was no serious bodily injury."

Heini sat in the waiting room, her eyes closed. When I asked if she wanted something to eat or drink, she just shook her head. I still got her some water and a chocolate bar from the vending machines.

"Only two more before you," I said when I returned. I had tried to get Heini past the line, but the response was curt: everyone had to wait their turn.

"The doctor will probably give you sleeping medication. Just go ahead and take it, even though you might not normally. Any trouble sleeping will just make you more depressed. I know from experience."

My words made Heini sit up a bit.

"What do you know? No one can know how I feel!" she yelled. She was moving from initial shock to the anger phase, and in that state, anyone would do as the target for her rage.

"I might know." I didn't want to relate my own experience in a public place, where there could be inquisitive ears. Though most of the people here were too focused on their own misery to eavesdrop on us. The others waiting to be seen included an old woman coughing violently into a towel, a worn-out looking young Russian woman whose toddler was whimpering and clutching his ears in obvious pain, and a drowsy drunk with a head injury who was mumbling to himself. A guard came to check every now and then to make sure the man wasn't making a scene. I hadn't told the guard I was a police officer, though it would be my duty to intervene if the intoxicated man started bothering the others.

"At the Girls Club, do you have the contact information for the rape crisis center and the Victim Support Society? Definitely get in touch with them, and you can always call me too," I said when the patient in front of Heini, the little old lady with the cough, had been in with the doctor for fifteen minutes. Just like Heini, I'd been able to recite from memory what a sexual assault victim should do and where to get help. Even so, I still ended up carrying the pain and shame inside for a long time, although support from my peers did help to lighten the load.

Heini's brother arrived at the emergency room a couple of minutes before his sister was called in to see the doctor. He was a little under thirty, and despite its being Friday evening he was dressed in a dark suit, spotless black shoes, and a blue tie with a Finnish coat of arms tie tack. He looked like he belonged to a different world than Heini did. The siblings didn't hug or touch each other, but the brother introduced himself as Kimmo and shook my hand.

"It was good that you were with Heini. The negotiation just went on and on, and I didn't want to tell my business partners where I needed to hurry off to. Who hurt her?"

"We'll talk about that soon enough," I said just as the doctor called number forty-seven to come in.

"Should I go with her?"

"It would probably be best for you to wait here. Heini, I'm going to go now. You know where to find me. Your brother will wait here."

I'd requested that the on-call psychiatric nurse attend Heini's physical examination. I would have wanted to be there myself, but regulations prevented it. Heini drifted into the office like an empty shell, and through the doorway I saw that in addition to a young female doctor, there was also an older woman in a nurse's uniform. Though the gender of a health care professional was no guarantee of empathy, it was better that neither of the people examining Heini was a man.

I asked Kimmo to come out into the hall where we could talk in private. I told him that Heini had invited an acquaintance she'd run into on the bus to her home for coffee, and that he had raped her. The perpetrator was now in police custody.

"Who is this guy? Will he go to jail? It's one of those ragheads, right? The ones whose sisters Heini mollycoddles over at that club of hers." Kimmo's switch from polished to furious was so fast that it took me a second before I managed an answer.

"I don't know what you mean by 'raghead.' The initial investigation is ongoing, but the suspect is Samir Amir, a Bosnian Muslim."

"How could Heini have been so stupid, inviting a guy like that into her place!"

I counted to three, then ten. I felt like grabbing his Finnish-flag-blue silk tie, but instead I directed all of my anger into my voice.

"The worst thing you can do to your sister right now is blame her. She hasn't done anything wrong."

Kimmo Korhonen blushed. "No, of course not. You never know about these Muslims, though. It's not smart having anything to do with them. Heini is too naïve. I guess this will teach her."

No sermon I could give was likely to have any effect on Kimmo's opinion of immigrants, so I let it be. I made him swear not to blame Heini. A rape wasn't the victim's fault.

Back in my car, my hands were shaking so much that I had a hard time getting the key into the ignition. I wanted to get home, safe behind locked doors. Even though I knew the man who had injured me was in prison, the feeling of fear still overcame me, and there was no way to rationalize it away. I finally got my breathing under control, using the alternate-nostril breathing technique I had learned, and drove home.

Once I was safely inside my house, I discussed the case over the phone with Ruuskanen. He thought that interviewing Heini Korhonen again could wait until next week. He was happy to leave it for me to do, since I was a woman, after all. We both reckoned that Ursula Honkanen would probably be too overzealous for the job, and the trainee, Jenna Ström, was still too inexperienced. There wasn't any talk of questioning Samir Amir, because he'd sunk into a reactive psychosis.

"Maybe he's just trying to avoid having to take responsibility for his actions," Ruuskanen said dubiously over the phone.

"I don't really think you can fake psychosis like that. He has an extremely traumatic past; he spent his childhood in a refugee camp. You name it, it happened there."

Ruuskanen just snorted. "My own father probably would have been certifiable by these new soft standards. He went to the front when he was seventeen and left one of his legs with the Russians. But he wasn't any more traumatized than anyone else who came back from the war. He went to school and graduated in mechanical engineering. He was still entertaining his grandchildren with his prosthetic leg when he died. Our Miro always begged Gramps to take his leg off so he could show it to all his friends. No one else had a one-legged grandpa."

My own kids' grandpa still had both of his legs, but his back was so sore that we finally asked a doctor to make a house call. He prescribed more pain medication and some exercises.

"We could get you home lying down in a taxi van, but let's wait and see how it is next week."

On Saturday night Antti and I decided to go into the city. My dad would be able to watch the kids, even though he couldn't move.

When someone from Espoo went "into the city," it meant going to downtown Helsinki. We made a compromise: first we went to a Scarlatti piano recital, which Antti enjoyed, but to be completely honest it put me to sleep, then we ate in an Italian restaurant, and finally we rushed over to Semifinal to see to a couple of my favorite bands. Antti got caught up bouncing with me to the music, and in the taxi we made out like teenagers. It was hilarious trying to sneak into the house without waking up my dad. We managed to do it, but Iida was still awake and followed us into our bedroom, looking serious.

"Mom, how can you go out partying when Heini was just raped!"

"Where did you hear that?"

"Everyone knows. We have an e-mail list at the Girls Club."

"Did Heini announce the news there?"

"No, but someone did . . . I don't know who. So, it's true!"

"Yes. We already have the perpetrator in custody, and I took Heini to the doctor."

"So, you knew yesterday?"

"I have to keep my work confidential; we've gone over this before."

"What difference does that make when everyone can read about it online?"

I was too tired to check up on that on the computer, and it took a good amount of time to calm Iida down. I sat next to her bed until 3:30 a.m., and by that time, the last of the alcohol I had drunk had disappeared from my bloodstream.

On Sunday I didn't get out of bed until noon, and still I felt like I hadn't had enough sleep. Iida was still dozing as I finished my morning coffee. I went into her room and gently stroked her teased-out hair.

"Time to get up, dear, so your sleep rhythms don't get all out of whack."

She looked like a little troll, and her expression was surprisingly similar to a three-year-old woken up from a deep sleep.

"After breakfast, I want you to show me that e-mail list. I don't normally track your conversations online, but in this case, someone has to step in."

"I'll start the computer right now if you bring me a cup of cocoa," Iida said as she got up and stretched. The skin on her back and arms was still smooth and free of pimples, but her breasts were already womanly under her thin nightshirt. I went to make some dark hot chocolate, with very little sugar. That was how Iida liked it. My dad had succeeded in turning onto his side on the mattress on the floor and was reading the morning paper, groaning occasionally. Antti had brought him bread, coffee, and fresh juice. Taneli had gone to the morning session at the rink with a friend, whose mother had picked him up. Antti had apparently been up since the boys left. I tried not to feel guilty—one parent was enough for sending a child out for the day.

"Heini posted it herself. Just look, Mom. Her username is HeiniK."

I bent over to look.

Warning to all girls: Never let anyone even the slightest bit unfamiliar into your home. Anyone can be a rapist. Anyone can take you by surprise. Anyone can hurt you.

And so on. Heini must have really gone haywire.

Instead of calling her, I called Nelli Vesterinen, who was the other moderator of the e-mail list. She hadn't checked the list since late the previous evening and was appalled to hear what had been posted there.

"Is it true?"

"Unfortunately, yes. You haven't talked to Heini?"

"No! She had Friday night off, since it was theater improv night, and we don't really do anything together outside of work. This is terrible! Who did it?"

I related the facts briefly, and I used the term "suspect" in reference to Samir Amir. I asked Nelli to take down the message and to delete all of the replies that had come in.

"Should I say that someone hacked the site using Heini's username? Heini never would have done this, upsetting the girls on purpose."

"Maybe not. I'll be in touch later."

Iida had gone downstairs, so I stayed at the computer. I did a search of the discussion boards using Heini's name. News of the rape was already on quite a few forums, including *Suomi24*, where the thread had already been cut off once, and also on the *Homma* anti-immigration forum. The opening post was the same on all of them:

> My name is Heini K. and I'm 29 years old. I was raped in my own home on Friday by 22-year-old Samir A., a Muslim refugee from Bosnia. I was crazy to let him into my home. I took pity on him because he needed someone who knew Serbo-Croatian. I do. It's almost the same language as Bosnian.

The message continued with a description of what the rapist had done to her. The username was different on every discussion thread, and none of them was HeiniK.

I tried to get in touch with Heini, but all I got was her voice mail. I left a message asking her to call me, and I also got in touch with the cybercrime officer on duty, who would have to deal with the legality of the messages with the discussion board moderators. There wasn't much more I could do.

Once I'd made lunch for Taneli after he'd returned from practice, I asked Iida to go for a walk with me. It was a sunny day, which, despite how much snow there was, still exuded a feeling of spring. Chickadees sang in the trees in the yard. Jahnukainen was sleeping on the porch and lazily opened his eyes when a bird came too close. Venjamin was entertaining Norppa, the little girl next door, by running after a branch she was dragging around. He was still such a kitten, and he must have been able to feel spring in the air too. Iida and I set off in the direction opposite of the police station.

"Thank you for telling me about what was happening online, Iida. Without you, those rumors would have been left to spread. Heini probably wasn't herself when she shared that with everyone."

"I hear it was posted other places too. Someone said so on Messenger. They're threatening to beat the person who did it if he gets free. How is that supposed to do Heini any good? Everyone just wants revenge and revenge and revenge, and it just goes on and on. Someone wrote online that we should borrow the Muslims' tradition of blood vengeance."

The sun shone straight into my eyes and made them water. I recognized the anxiety and anger of puberty in Iida. The black-and-white world of childhood was forever gone for her, even though plenty of adults seemed to return to that often enough nowadays. It was easy to label and pigeonhole, to cling proudly to prejudice, no matter what reality showed you. But I guess each of us has our own mental funhouse, though looking at our delusions in the mirror is more likely to make you want to cry than to laugh.

"Nowhere near all Muslims believe in blood vengeance. And even if some do, we shouldn't adopt something so absurd."

"Maybe Dad is right: all religions are evil," Iida said with a dramatic sigh. We arrived in the center of Kauniainen, a small town surrounded by the city of Espoo, and stopped at a kiosk to buy some salmiakki licorice. Iida especially liked the strong Turkish Pepper brand. I knew I couldn't make my daughter forget what had happened, not Noor's murder and not Heini being raped. All I could do was be there with her and listen, and answer her questions, however imperfectly.

On Monday morning, when I switched my work phone's ringer on, I found that Ruuskanen had called three times and Koivu once. The latter had also sent a text message: *Ruuskanen in headlines, both tabloids. Explaining why he hadn't announced Friday rape. Papers in the case room. Come read before morning meeting.*

I'd slept in for as long as possible, so now I'd be cutting it close. Ruuskanen must have tried to call to talk about my participation in the morning meeting, but then why hadn't he left a message? I was just glad that someone else was dealing with being the boss and under the reporters' microscope. I managed to get dressed, drink my coffee, eat a roll, and glance at the morning headlines in fifteen minutes. It only took five minutes to get to work by bicycle, though I almost had a wreck on a puddle that had frozen overnight. The surface was so slick that even my winter tires couldn't get any purchase.

Akkila was just taking down a crime report when I stepped into the vestibule at the station. The complainant had had a rock thrown through a window during the night—that was as much as I managed to hear as I walked by. The case room smelled like coffee, and Puupponen was unwrapping a cheese-filled baguette.

"I decided to have health food for breakfast today! Have you seen the papers?"

"Give them here."

Ruuskanen's mustache looked bushy; the picture was obviously a few years old and had been taken from a police yearbook. In both tabloids, the article itself was brief. Ruuskanen had been pressed on why the media hadn't been informed about the rape on Friday in Tapiola, and Ruuskanen had replied that it hadn't been necessary since the police already had the suspect in custody and didn't need the public's help in solving the crime. Another reporter had stated that the person in question was presumably a man, which Ruuskanen confirmed. Ruuskanen also said that the rape case hadn't been made public out of a desire to protect the privacy of the victim. After this Ruuskanen was asked whether it was true that the suspect had received a permanent residency permit in Finland and had a Muslim background. Ruuskanen had answered in the affirmative but declined to comment further. The headline of one tabloid asked the question "Police Covering Up Immigrant and Refugee Crimes?" and the other proclaimed, "Woman Raped in Tapiola—Second Act of Violence by an Immigrant in Espoo This Month."

"There isn't anything all that special about these. It was just a slow news day."

Koivu, who had just walked through the door with a sheaf of papers under his arm, said, "Yeah, but Ruuskanen is spitting mad because he's being accused of being a raghead ass-licker. And, of course, us cops are all the same. I'll probably have to start recusing myself from investigating immigrant crimes because I'm married to a Vietnamese Chinese woman who moved here when she was two. You got the request to come to the meeting at nine, right? Samir's family is pretty popular around here right now. Yesterday a fax came from the Bosnian police with Sara Amir's interview word for word."

"Fax? Don't they know how to use e-mail?"

"They're probably afraid that the Swedish Security Service will intercept the message," Puupponen said with a smirk. "Is there anything interesting in it?"

"Don't rush me—I'm reading." Koivu poured coffee into his stained mug, added two sugar cubes, and dug for his reading glasses in his jacket pocket. I flipped through one of the tabloids, realizing that I didn't know half of the people the gossip columns were talking about. Luckily the reporters had been kind enough to add descriptive titles: "familiar from *Big Brother*," "contestant on *The Apprentice*," "of *Bachelor* fame." Maybe it was high time for me to start updating my TV knowledge.

Koivu read with intense concentration. His reading glasses slipped down a little on his nose, and he pushed them back up. His wedding ring looked tight, and his gray corduroy jacket was worn at the elbows. Of all the men in the world, Koivu was the dearest to me after Antti—he was the brother I'd never had. I saw his eyebrow raise half a second before he opened his mouth.

"Well, well, well! I think we just cleared up why Sara is happy to be in Bosnia. Apparently, her brother had been molesting her and sometimes hitting her. Sara's parents thought it would be best for her to return to Bosnia so that her brother wouldn't lose his residency permit in Finland. Samir has a panic attack and hides in the corner and rocks back and forth—that's what it says here in the English translation—whenever he thinks that he'll have to leave."

I remembered what Samir had said about the "wrong boys" Sara had been spending time with. Had he come up with that explanation himself, or had it been fed to him? It would be up to the forensic psychiatrists to figure out how delusional Samir was. It would probably be my job to question his parents, which would help us determine who was ultimately responsible.

And that was precisely what Ruuskanen suggested when we sat down for our meeting. Because Samir Amir and the Girls Club staff were connected to the missing young women, our cell would add the rape case to our task list. It was an open-and-shut case, so all we'd have to do was get it ready for the prosecutor.

"But I'll handle the media myself. Is that clear, Kallio?"

"Crystal."

After the meeting, I contacted Jorvi Hospital to ask how Samir was doing. A nurse promised that the attending physician would call me back when he finished his rounds. Koivu contacted Samir's parents. They'd been extremely concerned when they hadn't heard from their son on Friday night. Samir was an adult, so no one had been obligated to notify his next of kin, but I had still assumed that the hospital would have contacted the parents of a psychiatrically ill patient. Based on Koivu's repeated sighs, the conversation was arduous.

"I'll contact you again. Samir is not in any danger. You don't need to go to the hospital. We will come to see you with an interpreter." Although Koivu's voice was calm, and he was speaking slowly and clearly, his face was getting red.

"I'm not sure Samir's father understood even half of what I said," Koivu said after hanging up. "He seemed to think that Samir had been in some sort of accident. We're going to need a Bosnian-speaking interpreter; apparently the mother doesn't speak a word of Finnish, even though the family has lived here for ages. Supposedly she knows English, but it seems a little dodgy to go talking to them in a language no one involved with this case speaks fluently. Where is our list of official interpreters?"

Heini Korhonen's name was on the list, but naturally Koivu had skipped over it. In the meantime I called Heini again. This time she answered her phone.

"Hi, this is Heini."

"This is Maria Kallio. How are you coping?"

Heini didn't answer for a long time. Her breathing was a little raspy, but I didn't hear any sounds of crying.

"Nelli called yesterday," she finally said. "She claimed I'd written some nonsense on the Girls Club e-mail list. It wasn't me."

"So, you didn't write about the rape online?"

"Why on earth would I do that? This is already hard enough without everyone finding out about it. I never could have imagined how terrible I'd feel. Never."

"Where are you now?"

"At Kimmo's place in Lippajärvi."

"Alone?"

"My brother's wife and kids are here. Väinö is three and Aino is six months. What has Samir said? Why did he do it?"

"We haven't been able to interview Samir yet."

"But he's locked up, right?"

Heini's voice was shrill. In the background I could hear a child singing, "Baa, baa, black sheep, have you any wool," and another child yelling out infant babble, mimicking the one singing.

"Yes," I answered, even though I didn't actually know what kind of room Samir was in—but I did know he was under guard. "Have you been in contact with any sort of support group?"

"Nelli stopped by yesterday. But no one can really help."

This made me even more concerned. Her reaction to what had happened was normal, but she shouldn't be left alone. I asked her about the security on the e-mail list, and she said that only Nelli and she knew each other's passwords and were able to remove messages from the discussion board. Heini didn't have any idea who could have gotten her password.

Her brother, Kimmo, had been furious about what had happened to his sister and had apparently managed to squeeze the details of the rape out of her. Could he have gotten her passwords too? When I asked where Heini kept her passwords, she answered that she memorized them.

"And they aren't just your birth date or phone number or anything like that?"

"Of course not! They're just random words."

Telecommunications fraud and identity theft weren't our responsibility, so I'd have to leave that for others to investigate. Still, I wasn't totally confident that Heini was telling the truth. What if she'd written the messages while in shock and didn't remember? The emergency room doctor had prescribed a week of sick leave, but Heini said she was going to the Girls Club that afternoon.

"I won't let what that bastard did destroy me. I'm going to continue with my life."

I didn't ask whether Sara had told Heini that Samir had molested her. That would have been too cruel. Instead, I told her I'd come by the Girls Club if I could.

Koivu announced that the Bosnian interpreter's child was sick, and the earliest we would be able to get her would be Tuesday afternoon, when her husband would be free to provide childcare. I had to laugh about how the simplest delays could make an investigation drag on endlessly. The physician attending Samir didn't have much to report: Samir was still in a psychotic state, and they hadn't been able to get through to him. He just lay there, so they'd been forced to put him on an IV. He wasn't even using the restroom, the doctor said.

"We're trying another medication now."

"Is there anyone in the hospital who speaks Bosnian or something related? That would be good if the hospital staff wants to contact Samir's parents," I said.

"The pediatric ward has a nurse who knows Serbo-Croatian. I'll see if she has better luck with the patient than the Finnish speakers have had."

Koivu and Puupponen left to continue interviewing the Ezfahanis. I poisoned my mind by reading the online discussion the username HeiniK had set off, until the mental nausea began to turn physical, and I realized I was hungry. I called Taskinen and asked him to lunch, but he was in Vantaa in a joint Helsinki-Espoo-Vantaa metro area coordination meeting. So, I went down to the cafeteria alone and ended up slurping my bowl of vegetable soup with the white-collar crime investigators and barely escaped being dragged into their Tuesday night hockey betting pool. The Blues were in danger of being knocked out of the playoffs, which seemed to be a catastrophe for two of the detectives but gave Kantelinen, who was from Turku, the opportunity to give the others a good ribbing.

On the bus ride to Tapiola I talked with my mom on the phone—she would be coming on Wednesday. My sister Helena's husband, Petri, had offered to outfit his van so Dad could lie down in it to travel home, but my mother was doubtful that the vehicle's suspension was good enough to transport someone with a back injury.

The door at the Girls Club was unlocked, even though the activity groups wouldn't be starting until four o'clock. I stepped inside and heard two women having a heated discussion.

"But that's what Ayan's mother told me!"

"Should we tell the police? She told them she didn't know anything about Ayan." I recognized the second speaker as Nelli Vesterinen.

"Hello," I said loudly and then stepped into the room like a deus ex machina that shows up at the end of the play to turn the situation on its head. "What should you tell the police?" The first speaker was Miina, who jumped when she saw me. She had on a white knit dress that went all the way down to her ankles, with a hood that she'd pulled over her head, covering her hair. She tugged the hood back from her forehead before answering.

"I met Ayan's mother yesterday by chance at the Cello Mall. I asked her if she'd heard anything about Ayan. She yelled at me and told me to go away and that she never wanted to see me again. She said Ayan had left because of me, because I'm evil and dirty. But I have no idea what she was talking about."

18

"So, you weren't lovers?" I asked Miina, who had fallen silent as she considered what Ayan's mother's words could have meant.

"No! Though you can love friends too." Miina's pale eyes looked at me pleadingly; her eyelashes were so white they were barely distinguishable from her skin. "Why would someone have told Ayan's mother we were in a relationship? Who would do that?"

"Maybe Aisha misunderstood. Did she say that she knows where Ayan is?"

"No, but she said that Ayan left because of me."

To me, Aisha had claimed she didn't know anything about Ayan. That had obviously been a lie. I thought back to our conversation. When she'd asked if Ayan had been found, she'd looked hopeful, and after I'd asked whether one of the male members of the family could have killed her, she'd clammed up entirely. Then we'd forgotten about Ayan in the aftermath of Noor Ezfahani's murder.

"Did she say that Ayan left or that Ayan was sent away? And by leaving, did she mean leaving the country—or dying?"

"I don't know. Ayan's mother—Aisha—doesn't speak Finnish very well, like you said. I can't be sure what she really meant."

"I've met her. Did you talk to her for long?"

"No, it was more like she was trying to brush me off." Miina had been in the big supermarket at the Cello Mall buying dish soap when she saw Aisha Muhammed Ali with her shopping cart. Miina had met Ayan's mother a few times when visiting her friend's home; Ayan only took her there when all of the men of the family were away. During her visits Aisha had been friendly and served tea, so Miina had no reason to expect her outburst of anger at the store.

"She only stopped yelling when she noticed that people were staring, and one man came to ask if I needed help. He probably thought that Aisha was attacking me. What on earth could she have been thinking? I'm no lesbo, even though some of the guys say that all of the girls in the club are."

I laughed. It was the same thing everywhere. Whenever women formed their own communities, close-minded men labeled the groups as breeding grounds for lesbians, but no one would dream of calling the Finnish Club a homosexual society because women were only allowed there on certain evenings.

The door opened and a cold blast of air swept through the room, followed by Heini Korhonen. She was walking strangely, stooped over and with her eyes flitting from side to side. The clothes she had on were the same ones I had taken out of her closet on Friday night. They stank of sweat. Nelli rushed over and hugged her, but Heini didn't respond. She just stood with her arms hanging at her sides, staring at something the rest of us couldn't see. Miina looked at me aghast.

"Hi, Heini. Is it wise for you to be here right now?" I asked. Nelli let go of her colleague, realizing the state she was in.

"You really don't look well," Nelli said. "You're on sick leave. Go home and get some rest! We'll manage just fine. I was just saying to Miina that she could lead your book group—she was going to use Merja Virolainen's new poetry collection, *I'm a Girl, Wonderful!*"

"No need. It's the same as when you fall off a horse. It's best to just get back in the saddle." Heini tried to smile, which looked even more dreadful than her previous apathetic expression.

"Have you spoken with Sylvia? She must not have read the message on the e-mail list, or else we would have heard from her."

"No. Why would I? This is personal business."

"So, Sylvia doesn't know anything?" Nelli asked.

I interrupted. "She's probably still in Hamburg with her friend."

"Friedrich Wende," Nelli said. Heini didn't react. She just sat down on the nearest chair and didn't say anything. The smell of sweat grew stronger. Forensics had finished their work on Saturday, so Heini could have gone home to change clothes by now.

"Sylvia won't like it if we don't tell her. Especially since you're on sick leave . . . ," Nelli continued.

"But I'm not going to take it," Heini muttered. "I'm safe here. The book is in the lounge. I need to make copies of the poems." She still didn't get up, though. She just sat there in her chair, eyes staring away from us like a blind woman's.

"Listen, Heini," I said, trying to put as much energy as possible into my voice. "How about I take you home? I'm sorry to be so blunt, but you stink."

When Heini didn't answer, I told Miina that I'd picked out the clothes for Heini on Friday. Heini claimed again that she was fine, then stood up slowly and walked to the back of the club. If her strategy for getting through this was returning to work, that was good enough. Nelli and Miina would be able to handle her.

I didn't want to torment Heini with any more questions. Miina promised to escort her home after the book club and then stay with her if she needed the company. As for me, I said I was going to have a chat with Ayan's mother, Aisha, to find out what she'd meant in the cleaning supplies aisle at the supermarket at the Cello Mall.

Nelli walked me out. She closed the outer door to the club behind her before saying, "I've been thinking and thinking about that e-mail on the list. Heini was at her brother's house overnight. Her brother is a bit . . . skeptical of immigration. Maybe he stole Heini's password somehow. He doesn't really like Heini's job. They're pretty different people."

She stopped and dug in her jacket pocket. "Damn it, no gum. I stopped smoking when I started working here. Sylvia said I was the right woman for the Girls Club otherwise, but that she wouldn't hire a smoker, because I had to set a good example for the kids. Sometimes I just want a cigarette so damn bad. You don't have any gum, do you?"

"Would salmiakki work?" I still had the candy Iida and I had bought in Kauniainen the day before.

"Yeah, that'll work."

I fished the box of Panther licorice out of the nether regions of my bag and told Nelli to take two. She threw one into her mouth and put the other in her pocket. "Or Heini wrote it when she was still a basket case and doesn't remember or doesn't dare admit it. Either way, it was one hell of a mistake. We'll see if she gets through the night without us having to call the men in the white coats. Later!"

Nelli went back inside, and I started walking toward the center of Tapiola. As I waited at a traffic light, a bus pulled up to a nearby stop. I watched the people stepping off, and among them was Tuomas Soivio. He blushed when he recognized me, but he still walked up to me, and together we set off across the street after the light turned green.

"How's it going, Tuomas?" He looked like someone had turned out the lights behind his eyes.

"Terribly. I never would have believed I could really feel like . . . this."

His words sounded familiar; Heini had used almost the same expression. I didn't tell Tuomas that time heals all wounds, because he wouldn't have believed me.

"My lawyer, Ljungberg, said that you're one of the biggest mother-fucking bitches he's ever met," Tuomas continued, his voice shrill. "He says you'll try to nail me to the wall and maybe even put me in jail if you can."

"You have a really bad defense lawyer if he thinks your first offense could get you a prison sentence. Maybe it's time for a change?" We passed a kebab-pizzeria that was giving off a scent that would have had Koivu inside ordering a double *döner* already. "Besides, I'm not the one who decides what the charges are—that's the prosecutor. I didn't even handle that investigation, as you know perfectly well."

"It was Miro Ruuskanen's dad, right? He was in charge?"

"Yes. You know Miro?"

Tuomas flushed again. "We sometimes run with the same crowd when we watch the Blues' matches. Have they. . . When is Noor going to be buried? Can I go when they do? I didn't know how much I loved her until now. Really. I was such a fucking idiot." Tuomas's eyes were full of tears. He didn't wait for me to answer, instead suddenly bolting off down the street toward his house.

I walked across Tapio Square to the bus stop and got on the 19, which happened to pull up just at the right moment. Hopefully Aisha Muhammed Ali would be home.

When I arrived, the yard in front of her building was full of children who could barely stay on their feet, running around in what was left of the snow in their squelching boots. The mothers were off to the side chatting, five or six different accents in their Finnish. There wasn't a single father in the group. Back in the fall I'd heard of a study that said nowadays women in their twenties consider stay-at-home dads unmanly. Sometimes progress moves in unexpected directions.

The elevator had been fixed since my last visit, but I still used the stairs. One floor smelled strongly of bergamot, but on the next one up it changed to lemon. I rang the bell at Ayan's apartment. No one came. I decided that the police always ring twice and pressed the button again. I heard steps inside the apartment, and the peephole went dark. The door chain rattled, and then the door opened.

"Hello, Aisha." Somehow it was easier for me to call Ayan's mother by her first name than to address her as Mrs. Ali. Hopefully she didn't feel it was disrespectful. "Detective Maria Kallio, Espoo police. We met a couple of weeks ago. Do you remember?"

Hope flashed in her eyes but then gave way to fear.

"You find Ayan, my Ayan?"

"We still haven't found any trace of her. But you seem to know why she left. What was she running away from?" I stepped past Aisha into the apartment. She had a man's white dress shirt in her hands, along with white thread and a needle.

I took off my coat and after a moment's consideration also my shoes, even though Aisha hadn't invited me in. I walked into the living room and sat down on the sofa. Next to it was a well-organized sewing basket full of bright spools of thread, scraps of fabric, and lengths of yarn. Aisha hesitated for a few moments, then sat down on the other end of the couch, which was next to the window. She arranged the shirt in her lap and continued mending a tear under one arm.

"I just saw Miina Saraneva," I said. "You shouted at her in the supermarket at the Cello Mall, because you thought it was her fault that Ayan disappeared. Where did Ayan go?"

Her needle was moving rapidly, and the stitches were so small that they were barely distinguishable. Aisha didn't look at me when she began speaking.

"I not know."

"Then why did you tell Miina Saraneva that Ayan's leaving was her fault?"

Her dark eyes glanced at me, uncertain, and then she turned her attention back to her needlework.

"Ayan always talk about Miina. Adey so beautiful, skin white as cream. I not understand. It terrible crime be with another woman like that. Is that what they teach there in your club, I ask her. She say she not understand. I say that Ali kill, boys Gutaale and Abdullah kill, all friends kill if hear shame like that; whole family go shame and hell, whole family bad Muslim."

She stopped sewing and looked outside. The sun had fallen behind the tall apartment blocks, leaving long shadows, one of which partially obscured Aisha's face. She shifted her position so the part of the shirt that needed mending was in the light again. The clean, even stitches continued. She didn't even have to look where she was putting her needle. She'd probably done the same thing thousands of times.

"I have beautiful amulet, got from Ali when we married. On it sura of dawn, Surat al-Falaq, our sura one hundred thirteen. It no sell, Ali say, no sell ever even if hungry. It always have hide when we come Finland, so no one take away, say sell jewelry first then get food money. I keep safe amulet. Many envy, neighbor Batuulo envy, want buy. They have lot money, somewhere they get lot money. I say give thousand euro, get amulet. Five hundred, say Batuulo. Eight hundred, I say then. Gave eight hundred. I give money Ayan, say go, go, go somewhere away here but write when there. Where I go, Ayan ask. Away from girl, far away. But the woman lie, Ayan say. Cry. I see how you look Adey, look wrong. I want you live. My other daughters die. Now you go."

The further Aisha's story progressed, the faster her needle went. After the last word—"go"—it stopped, because the seam was finished. She took a small, sharp knife and clipped the thread.

"Miina Saraneva swears that there wasn't anything going on between her and Ayan. They were friends, nothing more, nothing less."

Aisha stood and folded the shirt carefully on the coffee table.

"You want tea, coffee?"

"No . . . or, yes, a cup of tea would be lovely." Aisha went into the kitchen. I heard some jingling, and soon she returned with two cups and some small cookies. They were carefully arranged on a serving tray, which was covered with a decorative cloth. It was embroidered so heavily that the base white fabric was barely distinguishable.

"Tea ready soon."

"Did you embroider that cloth yourself?"

"Embroi—what?"

"Did you make that cloth?"

Aisha nodded.

"It's beautiful."

She nodded again and went back into the kitchen. I stroked the cloth with my fingers, thinking about how much time had gone into making it. The Girls Club had a sewing group, in which they taught traditional handicrafts from different cultures, but Iida hadn't been interested in it. She did hem her own jeans, but, to her, sewing on a button was drudgery. When Iida had still been synchronized skating, Antti and I had taken turns sewing sequins on her costume, even though both of us hated doing things like that. Luckily Taneli was content with black pants and a white shirt for his competition outfit.

Aisha returned with a teapot and a sugar bowl. She poured a rosy liquid that smelled like apples into the cups and offered me one of them. The tea was hot and sweet—Aisha had already put sugar in it. She took a sip from her own cup before continuing.

"That woman say my Ayan love Adey like man love woman. Walk holding hands and kiss. That not way in Finland unless wrong kind friend."

"What woman?"

"Woman at club."

"Miina?"

"Not Adey! Big blond. Boss."

"Sylvia Sandelin? The older woman?"

"No, no, no! Young woman! Not girl, woman. She in charge club."

"Heini Korhonen?" When I said the name, I could hardly believe my own ears. My mouth went dry. I sipped some more tea. Aisha looked at me again, straight in the eyes.

"It was her. Came my house, say know Islam no like two women lie together. It good for me protect Ayan. Send Ayan away."

"And you believed her—and not Ayan?"

Aisha nodded. I didn't know who to trust. Someone was lying: Aisha, Miina, or Heini. Had Heini misinterpreted Miina and Ayan's relationship and was so ashamed of her mistake that she didn't dare admit it to the police? Or had Aisha's imperfect command of the language made her imagination run away with her? I drank the rest of my tea but declined a second cup.

"So where did Ayan go?" I asked.

"I not know. She say hate me forever and leave. Not hear anything her after then."

I thought about the rumors about Ayan that had been spread around on the Internet. Had talk of a relationship with another woman gotten to her father and brothers? Had Heini told her story to them too? We would have to talk to her again first thing tomorrow, even if she wasn't back to full strength. Or had Ayan been so distraught by her mother's accusations that she'd taken her own life? Even though the water had been solidly covered in ice since the beginning of the year, there were still spots under the bridges that were melted enough to dive into. Sleeping pills and a frosty night in the woods were also a fatal combination, and if Ayan had managed to find a secluded spot, she wouldn't be found until spring, when people started wandering farther afield once again.

"Did you tell your husband and sons why Ayan left?"

"No, no, no! No tell! You not tell, right?" Aisha grabbed my wrist and squeezed. "Are you mother? You child?"

"Two. A girl and a boy."

"Only two. What if no more, if all die?"

The question made me shudder. I didn't even want to let a thought like that into my head. I focused on Ayan instead. Koivu and Puupponen had contacted all of the women's shelters in southern Finland after the young woman's disappearance. It was common for immigrant women to seek refuge, to get away from domestic violence. However, they hadn't found Ayan.

Was it wrong not to tell her father and brothers that there was hope she might be found alive? Ayan was an adult. She had made this decision herself.

"I know that you have been asked this before, but do you have any relatives or friends here in Finland to whom Ayan might have gone?"

"No . . . friends small . . . few, Sudanese. They would tell. Relatives no. All die Darfur. I think Ayan afraid of all man, so like Adey. In Darfur so many bad man kill Ayan's sisters. Gutaale come soon. Not like if here woman police."

I left my business card with Aisha and asked her to call me if anything else occurred to her. I wondered if she had a cell phone; I hadn't seen a landline in the apartment. On my last visit, the neighbors had said that the family kept to themselves, that they seldom had visitors. Aisha probably hadn't had anyone to talk to about Heini's assertions. Maybe that was why she was ready to believe a stranger's claims over her own daughter's assurances.

As I walked to the bus, I tried to reach Heini, but she didn't answer her phone. It was only four thirty, and the book group wasn't until the evening. I was completely exhausted and wanted to get my thoughts in order. The bus was full to overflowing—there were already two baby strollers in the aisle, and a woman dressed in a veil that only revealed her eyes was trying desperately to get a third in. I helped her lift the stroller and asked an antisocial-looking middle-aged man to move a little so we could fit.

"Can't she wait for the next bus? She can't be in a hurry to get anywhere; they don't work—they just breed more of their brats for us taxpayers to support," the man said.

"How about you just get out of the way and leave the political speeches for another time?"

The man gave me a look like the next thing to come would be his fist. The driver tried to close the door, but I yelled at him that there were still people trying to get on.

"C'mon, jerk-off!" It was a punk teenager, not much older than Iida. "You're the problem here, not the stroller."

The man flushed and moved closer to the boy, who was wearing a leather jacket covered in pins, and combat boots that were almost worn through. The man was taller and broader than him, but the boy didn't look afraid. I got the stroller in, and the mother crammed herself in too just as the doors closed again. Most of the passengers pretended not to have noticed the incident. Many had earbuds in, and one was immersed in a book. The man who'd been such a problem got off at the next stop, as did one of the baby carriages, and when a space freed up next to the punk, I went to sit by him. In Espoo it wasn't exactly customary to talk with strangers on the bus, and the boy had turned up his MP3 player so loud that I could hear the rumble of the bass through the headphones. It sounded suspiciously like the Dead Kennedys. I flashed him a smile and gave him a thumbs-up. He smiled back.

I leaned back and tried to relax. If the man had started to lay into the boy, of course I would have intervened, but luckily, I hadn't needed to. I got off in Leppävaara, where I helped the same stroller out of the bus. The woman had a smile in her eyes, but she didn't say a word. As the bus pulled away from the stop, the punk teenager gave me a thumbs-up through the window. Who said there wasn't any hope for the younger generation?

To my surprise my father was standing in the living room watching Taneli do practice jumps when I got home.

"This is a lutz. It takes off from a back outside edge—you can't really see without skates on—but on television you can pick it out because it's almost like the skater sits in a chair before he takes off like . . . this!" Taneli pushed off and turned two revolutions in the air.

"Mom, I'm trying to teach Grandpa to recognize jumps. The world championships are next month! Grandpa said he used to like a skater named Katarina Witt. Who was that?"

"A two-time women's Olympic champion," I answered, although my father had probably admired more about Witt than her skating prowess. I turned to him. "So, it looks like you're doing better?"

"Looks that way. It's so nice outside I think I may take a walk. Your mother says there's still three feet of snow in Arpikylä and more on its way tomorrow. But I don't think I should go any farther than the yard. Come out with me, Taneli. There's more room for jumping outside."

Antti had made a salmon chowder the day before, so all I had to do was heat it up and set the table. My work phone stayed silent all night, and the only call I received on my personal phone was from my friend Leena. She was at a weeklong rehabilitation training course at the Spa Hotel Peurunka and needed someone to talk to. I traded gossip with her for half an hour. Leena had been in a car accident and would never walk again, but she was still able to work at the Adaptive Sports Association. Apparently, the best thing about the course so far had been a male lecturer's candid talk on the mental health effects of becoming disabled.

Ayan's face showed up in my dreams that night. The cats were abnormally restless too—maybe there was a fox prowling in the yard. I woke up several times to their creeping about. In the morning I felt groggy, but sunshine and strong coffee helped. I was walking to the station when my work phone rang.

"Kallio here."

"Hi, it's Tuomas. Tuomas Soivio. I can't take it anymore. I haven't been able to sleep for days."

"Good morning. I'm glad you called, but if insomnia is your problem, I think a doctor will be able to help you better than the police."

"Nothing will help! There isn't any doctor or medicine that will take away my guilt over Noor's murder."

"Rahim Ezfahani killed Noor, not you."

"But the whole thing was planned. We meant for Rahim to kill Noor."

19

Tuomas's words awoke the same surreal feeling I'd experienced with Aisha. What was he talking about?

"Where are you now?"

"At home. I haven't been able to go to school since Noor's death. It doesn't matter if I never get to go to college."

"So, you're saying you have something new to tell the police about Noor's death?"

"I can't take it anymore! I have to talk to someone or my head's going to explode!"

"Come down to the station. Should I send a patrol car to pick you up?" I asked, because he was so all over the place that it seemed like he might need protection from himself.

"Mom's car is here because she's in Stockholm. I could take that."

"Ask for me by name downstairs, and I'll come get you."

I picked up my pace and tried to get the pieces to fit into place in my mind. I remembered how Tuomas had burst into the Girls Club and rushed into Heini's arms for comfort. It had seemed odd to me that they were so close, but nowadays some young people hugged more freely. Heini had criticized the girls' families for trying to use culture and religion to restrict the Girls Club's members' activities. Had she encouraged Tuomas to date Noor in order to irritate her relatives? Had Heini seen rebellion where there wasn't any, like in Ayan and Miina's relationship, and tried to support it? Had she invited Samir in for coffee because she was trying to get him to admit that he'd been molesting his sister, Sara?

I ran the last few hundred feet to the station. There wasn't any sign of Tuomas in the lobby. Puupponen was in the case room.

"Samir Amir is still psychotic," he said as I walked in. "I just spoke with his mother. She said Samir was made crazy by the war, that he isn't responsible for anything."

"What about the Ezfahanis?"

"We interviewed Noor's brothers again. They're mostly just worried about whether their residency permits will be revoked. The boys have applied for Finnish citizenship. The mother is just grieving for Noor. They buried her last Thursday, immediately after the body was released to them."

Tuomas Soivio hadn't made it to the funeral, but he likely wouldn't have been welcomed by the men of the family anyway. I'd seen a funeral procession in Afghanistan. Four men carried the deceased on their shoulders, without a coffin. There were a lot of people in the procession, mostly men. It was important for Muslims to participate in funerals, because it was an expression of respect to Allah and his will.

"We're interrogating Rahim's father, brother, and grandfather again today. Do you want to join us? I think it would serve them right to have a woman question them too. I can't really comprehend their mindset, that they think any woman in any situation is so alluring that she has to be covered in robes and veils. With all the tits and bras and bare skin in ads these days, I don't even register them anymore. And I'm just a regular guy who likes women," Puupponen lamented. He took a ruby-red grapefruit out of his pocket and threw it in the air, then lobbed it toward me like a volleyball. I caught the fruit and threw it back to him.

"I think the way they think degrades men even more than it does women. As if our brains were between our legs and we didn't have any ability to control our desires. But that is how Samir acts. A woman asks him into her home, and he attacks her. I don't want to think like a racist, because there's absolutely no way to do this job right if you have too many prejudices. They can't be *that* different from us. Religion is just an excuse for them, like it is for those Christians who won't accept female priests. Don't laugh, Maria. I've read the Quran. I really do want to understand. Would you recommend me for a language course if I wanted to study one of their languages, like Arabic?"

"Of course I would. No one can get by just knowing a little Swedish anymore."

"Koivu and I don't even really know that," Puupponen said with a groan, and at the same moment my work phone beeped with a pager code. Tuomas had arrived.

I went downstairs. Tuomas was standing at the reception desk, clipping a visitor's tag to his collar. He had on muddy black shoes and a black winter coat that went down to his knees. It looked too big on him. When he saw me, he flushed a deep red but still tried to meet my gaze. There were dark shadows under his eyes, and he didn't even try to smile. He didn't say anything beyond hello until we sat down in my office. Then he stared at his shoes for several minutes. He unbuttoned his coat but didn't take it off.

"What did you want to tell me?" I finally asked. "You claimed on the phone that Noor's murder was somehow planned . . . Planned by whom?"

"By . . . us. We don't have a name. Or I guess Kimmo called it Operation Eye-Opener, but he was probably the only one."

"Kimmo? Kimmo who?"

"Korhonen. Heini's brother. Maybe it's best if you just watch this video . . ." Tuomas took a thumb drive out of the breast pocket of his coat. "You should be able to open it on your computer."

I took the thumb drive from his hand, which was shaking like an old wino's. I got the video to work after clicking around for a second. There weren't any opening credits. The picture shook a little, and then it became apparent that we were in a normal Finnish living room, where a group of men in their twenties and thirties were gathered. A date from the end of the previous September showed on the screen.

"Who are these guys?"

"Mostly Kimmo Korhonen's friends. A lot of them play paintball together. I've been with them a couple of times. I don't know why I went to that meeting. I guess I didn't have anything else to do that night. I had a video camera with me, because I was supposed to be doing a project for social studies class. They wouldn't have let me tape, but I snuck it in and turned it on in the middle of things. Listen to what they're saying."

"And the Somalis had another fight with some Finns in Kivenlahti," one of the men said. "A gang of them jumped two teenagers for no reason. But the police won't do anything, and society pays for the spearchuckers' defense lawyers, so they don't get punished. I've had enough of this bullshit."

"My sister doesn't dare go near the Espoo train station at night. If she gets off work at ten, she has to take three different buses to avoid having to be around those Muslim rapists," a young man in a T-shirt with a Finnish lion on it added. "Do we have to take the reins because no one else will?"

All of the men growled in agreement. The picture was still bobbing around, and the sound quality was poor, but the men's rage was conveyed perfectly. They reminded me of the Taliban soldiers I'd met in Afghanistan—the anger that filled the room was just as explosive. Suddenly, a woman's clear mezzo-soprano rang out over the men's voices.

"Hold on a second, guys! You're saying that we need to get all these namby-pamby bleeding hearts to realize how immigrants are threatening our society. And that's true—the only way we can we stop our nation from slipping toward Islam is to get people to see the truth. But you aren't going to convince them by fighting with immigrants. You'll just make the liberals see them as victims."

"Yeah, and then we have to give them handouts, since they can't work because of their PTSD. Fuck me if anyone coddled my granddad after the war. He had to work construction even though he left a leg at the Svir River." The young man in the Finnish coat of arms shirt was speaking again. He seemed familiar. I paused the video.

"Who is that?"

"Miro Ruuskanen. But he doesn't play a lead role here." Tuomas pressed play again.

The woman, who the camera finally turned toward, didn't let Miro Ruuskanen's interruption bother her.

"Exactly. But even the libtards don't really want Sharia law here. A lot of them are Green Party feminists. They only protect the Muslims because they can use them to keep you Finnish men in your place. We have to show them what their little pets really are. They are men who don't value women at all, who beat them and rape them when they try to integrate with Finnish society." Heini Korhonen's eyes shone with the passion of a true demagogue.

"We know all that. They're so blind." This speaker had a refined, bookish tone and an Adam's apple the size of an orange.

"Opening their eyes will take effort from all of us. But it will be worth it. We'll have to act exactly the way the bed-wetting liberals want. We'll start befriending immigrants. We'll get to know them. Every guy here will get an immigrant girlfriend. The more traditional the family, the better. I have a few good candidates at the Girls Club. I can help introduce you. And we women will have to make even bigger sacrifices. In a war you don't ask what the price of victory will be."

Heini's voice was impassioned, but there were skeptical murmurs among the men. The one with the educated accent raised his voice again and asked if Heini was really suggesting that they start making friends with ragheads.

"We don't have anything against their women, so why not? They're kind of pretty under their veils," a small, dimpled young man exclaimed, looking excited about the idea.

"But they're all circumcised. What's the fun in that? Although, I don't really need a girlfriend, since I already have a wife." Kimmo Korhonen stood out from the group in his well-tailored suit. He didn't really seem to like that his sister had suddenly taken charge of the meeting.

"At least you know that you'll be getting fresh, tight meat," Miro Ruuskanen said with a laugh.

"This plan will take time. We won't see results immediately. And that's exactly why it will work, if we can just keep it quiet. The operation has to be secret. Can all of you keep your mouths shut? God damn it, put that phone away!"

Tuomas's video ended there.

"They didn't realize that I was filming too, but I didn't dare try again. That was where it started, Heini's idea. I knew Noor from school—there was no way not to notice a girl that beautiful—and Heini said that she would be a good candidate because her family was so possessive. And the plan worked . . . perfectly . . ." Tuomas broke down in tears.

I felt like shouting and breaking things, but my feelings didn't have a place in this investigation. I let Tuomas sob in peace and watched the video again. "In a war you don't ask what the price of victory will be." Did Heini still think that? Had she only pretended to be broken?

"So, your intent was to provoke hotheads like Rahim Ezfahani to violence and use that to turn public opinion in your favor?" I asked once Tuomas's sobbing had stopped.

"Yeah, we were supposed to write online and use that to influence people's attitudes. At first Heini's plan sounded reasonable. It just didn't seem to work. I was really the only one who found a girlfriend, and the others started to fade away. Heini made a list of the ones we should try with. Noor was on it . . . and Ayan Ali Jussuf. And that Sara girl . . . Have they been killed too? Why hasn't there been more talk about them? Heini was right about that, that the Espoo police only protect immigrants. Didn't you learn anything when Ibrahim Shkupolli shot those people in the mall?"

"So Aziza Abdi Hasan wasn't on your list?"

"No."

"Do you have the list?"

"No. Only Heini and Kimmo have it. Kimmo has an MBA and he's studied a little law too. He said he was going to make sure that none of us could be charged with anything. Guess how angry he was at me when I went to force Rahim to confess. But what else could I do? I couldn't let him beat the rap for her murder. But now I'm the prisoner, probably for the rest of my life . . ."

I sighed. This childish conspiracy was like something straight out of a video game, where everyone has six lives and you can always start over from the beginning. Tuomas was still a kid, of course, but he should have had some sense of what he was doing.

"Heini gave me instructions on how to approach Noor, but after the beginning I didn't need much help. She was a cool chick, but her homelife was screwed up. She wanted to live like the other Finnish girls. And I didn't realize how much I really loved her until it was too late. I didn't believe they'd really do it, no matter how crazy they are. After a couple of months of dating, I didn't remember anymore what the original purpose had been. I just wanted to be with her." Tuomas wiped his nose on the sleeve of his coat. "Heini told Noor that the best way to get rid of Rahim and his plans to marry her was to tell him that she wasn't a virgin anymore. And that made him kill her! Why am I such a fucking idiot!" Tuomas slammed his fists against his head.

"You did succeed at getting people talking. The Internet is full of calls for a lynching, and Rahim's time in prison is going to be hell on earth if I know that part of society as well as I think I do."

"I don't feel sorry for him at all. He's a total shithead. Maybe he would have killed Noor anyway, because she wasn't willing to marry him. I should have just taken her away from him. Maybe I could have asked her to come live with us!"

"Will you tell me the names of everyone who participated in your meetings and this 'operation'?" We might have been able to charge the group with incitement to racial hatred, but if the only evidence was a few minutes of poor-quality video and Tuomas's story, there probably wouldn't be any prosecutions. We would have to question Heini Korhonen regardless, and before we did that we needed as much information as we could collect.

Tuomas listed about a dozen names. Besides Miro Ruuskanen, none of them were familiar from work or elsewhere. In addition to Heini Korhonen, there was another woman in the group, a girl named Pia who was the girlfriend of Jasu, the one with the fancy accent.

"Does your attorney, Kristian Ljungberg, know about this?" I asked Tuomas.

"No. Why would I have told him?"

"In court Kristian should be able to shift the blame for Rahim's kidnapping from you to Heini. He isn't a bad lawyer, even though what he says about me is a load of bull."

"I want to die. I want to go where Noor is. I don't deserve to live," Tuomas said, heaving a sigh.

"Don't go ruining any more people's lives now. You're right, you've been an idiot. But it's good you came to talk to me."

"Heini said that you understand the Girls Club and that you really care what happened to Ayan and Sara. That through you we could make our voice heard."

A hum began in my head. Heini Korhonen had wanted me to be a part of her twisted game too, because she knew that I viewed the rights of immigrant girls the same way she did. Maybe the fact that I'd danced along to her choreography and started the investigation into the missing girls had set off this chain of events. I stopped myself midthought. No,

Heini had started refining her moves in the early fall, when I was still at the Police University College training Afghans. I'd just happened to cross paths with Heini through my work and Iida.

"If I remember right, it was Jaro, the short one who laughed in the video, who tried to make friends with Ayan in the fall, but Ayan wasn't interested, and then Jaro started badmouthing her. Heini was mad, because Jaro said that he'd only tried to hit on Ayan as a joke. Jaro told Ayan she was a fucking nigger lesbian, and Heini thought that it wasn't a good idea to keep Jaro in the group because he was unreliable. And then the group sort of dissolved. I was the only one who continued, and I didn't realize that I wasn't pretending anymore, that I really was head-over-heels for Noor, and I finally got her in bed. She wanted that too."

Once Tuomas got going, he talked and talked about the things he and Noor had done together, about Noor's dreams, about how Tuomas's parents had been delighted about Noor appearing in his life, because she valued her education and encouraged Tuomas to improve his grades. I wrote down the details, becoming increasingly apprehensive. All that was missing from this mess was for Noor and Rahim's male relatives to take revenge on Tuomas if knowledge of the provocation reached them. The cycle of hatred would only continue.

A knock came at the door. I stood up and opened it. Koivu was waiting in the hallway. His expression turned curious when he saw Tuomas. He motioned for me to follow him. I closed the door behind me, and we went into the case room.

"What is Tuomas Soivio doing here?" Koivu asked once the door clicked shut.

"He came to confess."

"Confess what? Rahim Ezfahani murdered Noor, and the other men of the family helped hide the body. We confirmed all that again in yesterday's interviews. Puupponen went home because he had a headache. No wonder, given the heavy stuff the Ezfahanis were telling us."

I repeated to Koivu what Tuomas had told me. When I got to the video about the meeting, Koivu suddenly sat down. After I was done, he sat silently for a long time before he spoke.

"So, in a way the Ezfahanis were right. They thought Tuomas was a bully who was trying to lure Noor away from Islam. But because Noor had transgressed so seriously against all of them, they believe Rahim's act was just, even though they understand that according to Finnish law he will have to go to prison."

"What were you coming to tell me?"

"I just came to ask if you'll have time for lunch in a couple of hours. They're serving chicken pesto lasagna in the cafeteria, and it's pretty damn good. Ville and me usually split an extra serving."

"Let's shoot for that. I'll come over to your office, but right now I need to keep going with this."

I didn't feel like leaving Tuomas sitting alone in my office for any longer than I had to. I hadn't shut down my computer completely, but I had left it in a state that would require a password to access anything. Although I hadn't had time to collect much in the way of files, I wouldn't have been surprised to see him flipping through the folder that had *Noor Ezfahani* written on the cover. But when I returned to the room, Tuomas was sitting with his hands covering his face, crying.

"Do you know if Noor has already been buried?" he asked when he finally regained control of his voice.

"Last Thursday. She was buried immediately after the body was released."

"Where?"

"There's a small Islamic section at the Kirkkonummi cemetery."

"Is there already a headstone at the grave? I have to go there; I have to get close to Noor."

"I don't know. You said your mother is in Stockholm. On a business trip? And your father?"

"He's probably at work. He has some sort of account-balancing thing going on. Mom was a little unsure about whether she could leave now with me just lying around the house, but then she said that I'm a grown man who has to grieve in his own way. And they can't help me. No one can."

The idea of putting Tuomas behind the wheel of a car was terrifying, especially if he decided to drive out to Kirkkonummi. After the intersection with the Ring III Beltway, he might meet a truck coming in the opposite direction that looked just a little too appealing.

"I'm going to say this one more time: you have acted like an irresponsible idiot. But Rahim killed Noor, not you. And maybe with the information you've given me we can still find Ayan Ali Jussuf. Heini lied to her mother—I'm sure of it now. Why do you think she's so afraid of immigrants?"

"She isn't afraid of immigrant women at all. She wants them to come here and be freed from the chains men and Islam put them in. That's how I've understood it anyway." Tuomas dried his eyes. "What will happen to me now?"

"Maybe it would be a good idea for you to tell your parents and your lawyer the truth about why you started dating Noor. Leave that memory stick with me. I'll write you a receipt for it. I'm going to have to talk with the officer in charge of the investigation. You'll have to repeat your story for the official record. And one more thing: Was Miro Ruuskanen actively involved in carrying out the plan, or did he just go to meetings?"

"Well, he didn't hit on any chicks, as far as I know. He mostly just hung around, listening, but he didn't say much. I haven't seen him around in the past few months. He's probably trying to stay on the straight and narrow since his dad's a cop."

If Miro had directly played a part in Noor's murder and Sara's and Ayan's disappearances, then their investigation would have to be moved away from Ruuskanen's unit—or at least from Ruuskanen. I had no desire to make an enemy of Markku Ruuskanen, though. The smartest thing would be to talk to him and Taskinen at the same time. Even though Taskinen might be annoyed by it, I wouldn't warn him ahead of time and would instead just invite them both to a meeting tomorrow morning. Our cell could always act independently, of course—we weren't under Ruuskanen's command. I reported directly to Taskinen.

"Sylvia's going to kill me and Heini when she hears about this," Tuomas said. "She probably won't ever speak to me again, and my grandma's going to be scolding me for the rest of her life. I guess I deserve it. Can I go look for Noor's grave now?"

I didn't have a way to prevent Tuomas from leaving. I told him that he could call if the guilt became too difficult to bear and he didn't have anyone else to talk to. He was an adult, so in theory I didn't need to notify his parents. I would be violating Tuomas's privacy if I did tell them, but that wasn't relevant at the moment. He needed support. I looked up his mother's telephone number, and when she didn't answer I left a message asking her to call me back. As the investigation proceeded, we would need to interview Tuomas's parents, because Noor had visited their home frequently, and Noor's relationship with Tuomas had been the main motivation for Rahim's attack.

Tuomas collected himself, becoming once again the polite boy his parents had tried to raise, and he shook my hand before he left. After I'd escorted him to the lobby, I returned to the case room where Koivu was engaged in his favorite activity, drinking coffee and eating the last piece of a pastry, which, based on the smell, had been a cream cheese Danish.

"Puupponen just called. He says his head feels like it does after drinking all night on May Day. The hospital called him to report that Samir Amir still isn't in any shape to be questioned. They don't know if he ever will be. His mother visited today but with no real results. Puupponen said he was going to take a thousand milligrams of ibuprofen and try to get some sleep. He'll come in tomorrow if the jackhammers have disappeared."

I told Koivu about my dilemma with Ruuskanen. Next I sent Ruuskanen and Taskinen the meeting invitation. Then I called Samir Amir's mother. Our previous meeting had been brief. Mira Amir had let her husband do almost all of the talking and only sat nodding by his side. Mira didn't have a cell phone, but she answered on my second attempt on the family's landline. She spoke good English, which she'd apparently learned during school in the still-unified Yugoslavia.

"Amir residence."

"Detective Maria Kallio, Espoo police. Hello. Do you have a moment?"

"Is this really the police and not another reporter? I'm not going to talk to any reporters, no matter what you promise to pay. My family doesn't need that kind of reputation."

"I can give you the Espoo police switchboard number, and they'll connect you back to me, if you'd like. And I want to talk about Sara, not Samir. Did you send her back to Bosnia because Samir was molesting her?"

It was quiet on the other end of the line, and when she finally answered, her English was somewhat less clear than before.

"I not understand what you mean."

"Was Samir molesting his sister sexually? Did he attack Sara?"

Mira didn't reply.

"Was Sara using birth control pills so she wouldn't become pregnant from her brother? Did Samir rape her too?"

"No! Samir sick, very sick. You can't send him back Bosnia. He is in bad, bad shape now. You know this. He not even recognize his own mother."

"Did Samir see rapes or other sexual violence as a six-year-old in the Srebrenica massacre? Since we can't speak with him, we need your help."

"He is my son, and I won't let him be deported! He can't go back to Bosnia. He saw too much, saw things that no child should see. I cannot talk about it. He saw his sister and aunt die, saw . . ." Mira Amir went silent and then hung up the phone.

I sat at my desk and took a few deep breaths. During my time in the police, I'd encountered dozens of women who had been raped, from girls who were barely teenagers to eighty-year-old great-grandmothers. The oldest rape victim I'd met was a woman who was turning ninety the next year and lived alone in a secluded cottage. She had been the victim of two burglars in their twenties. One of them had finally attacked her sexually after the elderly woman ignored their threats and attempted to call the police. The two friends were caught sitting in a car, surrounded by their plunder and emptying a bottle of cognac they'd pilfered from the old lady. Both were probably still in jail, since that was their sixth break-in.

I'd never needed to turn the screws on a rape victim to try to make her tell me how she had provoked the offender to carry out his act. Now I would have to do exactly that, and on behalf of all the victims of rape I had ever met before, I found myself hating Heini Korhonen.

20

"What sense is there in you going and getting in Heini Korhonen's face? We can't change what happened. How can we prove that she provoked Samir to attack her? We can't. She lied to Aisha about Ayan and Miina's relationship, but that isn't actually a crime either. Don't let your own experiences cloud your judgement, Maria."

I knew that Koivu was right. A healthy serving of chicken pesto lasagna had cooled me down a bit too. I still wanted to meet with Heini, though. I'd asked Koivu to go with me to track her down. Before that we'd put out an elevated-priority APB on Ayan Ali Jussuf. In addition to the police, alerts had been sent to hospitals, shelters, and girls homes throughout the Nordic countries. She had to be somewhere. She didn't have a bank account or any credit cards, and Aisha hadn't been able to say whether the eight hundred euros from the amulet had been Ayan's only money. That would hardly have lasted two months if she had to pay for room and board. Shelters weren't under any obligation to reveal their clients to the police, though. Maybe Ayan had forbidden them from notifying anyone of her whereabouts. I added to the bulletin that incorrect information received by the family was being corrected. Heini owed Ayan at least that much.

I reached Heini on her cell phone.

"Hello, Heini. How are you doing today?"

"I'm trying to work. I have a meeting with Sylvia today. The Girls Club advisory board is convening tonight." Heini's voice was robotic, completely devoid of emotion. Was she just acting?

"What time are you meeting her?"

"At four. The board meeting is at six."

"So, you should have time for a chat with me and Detective Koivu. Are you at the Girls Club now?"

"Yes. But I have work to do."

"We won't bother you for long."

I promised Koivu cinnamon buns at Kaisa's Café in Tapiola if he went with me. Of course, I didn't have to entice him with sweet rolls— I could have just ordered him, but this was an easy way to get him to agree without losing face. While Koivu was arranging a car for us, I read through the physician's report on Heini's injuries. There were strangulation marks on her neck and scrapes and bruises on various parts of her body. The strangulation marks had without a doubt been caused by someone else. Theoretically Heini could have caused the other contusions herself. The sperm found in Heini's vagina, which matched Samir Amir's DNA, was evidence that intercourse had occurred.

Heini had calculated right in calling me. I'd been on her side from the beginning. And she'd been lucky that Samir had gone mute. Of course, the fact that Heini had provided the opportunity for the act didn't reduce the seriousness of Samir's crime. The physician's report would speak loud and clear to the prosecutor.

The route to the Girls Club was already all too familiar. Traffic was backed up at a major intersection partway there, because there was a troop of children crossing the crosswalk toward the swimming center and preventing a tractor trailer from turning left. Half of the trailer was blocking the oncoming lane. Koivu and I looked at each other; this was clearly a moving violation. We didn't feel like getting involved, though, and just waited patiently for the next light, even as the drivers behind us honked like a two-minute delay was a major catastrophe.

It was easy finding a parking place this time, since it was the middle of the day.

"You be the good cop this time," I said to Koivu as we were getting out of the car. He nodded and looked like he was going to say something in reply, but then he closed his mouth again.

The door to the Girls Club was locked. I had to ring the bell three times before Heini came. She had on a dark-gray turtleneck and different jeans than the day before, this time light blue. It didn't look like she'd washed her hair. The bruise on her left cheek had lightened to a yellowish purple. That would get her some stares on the street. She didn't say hello or reply to Koivu's greeting.

I walked to the lounge, sat down, and took my computer out of my bag. Koivu and Heini followed behind. Koivu pulled over a chair for Heini and almost pushed her down into it. He stood in the doorway. He looked even larger than usual in the small room.

"We came because of this video," I said, turning the screen toward Heini. At first, she didn't show any interest in what she was being shown. After hearing a couple of sentences of dialogue, though, she clearly realized what she was watching, and when she heard her own voice, her face flushed. However, she stayed silent all the way through the clip. I took the USB drive out of the computer and opened the physician's statement.

"On this video you say that you're ready for any kind of sacrifice to advance your cause. Is that what was going on with Samir Amir? Did you guess that he would attack you if you invited him into your home?"

Heini didn't answer.

"We aren't accusing you of anything." Koivu took the third chair and sat next to Heini. "I know quite a bit about the things you were talking about. My wife's family came here as refugees. First, they had to move to Vietnam from China to escape the Cultural Revolution, and then they had to flee again during the seventies. Maybe you've heard about the boat people. Her family has done everything they can to adapt to life in Finland. My wife is a police officer too. She even changed her name to sound more Finnish. One of Anu's brothers is an engineer for Ericsson, and the other is a shop teacher. I understand perfectly well why you want immigrants to follow our rules."

Koivu had turned on the charm. It almost made me smile.

"Where did you get this video?" Heini's voice sounded just as apathetic as it had on the phone.

"That doesn't matter," I answered. "What does matter is that you tried to play god. Wouldn't the online commenting have been enough?"

Heini looked at me hollowly, but when she answered, life slowly returned to her voice.

"Don't you understand? If we're too meek, they'll take over the whole world. Think how Finnish women have fought for their rights. Do you want to start having to wear a veil? Do you want your female grandchildren to be barred from going to school? If we give in to them, soon we'll be back in the Stone Age. By all means let them come, but on our terms. Let them believe what they want, but let them also follow our laws. No headscarves or burqas, and jail time for female circumcisions. Are you a feminist?"

"Yes," I answered, even though my opinions weren't Heini's business. I was just trying to get her to talk herself into a corner. So far, she hadn't said anything that would allow us to charge her, but if she chattered enough, maybe she would fulfill the statutory requirements for a charge of incitement to racial hatred.

"So how can you think any differently? The Muslims want to take away our rights. You saw what happened to me with Samir. He didn't listen when I said no. He didn't realize that in Finland a woman can flirt with a guy and even touch him without it being a promise of sex. That's what they think, and even if you put them in jail they just repeat their crimes as soon as they get out. I'm fighting for us women—Finnish women and immigrant women. Open your eyes, Maria!"

"So, you were flirting with Samir and you touched him?"

Heini responded sharply. "I didn't say that. I just said that I told him no. What is Samir claiming?"

"Nothing right now. We haven't been able to interview him yet. Surely Sara Amir told you that her brother was molesting her."

"Can you prove that?"

"The Bosnian police found Sara. She's fine. She is going to school in a village called Bihać. The police are still talking to her. But Noor is dead, and Ayan Ali Jussuf's fate is still unknown. Maybe she killed herself because she was driven away from home. How does that help your plans? You convinced Ayan's mother that she was romantically involved with Miina Saraneva."

"I misunderstood." Now Heini was talking to Koivu. "They were together all the time; Ayan was always stroking Miina's hair and calling her by Arabic pet names. I didn't think there was anything wrong with it, but I'd heard what Ayan's brothers were like, and I didn't want her getting into trouble. Her Allah is even harsher on lesbians than our most conservative Lutheran God, after all. I've heard terrible things from these girls. The Girls Club is their last refuge. I had to do something . . ." Heini's last word was only a whisper. It was like the fire that had been burning in her had suddenly gone out. Koivu and I sat in silence. We should have made Heini repeat the details of the rape, tell us how her injuries had been caused.

"Why haven't you been able to interview Samir?" she finally asked.

Koivu looked at me. We didn't have the right to give out information about the health status of Heini's rapist.

"What did Samir do after he ejaculated? According to the patrol report, he was sitting next to the door to the balcony in your apartment and whimpering when you let the police in. Obviously, he let you go, because you were able to call for help."

"I don't really remember . . . Do I have to talk about it?"

"You seemed awfully ready to sacrifice yourself for your cause," I began, but Koivu glared at me. Silence descended over the room again, broken only by the periodic hum of the computer's fan and hard disk. I could hear the clock ticking in the next room.

"I know you're going to show that video to Sylvia, and I'm going to lose my job," Heini finally said, again in her robot voice. "None of it did any good anyway. I certainly didn't feel like a hero with Samir. There wasn't anything noble in that sacrifice. It was just horrible. I managed to write about it online, but I haven't had the energy to follow the discussions. I imagined giving interviews, but I can't. He destroyed me. Do you understand? I can never let a man touch me ever again. So much for heroism. I promised to tell everyone how dangerous it is to invite the wrong man into your home. So they would know. But I don't think I can."

According to the investigating Puupponen had done online, Heini had received a generous amount of sympathy, but of course there were also those who considered her a naïve feminist bitch who had gotten her just deserts. Heini had wanted to increase the level of hate, and at that she had succeeded brilliantly. Even I had to fight not to hate her, although for a different reason than the others.

"After Samir came, he stayed on top of me for a second and then strangled me again. I was sure he was going to kill me. I asked him not to kill me, begged him in every possible language. I said that I wouldn't report it to the police if he would just let me go. He did. I didn't dare move; I just waited for him to leave. I saw how he looked out the window, how he opened the balcony door. I started to get cold lying there on the floor. He looked like he was going to jump off the balcony, but he didn't. He just sat down on the floor and started to whine. I got the bread knife, closed myself in the bathroom, and called you. I'd heard that the emergency operators don't always answer, and I was afraid for my life. I didn't really mean . . . I didn't want him to attack me. When he came to my place, I thought I would just give him a cup of coffee and then ask him to leave. It was just a whim on the bus. I didn't really want this."

Koivu moved closer to Heini. She recoiled.

"I think you need a doctor's help, and sick leave. Maria, can I have a word with you?" Koivu stood up, and I followed him into the band room. He closed the door behind us.

"You recognize the symptoms? Korhonen is at the breaking point. No more pushing her. She's already paying for her stupidity."

"As are a lot of other people. But you're right. Maybe now isn't the best time to interview her. I'm not able to stay objective."

Koivu wrapped his arms around my shoulders. I believed Heini when she said that she would never be able to stand having a man touch her again. After my sexual assault, it had been a long time before I was able to let even my husband near me.

"It'll all be OK," Koivu said, trying to comfort me. "This is our job: other people screw things up and we clean up the mess. Someone has to do it. And now it really is time for a cinnamon roll. Maybe two."

The meeting with Ruuskanen and Taskinen the next morning was just as irritating as I had imagined it would be. Ruuskanen immediately went on the defensive.

"Miro is an adult! I'm not responsible for his politics!"

We were sitting in Taskinen's office. Outside it was snowing again. Winter didn't seem to have any intention of letting up. A snowplow was trying hopelessly to add snow to the nearly twelve-foot-deep piles outside. It would be a miracle if they melted by Midsummer.

"Of course not, but you have to understand that you can't investigate a case in which your son is involved," I said.

"Involved how? So what if he was at some meeting? What does that make him guilty of? As I understand it, in this country we have freedom of speech and freedom of assembly. And what is there to investigate at this point anyway? Ezfahani has already confessed and the evidence is solid, and Samir Amir is obviously guilty of rape. I would think the two of you would know not to waste time on cases that are already solved. Just send them both on to the prosecutor."

"We haven't been able to interview Amir yet," I reminded him.

"That isn't my problem; you wanted that investigation. Listen here, Kallio, Taskinen: this is starting to stink to high heaven. I might just make a call to the union. It's starting to seem like you want me out of the department before the end of my assignment. And I can guess who would be promoted to take my place."

"Markku, it isn't about that," Taskinen said. "I'm just going to take over the Noor Ezfahani homicide investigation until the case is ready for the prosecutor. As you said yourself, it won't be long. And you have no reason to worry about your position. Maria, it would be a good idea for you to get in touch with Security Intelligence. Isn't this homespun cabal more of their thing? A little time with some professional interrogators should scare some sense into these clowns."

Ruuskanen rose and closed the door carefully behind himself as he left. Taskinen shrugged. There was a framed newspaper article on his wall that I hadn't noticed before. I stood up to read it. The piece had been clipped from a December issue of the Christian newspaper *Homeland*, and it contained an interview with Lauri Johansson, the former leader of the Natural Born Killers gang, who was serving a life sentence for murder. He had found religion in prison and wanted to atone for his crimes.

"Some of them turn out like that," Taskinen observed calmly. "It's good to remember that when this rat race really starts to get you down."

Despite the uplifting message of the article, I walked home that night feeling despondent. I hadn't had time to tell Sylvia Sandelin about Heini's scheme yet. Koivu had been in touch with the Muslim communities in nearby countries, and I had checked possible human traffickers. After she ran out of money, Ayan wouldn't have anything to sell but herself. There certainly wouldn't be any shortage of buyers.

My mother had arrived, and when I walked in the door she was in the middle of giving my dad a lecture about how stupid he was. He just had to go lifting heavy things at his age, didn't he? Listening to her tone of voice was a trip back to my childhood. My parents had often said that constant nagging was just a way of speaking—"just sayin'," as Iida's generation would have expressed it—but I hadn't understood that as a child, so it still bugged me. The kids had their grandparents to keep them company, so I spent the evening doing laundry and mending the hanging loops on some of our hand towels. I would have liked to put my brain in the washing machine too—maybe the permanent-press cycle would work.

I drove my parents to the airport on Thursday. It wasn't possible to get to Joensuu or Kuopio, the larger towns near Arpikylä, by sleeper train anymore, so my parents would be flying with special disability status. My dad's back was still sore, but it hurt the least when he was either walking or lying down. The doctor had prescribed some strong pain medication, so Dad could get through the flight, though after taking a pill he could barely talk.

Helena was the only one of my sisters who still lived near our hometown. Eeva's husband's job had forced her family to move to Tampere. Helena's husband Petri's van would be waiting in Joensuu, outfitted with a bed. It felt eerie to me, watching the airport employee push my father in the wheelchair with my mother following forlornly after them. It was as if the scene was giving me a glimpse of the frailty and incapacity that would be coming for my parents over the next ten years.

Because I'd built up so much overtime, I didn't rush to work, instead sitting in the airport with a cup of tea, contemplating the hustle and bustle surrounding me. A gaggle of Japanese tourists, all wearing the same dark-blue sport jackets and red-and-white-striped scarves, was listening to their guide's instructions. Their money was more than welcome in Finland. A spaniel nearly had a seizure from happiness when its master entered the arrivals area. People shook their heads at its frantic barking. I read the list of departing flights and thought about where I'd like to disappear to right at that moment. Rome was the most tempting, since it would already be spring there.

The next clot of arriving passengers must have come from somewhere sunny, given that their faces ranged from a bright red to deep brown. A good number of them were dressed for entirely different weather, not mid-March in Finland, where temperatures were still well below freezing at night. Some of them looked like they didn't have the slightest desire to return to their normal lives, but others had clearly been missing their children or partners.

At first, I didn't pay any attention to a young woman in a headscarf with no luggage other than a Marimekko Arkkitehti shoulder bag. I had looked past her, shifting my gaze to the famous film actor who happened to be walking behind her. Everyone else was staring at him too. But then my brain registered what I'd just seen. I'd been staring at that scarf-framed face on the wall of our case room for the last couple of weeks. Aziza Abdi Hasan had just walked by.

I stood up so fast that I almost knocked down the plastic chair I'd been sitting on. Where had she gone? I couldn't see her in the terminal anymore. I ran outside. The line for taxis was only a few people long, and she wasn't in it. Had there been someone waiting for her? Bus 615 was at its stop. I ran to the door.

"Police," I said and showed the driver my badge. "I'm looking for someone." I climbed onto the bus, but there was no sign of Aziza there either. One of the blue local Vantaa buses was just starting up at the next stop over. If Aziza was going home, there wouldn't be any sense in her taking that one. I exited the bus and scanned the bus stops. No Aziza. Maybe she'd gone into the airport restroom.

I contacted the airport police and border guard officials. It took almost an hour to determine that no Aziza Abdi Hasan had entered

Finland from outside the Schengen Area. The flights Aziza could have arrived on were from Las Palmas, Stockholm, Frankfurt, and Athens. I asked them to send the passenger manifests to the Espoo Police Department. I borrowed a border patrol computer in the airport just long enough to log in to the department intranet and check Aziza's headshot. The expression of the girl in the picture had been vivacious, happy, lightly reddened lips smiling slightly. The girl who had arrived at the airport had looked frightened and hadn't been wearing any makeup, but it had clearly been the same young woman.

I called Puupponen and asked him to send out an alert to all of the buses and taxis that had left the airport between noon and one, and gave as detailed a description of Aziza as I could. Then I retrieved my car, which had managed to rack up a respectable parking fee in the short-term lot, and took off for Leppävaara. The drive took a painfully long time, because there was only one westbound lane open on Ring I due to an accident in which a car had rear-ended a semitrailer. Some of my colleagues from the Helsinki PD and the highway patrol were doing their best to direct traffic. The snowfall had escalated to near-blizzard conditions, and the ruts in the snow felt dangerously deep under my tires.

Aziza's family had paid the rent on their apartment through the end of March, and even though it had been practically empty the last time I had been there, perhaps the family had returned. There hadn't been any response to the official letter I left. Aziza would not turn eighteen until the end of December, so she was still under her parents' guardianship. Her family's residence permit was temporary but would last until the end of next year.

I pulled into the familiar parking lot, rudely leaving my car in the handicapped space and walking up the stairs to Aziza's door. No one answered when I rang the bell. I rang the doorbells of the neighbors living on the floor, and on my third and final try my luck turned.

An old woman opened the door. According to the plate on the door, her name was Mukhortova. I asked if she'd seen her Afghani neighbors recently.

"No one there for long time. Maybe traveling. Lady sometime drink tea with me. Not speak much Finnish, a few words Russian. Learn during war. Say we not need hate, even though countries then at war. Drink tea together. You want tea too?"

"Thank you, but no, Mrs. Mukhortova." I gave her my card and asked her to notify me if she saw the residents of number thirty-one.

"They haven't done anything wrong. I just want to talk to them."

I dropped my card through the mail slot at apartment thirty-one too. I saw it fall onto the stack of free papers and advertisements that had spread across the floor. I sat for a while in my car waiting for Aziza, but she didn't appear out of the driving snow. Maybe I'd just been seeing things.

However, at the station a message was waiting for me saying that a woman fitting Aziza's description had gotten onto Vantaa bus 61 at the airport. The driver had said he wasn't able to tell one headscarf from another, but had contacted us anyway. Maybe my eyes had been playing tricks on me. Maybe it hadn't been Aziza at all. I was probably just hoping too much.

I chatted with an agent from Security Intelligence about the video, which I'd copied and sent over to them, but he didn't think it provided cause for action since the cases had been solved. A few of the people in the group were already on their surveillance lists, including Kimmo Korhonen. I asked again if they had any information about the drug lord Omar Jussuf's son Issa Omar's connections to Finland, but of course I didn't get an answer, even after quoting Uzuri's e-mail message.

"I already deleted it from my computer," I lied when the investigator asked me to forward it to him.

The feeling of emptiness was still plaguing me. It was like I was grasping for birch branches waving in the wind but was only able to graze them before they escaped my reach. Home felt downright deserted because my dad wasn't lying on the hard mattress on the floor of the living room anymore, commenting peevishly on the day's events. I hunted for the thumb drive I'd used to store the pictures I took at my Police University College course and in Afghanistan. Uzuri reciting her poem, Muna smiling, me, Ulrike . . . That was the last picture taken of Ulrike. Vala's profile was visible in one of the snapshots. I was glad that he'd finally left me alone. I'd just breathed a sigh of relief when my phone rang. And who else could it be but Vala.

"Howdy, Kallio. I just wanted to tell you that I'm leaving tomorrow, back to Afghanistan via Frankfurt. Will you see me off at the airport?"

"I think I'll have to pass." I thought for a moment about whether to tell Vala that I'd imagined seeing the woman who was believed to be Issa Omar's bride earlier that day at the airport. But Issa Omar couldn't just waltz into Finland with the intelligence services of several countries on his tail.

"Too bad. Maybe we'll run into each other sometime. Or then again maybe not. Since I don't believe in life after death. They're rebuilding the police academy over there, the idealists. And we're going to try to give them a little protection. Command is transferring some of the Finns from Mazar-i-Sharif to the southeast, closer to the school. I'm going to be with them."

"Try to stay alive." My voice shook even though Vala didn't have any place in my life.

"That's the idea. Take care of yourself," Vala said and then hung up.

I gave up looking at pictures and went to roast the salmon that Antti had bought at the market the day before. Iida protested about my using pink peppercorns to season it, and Taneli told her she was being stupid. I threw a couple pieces of salmon skin to Venjamin and Jahnukainen, who then proceeded to drag them around the kitchen, playing roughly enough that scales got spread all over the floor. Time to mop again.

Because there was a good amount of commotion over all of this, I didn't hear the text message notification on my work phone, which I'd left in the bedroom. I didn't see the message until later when I was putting on my pajamas. The sender's number didn't show up on the screen, but the message was signed.

I got your messages. Home empty. I'm afraid. Can Finnish police help? Aziza

21

It was pointless trying to call Aziza, because she'd texted from an anonymous number. She must have dropped by the family's apartment and seen my note and calling card. It was already after ten p.m., but I still started to pull my clothes back on. Antti was reading in bed and didn't comment when I said I was going to go check on something.

While I drove, I tried to get in touch with Koivu, but he didn't answer his cell phone, and I didn't want to call his home phone so late in case it woke up the children. I left a message saying I was coming his way and would be in the building next door.

Of course, at that time of night the downstairs door of the building was locked, and there was no buzzer. I tried to figure out which window would be Aziza's family's. Then I thought of calling Information for Mrs. Mukhortova's number, but before I could, the light in the entryway switched on. A young man came out of the building, lighting a cigarette as soon as he got outside. The city building authority did not allow smoking inside rental units anymore, which the smokers probably saw as discrimination. The young man looked at me curiously but let me in anyway.

I rang Aziza's family's doorbell, and it seemed like the sound echoed through the whole building. I didn't hear any footsteps inside. The door opened immediately, as if someone had been waiting behind it. The same girl I'd seen at the airport now stood in the doorway. She had on a different headscarf than the one from earlier in the day. It was violet, and a dark curl had escaped behind her left ear.

"Are you Aziza Abdi Hasan?"

"Yes."

"Detective Maria Kallio, Espoo police. A missing person report was filed for you, and the police have been looking for you for over a month." I stepped into the apartment without being asked and closed the door behind me.

When I'd visited the apartment before, it had smelled of emptiness. Now there was a peppery smell, as if someone had just finished fixing food.

"Where is my family? What has happened to them?" Aziza asked.

"I don't know." I walked into the living room, but then I stopped in my tracks. I hadn't expected to see anyone else in the apartment, but on the couch in front of the bare window sat Major Lauri Vala.

"Well now, look at this, Kallio. I know you better than you know yourself. I guessed you would get your ass in gear if a damsel in distress called for help. And Aziza will be in distress soon if we don't help her." Vala leaned back, relaxing. The expression on his face was more contented than any I'd ever seen on him before. When he moved, I caught a glimpse of a shoulder holster strap. Vala was armed.

"What are you doing here?"

"Well, I've been sending you texts for one. I'm not on my way to Afghanistan after all. The purpose of that call was just to test whether you would be reachable later tonight. If you wouldn't have come, I would have had to go it alone. But it's better for there to be two of us who've stared death in the face before. Have you done that too, Aziza? How were you lured into this? Money or threats? Or do you love Issa Omar?"

Aziza didn't answer. She just stared at Vala. Did she understand more of what he was saying than I did?

"What exactly are you up to, Vala? How did you end up here, in this apartment?"

A smile spread across Vala's face.

"Did you think that it would be hard for me to find the building where Issa Omar's fiancée lived? It was almost too easy. And then I just started keeping an eye on her. This girl is going to lead us to Issa Omar. As soon as she gets what Issa wants here, she's going to go deliver it to his sidekicks in Malmö, and we're going to follow her."

Vala had clearly lost his mind. I would have liked to talk to Aziza in private and leave Vala to his secret agent games.

"Did you break in here by threatening Aziza with that gun?"

"I imagine showing her my revolver may have increased her desire to cooperate. But she's a good girl. She wants to get out of this mess and back to Finland for good, as soon as we've made our little trip to Sweden. You want to get Omar Jussuf too, don't you? He almost killed us, and he did kill dozens of people in the police academy explosion."

"Listen, Vala, even if you believe that one Finnish soldier is worth ten Russians, I think we're in deep enough water here that we should leave this to the real spies. What are they bringing Aziza, drug money?"

"No, but she does have jewels bought with drug money that are meant to be used for payment. You can get anything with money—falsified Finnish passports for example. I'm just dying to see what alias Issa Omar chose this time."

"How do you know all this?"

"The girl told me herself. She even showed me the Quran with the hollowed-out space the jewelry is hidden in and how she plans to smuggle the passports out. Even though no one is going to check a cruise ship passenger's luggage."

"Did Aziza tell you this after you threatened her with a weapon?"

"As I said, her knowing that I have a weapon increased her desire to cooperate."

"That's aggravated assault, Vala. I suppose you have a permit for that gun?"

Vala didn't answer; he just laughed. Aziza was listening to our discussion impassively. I asked her where she'd been the last two and a half months.

"In Sweden and Denmark," she answered quietly.

"In Malmö?"

"Malmö, Stockholm, and Copenhagen. There." Aziza obviously hadn't used Finnish while she had been away, and now it came out clumsily. I asked if she would rather speak Swedish, but she shook her head. *"Nej prata svenska."*

"What did you do in Sweden?"

"I got married," Aziza said. "Mosque in Malmö. My cousin Mohammad Hasan. Came to wedding from Afghanistan. Need Finland passport. I take now. Not want do wrong. This man say no can take passport. What police says?"

I sat down on a sleeping mat rolled up on the floor and crossed my legs. My phone jingled. A text message from Koivu: *Sorry, I was in the sauna. Are you still over there? Should I come?* I started keying in a response, a *YES* in all caps, but then Vala was at my side, grabbing the phone away from me. He had pulled the revolver out. He was pointing it at the ground, but only two feet from my right leg.

"Who were you texting?"

"A coworker. Police business. Give it back!"

"Let's concentrate on Aziza for now, and Issa Omar's passport." Vala calmly slid my phone into his pocket. I tried not to panic. Vala clearly hadn't deluded himself into thinking I was a subordinate who would humbly obey his commands.

"Give me my phone back. Do you want more charges piled on with aggravated assault?"

Just then some other cell phone started to ring, and Aziza pulled a small blue Ericsson out of her skirt pocket. She looked at the number and silenced the phone.

"Need to throw key down," she said quietly. "Can I open the window?" She was asking Vala for permission, not me, and Vala nodded. I thought about what he might have said to Aziza, who he was claiming to be. Aziza opened the window and threw the keys out, and a cold blast of air whipped in. The wind grabbed her scarf, nearly tearing it off her head, and she slammed the window shut hard enough to make the glass shake.

"Now the dude's on his way up. Let's go hide in the kitchen, Kallio. Then I'll surprise him. And you, Aziza, if you don't do what I tell you, things will go badly for your family." He added a few words in Persian, which of course he had picked up in Afghanistan. That was apparently the tool he'd used to get Aziza to let him in.

I followed Vala into the kitchen. I still had on my winter coat and felt hot. I just had time to take it off and throw it on the kitchen counter when we heard a key in the door. How long had Vala been in the apartment? Had he searched it thoroughly and found the bread knife I remembered seeing in the drawer on my previous visit? If not, I might be able to surprise him.

"Evening." The male voice spoke fluent Finnish. I only heard one set of steps. "Are you alone here?" the voice continued. I couldn't make out Aziza's response. Maybe she just nodded instead of using words. It was not completely dark in the kitchen because the streetlights shone through the windows. I could see Vala draw his weapon. He stepped from the kitchen into the living room. I stifled both a cry and the desire to rush him.

"Hands up!" he said. Aziza cried out, and I heard a quick rustling.

"Let the girl go." Vala's voice was tense.

"No," the man's voice replied. "Who the hell are you?"

I took the bread knife out of the drawer as silently as I could, even though I knew it would be little protection against a firearm. I peeked through the door, but I couldn't see Vala. Instead I saw the other man, who was holding Aziza in front of him, using her as a shield. He also had a firearm in his hand, a small semiautomatic with a silencer. A professional criminal's tool. He looked like a motorcycle gangbanger in his leather jacket, but I couldn't make out any insignia. He was thirty-ish and only about five foot six, but well muscled and solidly built. His long, light-brown hair was pulled back in a ponytail, and his beard was plaited into two braids that extended halfway down his neck. His face wasn't familiar. I hadn't run into him before, but it was obvious that this wasn't the first time he'd stared down the barrel of a gun.

"Whoever you are, you'd better give up while you're ahead. I have the passports, the girl, and the jewels. Put down your weapon, and I'll let you keep your life."

"Don't waste your breath," Vala answered.

I eased myself over to the window and looked down. We were on the third floor; it would be too dangerous to jump down. The outer wall was smooth, and there weren't any balconies on this side of the building. The ventilation window was narrow, so I would have to smash the larger window in order to get out, and that would certainly alert the man that there was another person in the apartment. Because I was able to see him through the crack in the door, he would also see me if I left the kitchen and tried to flee to the stairwell. It would be pointless to try to appeal to my authority as a police officer; for some motorcycle gang members, killing a police officer was a badge of honor.

"Do you know who that girl is working for?" Vala asked. "Omar Jussuf, who is killing Finnish soldiers in Afghanistan. Think about whether you want to be a traitor to your country."

"What the fuck does it matter? And come to think of it, you don't matter either," the man answered. I heard a dull thud, and both Vala and Aziza cried out. Then I heard someone collapse, though the rugs muffled the sound of the fall.

It took all I had not to rush in. The man with the passports had shown that he was prepared to kill any witnesses. I tried to burn his image into my mind. My heart was beating so hard I was sure he could hear it. I prayed that Aziza wouldn't give me away. She had started to sob.

"Nothing's going to happen to you if you give me what was promised. Where are the jewels?"

"In my pocket . . ."

"Good. Let me have a look." The man came into my field of vision again. He turned on more lights. I saw that he was holding a piece of gold jewelry with small stones shining in it. He inspected it carefully and then shoved his pistol carelessly under his belt and dug a magnifying loupe out of his pocket. After peering at the jewels for a moment, he nodded.

"Looks genuine. The passports are yours. Here . . . What the hell?"

Even though my field of view was limited, I could see Aziza holding Vala's weapon, which must have slipped out of his hand when he fell.

"No, Aziza!" I screamed at the same moment she shot the man straight in the chest. Vala's pistol didn't have a silencer. Fired from such close range, the bullet penetrated the man's body with violent force. Blood sprayed all around him. Aziza started to shriek. I opened the kitchen door, but the man's fallen body blocked my way. I started to ease him out of the way and got blood smeared on myself too. Finally, I succeeded in hopping over the body into the hall. The man's gunshot wound looked to be right to the heart. I had to turn my head away.

Vala lay on the floor. He was conscious, but just barely. He'd been shot in the stomach. My cell phone had flown out of his pocket onto the floor. It was covered in blood, so I wiped it off with my shirt.

First, I called dispatch and reported that there had been a shooting with two victims. Then I called Koivu, and thank God he answered.

I asked him to bring a first aid kit. I could hear noises in the hallway. The shot and Aziza's shrieking had apparently roused the building's residents. I went back into the kitchen to get my scarf out of the arm of my coat and with it tried my best to quell the flow of blood from Vala's belly. The wound was more or less where his appendix would be, but because of the amount of blood, I couldn't tell whether the bullet had passed through or remained lodged inside. The scarf wasn't enough by itself to staunch the flow, but it did slow it a little. Vala moaned quietly.

I checked the other man's pulse after binding Vala's stomach. It didn't seem like there was anything to be done for him.

The voices in the hall grew louder.

"Out of the way, I'm a police officer," I heard Koivu say on the other side of the door. "Maria, are you in there? Open up!"

I jumped over the dead body to the door. Koivu was wearing his pajamas with a winter coat on top. On his feet he had felt slippers with rubber soles. In his hand he carried a first aid kit, which I'd seen before in his car.

"No unauthorized personnel!" he yelled into the hall. "And don't close the downstairs door! The paramedics will be here any second."

I took the first aid kit from him. Aziza had dropped Vala's pistol and was now vomiting in the corner of the living room near the window. I undid the scarf, and blood gushed from beneath it. It took some effort to stifle my nausea as I bound Vala's wound as best I could. Koivu tried to resuscitate the man in the leather jacket, but his heart had already stopped pumping. Sirens began to wail outside, and in a moment the parking lot was full of blue flashing lights. The paramedics arrived, and I backed into the corner of the living room that wasn't covered in blood or vomit. I put my head between my knees. When I finally looked up, I saw Vala being taken away on a stretcher. He was being carried away headfirst.

As I'd guessed, the man who had brought the passports had been a member of a motorcycle gang. His name was Riku "Ricky Bruch" Konttinen, and he belonged to Gunners MC. He'd done some time for attempted murder and four shorter stints for drug dealing. He'd been free for the past year. According to intelligence from the National Bureau of Investigation, the Gunners had connections to the international drug trade and human trafficking, and forging passports was something they excelled at.

Konttinen had shot to kill. The only thing that saved Vala's life was that he'd received first aid within two minutes of being shot. I didn't feel like a hero. Quite the opposite. I'd gone along with Vala's games for too long. He'd come to Finland because his commanders had ordered him to take sick leave. The continuous close calls he'd experienced during the fall and early winter had gradually disturbed him to the point that he was no longer fit for duty. But he'd become fixated on Omar Jussuf, and when he heard through the grapevine that the drug lord might have connections to Finland, he decided to seek out Jussuf's second cousin's family.

After the explosion at the police academy, Issa Omar had fled to Sweden through Russia and Estonia. A Finnish passport issued in the name of Issa Jussuf Hasan had been intended for him. The passports had been in Riku Konttinen's breast pocket, and when Aziza shot him, they were almost completely destroyed. But Aziza told us everything she knew in our case room at the station. We'd stopped by Koivu's so he could swap his pajamas for a uniform, and I'd taken off my bloody blazer and sealed it in an evidence bag. I wore Koivu's bathrobe, which somehow made me feel more secure, the more so because it was so big on me.

Aziza had been married to her second cousin Issa in an Islamic ceremony. According to Swedish law, the marriage was not legal, because Aziza was underage. Issa had pressured Aziza and her parents into cooperating, threatening them with the loss of their refugee status or deportation to Afghanistan, where they were on the Taliban's hit list. After Aziza went abroad, the family had disappeared without a trace. State Intelligence had been aware of Omar's connection to his cousins, who had received residency permits in Finland, but predictably they hadn't seen fit to tell the regular police. Vala hadn't yet revealed where he'd gotten his information from, but someone had probably leaked it while he was hosting a SIS delegation in Afghanistan just before Christmas.

By around two in the morning, Aziza had become so pale that we started to worry. We took her to the lounge so she could lie down and rest. Koivu's eyelids were drooping, but I was wide-awake. I didn't dare drive home, though, so I shared a taxi with Koivu. At home I took my bloody shoes off outside and put them in an evidence bag I'd brought along. I went straight to the shower, where I washed my hair and poured half a bottle of verbena-scented shower gel over myself. Still, I felt like nothing could make the stench of blood go away.

The following days were taken up with answering inquiries from other colleagues and the media. The new homicide seemed to overshadow Noor's murder. According to the news reports, Aziza was either a cold-blooded terrorist bitch or a heroine. She would probably get to stay in Finland under the supervision of the child welfare authorities.

She was also in line for mental health treatment, but because hers wasn't an acute case, she would probably have to wait for the better part of a year.

"Finnish prison will be safe for me. Issa can't get in there. No one can get in there," she had said during the preliminary investigation, which of course I wasn't able to carry out because I was one of the parties involved in the incident. The trials would probably take years. But Aziza would be able to get out on bail while the process worked itself out. And maybe the prosecutor would decide she had killed in self-defense. Only I knew that she hadn't had any reason to kill Konttinen other than her own fear.

More and more people I saw walking on the street seemed to carry fear within themselves, and every new killing spread the anxiety further. I concentrated on investigating the case of the woman who had assaulted her brother. As I'd guessed, it turned out to be a case of incest: the brother, who was three years older, had been molesting his sister since she was ten years old. The sister said that she only regretted that she hadn't had it in her to kill him, and that her revenge had been incomplete.

Unfortunately, Heini Korhonen's group succeeded in their goal. The anti-immigrant conversation remained extraordinarily tense throughout the spring. After a few minutes online, which led to a headache and nausea, I stayed away from the Internet hate speech boards. Sylvia Sandelin fired Heini from the Girls Club for spreading false information about its members and exploiting them.

Sylvia looked old and frail when we ran into each other on the evening of the Tuesday before Easter, on a side street in the center of Tapiola.

"I've always considered myself a good judge of character," she said. "Having that pride was stupid. If I hadn't hired the wrong person, Noor would still be alive, and Samir Amir might not be lying in a mental hospital, more dead than alive. And Ayan—where is she, the poor dear? I was trying to do something good when I founded the Girls Club, but I created so much anger and sorrow. But Easter is a celebration of mercy. I'm trying to have mercy on myself. It will still be some time before I can forgive Tuomas. Hate is just so exhausting, though. It doesn't agree with me. Happy Easter, Detective. Come by for lunch sometime with your mother-in-law. Being around girls and young women can be exhilarating, but sometimes I feel the need for more experienced company."

Vala called me on Maundy Thursday. He was still in the hospital, but he'd been released from intensive care into a normal ward.

"I just wanted to say thank you. I went a little off my rocker there for a while. I was so sure that there was a secret message in the necklace Ulrike gave you, that it was supposed to tell you where Issa Omar was. I guess I was wrong."

"Totally off your rocker. It's just a necklace." I didn't feel like telling Vala that I'd almost believed his story and hidden the necklace in the freezer. I'd taken it out, ashamed, the day after the shooting.

"I started seeing enemies everywhere, at SIS, in our own ranks, all over the place. Those Swedes getting shot was the last straw. But I just tried to put my head down and keep going. What kind of Finnish man asks for help, especially one who believes he's as good as ten Taliban soldiers and eleven Afghan drug lords? But that attitude just doesn't work in war. If I'd met that chopper gang shit alone, I would now be picking up my air force wings at the Pearly Gates. It was good you were there."

"Lauri, I came to that apartment because of Aziza, not you."

"I know, and I'm not going to bother you anymore, Kallio. You have my word on that. Stay alive."

"You too."

"I hear they're transferring me to headquarters to push paper. The only thing people die of there is boredom."

When I hung up the phone, it was well past three p.m. The holiday was about to start, and it wasn't my turn to be on duty. I would glance at my e-mail again and then leave to enjoy the weekend. I had promised to teach Iida her great grandmother's *pashka* recipe.

A message had come from the police in Tampere, from a Sergeant Irma Halli-Rasila in their white-collar crime division. I remembered seeing the unique name before on an attendee list for some women's police event.

Detective Kallio,

Early last month we received an attempt-to-locate request from you about a young woman named Ayan Ali Jussuf. We recently found her here in our jurisdiction. We suspected a restaurant in the Pispala neighborhood of cooking their books. The restaurant owners are ethnic Afghans and Kurds. We conducted a raid on the restaurant last week. Ayan Ali Jussuf had been working there as forced labor, sleeping in a back room with three other women. She had been receiving two hundred euros under the table every month, plus board. She says she was recruited at the Tampere train station and went with the restaurant owner because she didn't have anywhere else to go. We plan to put her on a train to Helsinki in the next few days. Would the Espoo police like to interview her?

I answered briefly that no, we didn't, but I asked Halli-Rasila to tell Ayan that her mother now knew that Heini had been lying. I thought of Miina Saraneva. Was she still sitting at the Girls Club, jumping every time the door opened, hoping it would finally be Ayan? Adey would no longer need to wait in vain.

When the Tampere restaurant's financial shenanigans came to trial, the news media would squawk again about forced labor and immigrant criminals. The strains of hate were already ringing in my ears. A couple of thousand years ago, that same hate had nailed one Jew to a cross, but now the outcome of that event was celebrated as a triumph over death.

Even though finding Ayan alive was good news, I was still glum. It would do me good to try to forget work for a few days.

Taneli was home when I got there. We ate quickly so he could make it to his extra practice. A real figure skater practiced on Maundy Thursday too. The snow had finally started to melt, and the streets were in full flood. Taneli's own rain boots had gotten too small, so he borrowed mine. Boys' feet grew so fast.

I hadn't had a chance to check the mail, so I didn't notice the letter until that night when Taneli was already asleep. The postage stamp was familiar; I'd pasted the same ones onto the cards I sent from Afghanistan. There were two on this envelope, so it must have more than just a letter in it. I borrowed Antti's paper knife to open it. It was written in English.

> Hi Maria, I mean Detective Kallio,
> You may have been told that the rebuilding of the police academy has gotten off to a good start. We are thankful that the EU has granted more money despite everything. Everyone has been working night and day, from the director of the academy to the recruits and the new kitchen staff. The only professional builders are the electricians. We continue to mourn for the dead in the explosion, but that terrible event has brought the rest of us closer together. We know that this country needs us. We look forward to the time when it will be safe enough here for you to dare come to visit. It would be nice to see you again. Maybe we will get to go to Finland once more to learn new police techniques. The training city in Hervanta is something we can only dream about here in Afghanistan right now. Our first goal is to get all our new recruits to be able to read and learn a little English.
> Greetings from Afghanistan where the first fig trees of spring are blooming,
> Sayeda, Uzuri, and Muna

Folded into the letter was a picture of the police academy's new building site. Muna had a hammer in her hand; Sayeda and the academy director were carrying boards. In the background was a Massey-Ferguson tractor with Uzuri leaning on its side. Everyone was smiling.

I looked at the picture for a long time. Venjamin came to rub up against my legs. He meowed to be stroked and fed, and Jahnukainen peered from his favorite place behind the couch to see what was on the menu today, kibble or something special. I cut up a piece of pig heart for the cats, and Jahnukainen immediately began killing his own piece. A cat didn't think about whether its actions were justified.

Humans did, though. Even the homegrown Finnish punk music I'd been listening to since I was a girl wrestled with the subject. Pelle Miljoona sang about fear and hate, and Luonteri Surf asked whether we should love or hate. Maybe I was like Sylvia Sandelin—hate didn't agree with me. And I had a lot of people to love—and two cats, who were dragging pieces of a heart across the kitchen floor. I poured them some milk to wash it down and then went into the bedroom, where Antti was reading. I took his book away and kissed him. Easter vacation would start with love.

ABOUT THE AUTHOR

Photo © 2011 Tomas Whitehouse

Leena Lehtolainen was born in Vesanto, Finland, to parents who taught language and literature. At the age of ten, she began her first book—a young adult novel—and published it two years later, followed by a second book at the age of seventeen. The author of the long-running bestselling Maria Kallio Mystery series, which includes—most recently—*Derailed* and *The Nightingale Murder*, Leena has received numerous awards. Among them are the 1997 Vuoden Johtolanka (Clue) Award for the best Finnish crime novel and the 2000 Great Finnish Book Club prize. Her work has been published in twenty-nine languages. Besides writing, Leena enjoys classical singing, her beloved cats, and—her greatest passion—figure skating. Her nonfiction book about the sport, *The Enchantment of Figure Skating*, was chosen as the Sport Book of the Year 2011 in Finland, where Leena lives with her husband and two sons.

ABOUT THE TRANSLATOR

Photo © 2015 Aaron Turley

Owen F. Witesman is a professional literary translator with a master's in Finnish and Estonian-area studies and a PhD in public affairs from Indiana University. He has translated dozens of Finnish books into English, including novels, children's books, poetry, plays, graphic novels, and nonfiction. His recent translations include the first eleven novels in the Maria Kallio Mystery series, the dark family drama *Norma* by Sofi Oksanen, and *Oneiron* by Laura Lindstedt, 2015 winner of the Finlandia Prize for Literature. He currently resides in Springville, Utah, with his wife, three daughters, one son, two dogs, a cat, five chickens, and twenty-nine fruit trees.